Applause for L.L. Raand's Midı

The Midnight H
RWA 2012 VCRW Laurel Wreatl
Night Hunt
The Lone Hunı

"Raand has built a complex world inhabited by werewolves, vampires, and other paranormal beings...Raand has given her readers a complex plot filled with wonderful characters as well as insight into the hierarchy of Sylvan's pack and vampire clans. There are many plot twists and turns, as well as erotic sex scenes in this riveting novel that keep the pages flying until its satisfying conclusion."—*Just About Write*

"Once again, I am amazed at the storytelling ability of L.L. Raand aka Radclyffe. In *Blood Hunt*, she mixes high levels of sheer eroticism that will leave you squirming in your seat with an impeccable multi-character storyline all streaming together to form one great read." —*Queer Magazine Online*

"*The Midnight Hunt* has a gripping story to tell, and while there are also some truly erotic sex scenes, the story always takes precedence. This is a great read which is not easily put down nor easily forgotten."—*Just About Write*

"Are you sick of the same old hetero vampire/werewolf story plastered in every bookstore and at every movie theater? Well, I've got the cure to your werewolf fever. *The Midnight Hunt* is first in, what I hope is, a long-running series of fantasy erotica for L.L. Raand (aka Radclyffe)."—*Queer Magazine Online*

"Any reader familiar with Radclyffe's writing will recognize the author's style within *The Midnight Hunt*, yet at the same time it is most definitely a new direction. The author delivers an excellent story here, one that is engrossing from the very beginning. Raand has pieced together an intricate world, and provided just enough details for the reader to become enmeshed in the new world. The action moves quickly throughout the book and it's hard to put down."—*Three Dollar Bill Reviews*

Acclaim for Radclyffe's Fiction

2013 RWA/New England Bean Pot award winner for contemporary romance *Crossroads* "will draw the reader in and make her heart ache, willing the two main characters to find love and a life together. It's a story that lingers long after coming to 'the end.'"—*Lambda Literary*

In **2012 RWA/FTHRW Lories and RWA HODRW Aspen Gold award winner** *Firestorm* "Radclyffe brings another hot lesbian romance for her readers."—*The Lesbrary*

Foreword Review Book of the Year finalist and IPPY silver medalist *Trauma Alert* "is hard to put down and it will sizzle in the reader's hands. The characters are hot, the sex scenes explicit and explosive, and the book is moved along by an interesting plot with well drawn secondary characters. The real star of this show is the attraction between the two characters, both of whom resist and then fall head over heels." —*Lambda Literary Reviews*

Lambda Literary Award Finalist *Best Lesbian Romance 2010* features "stories [that] are diverse in tone, style, and subject, making for more variety than in many, similar anthologies...well written, each containing a satisfying, surprising twist. Best Lesbian Romance series editor Radclyffe has assembled a respectable crop of 17 authors for this year's offering."—*Curve Magazine*

2010 Prism award winner and ForeWord Review Book of the Year Award finalist *Secrets in the Stone* is "so powerfully [written] that the worlds of these three women shimmer between reality and dreams…A strong, must read novel that will linger in the minds of readers long after the last page is turned."—*Just About Write*

In **Benjamin Franklin Award finalist** *Desire by Starlight* "Radclyffe writes romance with such heart and her down-to-earth characters not only come to life but leap off the page until you feel like you know them. What Jenna and Gard feel for each other is not only a spark but an inferno and, as a reader, you will be washed away in this tumultuous romance until you can do nothing but succumb to it."—*Queer Magazine Online*

Lambda Literary Award winner *Stolen Moments* "is a collection of steamy stories about women who just couldn't wait. It's sex when desire overrides reason, and it's incredibly hot!"—*On Our Backs*

Lambda Literary Award winner *Distant Shores, Silent Thunder* "weaves an intricate tapestry about passion and commitment between lovers. The story explores the fragile nature of trust and the sanctuary provided by loving relationships."—*Sapphic Reader*

Lambda Literary Award Finalist *Justice Served* delivers a "crisply written, fast-paced story with twists and turns and keeps us guessing until the final explosive ending." —*Independent Gay Writer*

Lambda Literary Award finalist *Turn Back Time* "is filled with wonderful love scenes, which are both tender and hot." —*MegaScene*

By Radclyffe

Romances

Innocent Hearts	Turn Back Time
Promising Hearts	When Dreams Tremble
Love's Melody Lost	The Lonely Hearts Club
Love's Tender Warriors	Night Call
Tomorrow's Promise	Secrets in the Stone
Love's Masquerade	Desire by Starlight
shadowland	Crossroads
Passion's Bright Fury	Homestead
Fated Love	Against Doctor's Orders

Honor Series

Honor Series	Justice Series
Above All, Honor	A Matter of Trust (prequel)
Honor Bound	Shield of Justice
Love & Honor	In Pursuit of Justice
Honor Guards	Justice in the Shadows
Honor Reclaimed	Justice Served
Honor Under Siege	Justice for All
Word of Honor	
Code of Honor	

The Provincetown Tales

Safe Harbor	Winds of Fortune
Beyond the Breakwater	Returning Tides
Distant Shores, Silent Thunder	Sheltering Dunes
Storms of Change	

Visit us at www.boldstrokesbooks.com

SHADOW HUNT

by

L.L. Raand

2015

SHADOW HUNT
© 2015 By L.L. Raand. All Rights Reserved.

ISBN 13: 978-1-62639-326-4

This Trade Paperback Original Is Published By
Bold Strokes Books, Inc.
P.O. Box 249
Valley Falls, NY 12185

First Edition: March 2015

Credits
Editors: Ruth Sternglantz and Stacia Seaman
Production Design: Stacia Seaman
Cover Design by Sheri (graphicartist2020@hotmail.com)

Acknowledgments

When I first started the Midnight Hunters series five years and six books ago, I began a new adventure in my writing career—writing paranormal romance. Many of the elements of the genre were familiar: the structure of a romance has recognizable elements regardless of the time, place, plot, or theme. Characters meet, fall in love, grow, change, and shed their shields to embrace their true selves, realize their goals, and celebrate love and desire. The paranormal romance demands we create characters and worlds different from our own but which we recognize on some fundamental level—we must be able to sympathize with our heroes' plights and invest in their journey. As authors who write series know, the characters become very familiar to us in a way that doesn't happen in a stand-alone romance. We spend much more time with them, not just in the subsequent books we write about them, but in the days, months, and years in between. Even when we are writing something new, their unfinished stories remain in the backs of our minds, teasing us to return.

Every series needs a goal, just as the characters do, and sooner or later that goal must be reached. Happily, we need not write "the end" in capital letters, but can leave the door open for return adventures. This is a world I have enjoyed building, and with each new book, I've discovered more about it and its inhabitants that intrigued me. As I wrote the final words on the last page, I caught glimpses of other stories waiting to be told. Thank you to all who have encouraged me to tell these.

Many thanks go to Sandy Lowe for her professional expertise and essential personal support, editor Ruth Sternglantz for skilled advice and insights, editor Stacia Seaman for attention to the final drafts, Sheri Halal for the expert graphic work, and my first readers Paula, Eva, and Connie for encouragement and inspiration.

And as always, thanks to Lee, who helps build the world that makes all this possible. *Amo te.*

Radclyffe, 2015

To Lee, who never quakes at shadows

Early Morning Edition: Albany Gazette

NEW HEAD OF VAMPIRE LEAGUE ANNOUNCED

In a surprising development announced at a predawn gathering at the state capitol building in Albany, New York, Zachary Gates, leader of the Night Hunter Vampire Clan, was named Chancellor of the City and the new Viceregal of the Eastern Territory. The Eastern Vampire seethe, as the loose association of Vampire Clans is called, is the largest in the continental United States and holds considerable power in terms of ruling judgment over all North American Vampires. In addition to managing the many financial and corporate holdings that support the Vampire community, the Viceregal enforces Vampire law and exerts deciding judgment over the other Clan heads in matters of diplomacy and dispute. After formally accepting his new position, Viceregal Gates assured the public he would continue in his efforts in association with the other Coalition members to work toward a "smooth and mutually beneficial" integration of the Praetern species with the human population. He declined to comment on his opinions regarding Praetern sovereignty and the establishment of independent Praetern nations, much in the way Native American tribes have preserved self-governing powers. Francesca, the previous Viceregal, was not available for comment.

The matter of Praetern rights and what governing powers, if any, the Praetern species will hold has led to vocal and, occasionally, physical confrontations between factions on both sides of the debate in Washington and state capitals across the nation. The Humans First movement, opposed to any independence for or civil recognition of Praeterns, has gained a groundswell of popular support in recent weeks, polarizing lawmakers at the highest level of government. Daniel Weston, Conservative senator from New York and head of the House Committee on Praetern Affairs, stated the pending bill under consideration granting full citizenship for all naturalized Praeterns as well as granting a host of accompanying civil liberties and protections had been tabled in light of recent developments to allow a re-assessment of "many complex factors." He pledged, however, a "fair and unbiased review" of all sides of the issue and welcomed the input of the Coalition members who represent the five Praetern species.

Coalition head Sylvan Mir, the wolf Were Alpha, was present at Viceregal Gates' official instatement and voiced the support of the Timberwolf Pack for the new Viceregal. Mir herself has been the focus of violent attacks in recent weeks, sustaining the loss of a high-ranking member of her guard in an assassination attempt and damage to Mir Industries as a result of sabotage. When asked directly about the Coalition's present stance on the issue of Praetern sovereignty, she said, "These issues demand careful consideration by the Coalition members as well as all Praeterns. Our goal has always been to achieve a mutually beneficial relationship with humans, but our first priority must be to protect the welfare of our populace."

For further breaking developments, stay tuned to the Land Report.

—Rebecca Land, investigative reporter

CHAPTER ONE

Drake's wolf raked at her insides, searing her flesh. Pelt prickled beneath her skin. Her fingertips throbbed where claws threatened to burst free. Sylvan should have returned by now. She must find her, protect her. She needed to shift, to run, to hunt, to claim her mate.

She couldn't. The Pack needed her. She was Prima. She could not leave them leaderless. Until Sylvan returned, she was their strength.

Drake surged to her feet, sped down the wide timber stairs from Sylvan's office, and headed to the one place where she could find her balance. She shoved open the heavy oak doors and Jace, the *centuri* assigned to guard her, jumped to attention.

"Prima, where—"

"Stay here," Drake ordered. "Await the Alpha's return."

"But—"

"Do as I say."

Jace shuddered and ducked her head, whining softly in the wash of Drake's aggressive pheromones. Her sky blue eyes clouded with misery.

Drake slowed, cupped Jace's face. "I'll be in the nursery. I will be well protected in there. Keep watch out here and alert me at any sign of trouble."

She didn't need to tell Jace to alert her if Sylvan returned. She would feel her mate when she was still miles away. Their hearts and minds and bodies were attuned, chemically and psychically connected. When they were apart, their primal instincts drove them to reunite. But for now, she must fight her urges and remain behind. The entire Compound was in a state of high readiness after the battle at Nocturne twenty-four hours before. The Vampires were under new rule, Sylvan had killed the Blackpaw Alpha and annexed the Blackpaw wolf Pack, and the Fae had joined the fight—although whose side they might ultimately support was unclear. Retaliation might come from any quarter at any time. The Pack was surrounded by enemies, or the enemies of their allies. Despite the danger of another assassination attempt, Sylvan had insisted on showing her support for the new Vampire regime by attending Zachary Gates's de facto coronation.

Now Drake must set aside her anxiety over Sylvan's absence and wait in the safety of the Compound for her mate's return. She must do her duty as Prima of the Timberwolf Pack. She nodded to the *sentrie* posted at the double doors leading to the nursery wing at the center of the Compound. The young blond-haired, blue-eyed Were snapped her fist over her heart in salute. "Prima."

"As you were, Sima." Drake pressed her palm to the sensor on the wall and the reinforced steel doors swung open. She strode down the hall past sleeping quarters where maternals and beta caregivers slept in rotation while assigned to the young who resided in the nursery until they were old enough to shift at will and join the older offspring in the barracks. Another door at the end of the hall was likewise guarded. The *sentrie* rocketed to rigid attention as she passed. Beyond the inner door, a huge earthen-floored atrium several acres square extended beneath a retractable roof that currently was open to the fading dawn. The mountains rose high above them, evergreens interspersed with fir and beech and maple, their leaves a riot of fall colors. Woodsmoke drifted in from huge fire pits in the center of the Compound yard, and the breeze carried the scent of wildlife: fox, deer, squirrel, rabbit, and other prey. The hard-packed stone and pine covered floor radiated the rich odor of fertile soil and living things. The wolf pups' first awareness after that of their Alpha and the Pack would be of their natural habitat, the forests of the million acres of Pack land.

The nursery held six young now, with two more expected at any time. Each was precious to the Pack, and every Pack member would protect them with their lives. Roger, a beta wolf and *magister*, teacher and guider of the young, sat on a rocky outcropping watching Drake's young tumble and tussle. Both were in pelt. Kira, the larger silver pup, had her jaws clamped onto Kendra's neck, growling and tugging. Kendra, midnight black like Drake's wolf, dug her paws in and steadily, calmly, pulled back, wisely reserving energy. Drake smiled and stopped at the far side of the clearing to watch the mini-battle. Kira was much like Sylvan already, a warrior whose power sprang from her speed, ferocity, and supreme confidence. Kendra, like her, was more studied, content to hold back and wait for just the right moment. When they scented her, they broke apart and raced toward her, yipping joyfully. The mantle of darkness lifted from her shoulders and she dropped to her knees, opened her arms, and caught them as they launched themselves against her chest. Rubbing her face against their soft fur, she inhaled their unique scents, blends of hers and Sylvan's and their own. They licked her throat and when they would have nipped, she shook them both lightly, laughing, and set them down.

Roger drew near. "I didn't know you were coming, Prima, but they did. They shifted moments before you arrived." He smiled shyly. "It's…good to see you."

"Yes," Drake said, rising. She slid an arm around his shoulders and drew him close. He relaxed against her body for a second, absorbing strength and comfort as all Weres did from physical contact. She leaned against the outcropping as the pups raced around her. "How are they?"

Roger drew back, his rich brown eyes smiling. He would know she meant all the young, not just hers. The young were the joy of every Pack member. They had so few, and the future depended on them.

"Everyone is doing very well. Adam shifted for the first time this morning when Callan came to visit. The two youngest have not yet, but they are growing steadily."

"Wonderful news. When the Alpha returns, we'll take Adam and our two out for a run."

"Will that be soon?" Roger asked.

"I expect so." Drake couldn't let her anxiety show. The wolves were always unsettled when Sylvan was away, even when the Pack was not in danger. Sylvan was the strength that held hundreds of natural predators together in community, leading them, guiding them, establishing order and discipline, and allowing them to live in harmony. The longer she was away, the more uneasy everyone became. None more than Drake. Her wolf cared nothing for politics or power struggles. She only wanted her mate by her side, where she could protect her and defend her. But for the good of the Pack, she pushed her wolf down. When she'd mated the Alpha, she'd accepted the same responsibility Sylvan bore to bring harmony and unity and safety to those who depended upon them.

"I'll leave you to these two," Drake said after one more hug for each of her young. The familiar ache began before she'd even reached the inner doors. She trusted Roger and was grateful for the training he gave Kira and Kendra, recognizing the importance of their living in community with those they would one day lead, but every time she left the nursery, a part of her bled. This morning, though, she must be more than a mother, she must stand for Sylvan in her absence and see that all in the Pack were cared for. There were wounded in the infirmary, infected humans in the isolation room, and a detainee in the holding cells—all of whom needed her attention.

The courtyard had filled with Weres while she'd been inside: *sentries* in black BDUs congregated around huge open fire pits sharing food and coffee, mated pairs—many of them naked after a morning run—bounded out of the forest, and the adolescents in *sentrie* training exploded from the barracks in a cloud of sex hormones, pheromones, and raucous noise. Squads of Weres headed for the huge mess hall adjoining the sleeping quarters.

Callan, captain of the guard, approached and she slowed. "All quiet?"

The wiry, dark-haired Were nodded curtly. "Nothing out of the ordinary, Prima. A few reports of cat sightings along the northeast perimeter, but no engagements."

"Good." She wondered if the cat Weres were searching for Raina, the cat Alpha who had recently sworn an alliance with the Timberwolves and was now set on unifying the rest of the cat Weres scattered throughout Vermont. That would be no easy task. Many of them were renegades and next to feral. "Friend or foe?"

"We couldn't tell, but none attempted to cross into Pack land."

"They'll need to be watched. What do you hear from the Blackpaws?"

Callan lifted a shoulder. "Some of their lieutenants have returned after the battle, under escort from our warriors."

Callan looked uneasy.

"What is it, Captain?"

"They swore allegiance under duress when the Alpha killed Bernardo, but who is to say if their oaths are true? They left their betas and maternals without protection to feed and couple with Vampires." His canines punched down and his eyes sparked gold. "They are cowards and not to be trusted."

She slung an arm over his shoulders, dragged him close. "You are right. But they are wolves and your Alpha has declared them Pack."

"I ask permission to leave a cadre of warriors in the Blackpaw camp until we are sure."

"We'll need to supervise the transition. When the Alpha returns, we'll decide on the logistics. For now, make sure we have enough warriors there to maintain order."

Callan brushed his cheek over her shoulder, some of the tension leaving his body. "As you command, Prima."

The sun moved higher in the sky as Drake crossed the Compound to the infirmary. A pair of *sentries* guarded the door, and a young female pushed open the door as Drake bounded up the stairs. She passed through into the well-lit, wide corridor, drawing in the familiar scent of medicinals, compassion, and pain. Before she turned, she'd been a human physician, and the odors were familiar to her, but so much more acute now than they had been then. Not only were her senses heightened, but as the Alpha's mate she was connected to every Pack member on a psychic and physical level. The joy and pain, need and desire, of every Pack member was in some part hers, and magnified for Sylvan. The responsibility was enormous and the reward just as great.

She stopped first at the treatment room where she detected a medic treating one of the warriors injured in the recent battle. When she entered, the shirtless male stretched out on the treatment table attempted to rise. She held up her hand.

"No, stay. How are you, Ivan?"

"Fine, Prima," he said, despite the open wound on his right shoulder and the gouges on his chest.

Elena, the dark-haired chief *medicus*, looked up from cleansing his wounds and shook her head as if she had heard that statement too many times over the last days. "He would be a lot better if he'd come in immediately instead of waiting almost a day to shift."

"I was on guard duty," he said as if that were all the explanation required.

"He'll be fine after a shift, a large meal, and a day's rest," Elena said.

The male growled. "I will be fit for duty as soon as Elena stops fussing."

"You will do as the *medicus* says," Drake said firmly.

He ducked his head but didn't completely stop growling.

"And next time don't delay seeking treatment." Drake suppressed a smile. Maintaining order over the hundreds of Weres who lived within the Compound and the surrounding mountains was a constant challenge, and now, when they were under nearly daily assault, the warriors were on constant alert and ready to fight with anyone, including each other, at the slightest provocation. "Elena, if he gives you any trouble you let me know."

Elena's eyes sparkled. "I will, Prima."

Drake moved farther down the hall to the isolation ward and let herself into the large room where two frail young females occupied the only beds. Both had been removed from life support but remained in comas. Sophia, the senior *medicus*, checked the vital signs on the smaller of the two, a redhead with milky skin so white it appeared translucent. No one knew their names, or how they had come to be imprisoned deep within the bowels of a secret laboratory facility. All anyone knew was they had been experimented upon and were now in the throes of something resembling Were fever, a deadly viral infection that generally proved fatal to Weres. This, however, was something different—something manufactured by humans and perhaps their Praetern allies.

"How are they?"

"Not much change. Both still with fevers, although slightly lower." Sophia pushed long strands of platinum hair away from her face. Her hands trembled.

"You need rest. You've been caring for the wounded and ill for two nights without sleep."

Sophia's eyes flashed. "The warriors are still on duty, so are you, so is the Alpha. There is still work to be done."

"And you are essential—we have only a few with your ability in the Pack. When all the wounded have been stabilized, I want you to get some rest."

"Yes, Prima." Sophia sighed. "Have you heard from them?"

She meant Niki, her mate and Sylvan's second, who had accompanied Sylvan into the city as part of her guard. "Not yet."

"Do you think they're out of danger? They only kept a small security force with them."

"Sylvan could hardly be interviewed for the international media surrounded by warriors." Drake grimaced. "And she did not want to reduce our forces here."

"How much longer must we pretend to be other than who we are?" Sophia asked in a rare flare of temper.

"Until it is safe to be ourselves."

CHAPTER TWO

B ecca kept an uneasy eye on the blackout shields that covered the floor-to-ceiling windows on both sides of the vaulted ballroom. Not a glint of daylight pierced the metal barriers set into the thick natural stone walls. Sconces with amber glass shades provided the illusion of warmth, but the room remained cold and, despite the elaborate wall hangings, glittering chandeliers, and opulent furnishings, soulless. She shuddered inwardly, thinking the room reflected its master. She'd never been inside Zachary Gates's mansion before, although technically, she supposed she was his daughter-in-law. The Vampire family structure resembled what she was used to in name only. Jody rarely spoke of her sire, and seeing the two of them together, Becca couldn't reconcile that they *were* father and daughter. Zachary looked only a few years older than Jody, although they shared the same midnight hair, dark eyes, and rapier-thin build. Now that Jody was Risen, her eyes, like her father's, never lost the shards of crimson that slashed in their depths. The blaze of hunger in Jody's gaze was impossible to ignore, but Jody's features held a subtle softness Zachary's lacked. That glimmer of empathy perhaps explained why Jody was capable of love, despite Jody's warning that Risen Vampires felt nothing beyond hunger and the drive for pleasure. Becca had not been frightened off by Jody's dire predictions. She refused to believe she could lose Jody to the insatiable lust for blood and power that seemed to rule all the Risen. She would never let Jody forget she was loved, or the pleasure of loving.

Becca was never more aware of being among predators than she was at that moment, surrounded by Vampires, their consorts, and human servants, although she recognized the mayor, the lieutenant governor, and quite a number of business moguls who were human like her. Regardless of species, most were present to garner favor with the new Viceregal in the obscure world of Vampire politics or the equally murky universe of human power struggles. Unlike many of the ruling Vampires who, at least if rumor was to be believed, made their fortunes through nightclubs and casinos and less savory, illegal enterprises like prostitution, protection, and drugs, Zachary had made his fortune through legitimate military and government contracts. Most human politicians and business tycoons paid lip service to supporting Praetern freedoms out of fear that the Vampires might pull their funds from critical projects. But she doubted the pretense would last very long once Praeterns began to openly exert their true economic power.

"The Liege is now next in line to be Viceregal," a cool voice murmured.

Becca regarded Zahn Logan, the head of Jody's security forces and a human servant whose lineage stretched back as far as Jody's. Blond, blue-eyed, and dangerous looking in black shirt, pants, and calf-high leather boots, she carried an automatic pistol in a shiny black leather holster against her slim torso. "I didn't know the position was inherited."

Zahn's graceful lips thinned. "If Viceregal Gates steps aside, his heir would assume the mantle unless she was…deposed…by other Vampire factions."

Deposed. Meaning killed. "I suspect that Zachary will rule for a very long time."

"The naming of a new Viceregal always leads to instability." Zahn's glacial gaze flickered from Zachary to Jody, her cool elegant features registering the faintest hint of disdain. "Decades of revolt, assassinations, and power struggles followed Francesca's ascension. The new Viceregal may not be viewed as a friend by all, especially if he accepts the yoke of human rule."

Becca's heart sped up. The last thing she wanted was to see Jody caught in the middle of a civil uprising, and she wasn't at all sure she wanted Jody to assume the mantle of the most powerful position in the Western Hemisphere when that would make her more of a target than she already was. "I'm sure Viceregal Gates has ample protection and will not be outwitted by his enemies."

"Perhaps," Zahn said mildly, tracking Jody as she moved through the crowd.

"Don't those windows make you nervous?" Becca asked. However much Zahn resented Jody taking a human consort, Becca didn't doubt Zahn's devotion to Jody. She thought Zahn might be secretly in love with Jody, but she was new to the Vampire world and could be misinterpreting loyalty for something else. No matter what tensions lay between them, she wanted to learn as much as she could about Jody's world and how to keep her safe. If she had to live with Zahn Logan's superior attitude, she would.

"Nothing makes me nervous." Zahn paused. "But I don't think it wise for the Liege to be above ground after dawn and have advised her of such."

Becca's chest tightened as she considered the kind of target a roomful of some of the most powerful Vampires in the world would make. "And what if the electrical system fails and those occlusive shields open?"

"I'm sure the Viceregal has backup generators, but if the worst were to happen, every one of Liege Gates's personal guard knows what to do. She would be exposed for a few seconds at most."

"And her guard?"

"Some would burn."

"I think it's time we went home."

"Don't let anyone know you fear for her. It weakens her position, and having a vulnerable consort weakens her enough already."

"You're human too," Becca pointed out.

"I am more than human." Zahn turned on her heel and slipped away into the crowd, her speed and elegance nearly equal to that of a Vampire. Jody had said that certain familial lines of humans were evolutionarily attuned to their Vampire hosts and, through centuries of sharing blood, were not only exceedingly long-lived, but had acquired other Praetern characteristics.

Becca wasn't particularly fond of Zahn, but she didn't need to be. She was glad someone so skilled and ruthless was in charge of Jody's security. All the same, she'd had enough of Vampires for one morning. She threaded her way through the crowd and slipped her arm through Jody's.

"Have you done your duty yet?" she murmured, skimming her mouth over Jody's neck as she leaned close.

Jody's eyes glinted. "It's been a long night and the sun has been up for more than an hour. I hunger."

Becca gasped. Jody's need flamed through her like wildfire. "Then let's go."

"I must take my leave of the Viceregal."

"I'll go with you."

Together they slipped through the crowd and found Zachary talking with a small group of human politicians. When he saw them coming, he broke away and walked to meet them.

"Becca," he said in a tone so intimate her skin heated.

She tightened her hold on Jody's arm and kept her gaze fixed on Zachary's. "Congratulations."

Zachary smiled, his face unspeakably beautiful and unbearably cold. "I understand I have Liege Gates and some of her…allies to thank for this unexpected honor."

"I came to the aid of my wolf Were allies," Jody said. "The transfer of power from Francesca to you was not my goal."

"Are you saying you are displeased?" Zachary showed no signs of annoyance or concern, merely curiosity.

"I'm not sure it's the best time for a new regime, but I'm sure you will represent us well."

"You have learned some diplomacy, it seems." Zachary laughed, his dark eyes locked on Becca's.

Becca trembled as the sensation of a soft caress whispered down her spine. She pressed closer to Jody and stroked her arm. "Jody, it's time to leave. I hunger too."

"Of course. I should not have kept you waiting so long." If Jody was surprised by her forwardness, she gave no sign of it. She nodded to her father and guided Becca toward the nearest entrance. Zahn and her soldiers fell in behind them.

"What is it?" Jody murmured.

"I…" Becca shook her head. "It's nothing."

"It's all right. Tell me."

"I felt as if your father was trying to enthrall me."

"Sexually?" Jody hissed softly. "It wouldn't be the first time he competed with me, but he must know we are blood-bonded and you would not be open to his call."

"It wasn't sexual exactly, or not *just* that. It was more like he was…searching my mind."

"He is very old and very powerful. Even I did not detect his probing, but I'm not surprised. I'm sorry."

The limo was waiting for them at the end of a long enclosed walkway, shielded like the windows to keep the ultraviolet rays away from the Risen as they departed. Jody handed Becca into the rear seat of the reinforced limo, its opaque glass completely filtering all ambient light. When the door shut them in and Becca felt safe at last, she leaned her head against Jody's shoulder. "You have no need to apologize for your father's actions. But what do you think he was trying to discover?"

"You're an investigative reporter, remember? We hold official Friends of the Pack status. I'm sure he hopes to learn something that will give him an advantage in his new position."

"Do you think he was able to tell anything?"

Jody's hand tightened over hers. "Ordinarily, I would say absolutely yes. But you are no ordinary human. The fact that you could recognize his thrall is unusual. Already you are able to perceive my thoughts and shield yourself from others. He knows that now."

"But he's your father. Surely, he wouldn't—"

"He is my sire. I carry his lineage, but my connection to him is only important as long as I follow his edicts and pledge to secure our dynasty no matter what. I don't know that I can do that."

"And if you break with him?"

Jody's jaw tightened. "Then he would declare me *deshert*— severed from the line of succession. And I would become expendable."

❖

Drake made her way down the long tunnel under the Compound to the holding cells. The simple stone rooms, barricaded with silver-impregnated bars, were designed to detain rogue Weres awaiting the Alpha's judgment and punishment. The lone prisoner was a Were, but a renegade, not a rogue. She and two others had been part of a raiding party that had trespassed on Pack land, attacked a patrol, and later attempted to ambush Sylvan's war party. Her punishment should be death, but circumstances were not always black and white, even though wolf law was.

"Wait down the hall," Drake said to Beryl, the muscular lieutenant on guard duty.

"Yes, Prima."

"I am the Timberwolf Prima," Drake said to the young female crouched on the bare iron shelf bolted to the wall. She'd been given clothes—standard *sentrie* garb—black T-shirt and BDUs. She was barefoot, her cinnamon hair tangled about her long sleek neck. Even in the dim light from the wall sconces, her green eyes glowed with wolf fury.

"I remember you," the prisoner said.

"Yes. We fought."

"Yes."

Drake respected the young Were's courage. She did not deny the crime for which she should die. "How are your wounds?"

The prisoner dropped her chin so her gaze fell on Drake's chest. "Healed."

"Good. What is your name?"

"Tamara."

"Tamara, tell me what Bernardo said about the missing pregnant females."

"Why? You won't believe me."

"You are alive," Drake said. "Doesn't that tell you something? You attacked our patrol. You attacked me, and yet the Alpha has not killed you yet."

"I know." Tamara's belligerent tone softened with confusion.

"The Alpha has annexed the Blackpaws. You are ours now."

"What does that mean for me?"

"That is for the Alpha to decide, but she will treat you fairly if you tell us the truth. What did Bernardo say?"

"He told his lieutenants that the Timberwolves had abducted our females because you wanted our young."

"When did they go missing?"

"I'm not sure—not long ago. My uncle is…was one of Bernardo's lieutenants. One of the missing females was a cousin of mine."

"And that's why you trespassed on Pack land."

"Yes." Tamara growled softly. "Retribution was owed."

Beryl took a step toward them, a warning rumble rolling from his chest.

Drake waved him off. Tamara was right. Wolf law was simple and clear. When a crime was committed, retribution was expected. Wolf Weres might be rational, but at their core they lived and ruled by strength and will. Even the most submissive Were was capable of tremendous physical violence, and only the power of the Alpha prevented Were society from shattering and primitive instincts sending them all into chaos. "Retribution is due only if the accusations are just. They're not."

Tamara stopped growling but her eyes still blazed. "Gray said that too."

"She's right. We do not prey on other wolves. We do not endanger pregnant females or young. In time, you will believe that. Now, tell me about the females. Who are they, and when were they due to whelp?"

"Both were mated to soldiers and should have whelped any day."

"Were they or their mates out of favor with the Alpha?"

"The mates were lieutenants, but they weren't part of the Alpha's guard."

"What was your role in the Pack?"

"*Sentrie*, Prima."

Drake wondered at that. The young female was a ferocious fighter, but her scent was not that of a typical dominant. "You're unmated."

Tamara stiffened. "Yes, Prima."

"The Alpha will want to speak with you. In the meantime, make sure you eat and regain your strength."

"Why?"

"Because I am your Prima, and I ordered it so."

Tamara shuddered. "Yes, Prima."

Drake signaled to Beryl. "See that she is fed."

Beryl's lip curled but he nodded curtly. "Yes, Prima."

As Drake climbed the stairs back to ground level, her skin electrified and heat washed over her. Howls rose from the ramparts. Sylvan was near. Bounding up the remaining stairs, she burst out into the Compound. A warrior called down from atop the stockade, "The Rover approaches."

Drake strode to the center of the Compound. "Open the gates."

Soldiers rushed to carry out her orders and the tall, heavy gates swung wide. The Rover barreled through and pulled up a few feet away in a shower of red dust. Sylvan jumped out, her golden gaze locked on Drake. Power rushed throughout the Compound and the wolf Weres welcomed her back with a chorus of shouts and growls and wolf calls.

"You're late," Drake said, caught in the fierce pull of Sylvan's gaze.

Sylvan's hand came around her neck, clasped her tightly, and dragged her close. Sylvan's mouth covered hers, hot and hard and tasting of cinnamon and pine.

Drake gripped the back of Sylvan's shirt, her blunt claws puncturing the fabric to claim flesh. "I missed you."

"First I want you," Sylvan murmured, "then we'll talk."

❖

Dr. Veronica Standish arched as another orgasm tore through her, her throat constricting on a silent cry of anguish and unbearable pleasure. Luce fed at her throat, while between her thighs Francesca pierced her sex and drank of her blood and essence. She'd lost track of time, lost track of everything except the endless sea of release.

Distantly she heard Francesca say, "That's enough for now."

Veronica tried to grasp Luce and keep her at her vein, but she couldn't move. "Please, just a little more."

"Not just yet." Francesca leaned over her, her milky complexion flushed with the blood Veronica had given her, her turquoise eyes flaming with lust and power. "We must take very good care of you."

Francesca kissed her, and the surge of erotostimulants flooding her blood pushed her to the brink again. She writhed, desperate to orgasm as Francesca trailed a scarlet nail down her throat.

"After all," Francesca said, her voice a steely purr, "you are our best chance to destroy Sylvan and all her followers."

Chapter Three

"Tell me," Sylvan said in a low growl as she pulled Drake up the broad stairs to the second floor and into her office. She slammed the door and pinned Drake against it, her mouth on Drake's neck an instant later. "Is everything all right?"

Drake tipped her head back, exposing her throat even more. Sylvan's canines, large and lethal, pressed against her jugular. "It is now."

Sylvan raked a blunt-tipped claw down the center of Drake's chest, slicing open her black T-shirt. A hot mouth closed over Drake's breast and fire churned deep in her belly. She gripped the back of Sylvan's shirt and tore it from collar to hem, ripping at the shreds with both hands until Sylvan's slick skin pressed against her nakedness. Her wolf's restless anxiety drained away, replaced by a cell-deep urge to bond, to reclaim her place by her mate's side, to complete their union. With Sylvan back on Pack land and her power radiating to all within miles of the Compound, the Pack would calm too. And Drake would be filled.

Reading her as she always did, Sylvan looked up and murmured, "I would never stay away if I could help it."

"Show me," Drake said, scraping her teeth along Sylvan's jaw.

Sylvan's lips drew back in a feral grin, a supremely arrogant glint in her wolf-gold eyes, and she dropped to her knees. She pulled the snap and zipper on Drake's BDUs apart and shoved the pants to the floor. Drake barely managed to kick one leg free before Sylvan took her distended clitoris deep into her mouth. Heat flashed up her spine, her abdomen tensed, and pelt rolled beneath her skin. Drake readied, and at the first press of Sylvan's canines to the base of her clitoris, a shattering release cascaded through her. Her claws burst from her fingertips, and she raked Sylvan's shoulders, needing more.

Hearing her silent call, Sylvan lunged to her feet, pushing her clothes off with one hand and spreading Drake's legs with the other. She thrust her hips between Drake's thighs, her clitoris notching seamlessly beneath Drake's. With a tilt of her hips and a sharp thrust, she locked them, ensuring their essences would blend when she came. Gripping Drake's wrists, she held her against the rough wooden door and kissed her hard, too close to wait. She'd waited too long already, and the primal drive to mate ruled her. One thrust, two, and her abdominal muscles clenched. Her release was fast and furious, a thousand claws rending her soul. She threw back her head with a howl and spent herself in Drake's depths. When Drake's canines slid into the mate bite on her chest, she came again. Panting, emptied, she collapsed and felt her mate's arms come around her, shielding and welcoming her.

Drake stroked the damp hair on the back of Sylvan's neck and cradled Sylvan's head against her shoulder. She throbbed inside, feeling Sylvan's power fill her. "I love you."

Sylvan sighed and kissed the pulse in Drake's throat. "I love you. How are the young?"

Drake threaded her fingers through Sylvan's hair and kissed her temple. "Strong and well."

"I wish I never had to be away from any of you."

"I know." Drake caressed Sylvan's back, tracing the planes and muscles as familiar to her as a reflection of her own face. Still, every touch was a miracle. Sylvan was hers—hers to guard and defend and love. And hers to support. "But you must do what is needed for the Pack. If I can't always be with you, I will always be here when you return."

"I couldn't do this without you." Sylvan pushed back, her thighs still trembling, the thunder of blood in her pelvis still reminding her of a need greater than any she'd ever imagined.

"You'll never have to."

Sylvan kissed her, ending with a sharp nip on her lower lip. A reminder this quick coupling was only the beginning. "Come. Tell me what's been happening here."

"All right, but I'm not ready to let you go yet."

"You never have to let me go."

Drake licked the side of Sylvan's jaw and tugged a bit of skin with her teeth until Sylvan growled and gold danced in her eyes. Satisfied, Drake pulled off the remnants of their clothing and headed for the closet. She found shirts and pants for both of them and, taking Sylvan's hand, led her to the leather sofa in front of the huge stone fireplace. Reclining next to her, she said, "All the young are fine. Callan reports a few scattered cat sightings, nothing organized, along the northeast corridor. No perimeter breaches. And I've talked with the Blackpaw prisoner about the raid and also the reportedly missing females."

Sylvan's eyes sparked. "Your assessment?"

"I believe she's telling the truth—that there are missing pregnant females and Bernardo lied to his lieutenants by telling them we were responsible. He might not have intended for them to attack us, but he knew of the abductions. I think he was involved."

Sylvan growled and her canines lengthened. "How could any wolf, let alone an Alpha, betray his Pack and put a pregnant female at risk?"

"I'm afraid it's worse than we thought. They were ready to deliver, and I'm worried about who has the young." She paused, sensing Sylvan's control thinning, and rested her palm on Sylvan's chest. They'd been in battle mode for weeks, still had injured Weres recovering in the infirmary. Sylvan had been wounded, so had she, and the imperative for Sylvan to safeguard the Pack was enormous.

"Tell me the rest," Sylvan said.

"The immune systems of newborns—any newborns—are immature. If you wanted to use a viral mutagen or a chemical agent to produce the Were fever syndrome, then a newborn might be the perfect subject."

Beneath her palm, Sylvan's body shuddered. Fury loosed her wolf. The bones and muscles in her torso slid and shifted, enlarging and growing heavy. The sharp planes of her face and angle of her jaw thickened. In half-form, midshift, she was larger, more muscular, more brutal, than any Were alive. Drake shared her rage, but she needed to calm her. Sylvan in battle frenzy would incite every Were within range and the dominants would end up fighting each other if no enemy presented itself and Sylvan was not there to channel their aggression. Everyone in the Compound would be at risk.

Drake stroked Sylvan's chest and the cleft between the thick columns of her abdominals. When silver pelt burst free beneath her fingers and trailed down the center of Sylvan's stomach, she slid her palm beneath the waistband of Sylvan's pants, cupped her sex, and massaged the heavy glands buried deep on either side of her clitoris. Sylvan groaned, her claws tearing at the leather. Pushing down between Sylvan's legs, Drake opened Sylvan's fly, uncovered her, and took her deep. Sylvan thrust and Drake slid one hand between them to massage her while she sucked until, with a guttural growl, Sylvan released again.

Drake caressed her with her mouth until the rigid columns of her thighs softened. "Your wolf needs to run. This is not enough."

"You're always enough. You settle my wolf," Sylvan gasped. "But you're right. As soon as I can, we will run."

Drake held herself above Sylvan on both arms and kissed her. "Then make it soon. We both need it, and so do the *centuri*."

"I will. But we must find those females."

"Yes, and we need to integrate the Packs," Drake said. "The Blackpaws need a strong leader now."

"I've left warriors at the Blackpaw camp. I'm not sure Bernardo's lieutenants can be trusted."

"I agree," Drake said. "The prisoner—Tamara—tells me she is a *sentrie*, but I sense she may be more."

"What do you suggest?"

"Keep her and other young soldiers like her here, train them with our *sentries*. Then we can promote from within and replace any of the lieutenants whose loyalty is suspect."

"A good plan, but it will take time." Sylvan's wolf had calmed and her eyes had lost their gold sheen of ferocity. She pulled Drake down against her chest. "What of Torren?"

"I've not heard from her since she left Nocturne after the battle. She has returned to Faerie with the souls she'd claimed."

"And Misha? Has she heard?"

Drake sighed. Torren was ancient, the Fae Master of the Hunt and one of the most powerful of the Fae royals. Misha was a dominant young wolf, barely out of adolescence. A mating between an ethereal Fae and an earthbound wolf should have been impossible, but the old barriers seemed to be breaking down as Vampires bonded with Weres, wolf Weres with cats, and, apparently, Fae with Weres. "She is here, but I have not questioned her. I thought it best for you to speak with her."

"Yes, that is for me to do."

"Our first priority must be to find the Blackpaw females and their young."

"Yes." Sylvan pushed upright, firmly back in control, although the gold never completely left her midnight-blue eyes. "And this time, whoever is responsible—human or Praetern—must be held accountable."

❖

Gray finished breakfast crouched on a huge log by the fire pit with some of the other *sentries*. The warriors sat a little apart, talking in low tones about the way the Alpha had led the attack on the Blackpaw camp—about what they'd all done and how the Blackpaws had submitted. Gray ate without tasting her food, wishing she'd been there to see Barnardo defeated. No one talked very much about the battle at the Vampire club when the Alpha had finally killed the Blackpaw Alpha, but they'd all seen the wounded when the Prima and the medics had brought them back in the Rovers. There'd been a dozen injured at least, some torn and savaged by renegade Weres, others bearing the slashes and razor-thin bites of the Vampires. She hadn't been with the hunting party that had set out to find Katya and finished with a battle that rocked the Praetern world. She kicked a burning ember back into the pit with the heel of her heavy combat boot.

Katya was gone more than she was here now, mated or bonded or whatever it was a Were did with a Vampire. Gray still couldn't understand that. How Katya preferred one of them over another wolf Were. How could she, after what had been done to her, to them both? She remembered the way the Vampire had struck at Katya's neck when she'd been chained, helpless, unable to defend herself. Any predator who would take prey like that had no honor. But Katya didn't see it that way. Gray rose, surrounded by her Packmates, but feeling adrift. Alone. She and Katya had spent weeks locked in a torture chamber, suffering abuses she could barely recall and that no one would ever understand. Sometimes she'd felt like surrendering to the fear and helplessness, but Katya had been there, giving her someone to hold on to in the pain and the dark. Now Katya was gone, and she had no one who knew what she had known.

For an instant when she let herself into her dark barracks room, she thought Katya had returned. And then she smelled the wolf standing with her back to the window.

"What are you doing here?"

Misha turned from the open window, sunlight striking her ebony hair and making it shimmer like black gold. Her deep brown eyes were haunted, a look Gray had seen in her own eyes before she'd stopped looking in the mirror.

"I'm not sure, really," Misha said. "I just didn't feel like being alone."

Gray leaned with her back against the door and slid her hands into her pockets. They were friends, but a lot had happened to both of them and she didn't know how to talk to her anymore.

"I can go," Misha said.

"No need to." Gray gestured to the bed against the wall. "Katya's not here and probably won't be. She isn't much anymore."

Misha glanced at the bed but settled on the floor instead and put her back against the wood frame. "She's with Michel, isn't she?"

Gray dropped onto her own bed and kicked back against the wall, folding her arms over her chest. "Probably. She hasn't been back since the night the Alpha went to rescue her."

"She will be. She won't be able to stay away from Pack forever."

"What about…" Gray was about to say *the Fae*, but thought better of it. She didn't want to talk about Misha's bedmate.

"Torren?" Misha let out a long sigh. "I haven't seen her since the night we tracked Katya to Nocturne."

"You could ask the Alpha—"

Misha snorted. "Oh yeah. Right."

"What's it like," Gray asked, "being with, you know, one of them?"

Misha half-smiled. "Not all that different except—"

"That's all right, you don't have to talk about it." Gray wasn't even sure why she'd asked. What did it matter what others felt? She didn't feel anything, at least not the way she had before. And just as well.

"No, I don't mind. It's just kind of hard to explain. It's physical like you'd expect, intense, good—great, but it's more too, like traveling somewhere in a dream, a dream you didn't know you wanted until you were in it. And you can smell and feel and touch everything, and you never want it to end." She stared down at her hands. "I'm afraid she's not coming back."

"Maybe she can't, just yet."

"If she doesn't soon, I'm going to find her."

Gray didn't say anything. Misha wouldn't get very far before the Alpha sent someone after her. What would it be like, to care that much for someone, to risk the Alpha's wrath? She was glad she'd never know. The only thing she wanted from anyone else was sex. Her wolf demanded it, needed it as much as air or food, but that was all. No bond, no mate, no young. She would live in the Pack, but in her heart she would be a lone wolf.

The hairs along her arms and the back of her neck stood up and her belly tensed. She jumped to her feet. "The Alpha is coming."

Misha lurched up. A sharp knock on the door was followed by the creak of hinges as it pushed wide and the Alpha strode in, the Prima at her side. Power flooded the room and Gray's clitoris tensed.

"Misha," the Alpha said.

"Yes, Alpha!" Misha straightened to attention.

"Do you know how to reach Torren?"

Misha blanched. "No, Alpha."

"Do you know where the Faerie Gates are located?"

"No, but..."

"Speak," Sylvan said.

"I...I'm not sure, but I might be able to sense her if I'm close to where she has been recently."

The Alpha glanced at the Prima. She didn't say anything, but the Prima nodded.

"We'll start at Nocturne," the Alpha said. "We need to reach Torren."

"Come," the Prima said. "We'll get the Rover."

"Yes, Prima." Misha hurried to the Prima's side.

Gray shivered, waiting for the Alpha to speak.

"I have a job for you."

"Yes, Alpha."

"I'm putting you in charge of the training of a new *sentrie* recruit. You'll both obey the orders of your lieutenants, but you will be responsible for her."

Gray frowned. "Alpha?"

"I'm releasing the Blackpaw from confinement today. See that she doesn't try to escape."

CHAPTER FOUR

"Let the human sleep," Francesca said, stepping naked from the tangled sheets and catching a sheer pale blue silk dressing gown in her fingertips. She slipped it on and headed for the door. "Come."

"Yes, Mistress." Luce rose in one fluid motion and followed soundlessly in Francesca's wake through the twisting halls of the lair beneath the old mansion on the outskirts of the city. "Do you hunger still? Shall I call for a servant?"

"Not just yet." She drew a deep breath and smiled at the scent of blood and arousal growing stronger with each step. A handful of her faithful had followed her when she'd escaped the carnage at Nocturne. The servants and blood slaves, human and Praetern, provided blood, and the handful of guards secured them during daylight hours. Still, she would need to recruit more fighters and more food sources before she and her Vampires exhausted their blood supply. Hunting in the open now would be dangerous.

Francesca threw open the door to her private quarters, luxurious by human standards but pitiful and small compared to the elaborate quarters she had occupied for decades beneath Nocturne—the lair now occupied by her previous *senechal*. She hissed, imagining Michel in *her* boudoir, surrounded by her blood slaves, her human servants, her guards; imagining Zachary Gates ruling the Dominion that had been hers for centuries. She wasn't sure which was the greater insult, Gates usurping her position or Michel—her enforcer, lover, and confidant for millennia—betraying her for the fleeting pleasure of a young Were in her bed.

Katya. *She* would be one of the first to die.

Fury seared her breast as she pictured Michel feeding mindlessly from the throat of the beautiful young—*truly* young—wolf. She comforted herself in the knowledge Michel would soon lose interest in the pitiful weakling, and then where would she turn? To one of the traitorous Vampire guards who'd remained behind, a nameless lackey with a tenth of her power? Of course, by then, Michel would have far more to concern her than the source of her next feeding. Francesca would soon regain control of what was hers, and Zachary Gates, his treacherous daughter Jody, Michel le Clare, and all those who had turned against her would die. Slowly, and by her own hand.

She glided into the marble-floored room, its walls draped in thick velvet brocade, with Luce by her side. Daniela, ever faithful, waited for them naked in the oversized four-poster bed, the thick silk coverlets thrown down to expose her lush body. She was recently Risen and had not yet been honed to the razor-like sleekness of an older Vampire. Her auburn waves spread out on the pristine pillow covers, her milky breasts full and flushed a lovely rose. Daniela had fed, from the looks of the high color in her cheeks, but she hungered for more than blood. She was young and her control fragile, especially now with her sexual potency at its peak after feeding. The scent of need was heavy in the air, but she would have to wait.

"We must be careful with Dr. Standish," Francesca said as she settled onto a mound of pillows next to Daniela. "We need her to continue her work. If she is too weak or too addicted, she won't be able to complete her work on the contagion."

"She should be easy to control now." Luce stretched out by Francesca's feet. "She'll do whatever we want as long as we feed from her."

"Then see that she returns to her laboratories."

"Yes, Mistress."

"What about restoring our forces—have you begun recruiting?"

"Yes, Mistress. I've sent our human servants to make contact with a number of midlevel Vampires in the other Clans. Ones whose chances of advancement are slight. They should be eager to move up by joining us."

"Good. Let it be known that we will be especially generous to anyone who leaves *Chasseur de Nuit*."

"It shall be done."

Francesca had already begun to mobilize the financial reserves she'd sequestered over the centuries for just this kind of emergency. No Vampire in a position of power ever expected to hold it without a fight at some point, and she had secreted funds to rebuild her power base in the eventuality of a setback. Fortunately, she was owed many favors and intended to call upon all of them. But she had to move slowly to avoid detection until she was at strength again.

A knock sounded at the door and Simon, one of her human servants, requested entrance.

"Come," Francesca said.

The door opened and a svelte young male entered. His gaze jerked to Daniela and an erection sprang up in his tight black trousers. Wisely he instantly diverted his attention to Francesca.

"What is it?" Francesca asked impatiently.

Simon started, a cloud of lust lingering in his eyes. "Forgive me, Vice...ah, Mistress, but a cat Were requests an audience."

Francesca trailed her fingertips down her breast and over her nipple, enjoying the tightening as she anticipated her visitor. "Send her in. And Simon, wait outside. We may have need of you."

His eyes gleamed and his erection lengthened further. "Yes, Mistress."

She flicked her fingers and he stepped backward, out the door. An instant later, a leonine female in brown leather pants and a body-hugging tan shirt strode in. Her green eyes swept the room, passing over Daniela with only a second's hesitation before fixing on Francesca. Her tawny skin was coated in a gleaming shimmer of sex-sweat. Powerful musky pheromones surrounded her.

"Dru," Francesca purred, "have you been hunting?"

"Yes, my Queen."

"And do you bring us news?"

"I do, but I would rather serve you with my body before words, my Queen."

Francesca laughed, delighted at her arrogance. She rarely employed Weres but still remembered a time when wolves and cats were hers to call and command. Dru resisted command, but that was part of her appeal. That and her insatiable lusts.

"Approach."

Dru strode past the end of the bed and planted herself beside Francesca, legs spread wide.

"Tell me." Francesca leaned over on one elbow and slowly unbuttoned Dru's shirt, making sure her razor-sharp nails etched a faint blood trail over the inner curve of Dru's breast. Pain was foreplay to a cat like Dru. The muscles in Dru's belly separated into hard squares and golden pelt streaked the centerline between the etched columns, disappearing beneath the waistband of her pants. Francesca leaned closer and licked the tawny fur. Dru's hips jerked and Francesca purred again.

"I've been...scouting, my Queen. I saw several small groups of cats moving north along the border between the Catamount Pride lands and the Timberwolf territory."

Francesca licked her way upward to the undersurface of Dru's breast and bit lightly. "Why?"

Dru's claws burst from her fingertips. "I suspect the bitch Alpha is calling the cats to her, organizing them or trying to."

"Is that of any concern to us?" Francesca found a nipple and squeezed. Dru snarled softly.

"Possibly," Dru said, "especially if the mercenaries who had previously hired out to the humans join her. Or word of them comes to her."

"Do they know of the laboratories?"

"Some of them."

Francesca opened Dru's pants and pulled them down to midthigh. She licked the base of her extruded clitoris, letting her incisors glance over the blood-filled shaft. Dru shivered. "Then we must see she doesn't succeed."

"She is allies with the wolves," Dru said, her voice gravelly.

"Then we must find a way to drive a wedge between them if you cannot find a way to dispose of her yourself."

"As my Queen commands."

"Your Queen commands you join me." Francesca reclined on the pillows, her gown parting to expose her breasts and belly. "Luce, bring in Simon to serve Daniela. Then you may serve me."

"Yes, Mistress." Luce slid from the bed like water over smooth stones, not even disturbing the air.

Dru pushed off the rest of her clothes and climbed onto the bed, moving between Francesca and Daniela at a wave of Francesca's hand. A moment later Simon, naked and rampant, settled onto the far side of the bed beside Daniela. Francesca parted her legs so Luce could lie between them. Daniela, her eyes simmering pools of lava, opened her thighs and Simon knelt between them, his face a grimace of need. Francesca gripped him and slowly guided him into Daniela, whose incisors gleamed, her hunger a living beast.

"You may feed," Francesca decreed, and Daniela struck Simon's throat. His hips jerked and his face went slack. Luce's mouth closed around her, and Francesca turned to Dru as the orgasm built inside her. "The first time I will take your throat, then your breast, then your thigh. And if you are as strong as you pretend, I'll finish with your essence in my mouth."

"I am all that and more," Dru hissed. Her face had partially shifted, her expression stark and brutal, her beast a feral creature hungry for release.

Laughing, Francesca struck deep, not bothering to blunt the pain. Dru arched as if electrified and spent against Francesca's thigh. Francesca drank, savoring the rich nectar of Were blood. Yes, an army of Weres would be very useful in more ways than one. All she needed was a way to control them, and what better way than the threat of extinction?

❖

"I should go to Nocturne," Drake said as Misha and the *centuri* went to get the Rover.

Sylvan planted her feet and shook her head.

Drake ignored the silent no, expecting resistance and understanding the cause. Still, she had to be an equal partner—Sylvan needed that, and so did she. "Both of us should not be out of the Compound at once, and you have already been absent for too long."

"We don't know how secure Michel's power is, and the place is filled with Vampires and Weres of uncertain loyalty."

"I'll take guards. Besides, it's daylight, and Michel and the other Vampires won't be at full strength."

Sylvan's jaw set. "I should be the one to go."

"You're needed here. The warriors need to be organized, we ought to contact Jody and find out how the Vampire Clans are reacting to the transition, and the wounded will fare better with your strength to draw on."

"You seek to outmaneuver me, mate," Sylvan said, an edge to her voice.

She was the Alpha, and not used to compromising. Drake caressed her chest. "I know. But we have young and there will be times when we will have to fight this war separately. If I find the Faerie Gate, I'll contact you. I'll be safe enough."

"I don't want you in danger."

"I'll have guards. And I have proved myself in battle, have I not?"

Sylvan's lip curled but she didn't argue in the face of truth.

Drake kissed her. "I won't be gone long."

"Two hours—and then I'm coming after you."

"I'll be fine. Trust me."

Sylvan yanked her hard against her chest, the heat of her body a furnace searing Drake to the bone. "I do trust you. But I need you more."

"Then I won't go far."

Sylvan let her go and Drake climbed into the Rover. Jace, one of the *centuri* assigned to her, was behind the wheel. Misha sat in the rear behind her next to Jonathan, Jace's twin.

"Let's go." Drake didn't look back. She didn't need to. Sylvan watched her until the Rover passed out of the Compound and moved off into the forest. Even when out of sight, Drake could feel their connection, a tie between their hearts that never weakened.

Jace maneuvered the Rover along the rough single track hidden from aerial view by the thick forest canopy and eventually emerged from Pack land onto the interstate heading south. Thirty minutes later they reached the city and entered a warren of abandoned factories and refineries along the highway bordering the river. Nocturne crouched by the water, separated from the highway by a huge expanse of concrete parking lot, long abandoned to the elements. During daylight the lot was empty, but after dark it would be filled with luxury vehicles and limos side by side with pickup trucks and motorcycles belonging to the patrons who sought out the club for sex and blood. Jace pulled the Rover behind the building, where it was hidden from passersby. Drake and Misha slipped around to the front door set into the windowless plain black facade. Jace and Jonathan followed on either side. Drake tried the door and it swung open. Inside, the cavernous club was shrouded in semi-darkness. A short-haired blonde wearing a leather halter and low-cut black leather pants stood behind the bar. A spiraling red and green tattoo climbed from beneath the black leather covering her breasts onto one shoulder and down her arm. Bite marks decorated her throat. She watched them expressionlessly as Drake crossed to her.

"Would you tell your Liege the Prima of the Timberwolf Pack seeks an audience," Drake said.

"That won't be necessary," a cool, smoky voice said from the depths of the darkness beyond the bar. Michel whisked into view, a knife's edge carved from obsidian—black hair, slender body draped in black silk shirt and pants. Katya, blond hair loose and tousled, stood by Michel's side, one arm draped around her waist. Her eyes glowed gold and a hint of wild wolf prowled beneath her skin.

"I'm sorry to disturb you," Drake said, "but it couldn't wait until this evening."

"You are always welcome here at any time," Michel said.

"How is it you're awake?" Drake asked. Michel must be ancient indeed and very powerful to be awake during the day.

The blonde behind the bar gasped.

"Have I breached some protocol?" Drake asked. "My apologies, then."

Michel laughed softly and ran her fingers through Katya's hair. Katya growled and rubbed against her. Sex pheromones clouded the air. Katya was in heat. Drake wasn't certain how the mate bond between a Were and a Vampire would express itself, but they were mated without any question and she had no doubt Michel would fulfill Katya's needs. Beside her, Jace and Jonathan whined and shuffled restlessly, responding to Katya's call.

"Wait outside," Drake said.

Jace's eyes widened but she did not protest. She and Jonathan backed away and slipped outside. Beside her Misha was still calm. A bonded Were would not respond to another Were in heat.

"I'll sleep later," Michel said by way of explanation. She smiled at Katya. "Much later."

"We won't keep you."

"How may I be of service?"

"We're looking for Torren," Drake said.

"And you need to find a Faerie Gate."

"Yes."

Michel stroked down Katya's arm and cupped her breast. Katya turned into her body, straddling her hip and rubbing against her.

"I don't know where it is," Michel said, "but I suspect there is one nearby. When Torren escaped, we tracked her to the river before losing her."

"If you would give us leave to explore the club, we might be able to track her scent."

Michel hissed as Katya scraped her claws down the center of her chest, drawing blood. Katya nuzzled between Michel's breasts and slowly licked the rapidly healing cuts. Flame eclipsed Michel's eyes and her incisors glinted. "You have my leave."

"Thank you." Drake waited until Michel and Katya disappeared before nodding to Misha. "Time to hunt."

Chapter Five

A sharp scrape of heavy wood on stone, a faint glimmer of light, and the scent of Were spurred Tamara's wolf to attention. Footsteps approached her cell, and she steeled herself. They called it a holding cell, but it was a prison. What else could it be with silver-impregnated bars that kept her confined for days where she couldn't smell the forest, couldn't see the moon at night, couldn't feel the heat of sunshine at midday? They'd fed her, hadn't beaten her, no one had taken claw or tooth to her, but she'd been chained all the same. She might as well have been tortured. Chaining a wolf was worse than death.

Something was happening—the air vibrated with pheromones that had her belly tight and her skin slick. She wanted to fight or tangle or run. Anything to let her wolf breathe again. She hated being locked away from the Pack. She didn't know if a battle was coming or if the Pack was going hunting. All she knew was she didn't want to be alone and had no one she could trust. The last visitor had been the Alpha, and she still burned with shame that she had cowered in front of her. She'd thought she'd known what to expect when she confronted the Timberwolf Alpha, but Sylvan was nothing like Bernardo. He ruled with violence and fear. Sylvan didn't shout or debase or humiliate. She didn't beat or mount or dominate. She'd just stood outside the bars, her arms crossed, her legs spread, her wolf-touched eyes unwavering, and power beyond reckoning had lashed through the air and driven Tamara to her knees.

Sylvan exuded more force at rest than Bernardo had ever wielded with his weight upon her back. She shuddered, remembering his punishments. She'd answered the Alpha's questions, giving her the same answers she had given the Prima earlier. She'd given the truth because the Alpha asked for it and obedience to the Alpha ran bone deep, *soul* deep. Besides, she owed no allegiance to the Alpha who had abandoned them.

The guard appeared, the one named Beryl, the one who usually growled at the sight of her. Gray was with him, his expression unreadable.

"Today's your lucky day," Beryl said and unlocked the cage. He swung the door wide and beckoned. "Out."

Tamara looked from him to Gray, searching for the trick. If she walked out, would they club her to the ground and throw her back inside?

After a second, Gray said, "Come on. The Alpha has released you."

Slowly, Tamara rose, ignoring the stiffness in her cramped muscles. She strode forward, refusing to cower before these two. Still, she readied herself for a blow or a kick or a bite. None came.

"The Alpha has assigned you to *sentrie* duty, once you are declared ready," Gray went on, walking toward the light at the end of the hall. Stairs appeared out of the gloom.

"What does that mean—ready?"

"Fit to fight with the Timberwolves," Beryl said. "Assuming you can be trusted."

"We should eat," Gray said. "You can't start training until you're at full strength, and your wounds are still healing."

"I'm not hungry. And I'm fine."

Gray snorted. "A wolf is always hungry. And your ribs are showing."

Tamara followed up the stairs, alert to Beryl behind her, waiting for the prod of a gun barrel in her back. Beryl never touched her. When she stepped out into full daylight, her wolf prepared to run. She was free. This might be her only chance.

The Compound was huge, easily three times the size of the Blackpaw camp. The grounds were clean, the buildings in good repair, and dozens of Weres moved in orderly fashion everywhere—patrolling, training, performing routine maintenance chores. The high stockade fence was two hundred yards away. Even in pelt she'd have to be very fast to reach it before one of the guards stopped her. By the time she shifted and eluded Gray, some bigger, stronger wolf would be on her.

"The Alpha killed your Alpha," Gray said. "You are a Timberwolf now. There's nowhere to run."

"Just because your Alpha—"

"*The* Alpha." Gray's voice vibrated with pride.

The sense of unity and community was heavy in the air. This Compound radiated none of the fear and anxiety that always simmered beneath the surface in the Blackpaw camp. Everyone, from the captains to the most submissive wolf, lived in fear. But they were her Pack, not these strangers.

"Where are the other Blackpaws?" Tamara said.

"Some are at your old camp, I guess. You're the only one here right now." Gray angled toward a long low building from which emanated the sounds and scents of food being devoured by scores of Weres. Tamara's stomach hollowed and she kept pace. With nowhere else to go, regaining her strength at least gave her a purpose. She'd eat and train and when the time came, she'd escape. Halfway across the yard, three young Weres, two females and a male, approached them. The three spread out, one headed for her, two angling in on either side.

Tamara stiffened and prepared to fight. She was used to fighting— fighting for her position, fighting for food, fighting for a place to sleep, fighting not to tangle when she didn't want to. Gray slowed and a rush of disappointment burned in Tamara's belly. Gray was giving her up to them, and why shouldn't she? She was not a friend or protector. She was just another form of jailer.

"Where'd you find the cur, Gray?" the taller female asked. Her short blond hair framed a hard-edged face with green eyes the color of summer grass. Her muscular shoulders were broad, her torso thick. A dominant female and the leader of the trio.

Tamara eyed the female and growled softly. Her canines and claws lengthened.

"Tamara is in *sentrie* training," Gray said, casually bumping the smaller female aside and easing up to Tamara's left flank, blocking her from attack. "We're busy."

"Oh yeah?" The male, a heavyset redhead with a scar across one cheek, narrowed his eyes. "The whelp is looking for a fight."

The blonde bumped her shoulder against Tamara's, hard enough to jostle her but not to knock her down. "She looks too small to do any damage."

Testing. Trying to draw a challenge.

Tamara growled and swung her head around, meeting the green-eyed gaze of the female. She wouldn't show her belly, not until she couldn't draw enough breath to stand. "Touch me again and you'll find out."

"I'm ready whenever you are." The female grinned and the hardness disappeared from her eyes for a second. "But maybe you'd rather tangle than fight."

The other two Weres laughed. The blonde let her canines show. She was strong, her call potent.

"Leave her alone, Mira," Gray said.

"Ooh," the smaller female crooned. "Maybe Gray has already claimed her. Finally found someone you want, Gray?"

"No one claims me," Tamara said, pushing into the face of the taunting female. The female met her gaze for a second, then dropped her chin and backed away. One less to worry about.

"She talks like a dominant," the male said, leaning over to sniff her neck. "Smells like one too, but she"—he licked her throat—"doesn't taste like one."

Tamara straight-armed him in the chest, knocking him back a step. She followed close on her strike until her chest touched his. "Why don't you try me and find out?"

He was taller than her by two inches, and his blue eyes danced with merriment. "I heard all the Blackpaws were submissives, but you aren't, are you?"

"What do you think?" She'd played this game a thousand times before, from the moment she'd reached adolescence and had to find her place in the hierarchy. She'd fought almost every other adolescent and quite a few adults to prove she was worthy of being a warrior. Warrior rank automatically conferred dominant status, and no one questioned her. She'd kept her secret. And now she'd have to do it again.

Gray stepped up beside Tamara. The others were trying to get Tamara to fight, to force her down the hierarchy, or to get her to tangle. They'd do it to any new *sentrie* recruit. It had been done to her. But Mira was one of the strongest females in her squadron, and she didn't want to see Tamara under her. The image of Tamara on her back and Mira between her legs made her belly burn. "You're being a jerk, Aaron."

Mira pressed shoulder to shoulder with Aaron, her canines gleaming against her lower lip. Dominance rolled off her in thick waves, overpowering Aaron's scent and that of the other female. She smiled at Tamara, golden pelt rippling in the center of her stomach in the gap between her shirt and pants. "She's not for you, Aaron."

Tamara's clitoris stirred, responding to Mira's call. She lifted her chin. "No."

A growl rose from the female's throat, a challenge and an invitation.

Tamara's clitoris lengthened, the natural response to the demands of a dominant wolf. She'd fight her before she'd submit to her, no matter what her body urged. She knew what happened when she submitted—she'd seen how the submissives were treated. She held the female's gaze while pain lanced through her. Keeping her head up while fighting the building heat in her loins was like a thousand hot irons piercing her flesh. She didn't want her, but she'd been caged so long, kept down so long. Her wolf needed release.

Gray pushed between them. "Leave her alone. She's a Blackpaw warrior and too dominant for you to roll."

Tamara shuddered at the clash of power. Gray and Mira were of the same size and age, but Gray's power had a force like that of a much older Were. Her call was a knife buried in Tamara's depths.

Mira snarled and backed up a step. "She said no, but I can feel her need."

"If she doesn't want you, she doesn't want you."

"So she's got a defender." Mira laughed. "We'll see how long that lasts. Look me up when you're ready for a real tangle, Blackpaw."

The three sauntered off, leaving Gray and Tamara standing alone.

"I don't need you to defend me," Tamara said, fighting Gray's power. Her skin rippled with the press of pelt and her canines throbbed. She wanted her but she'd want any dominant right now.

"You better get used to being challenged. You're new, you know how it is."

"Oh, I know. And like I said, I don't need you to defend me."

"The Alpha said I was responsible for seeing you were trained. I need you in one piece for that. That's all it is." Gray's lip curled. "Unless you'd rather roll over for Mira."

Gray stalked away and Tamara hung back until she had control of her wolf. When the pressure in her loins eased, she followed. She had no choice, at least not yet.

❖

Cars, tractor-trailers, and construction trucks sped by on the highway outside Nocturne as Drake jogged along with Misha loping beside her. No one in the passing vehicles paid any attention to a jogger with a big German shepherd or likely noticed how quickly they were running. Misha tracked along the river for half a mile and then sprinted across the highway during a break in traffic. Drake followed her into an alley between several deserted factories. Rubble, broken glass, and cracked bricks littered the uneven pavement. Here and there a vagrant huddled in a doorway, drawing their legs closer beneath them as if recognizing Misha was no ordinary dog. Now and then a car passed on a cross street, but none slowed. They made rapid time moving toward a bedraggled park that divided the industrial section from a working-class neighborhood of side-by-side nondescript row houses, flat faced and gray and as weary as their inhabitants.

At the edge of the park, Misha slowed and circled, whining softly in her throat.

Have you lost her? Drake asked.

I'm not sure. Her scent is confusing. Changing, somehow.

Drake looked around. A few more people occupied the streets. If Torren had come this way during daylight, she would have wanted to be invisible or at least blend in, in some way. Drake had no idea how the Master of the Hunt carried souls back to Faerie, but Torren wouldn't have wanted to be seen on the streets in the form of a huge, leathery-skinned Hound with enormous claws and fangs as long as Drake's forearm.

Does she have another animal to call?

Misha raised her head and sniffed. Her lips pulled back in a wolf facsimile of a grin. *Hawk.*

Drake grunted. Tracking a bird might prove to be impossible.

Misha circled excitedly. *I can feel her in the air.*

Of course. They were bonded and Misha was connected to all of Torren's forms.

Go.

Misha trotted into the park with a determined air. Drake kept pace, moving deeper into a wooded section thick with undergrowth and crisscrossed with narrow paths where only the strongest of heart would venture even during daylight. Discarded refuse, broken needles, and used condoms decorated the ground. Wherever they were headed, it wasn't any place one stumbled upon by accident.

Eventually, Misha slowed in front of two huge oaks whose trunks bent together twenty feet or so above the ground in a natural archway. The configuration wouldn't be visible to anyone not looking up, and even if it was noticed, wouldn't mean anything. But the space between the trunks and the entangled boughs above resembled a gateway.

Drake glanced at Misha. *Do you sense anything?*

Misha padded back and forth, sniffing the ground, the trunks of the trees, the air with an anxious whine reverberating in her chest. She shook her head.

If this was a Faerie Gate, Drake had no idea how to request access. Torren had said Weres passed into Faerie when the Fae bred with Weres to strengthen their bloodlines, but she hadn't explained how the Weres were chosen or if they ever returned Earthside. The Fae, Drake was learning, rarely answered a question or explained anything without leaving more questions.

Drake buried her fingers in the ruff behind Misha's ears. If there was a way in, Misha would be the key. *I'm going to let the Alpha know what we found. Reach out to Torren along your bond. She'll know you are near.*

Misha pressed close to Drake's thigh while Drake dug her cell phone out of her cargo pants. She had no service and couldn't even reach Sylvan's number to leave voice mail. Slipping the phone back into her pocket, she opened herself wide to her connection to Sylvan. She could always feel her, no matter where they were. Sylvan had once told her their bond would reach beyond distance, but psychic communication was spatially limited. She couldn't talk to her from this far away, but she might leave an impression. She wasn't ready to quit. The Pack was under attack and the Fae might be able to identify their enemies.

She tightened her grip in Misha's ruff. *Let's get up close to the space between the trees. Call to Torren. Let her know her mate has come. If the Gate is there, she'll hear you.*

Slowly, they stepped closer to the archway.

Nothing happened. Drake couldn't sense anything different about the air a few inches in front of her or the ground beneath her feet. She sighed, out of ideas. "Let's wait—"

Her vision blurred and she strode forward, although she was certain she hadn't moved her feet. Misha growled. A light so sharp her brain recoiled surrounded her. Drake's wolf struggled to resist as night descended and midnight carried her away.

Chapter Six

"Niki, Callan," Sylvan barked as she left the infirmary after seeing to the wounded, "with me."

Niki stopped pacing and jumped down from the porch to follow. Callan trotted across the yard and fell in on the other side. Sylvan needed to get out of the yard before her agitation put every Were in the vicinity on full alert. Drake had been gone too long with no word. Her wolf wanted to hunt for her. Now. Nothing else mattered.

Only Sylvan knew many other things mattered, and despite the urgency pounding through her to run, Sylvan slowed when warriors called to her and younger Pack members cautiously approached, each seeking a moment with her. A brief look, a fleeting touch, the merest connection of Alpha to wolf bound them together. She ruffled the hair of a stout warrior who had seen more battles than her but unstintingly followed her command, briefly hugged a young maternal she'd seen in the nursery and whispered her thanks, and gave a nod of approval to two *sentries* who stood at attention, eyes bright with the desire of youth to serve. By the time she reached her headquarters and bounded up the stairs to her office, her pelt brushed the undersurface of her skin and her wolf rode hard along bone and sinew.

"Close the door."

She strode to the wide double windows she always left open and drew deep, searching for the scent of her mate. So many familiar spoor came to her on the crisp late-day breeze—falling leaves, burrowing animals, the icy breath of coming winter. Hundreds of Weres moved below her in the Compound and farther out into the forest and mountains, their hearts beating in her blood with the primal rhythm that drove her every moment. Amongst all those familiar scents and beating hearts, she could not find the single one that meant more to her than any other. Drake was late.

Sylvan snarled, chaining her wolf until she had done what needed doing. "Give me the status of our defenses."

Callan straightened. "Strong, Alpha. We've doubled patrols at all the outposts and brought up reinforcements from the barracks—"

Sylvan spun around, the specter of Andrew dying despite all her efforts haunting her still. He was a *centuri*—what chance would young recruits have? "*Sentries?* Barely trained?"

He dropped his gaze. "Untested, it's true, but well trained, Alpha. And I've sent lieutenants to oversee the squadrons, so a senior commander is available in case of escalation."

Sylvan flicked her glance to Niki. Hard bodied, utterly disciplined, ruthless in battle, Niki was her second and her general because she lived to fight and was a brilliant strategist. Until recently, when she'd mated, she'd also been reckless with her own life. Never though with those she commanded. "You concur?"

"With Bernardo neutralized and the cats disorganized, I think the only risk of attack on our borders is from humans, and thus far they've never done anything so blatant. So yes, I think Callan's measures are adequate until something changes."

Sylvan stalked to her desk and dropped into her chair. "Until now, we've been reactive. We've waited, tried to negotiate, and all that's gotten us is one dead *centuri*, several badly traumatized young, an infirmary full of injured warriors, and an entire Pack of Blackpaws who need discipline and care. We've been fighting shadows."

Niki shrugged. "Until now we haven't had any choice. Your focus since the Exodus has been convincing the humans we should be legally granted the rights we've had all along."

Niki had always been opposed to negotiating. Her first instinct was always to fight. From any other wolf, Sylvan would have taken Niki's subtle criticism as a challenge, but Niki was as close to her as blood. They'd been raised as littermates, learned to fight and hunt together, learned to rule as Alpha and *imperator*. None other than her mate was more trusted. "And you think that goal has changed?"

"I think the Coalition is doomed," Niki said. "Zachary Gates will have his hands full preventing a Vampire revolt from those who remain loyal to Francesca—if she still…exists—"

"I am sure she escaped us somehow," Sylvan snarled, "and she is likely rebuilding her forces even now."

Niki nodded. "Who knows what the Fae are doing. Their only goal is to secure their own welfare, at any cost. The other Praeterns are small in number, most like humans, and they are likely to fade into the human population—and would probably prefer it that way."

"I know you've never been in favor of negotiation," Sylvan said, "but if we precipitate a war, we'll be outnumbered and in all likelihood destroyed."

"I'm not proposing a war." Niki's green eyes gleamed and her heavy canines glistened against her sensuous lower lip. "At least, not a frontal assault. If we can identify and neutralize our enemies, you and whatever remains of the Coalition will have a better chance of achieving some kind of recognition for us. Until then, we live as we always have—by the law of the Pack."

Sylvan leaned forward and pressed her fingers to the desk. Her claws gouged holes in the hard oak. "We will *always* live by the law of the Pack, no matter what the Coalition does or doesn't achieve. That is part of who we are."

Niki tapped her fist to her heart and her smile was lethal. "Yes, Alpha."

"What do we know of our enemies?" Callan asked.

"We know two for certain." Sylvan's wolf snarled deep in her belly, claws raking, teeth rending, demanding justice. "Nicholas Gregory and Francesca. Gregory has been involved for years in research specifically designed to destroy us. Everything about these most recent experiments points to him."

"He's human," Niki said with disdain. "Give me leave, and I'll see that he's not a problem any longer."

Sylvan shook her head. "If it were that easy, I would've done it myself for his part in Andrew's death. But he's a visible and powerful public figure, and we still have no proof. If he were to suddenly meet with a suspicious death, we would be the first accused. The humans would have their excuse to retaliate."

"We will be suspect under any circumstances," Niki said.

"Yes, but if we can expose his illegal actions *and* ensure that the humans have no proof of our involvement, any investigation of us will likely lead nowhere."

Callan growled. "And if there are reprisals regardless of proof?"

"Then we will defend ourselves," Sylvan said.

Callan squared his shoulders. "Then we must discover what he's doing and act quickly. Illicit enterprises like this require support—

money will need to change hands for supplies, labor, transport, protection. Fala could reach out to her contacts."

"I want her to," Sylvan said, "but she needs to be careful. She's a Were police officer surrounded by human officers who may not trust her, who might be looking for a reason to be rid of her. Who might even be part of the movement to quarantine us."

"My mate can handle a human."

"I know she can," Sylvan said, "but I still want her to be careful."

"Yes, Alpha."

"I'll talk to Liege le Clare," Sylvan said. "If anyone knows of some long-range plan to destroy us, it will be the Vampires, and Michel was Francesca's second. When Torren showed me an image of the secret meeting of those she called the Shadow Lords, Francesca was there."

Niki's lip curled. "And where Francesca goes, Michel follows."

"Not any longer," Sylvan said.

"That's what she says," Niki said dismissively.

"Until she proves otherwise," Sylvan snapped.

"As you command, Alpha."

Sylvan had had enough talking. "Callan—find Max and have him report in. I want to know what the human resistance members have discovered about the locations of the remaining labs."

"Yes, Alpha," Callan said.

"Niki, we're going for a run."

Niki gave her a questioning look.

When Callan had left, Sylvan said, "Drake should have contacted me by now."

"I'm read—"

A knock sounded loudly on the door. Dasha, the newly promoted *centuri*, called, "I'm sorry, Alpha, but the Revniks are here and seek to speak with you."

Niki stiffened. Leo and Nadia Revnik were scientists and her mate's parents. And they'd been studying the mutation responsible for both the Prima's and her mate Sophia's turning.

"Tell them to wait," Sylvan said.

"They say it's urgent."

Sylvan frowned and came around her desk to stand by Niki. "Send them in."

Leo Revnik and his mate Nadia were blond and blue-eyed and usually calm in any crisis. When their lab had been about to be blown up by a terrorist's bomb, they coolly stayed until the last second, downloading their experimental data. Both were now agitated and, when they saw Niki, stress hormones clouded the air.

"If we might speak with you alone, Alpha," Leo said.

Niki stepped into his space, aggression pouring from her in waves. "You keep trying to come between me and my mate. I've allowed it until now for Sophia's sake—"

"Niki," Sylvan said, "stand down. Leo—if this is about the basis for Drake and Sophia surviving Were fever, Niki should hear."

Leo sighed. "It's not Were fever—not as we know it. It's a mutagenic gene-splice that produces symptoms similar to native Were fever and has as high a fatality rate. Thus far."

"We know this," Sylvan said, her patience fraying.

"Sophia survived because she was young and her biological parents probably tried an antidote when they realized they had all contracted the disease. She didn't develop resistance to the disease, but she achieved a form of equilibrium." Leo focused on Niki. "We can't be a hundred percent sure, but we believe Sophia is incapable of transferring the disease."

"What are the odds?" Niki asked, her voice a broken growl.

"We believe there's at least a seventy percent chance she could complete the mate bond without infecting you."

"And Drake?" Sylvan asked, her stomach churning. "She contracted the disease as an adult."

"That's what you need to know," Nadia said. "Drake isn't just free of the disease, she's free of any expression of the mutation. We believe her immune system targeted the mutation locus and deactivated it."

"What does that mean?" Sylvan asked.

"The Prima might be the source of an antibody to the manufactured mutagen—and possibly even the natural contagion."

"Drake might be the source of a cure for Were fever?" Sylvan asked.

"Yes." Leo grimaced. "And if our enemies were to discover this, they would stop at nothing to destroy her."

Sylvan held back a howl of frustration and rage. Her mate was in mortal danger, and she had no idea where she was.

❖

Drake awoke to the taste of honey. The delicate trill of a lute floated on the breeze. Her skin tingled as if kissed by sparkling dew. Deep within, her wolf slumbered, her paws twitching as she ran through sun-drenched glades and pine-strewn paths, chasing the flicker of whitetail deer, muzzle lifted to the sky, nostrils filled with the scent of freedom.

No. Not freedom. A dream. A paralyzing illusion. Freedom was Sylvan and their young. Freedom was Pack. Drake forced herself through the misty cloak of pleasure and magic and staggered to her knees, her wolf rousing with her, growling a challenge. The music hadn't been an illusion—the air was filled with notes, playing over her skin like thousands of teasing fingers. The glade was familiar, only a hundred times more beautiful than it had been Earthside—the tall oaks arched, branches full and leafy green. Bushes swaying with heavy blossoms, riots of pink and white and blood red, framed the clearing. The sky was a blue more exquisite than any shade she'd ever seen before—except perhaps in Sylvan's eyes—a shimmering cobalt cut through with silver. The world resembled a painting of a dream, vibrant and achingly untouchable.

Misha lay curled beside her in pelt, her muzzle pillowed on her paws, one ear flickering as if she too were running in her sleep. Drake stroked her.

Misha. You're dreaming. Come back.

Misha didn't stir and Drake sent her power into the sleeping wolf, the power of Pack, the power of the Prima. Misha's legs twitched and she whined, struggling to free herself from an invisible trap.

Misha. Come.

The gray-and-white wolf trembled, the air around her shimmered, and Misha reached out an arm for her.

Drake clasped her cool fingers. "You're safe."

"Prima?" Misha's eyes were dazed. "Where—"

"Faerie," Drake said.

Misha's jerked and looked around. "How?"

Drake gestured across the glade to where two figures stepped from a mist she hadn't seen before. "Perhaps they'll be able to tell us."

They were garbed in emerald cloaks clasped at the throat with gold wings, butter-yellow leather trousers that hugged their long slender thighs, and gold boots with laces crisscrossing to just below their knees. Each was at least six feet tall, golden haired and raven eyed, with long, elegant features. Their skin was the color of purest ivory. The female was nearly identical to the male, with the exception of the swell of her breasts visible between the laces of her rust-colored vest. Both were almost too beautiful to look upon.

Drake didn't waste time on their faces, but focused on the long spears tipped with glimmering points at least as long as her arm, and the long swords belted at their waists, elaborately tooled hilts inset with precious jewels in gleaming silver. She wagered the blades were silver too, just like the points of their spears. The Fae guards were armed to kill Weres.

Drake got to her feet and Misha, naked, stood beside her, head up, a proud young warrior.

"I am Drake McKennan, Prima of the Timberwolf Pack." Drake kept any note of either apology or challenge from her voice. "If we have trespassed, we meant no offense."

"Come with us," the female said, her voice rich and sparkling like wine poured into a crystal goblet.

Drake held her place. "We seek an audience with Cecilia, Queen of Thorns."

The male lowered his spear in an arc that ended halfway between them, the point directed just above Drake's shoulder, enough to be a challenge, but not a threat. Drake's wolf snarled and prepared to spring.

The air behind the guards shimmered and Torren stepped into the glade. Misha gasped.

"Forgive our guards, Prima," Torren said, striding forward. Like the guards, she was long and lean and spectrally beautiful, with dark hair and brilliant, almond-shaped blue eyes. Her cloak was magenta, her trousers midnight blue, her thigh-high black leather boots gleaming as if polished with moonlight. A sword hilt shimmering with rubies protruded from a hammered silver scabbard at her waist. "Aryn, raise your spear."

"As you so order, Hunt Master."

Torren removed her satin cloak with a swirl and draped it around Misha's shoulders. Her eyes lingered on Misha for a long moment and she smiled whimsically. "It has been a long time since a Faerie Gate has been breached. Your power is strong indeed."

"Your power over me," Misha murmured.

Torren stroked the edge of her jaw. "Perhaps it is the other way around." She turned, met Drake's gaze. "Cecilia, Queen of Thorns and All of Faerie, Ruler of Dark and Light, Mistress of All Seasons, welcomes you to Faerie."

"The Prima of the Timberwolf Pack thanks your Queen."

"Walk with me," Torren said, turning and gesturing to Drake and Misha to follow. "It may take some time to arrange an audience."

"I must get a message to Sylvan," Drake said.

Torren inclined her head. "I'm afraid that might take some time as well."

Chapter Seven

With the cold night wind ruffling her pelt and streaming over her muzzle, Tamara raced along the twisting forest path toward the deeper shadows at the foot of the mountain. Her senses filled with a thousand fragrances of freedom. She was alone as she had been for days, but now she was free or would be soon, and the solitude was a gift. Gray had escorted her outside the stockade, ordered her to shift, and walked away. Maybe she'd been wrong, maybe Gray was her friend after all. Maybe Gray understood the terror of being chained. Whatever the reasons, she'd set her free.

She lifted her head to the sky and howled at the rising moon, joy illuminating her. Her loins filled, her heart pounded, and she gulped the air, tasting freedom on her tongue. She skidded around the bend in the path and raced down a moonlit slope toward a mountain stream where silver glinted on the clear surface. She could already taste the icy crystals in her parched throat. She bounded over a fallen tree and the world went spinning.

The blow took her legs out from under her and she landed on her back ten feet from the path. Instinctively she pulled her legs tight to her belly and raked the air in search of her attacker. Jaws clamped onto her throat, closing around her windpipe. She scrabbled faster, felt her back claws slash through fur and flesh, heard a sharp howl of pain. Her lungs burned, her muscles screamed, and the moon above her dimmed.

Escape or die.

She snapped and thrashed and growled and clawed. Claws dug into her shoulder and the relentless pressure on her throat never wavered. Her limbs grew heavy and the moon winked out.

Tamara came to, gasping, her throat on fire, her left shoulder a mass of burning agony. A heavy weight pinned her to the ground as strong thighs clamped on either side of her hips and fingers dug into her wrists. She blinked and struggled for air. The figure backlit by the moon was unmistakable.

"You bitch," she gasped.

Gray stared down at her, blood as black as night streaking her cheek from a slash in her temple. Sweat gleaming on her bare torso, the light in her eyes as wild as the sky. "Where were you running, whelp?"

"Fuck you."

"Not yet."

"Not ever." Tamara's eyes brimmed with fury.

Gray panted through the pain. The gouges in her side throbbed and bled, but the pounding in her loins was worse. The chase, the capture, the fight left her wolf wild. Her clitoris throbbed against the hot slick surface of Tamara's tight belly. Gray leaned down and raked her canines down Tamara's throat. Tamara had fought well, and her wolf had not submitted. Not yet. "You lost. Submit."

"Fuck you."

Gray rocked her pelvis on Tamara's belly, coating her with her scent, letting her feel her power. Soon she would coat her with *victus*. Tamara whined and thrashed and Gray squeezed her thighs tighter to stay mounted. "I smell your need."

"I will never submit."

Laughing, enjoying the challenge, Gray licked her neck. "Why not? You lost."

"Then kill me." Tamara's eyes were as empty as her voice. She surrendered, but she did not submit.

Stunned, Gray loosened her hold and sat back, breaking the ecstatic contact between her engorged sex and Tamara's belly. "Why do you fight it?"

"Why did you let me run?"

"Because I wanted to see what kind of warrior you were. How fast you could run, how well you could fight." Gray shook her head, snarled softly. "You let me take your flank. You didn't know I was there, did you?"

Tamara said nothing.

"What if I hadn't been alone? What if I had been part of a raiding party? We would've torn you apart."

"Then why don't you?"

Gray didn't want to hurt her. She'd been bested herself by older, stronger wolves dozens of times. Had given her belly and offered her body, been mounted and ridden and had spent in submission. Until she couldn't be beaten, couldn't be taken down, couldn't be submitted. And then she'd been captured and she'd been worse than submitted. She'd learned to crave the humiliation. She would never do that to another wolf. "How did they train you, if you could lose your head alone in the forest like this?"

Tamara's eyes glazed for a moment, as if she were still running. "I've never been chained for so long. My wolf only knew the taste of freedom."

"What do you mean, chained?"

"Sometimes when we were disciplined, we would be shut away."

"Who did this?" Gray's wolf raised her hackles and snarled.

"The lieutenants."

"Which lieutenants?"

Tamara shook her head. "It doesn't matter. You let me run so you could dominate me."

"No. I let you run so we could fight."

Tamara frowned. "Why?"

"We fight to teach, to learn"—Gray grinned—"and tangle. It's not a punishment."

"I still won't submit."

"You want to tangle." Gray skimmed her fingertips down the center of Tamara's torso and held up her dripping hand. "Look at you. You're covered in sex-sheen."

Tamara thrashed, her clitoris on the edge of bursting. Gray was right. She wanted to tangle. In one breath she wanted to claim, and the next she wanted to be claimed. Gray would sense her need and she would know. "Please. Don't."

"If you go back to camp like this, Mira will take you. You know that."

"Then help me. Please," Tamara gasped, hating herself for saying the words.

"If I try," Gray said, need like a stranglehold in her throat, "I can't promise what I'll do."

"I don't care. Just…do what you want."

Gray pushed a hand between them and separated Tamara's thighs. She forced her hips into the space between Tamara's legs and groaned when her clitoris pressed into Tamara's. She gripped Tamara's upper arms and arched her back, working her clitoris in short hard thrusts over Tamara's. She should have been able to ride her until they both released, but her sex clenched and pain shot down her thighs. She couldn't change what she needed, and she needed more. "Bite me."

Tamara jerked. "What?"

"*Bite* me."

Tamara slid her hand behind Gray's neck, gripped a handful of hair, and jerked her head to the side. The pressure between her thighs drove thought from her mind. Need was all she knew. She buried her canines in Gray's shoulder and felt the hot gush of Gray's release flood her sex. Her hips jerked in response and she thrust until the pressure on the glands deep within her forced an explosion. She released without submitting, without dominating, without connection. She gasped, the pain in her belly finally easing. She panted, dazed and spent, until she realized she was stroking Gray's back. Gray lay heavily upon her, gasping as if she had been the one who had submitted.

"What just happened?" Tamara said.

"Nothing." Gray pushed up, her arms trembling. Her belly heaved, gleaming with their shared essences. "Agreed?"

Tamara licked the sweat from Gray's throat. Her wolf rumbled, pleased, when Gray shuddered. Secrets were another form of power. "Agreed."

❖

Niki and Sylvan sprinted shoulder to shoulder along the river, Alpha and *imperator,* Pack leaders, unbridled, unstoppable. Niki breathed deep of the power flowing from Sylvan with every leap, fortified by her presence. Dasha and Daniel, a newly minted lieutenant, followed a hundred yards behind them, ready to alert them of any danger from their rear. Nocturne by night was as dark as all the other abandoned buildings along the waterfront and would have appeared as deserted if not for the hundreds of vehicles surrounding it.

Sylvan nudged Niki's shoulder. *Over there. The Rover.*

They changed direction and skirted the lot to where the Rover was partially hidden from view beneath a cluster of pines. As they drew near they shed pelt. The doors opened and Jace and Jonathan jumped out.

"Alpha," Jace cried, saluting briskly. Relief flooded her face. "We—"

"Where is the Prima?" Sylvan's snarl was a whiplash in the cold dark.

Jace flinched and Jonathan whined plaintively.

"She has not returned, Alpha." Jace's voice quavered.

"From where? *Why aren't you with her?*"

Sylvan growled and her warrior form emerged. She grew taller, heavier, fiercer as bones and muscles reshaped and claws and canines jutted forth. Her rage struck like cannon blasts, and Niki jerked. Dasha and Daniel crouched by her side, shivering. Jace and Jonathan verged on shifting, ready to submit before the Alpha's fury. In another second Sylvan would lose control.

Niki crowded next to Sylvan, careful not to get in front of her. "Jace, tell us what happened? Quickly now."

"The Prima ordered us to wait outside." Jace blurted out the events of earlier.

"How long has she been gone?" Sylvan's growl punctuated every word with menace.

"All afternoon."

"Dasha," Niki said quickly, "get clothes from the Rover." She turned to Sylvan, partially shielding Jace and Jonathan. Sylvan had never hurt a Pack member unjustly, but her mate was in danger and she'd been battle ready for days. "They were following orders, Alpha. Her trail will be clear."

Sylvan shuddered, her warrior form slowly receding. "We can save time if Michel knows where she was going." She gripped Jace and Jonathan by the backs of their necks and dragged them close. "You should have contacted me when she was gone this long."

The twins shivered in her grasp.

"The Prima is strong, but these are uncertain times. Next time, you will know."

"Yes, Alpha," the twins replied.

"Stay here. Guard the Rover." Sylvan turned to Niki. "Let's see the Vampire."

Niki motioned to Dasha and Daniel to escort them. Daniel, dark skinned, dark eyed, and muscles bulging beneath his tight black T-shirt, had never been to Nocturne. Niki dropped back next to him. "The Vampire guards will be dressed in black, and they won't be feeding. They may or may not be our friends, so watch them when they are anywhere near the Alpha. The other Vampires will be hunting—and they like the taste of Weres."

"I'll be fine, *Imperator*," Daniel said in a deep baritone. "I prefer Weres in bed and everywhere else."

Niki smiled grimly. She'd felt the same once. "All the same, be on guard."

He saluted. "Yes, *Imperator*."

Niki caught up to Sylvan at the door to the club. Although it was only an hour after sundown, already the club was filled with Vampires and Weres and humans, many already in the throes of hosting and feeding. The sex and blood pheromones sizzled on her skin. Vampires and Weres and humans parted for Sylvan, even those who did not know her. Her power cleared their way, broadcasting a sense of danger and warning that triggered their primal defenses to run from an apex predator.

On the way toward the bar at the back, Niki stepped over a male Were sprawled on his back against a sofa while two female Vampires fed from his neck and groin, one slowly stroking his erection as he released in steady spurts over his chest and belly. She didn't recognize him, but he smelled like Blackpaw. She growled, her dominance failing to penetrate his dazed mind. He grinned up at her, his canines bared, and met her gaze with an arrogant smirk. She leaned down. "Look me in the eyes any longer, you pathetic whelp, and I'll tear out what's left of your throat."

He whined and looked away. "I'm sorry. I didn't recognize you."

"Leave him," Sylvan said. "He's within his rights to host and not worth our time."

Niki snarled and turned away. She might've been him. *Had* been him, desperate for the release and oblivion the Vampire's bite could give her. Her shame was not his fault. She straightened her shoulders. "Yes, Alpha."

A male Vampire guard stepped forward and bowed. "Alpha Mir, we weren't expecting you. How may we help?"

"I wish to see your liege."

"One moment." The handsome male, indistinguishable from so many of the other ethereally elegant guards, gestured toward a room to one side of the bar. "If you would like a private moment with one of the blood servants, we can provide you entertainment while you wait."

Sylvan snarled. "No."

The guard glanced at Niki with a raised eyebrow.

"You heard the Alpha." Niki recognized him. He'd fed from her on one of her trips to Nocturne. She couldn't remember anything other than the exquisite pleasure. He nodded and turned away.

"You have nothing to regret," Sylvan said.

"It's all right," Niki said. "The memory makes me stronger."

"Good." Sylvan paced. "I was wrong to let her go alone."

"She is capable, Alpha."

Sylvan rumbled dangerously. "I—"

Michel materialized from out of the shadows. "Alpha. If you follow me, we can talk where it's less…chaotic."

She gestured to a hallway behind the bar and led them downstairs to what had once been Francesca's lair. Francesca's sitting room remained the same, although many of the elegant trappings had been removed. Sleek leather sofas had replaced the brocade divans. The antique furniture remained and a coffee service sat upon the sideboard. A door at the far end of the room opened and Katya emerged from the adjoining boudoir, naked except for a tight pair of black leather pants open at the waist. Her skin shimmered with slowly receding dusty pelt. The scent of Weres—more than one—emanated from the room beyond. Her eyes widened, and she lowered her head. "Alpha, *Imperator*."

Sylvan nodded, her focus on Michel. "Drake was here."

"Yes." Michel lifted an arm and Katya went to her side. She caressed Michel's stomach through her tight silk shirt and slipped her hand inside the waistband of her black pants. Michel stroked her bare arm. "This morning. Looking for the Fae."

"Did you tell her where to go?"

"No, but I suggested the river would be my guess for locating the Faerie Gate."

"Specific location?"

Michel shook her head. "The servants who tracked her are either dead or defected with Francesca."

Sylvan grimaced. "Thank you." She paused. "If Katya conceives, she should be at the Compound."

Michel's eyes flamed. "I can protect her here."

"Perhaps. But she is still my wolf."

Michel cradled Katya's jaw and lifted her head, displaying the fading bite marks along the column of her throat. "She is mine by her choice."

Niki took a step forward. "What choice did you give her?"

Katya growled. "You forget yourself. She is my mate."

Sylvan clamped a hand on Niki's neck. "Enough." She sighed. "What of Francesca?"

Michel hissed. "We have no word, but a new power is recruiting forces."

"A new power?"

Michel's smile thinned and her incisors glinted. "Francesca is raising an army of Vampires."

"And Weres?"

"Undoubtedly."

"What happens if she is found?"

"She will be forced to submit to Zachary Gates's rule or fight a challenge."

"She has information we need," Sylvan said. "And so do you."

Michel continued to stroke Katya's arm. "I am at your service."

"Tell me who requested your presence in that laboratory the night we set Katya free."

"Veronica Standish."

Chapter Eight

Veronica woke to a terrible thirst. She threw off the rumpled, sweat-soaked sheet, unable to stand even that light touch against her burning skin. Her stomach cramped and she swallowed hard against the urge to vomit. Her head pounded, and when she tried to focus on the clock across the room, the red digits blurred and all she could see was blood. *Her* blood, painting Luce's lips, adorning Francesca's pure white incisors. Her blood had never seemed so sensuous, so alive. She could feel it flowing through her arteries and veins, collecting in the chambers of her heart, pumping out to the great vessels and into her lungs and her belly and her limbs. Filling her sex with urgency and excitement. She cupped herself, squeezing the hot, swollen flesh. The pressure made her back bow, and she moaned. The sound in the gloom resembled that of a wounded animal.

She brushed her rigid clitoris with her thumb and whimpered. So perfectly pleasurable, so exquisitely painful. The featherlight strokes made the tension in her loins worse, and she pulled her hand away. She sat up on the side of the bed, instantly dizzy, and gripped the mattress on either side of her hips.

She needed food, that was all. She hadn't eaten since before Luce drove her here the night before. Or was it the night before that? Taking deep breaths, ordering herself to concentrate, she tried to remember the events of the last few days, but everything was so fragmented. Images of her and Luce and Francesca and…others…sliced and scattered by the relentless hunger clawing through her. Forcing herself to her feet, she staggered to the window and pushed it open. An icy breeze wafted over her naked skin, making her nipples harden and her skin pebble, and still she burned.

Nothing outside looked familiar. The nearly full moon approached its apex and illuminated an expanse of lawn ending in a stand of pines a hundred yards away. No other lights shone, and if there were surrounding buildings, they were dark. From what she could see of the house by craning to see out the window, it was an enormous four-story stone mansion with no signs of life in the adjacent rooms. Somewhere a dog howled. She thought it was a dog. Maybe it wasn't. Maybe it was one of them. She shuddered.

Them. She was studying them—the animal mutants, teasing out the secrets they'd hidden for millennia. The truth lay in their genetic codes—what made them different, what made them dangerous—not in the facades the more cunning of them presented. Sylvan Mir and Raina Carras and the other so-called Alphas pretended to be like humans, but she only had to look in their eyes to see the animals waiting to spring. Once she knew which sequences controlled those animal parts, she could neutralize them. Suppress the dangerous elements that gave them power, tame them, like any other beast—domesticate them, perhaps. Like a dog or cat or horse or cow. She laughed at the image of a docile Sylvan Mir coming when she called, doing her bidding. And if the chemical sterilization rendered them incapable of reproducing, they would die off, like the bison or the carrier pigeon or the dodo.

She laughed again and gripped the windowsill as a spasm shot through her. Should the selective deactivation of certain loci prove impossible, she would soon have the means to infect the entire population with a deadly contagion. All she had to do was modify the virus and test it in the right subjects. Her mind cleared and she remembered the newest subjects. The lab. They were in the lab, and she needed to get back to her work. Food and a shower and her work. She'd be all right then.

The door behind her opened and she spun around. Her heart leapt and the pain in her belly grew so sharp she moaned. "Luce. Thank God. I need—"

The Vampire, dark and beautiful and so powerful, glided into the room. Her white silk shirt was unbuttoned, revealing small china-white breasts and a long, slender torso. Her hips were encased in black silk, her feet in gleaming leather. "Whatever your needs, I am here."

Luce's smile, sensuous and slow, sent a ripple of heat streaking up Veronica's spine. She was instantly wet, so achingly aroused she wanted to weep. Luce wasn't alone. A muscular blonde stepped in behind her, the light from the hall illuminating the hard, bold edges of her cheeks and jaw. Specks of gold glinted in her sea-green eyes.

She was beautiful in a fierce kind of way. Her dark brown leather vest parted as she moved, baring her breasts and abdomen.

Veronica stiffened. The blonde's tight, tawny belly was etched in hard muscle and dusted with a faint sheen of gold visible even in the dim light. Were. The line of gold down the center of her abdomen thickened as Veronica watched, and her skin tingled. She's seen these signs of arousal in the young female Weres she'd studied, remembered the pleasure of knowing she'd incited the reaction. Sex was power, and despite their superior strength, these lesser forms could be controlled by it.

Veronica smiled at the Were and was rewarded with a flicker of her wide, seductive mouth and a glint of canines. Oh yes, she could control her. She stepped close to Luce, pressed her breasts to her chest. "I'm so glad you're here. I need—"

"This is Dru," Luce said as she kissed Veronica. "Your new bodyguard."

The taste of spice and some exotic flavor skimmed across Veronica's tongue and soothed the burning in her throat. Her nipples hardened and the ache in her loins pulsed like another heart. "Why do I need anyone besides you?"

Luce played her incisors over the bounding pulse in Veronica's throat. "Because I can't always be with you at the laboratory, and we have important work to do there."

"Yes, yes. I know." Veronica pushed her fingers through Luce's hair and devoured her mouth, wildly searching for her tongue and the taste she hungered for, the taste that flooded her blood and her brain and released the terrible pain. The lab and work and food—everything melted away. "Whatever you think is necessary. But first, please, I need you."

Luce stroked her back and the curve of her ass and cupped one breast, her thumb teasing the already taut nipple. "Not until morning. You need to eat and drink and regain your strength. You need to sleep."

"I can't, not yet." Veronica writhed, already so close to the perfect pleasure if only Luce would help her. Just a little. "Just a little taste. Please."

"Only for a moment." Luce turned Veronica toward the bed and backed her up until they fell upon it.

"Yes," Veronica gasped. She closed her eyes, tilted her head to expose her throat, and opened her legs for Luce to settle between her thighs. "Yes, all right. Hurry."

A hot, firm, naked body pressed between her legs. Hot and hard, not cool and slim. Veronica's eyes flew open and she nearly drowned in the green depths of the Were's eyes. Canines gleamed inches from her face.

Veronica jerked away and the Were smiled.

"Luce has fed from me," Dru said, slowly rocking the prominence of her sex between Veronica's thighs. "She may not be hungry any longer."

Veronica whimpered, the pressure on her clitoris bringing her to the brink of orgasm. Luce lay beside her, stroking her breasts. "What do you want me to do?"

Luce smiled. "Only what you've always done. Help us find a way to control our enemies." She let her incisors pierce Veronica's throat for an instant and pulled away. "But not all Weres are our enemies. Dru will show you."

Veronica wrapped her legs around Dru's hips. "Yes, yes. Please. Now."

Luce struck as Dru thrust, twin shafts of pleasure piercing her to the core. Feeding hormones surged into Veronica's blood and Dru's essence coated her sex. Veronica exploded, lost in the wild green of Dru's eyes.

❖

Time was hard to measure when the very air seemed to be a living presence, but Drake judged several hours had passed since Torren had led them out of the glade and into a valley ringed with terraces of fruit trees and flowering bushes and running waterfalls. Sunlight drenched the landscape, although when she searched the turquoise sky she could not find the sun. Animals skittered in and out along the winding paths, seemingly unafraid and undisturbed by their presence. Some she recognized—hare, squirrel, and even a fawn or two. She caught glimpses of others she could not name—some small and furred with upturned ears and long, thin snouts, others resembling willowy deer but for the curving swirls of ivory-like horns in wreaths about their heads. Everywhere she looked, rainbows danced as if the air was filled with microscopic prisms.

At the far end of the valley beside a slow-moving stream that murmured in her ear like a long-ago lover's call, an archway appeared at the foot of a huge vine-covered earthen mound. She'd heard of Faerie Mounds, but thought them only myth.

As they drew nearer, the light around the mound shimmered, and when they stepped through the archway, rather than being inside the earth, they were in the center of a great hall easily a hundred feet long. Marble columns, intricately carved with twining stems and leaves and fruits, lined each side of the hall and soared high into the recesses above. Tall, narrow windows with crystal panes stretched from floor to ceiling all along the hall, and at the far end, a throne carved from some ancient wood and adorned with thorns sat on a dais. More glinting crystals hung down from the ceiling and swayed in long, rhythmic arcs, emitting a haunting melody as their delicate bodies touched.

The music drenched Drake's senses and her wolf paused, listening, head cocked and ears flickering with curiosity. Drake shook herself mentally and called her wolf to alert. They were being seduced into unwariness—a raw recruit's mistake and not one the Prima of a wolf Were Pack should ever make.

"This place is dangerous," Drake said softly to Misha.

Misha took an unsteady breath. "Torren will protect us."

"If she can." Drake did not add *if she wishes*, but she could not be sure of anyone or anything in this place. "But be alert."

"Yes, Prima," Misha said.

Torren murmured, "Your Prima is wise, my strong young wolf. Trust only what you can touch, and even then, only what touches you where none other can."

Misha's chin came up. "Then I trust you."

"Trust me now, then."

A row of helmeted guards in scarlet tunics, tight leather pants, and shining black boots stood at attention along the hall leading to the throne. Their gold faceplates extended from brow to midface, hiding their features except for their sensuous mouths and regal chins. They carried ceremonial spears carved from shining wood and tipped in triangular silver points two feet long. Their silk tunics were decorated in gold leaf down the loose flowing sleeves, and carvings of vines adorned with spines curled over their metal breastplates.

As Torren led Drake and Misha along the hall, the first pair lowered their spearheads, crossed spears forming an archway.

"Come," Torren said.

Misha and Drake kept pace by her side, and each guard in

succession crossed spears above their heads so they walked beneath an arch of silver to meet the Queen of Thorns. When they'd passed beneath the last pair of spears, Torren stopped. Her voice rang out like the peal of a thousand bells.

"May I present Drake McKennan, Prima of the Timberwolf Pack, and Misha"—Torren glanced at her and smiled—"soldier and escort to the Prima."

Drake caught only a glimmer of sparkling light where the throne had been empty and, in the next second, was not. She suspected Cecilia had been there all along, hidden by glamour. Drake had seen photos of Cecilia Thornton in newspaper accounts of Coalition events, but those images of a voluptuous blonde in figure-hugging dresses barely suitable for public were not of *this* being. The Queen of Thorns was beautiful in the way a perfectly pitched note or ray of sunshine was beautiful—impossible to describe or capture. Age was a concept that didn't apply to her—or any of the Fae—their translucent skin flawless, their fathomless eyes the purity of rare gems. Cecilia's emerald eyes were set in a delicate alabaster face above a thin nose and sinful mouth. Her wide ruby lips pursed into a smile that floated on the air like a kiss, and for an instant, Drake felt a stirring deep in her loins, and the enchanting music she'd heard upon awakening intensified. She lifted her chin.

"I'm honored to meet you, Cecilia, Queen of Thorns. I believe we have common cause and seek your friendship in the name of the Timberwolves."

Cecilia smiled. "So you are Sylvan's mate."

"I think you know that," Drake said, "and you know too, I am not susceptible to persuasion, no matter how beautiful or desirable the persuader."

Cecilia laughed. "Yes, you are Sylvan's mate." She turned her gaze to Misha. "But this one. She is young and not yet so claimed."

Misha said, "I am—"

"She is a guest, my Queen." Torren placed a long, elegant hand on the small of Misha's back. "They are both here as my guests, my Queen."

"Oh, my dearest Torren, you have been Earthside too long." Cecilia laughed again, a sound like a fragile chime in the morning breeze. Delicate and delightful and mesmerizing. She flicked a hand. "But that's a discussion for another day." She rose, her satin gown flowing from her breasts to the floor in a cascade of purest white. "Come. We shall share wine and food."

"Your hospitality is appreciated," Drake said, taking care not to express overt thanks and unwittingly indebt herself in some way. "But I'm afraid our time is very short and we are expected to return soon. If we could speak—"

"You'll find, Prima of the Timberwolf Pack," Cecilia said, "that time here in Faerie is different than what you're used to. We'll talk. Soon."

"Then I must contact the Alpha—"

Cecilia was gone. Drake turned to Torren.

"Sylvan will search for us."

"I have no doubt," Torren said, "but she will not find you until the Queen wills it so."

CHAPTER NINE

"Alpha," Niki said, "this could be a trap. We should return with a squad. Then we can spread out to search—"

Sylvan rounded on her, her snarl a lash that cracked the air and nearly brought Niki to her knees. "She's here. I can feel her."

The sun rose behind Sylvan's back, casting the shadow of her warrior form across the barren patch of ground where she had paced all night long. Her massive torso and heavy claw-tipped limbs created shifting forms on the ground that seemed to have a lethal life of their own. Dasha and Daniel crouched in pelt at the edge of the desolate clearing, guarding against anyone's approach. Niki grew more uneasy with each passing hour. They were too far from any reinforcements and vulnerable to attack.

"The Faerie Gate must be near here," Niki said again, careful not to hint at challenge. Sylvan radiated battle frenzy and the slightest confrontation would trigger an attack. Still, Niki knew her duty. "We don't even know the location of the Gate, and if the Fae come through in force we will have no warning. We cannot fight shadows. If we have a squad at our back we can be ready—"

"She is on the other side, and I will find a way in." Sylvan gestured to the overgrown path they'd followed into the small clearing. "Take the *centuri* back to the Rover. Call Callan—"

"No. Even if you find the Gate, you cannot go alo—"

Sylvan was upon her before she saw her move. Sylvan's face was inches from hers, her eyes the color of a molten sun. The grip on her throat cut off her breath but she did not struggle.

"She is my mate and your Prima. I will find her."

Niki cast her gaze down. The pressure on her throat loosened. "Yes, Alpha."

Sylvan dropped Niki and stalked back to the point where she had lost Drake's scent. She had followed her easily at first, her scent strong and clear. And then it was as if she had simply vanished. Frustration boiled through her belly, driving her wolf to madness. Her mate was here, somewhere, but she could not sense her. The connection that was part of every breath she took was obliterated between one step and the next. The shape of her world twisted before her eyes, and a void that threatened to swallow her opened before her. The dark was so absolute her wolf stumbled, uncertain and lost. She roared and howled and sent all her power in search of her mate and could not find her. Drake was somewhere other than this world, and she would not rest until she found her. Fear lashed through her and her wolf fought back, panic consumed by fury. She stalked back to her *imperator*. "We must find someone to take us through the Gate."

"Only Fae can—"

"I know that," Sylvan snapped, "and I know where to find one. Stay here and keep this area safe in case Drake returns."

Niki sidled into her path. "I should go with you."

"You should obey my orders, or have you forgotten who rules this Pack?"

Niki kept her eyes below Sylvan's but did not give way. "I have not forgotten, Alpha. Nor have I forgotten my duty. You cannot go alone."

"I need you here to protect the Prima when she returns."

"Once she is through the Gate, she will be safe with the *centuri*," Niki said. "We can send reinforcements to assist Dasha and Daniel in protecting the Prima, but if you are lost to us, the Pack will not survive."

Sylvan rumbled, unable to argue with her trusted second. "Fine. Come. Arrange for a patrol to secure this area while we pay a visit to the head of Cecilia's embassy."

When they reached the Rover, Niki ordered Jace and Jonathan to join Dasha and Daniel and got behind the wheel of the Rover. As they drove into the city, she called the Compound and instructed Callan to organize a patrol to join the others in the clearing. Aggression poured from Sylvan and filled the vehicle with the taste of copper and smoke.

"The Fae Queen will not be happy if you kill her ambassador," Niki said mildly.

"I'm not concerned with Cecilia's opinion."

"If you have another option, it might be wise to negotiate."

"My mate is missing, Niki."

"I know. And we will find her. I swear to you."

Sylvan regarded her at the wheel. She was as she had always been—hard-bodied, compact, honed to a killing edge—but different than she had once been when fighting was all she lived for. "What would you do if it was Sophia?"

Niki's canines glinted as her lips pulled back in a snarl. "I would tear the world apart." Niki glanced over. "And you would probably lock me in a cage until I found my reason and hunted like a wolf should—with heart *and* head. And Pack."

"You have grown wise since you've mated," Sylvan said.

"No," Niki said, pulling into the park that bordered State Street with its brownstone mansions and civilized veneer. Many of the high-ranking Praeterns kept residences there, disappearing among the privileged humans as they carried out business and entertained political allies. "I have earned my place as your second in more than just battle."

"You have always belonged there." Sylvan glanced at the four-story town house, wondering how many inside she would have to kill. She bounded from the Rover and loped across the grassy expanse to the narrow street lined with luxury cars and an occasional limo.

Niki joined her at the foot of the stone staircase leading to the discreet white door. "Where are the guards?"

"There are none when Cecilia is not in residence." Sylvan climbed to the landing. "Although the ambassador will likely have security."

"Who are not going to allow—"

Sylvan rang the bell.

The maid who answered the door stared at Sylvan and Niki, both in black T-shirts and cargo BDUs and boots. "I'm sorry, you must have the wrong—"

"Is Ambassador Lutin at home?" Sylvan said.

The maid made a startled sound and her eyes widened. "Yes, but he's not up—"

A broad-shouldered male with close-cropped black hair and startling bright green eyes stepped up beside the maid. "The ambassador does not receive visitors here."

Sylvan leapt through the door and grasped the guard by the throat while Niki moved the maid aside and scanned the hall. Sylvan lifted the male off the floor as the maid squeaked. "He'll see me. Where?"

The guard grunted and Sylvan felt the flesh beneath her fingers undulate and twist. Not human, Fae. She squeezed harder, slammed him against the wall, and let his limp body slide down to the floor.

"Never mind." Sylvan stalked the length of the first-floor foyer past gleaming antique armoires and elegantly upholstered divans to a staircase that rose in a gentle curve to the second floor. Following the scent of vanilla and oranges, she bounded up three steps at a time with Niki close behind. A second male appeared at the top of the ornate staircase, and she buried her claws in his throat. He went down to his knees, clutching his neck. Not fatal for a Fae, but he wouldn't be a problem for a few minutes. The hallway was carpeted with a plush oriental runner, and her steps made no sound as she moved quickly past rooms that smelled empty. Tall hand-painted vases holding fresh flowers were arranged on a marble-topped sideboard, but their sweet fragrance could not overpower the seductive scent of magic.

At the end of the hall, she pushed open a walnut-paneled door and stepped into a bedroom. Morning light filtered through gauzy curtains and fell upon a broad raised bed with carved head- and footboards of the same rich dark wood as the door. A male rose from a mountain of creamy satin pillows as she entered.

"Alpha Mir," he said graciously, as if an early-morning visitor in his bedroom was a common occurrence. The human female beside him gasped and pulled the heavy ivory coverlet up over her naked breasts. The ambassador slid naked from beneath the sheets, his lithe, ageless body glowing in the dim light. He pulled a deep purple robe from a divan beside the bed, slipped it on, and casually tied it at the waist. "How may I be of service?"

"I need you to come with me."

His gaze flickered over Niki to the empty hallway beyond the open door, and back to Sylvan. "I am of course available for your needs, but if you could wait until—"

Sylvan gripped the silk gown in her fist and drew him up until his topaz eyes were on a level with hers. "My mate is in Faerie. I want you to take me through the Gate."

His eyes widened. "I would be happy to assist you in any way possible, but I cannot take you—"

She flipped the gown open and slid her claws slowly into his lower abdomen. Something old and dark swam in his eyes. "I could tear your guts out with a flick of my wrist. I doubt even Fae magic would heal you in time for you to get to Faerie."

"It is forbidden for me to bring an Earthlander to Faerie."

"I am not an Earthlander," Sylvan said softly. "I am the Were Alpha. And Cecilia does not want to make an enemy of me." She pushed her claws deeper and he smiled. Sylvan caught a glimpse of something beneath the perfect surface of his face that might have crawled from the sea a long time ago. "I will kill you and move on to every member of Cecilia's staff until someone does what I ask. Would you die for nothing?"

"Death by your hand would be nothing compared to what my Queen would do if I brought you through the Gate."

"If you prevent a war, your Queen might well reward you. I will see that she knows that."

His face transformed into the most beautiful image Sylvan had ever seen. Delicate, ethereal, rare—

"Do not seek to persuade me," Sylvan whispered, her canines grazing his throat. She pressed close until her body covered his and let her power rise. He shuddered and she smiled. "You cannot influence me, and I want nothing more than to rend your flesh from your bones. Now, what is your decision?"

❖

"Come," Francesca called when she sensed Simon approaching in the hall outside her boudoir. The door opened and he slipped inside. He was paler than usual—all the human servants were being overused. She must rebuild her seethe, and quickly. "What is it?"

She was about to feed and impatient to taste the rush of vitality that followed. The sun was up, and while she did not need sleep, the changing cycles of the day triggered her hunger. The blood slave beside her was ready for her, her eyes glazed and belly heaving with anticipation. Her arousal was sweet on Francesca's tongue. She trailed her nails over the smooth skin of the slave's breasts and circled the tight pink peaks of her nipples. The slave whimpered and parted her thighs, moist and full and eager. "Be quick."

"I'm sorry, Mistress," Simon said. "There is a visitor. He insists on seeing you."

Francesca sighed but her curiosity swelled. "Who is it?"

"Nicholas Gregory."

Slowly, Francesca smiled. Nicholas obviously thought to take her at a disadvantage, arriving after sunup. His human arrogance prevented him from having learned anything of Praetern power. That misplaced superiority would one day bring about his death. "I see. Then show him in."

Simon glanced at the slave writhing next to Francesca. "Should I wait until you've finished feeding, Mistress?"

"No."

"Yes, Mistress." He dipped his head and backed out.

Francesca opened her dressing gown and sat up, draping the naked female across her lap and cradling the slave's head in the curve of her arm. The door opened and Nicholas, imperious with his silver hair and his customary three-piece suit, marched in. He stopped abruptly and stared. "What—"

"Nicholas, darling," Francesca purred, indolently caressing the slave's breasts. "It's so good to see you."

"I received word from a mutual friend that you were here. I was quite happy to hear the rumors of your...demise...were unfounded."

"Completely." She stroked down the center of the slave's abdomen and cupped her sex. The slave whimpered and rolled her hips. Nicholas followed the motion of her hand, a respectable bulge appearing along the inside of his left thigh. "As you can see."

"My understanding was that Zachary Gates has replaced you."

Francesca slipped one finger between the swollen lips of the slave's sex and massaged her. "And has he replaced me in your service, Nicholas? Have you taken him into your confidence as to your long-term plans?"

Nicholas's hands tightened at his sides and color suffused his neck. "No."

"I thought not. Then we still have the same goal, don't we?"

"My plans have always been the same," he said roughly.

Francesca lifted the female until her throat was within striking distance. "Then I'm so happy to know we're still on the same side." She struck, and the female convulsed in her grasp. She watched Nicholas as she fed, her orgasm a pleasant undercurrent to the flush of power. She wondered how soon after leaving her he would relieve himself of the erection straining his trousers. Enjoying the trickle of sweat that rolled down his cheek, she sent an image of him fucking the slave, his hands around her throat, her screaming as he battered inside her.

He twitched and whispered, "God."

Pleased that she had guessed his secret, she raised her head and licked closed the punctures on the slave's throat. "Dr. Standish is ready to go back to work. She will likely need further specimens. We must see that she receives them."

Nicholas blinked, his face slack. "What do you mean?"

"Sylvan has just destroyed Bernardo's Pack, and not all the Blackpaws are happy about the new leadership. We can use them to strike where we cannot, and with your resources, we can see that their attacks serve our ends. Sylvan will not be expecting any kind of organized retaliation so soon."

Nicholas's chest heaved and he tugged his suit coat closed in an attempt to cover the evidence of his excitement. "Are you ready to go to war with the Weres?"

"We are ready." Francesca pushed the spent slave aside, stepped from the bed, and glided to Nicholas's side. "Aren't you?"

"I have been ready for thirty years." He swallowed, his eyes on the naked female splayed out on the bed.

"With Sylvan gone, the Weres will scatter." Francesca drifted her hand along his thigh, giving his erection a teasing stroke as she captured him in thrall. "I have business to see to, but you are welcome to stay here while you consider my plan."

"She is not easy to kill, we've tried," Nicholas murmured, taking a step toward the bed.

"Sylvan's weakness lies in those she loves. That is where we must strike." Smiling, Francesca slipped into the adjoining room, turned on the cameras, and stretched out on the divan to watch.

Chapter Ten

S quad leaders, report in," a recruit yelled down the hall in the barracks.

Gray jerked upright on her bunk and reached for her boots.

"What's going on?" Tamara said from the opposite cot.

"I don't know. I'm going to find out."

Tamara stood. "I'm coming with you."

"They're only calling for squad leaders."

"You're not a squad leader."

Gray grinned. "I am now that you're assigned to me. It's just a small squad."

Tamara huffed. "I wonder if your captain will buy that argument."

"Worth a try."

Tamara kicked into her boots and followed Gray to the door. "Is there any law against me standing out on the porch?"

"No, but be prepared to get shouldered around. Remember—"

"Oh, I won't forget. I'm just a whelp to everyone."

"Everyone else maybe, but not to me," Gray said, surprising herself.

"Why not?"

Tamara sounded genuinely confused and her uncertainty hinted at a vulnerability Gray understood. She'd been raised to be strong, to show no fear, to fight for her place in the Pack—to be proud. Weeks of captivity had tarnished her pride and shaken her faith in her strength and made her unsure of where she belonged. Tamara must be feeling much the same. "Because you won't submit, even when you want to."

"What makes you think I want to," Tamara said on a growl.

Gray stopped, crowded her against the wall as a bevy of *sentries* hurried past. She pressed full length against her until Tamara dropped her head back and moaned.

"That's why," Gray whispered. Since they'd gotten back from their run they hadn't talked much, just caught some sleep in their shared room or pretended to. But she'd been aware of Tamara's breathing, as fast and uneven as her own in the warm stillness. She'd scented the lingering arousal too, the same simmering need she was broadcasting. Her body still pulsed with the excitement of the run and the tension of the tangle. The release had been short and hard and not nearly enough, and every time she thought of Tamara just a few feet away, as ready as she was for more, her clitoris tensed and ached. But now wasn't the time for thinking about tangling. If Callan was calling the squad leaders, it could only mean action was near. She bolted for the porch. "I'll be back as soon as I can."

Gray joined the others hurrying toward the Compound parade ground, aware of doors opening and closing along the hall as others trailed behind, curious and excited. Callan stood at the foot of the barracks stairs, and the squad leaders formed a ring at the top facing him. Gray edged onto the end of the line and caught Mira giving her a look with a raised eyebrow. She looked away—not to avoid a challenge, but to prevent drawing attention to herself.

"A platoon of Blackpaws have disappeared from the Blackpaw camp. They took weapons and equipment. They may be sending raiding parties across our borders. Ready your squads and assemble in fifteen minutes for your assignments."

"Are we going after the renegades?" Mira called.

Callan shot her a look. "Assemble your squad, Corporal. You'll know your mission when I give you your orders."

Mira grinned cockily and saluted. "Yes, Captain."

As the squad leaders headed back inside to organize their soldiers, Mira bumped Gray hard enough to throw her off stride. "What are you doing here?"

"The same thing as you." She'd been expecting Mira's challenge and shoved back.

"You're not a squad leader. You're just a—"

"She is now," Callan said, landing on the porch next to them. "Gray, take Tamara, Bryce, Loren, and Fen. Report with the others."

Gray shot Mira a grin. "Yes, Captain."

When Callan was out of earshot, Mira muttered, "The perfect

squadron—three whelps, a renegade Blackpaw, and a leader who can't control her wolf."

Gray drove her shoulder into Mira's midsection and sent her sprawling through the open barracks door into the hallway. She landed on top and they rolled in a snarling knot of arms and legs and canines and claws.

Mira was heavier, more muscled, but Gray was fast and she'd survived far more abuse than the bites and bruises Mira was giving her. She dug her claws into Mira's ribs and raked upward, drawing first blood. Mira's eyes flashed gold and she verged on shifting. Gray's wolf smelled blood and suddenly she was back in her cell, chained and tormented, the electric prod driving her to frenzy. She gripped Mira's throat and, when Mira tried to roll free, mounted her. Mira caught her arm and twisted, and Gray's vision dimmed. Her wolf would not be beaten again.

"Stop, both of you!" Tamara dropped to the floor beside them and pushed in between them, heedless of the blows and slashing canines. "You have an enemy to fight, and this is not the time to waste blood on each other." Tamara grasped the back of Gray's neck. Her hand was firm and cool, ice to her flame. Her voice was steady and calm—defusing the storm clouding Gray's senses. Tamara's dark eyes held Gray's, strangely warm and accepting, before moving to Mira. "Or are you more interested in petty quarrels than your duty?"

Gray straddled Mira's midsection and sat up, her chest heaving, her skin dripping battle fury. Mira's shirt was torn and bloodied, her wolf-shot eyes half-mad. Tamara gripped Mira's shoulder.

"You have soldiers to command. An example to set. Is this what you want them to see from their leader?"

Mira's face slowly lost its wolf edges and the gold sheen faded from her irises. Her belly slowly softened beneath Gray's hips as she stared at Tamara. "What do you know of leading soldiers?"

Tamara's smile was rueful. "I have fought with warriors, and I've seen bad leaders more often than not. What you do, how you lead, will decide what kind of soldiers your squadron will become."

"This time, I'll heed your request." Mira bucked her hips and Gray gave way, sliding off and getting to her feet. Neither had submitted, neither had lost face. Mira slowly got to her knees and slid her hand into Tamara's hair. She nuzzled her neck and licked her in a long searing stroke. "I told you to come find me when you were ready. Don't wait too long."

Tamara's skin misted and she shivered, but she just shook her head and moved away.

Mira glared at Gray. "You should remember your place, and it's under me. She is not for you."

"That's not for you to decide." Gray bounded up. "You have no claim—"

Tamara snarled. "Neither of you has a claim."

"We'll see." Mira shoved past Gray and stalked out the door. The recruits who'd stood around to watch the fight slowly drifted away until Gray and Tamara were alone.

"Are you hurt?" Tamara asked.

Gray swiped with the tail of her T-shirt at blood on her forearm. The gouge stung but all she felt was the odd peacefulness warming her insides. "No. I would have beaten her."

"Does it matter?"

"You know it does."

Tamara shook her head. "She's just looking for a fight because everyone else is afraid of her. You have nothing to prove."

"I have everything to prove."

Tamara brushed her thumb over a scrape on Gray's face she hadn't known was there until the pain disappeared. "Not to me."

Gray caught her hand, rubbed her cheek against Tamara's palm. The scent of fallen leaves and crushed mint settled deep in her belly, soothing and exciting. She shuddered. "I know what you did."

"You don't know anything." Tamara pulled her hand away.

Gray caught her arm. "Why are you ashamed?"

"I'm not ashamed. And you don't know anything."

"Did you hear Callan?" Gray understood secrets. She could be patient. "Outside in fifteen minutes. We're going out on patrol."

"You really think the others will stand for me in the squad?"

"The others will do as I say."

Tamara sighed. "Do you expect me to fight my Pack?"

"No. I expect you to fight *for* your Pack. You are Timberwolf now."

❖

Dru readied to spring as the door opened, casting light across the bed where she lay entwined with the human and the Queen's second. A servant stood in the doorway.

"Forgive the intrusion, but the mistress requests the presence—"

"One moment." Luce sat up and lifted Veronica's arm from around her waist. Veronica moaned softly but did not stir, her body lax and coated with streaks of Dru's essence and her own blood. The whites of her eyes showed through her slitted lids. "I'll be—"

"I'm sorry, Liege," the servant said. "The mistress requests Dru."

"I'm not your liege." Luce turned to Dru with a slow smile. "You are favored, it seems."

"Only rewarded."

"As are we all," Luce said smoothly as she slipped into her trousers.

Dru smiled to herself and pulled on her pants, purposefully leaving them open at the waist. She knew why the Vampire Queen favored her—at the moment at least. She offered two things the Queen valued—a ready source of blood and no objections to who she had to kill. When her skills and her body were no longer needed, she would be just another servant. But that time had not come, and before it did, she would be gone. And she'd have even more information to sell to the next employer.

She followed the servant through the halls to a room she had not yet visited. At the servant's knock, Francesca bade them enter. The sitting room was far smaller than the one in Francesca's previous lair, but still opulent compared to some of the places Dru had spent the night. Francesca, draped in a long pale blue silk robe, lounged on a divan the color of blood, the gown loosely tied at her waist and revealing more than it covered. Her complexion was high, so she'd been feeding. And feeding always made Vampires sexually ravenous. Dru bowed her head. "You sent for me, my Queen."

Francesca's heated gaze roamed over Dru's face and chest. "I see you've been busy."

Dru brushed her fingers through the sex-sweat still drying on her chest and belly. "Merely entertaining your guest, as you commanded."

"And how is the good Dr. Standish?"

"She seems well-satisfied at the moment."

"I wouldn't imagine otherwise. And what about you? Are you well-satisfied?"

"That would be for you to say, my Queen." Dru widened her stance and let the muscles in her belly flicker. "I am here to serve."

"And you do so very well." Francesca gestured to the sofa beside her. "Come, sit with me."

When Dru settled beside Francesca, she had a full view of the monitor where a male she recognized from television, his trousers pushed partway down his thighs, knelt between the splayed legs of a naked female. She hissed softly as he forced her knees apart and plunged into her. "I see another human has joined us."

"More like revealed himself," Francesca said with a soft purr of pleasure. "I believe Nicholas will be useful for a while longer. For now"—she ran her hand lightly up and down the inside of Dru's thigh—"I have another job for you."

"Of course, my Queen." Dru leaned back and Francesca lightly scratched her nails over the mound at the apex of Dru's thighs. Dru growled softly.

"Luce's sources report there is unrest in the Blackpaw Pack and talk of rebellion. While Luce is busy replenishing the ranks of my Vampires, I need you to raise an army of Weres. You can start by recruiting the Blackpaws to our side."

"The wolves and the cats are not natural allies, my Queen," Dru said cautiously.

"Under ordinary circumstances, I would agree, but necessity sometimes makes friends out of enemies." Francesca squeezed lightly and massaged Dru's clitoris with her thumb.

Dru lifted her hips and hissed. She had spent herself more than once with the human, but Francesca's thrall was a knife in her belly, a twisting pleasure that forced her to fill and ready again. "I will do what I can, but they will be bent on retribution for Bernardo's death before anything else."

"That could work to our advantage." Francesca continued the rhythmic strokes, fondling the deep nodes on either side of Dru's clitoris. "If they attack the Timberwolves, they may very well be able to do what others have so far failed in doing, and we will not be responsible."

"The chance of their succeeding is slight." Dru stroked the thickening pelt down the center of her abdomen.

"Any losses are worthwhile. Besides"—Francesca gripped Dru in her palm and increased the speed and pressure of her ministrations—"these guerrilla tactics will eventually draw Sylvan out, and our new allies will be only too happy to target her."

Dru's thighs tightened. "It is my pleasure to serve, my Queen."

Francesca smiled and bore down until Dru snarled and the leather beneath her palm heated with the flood of Dru's release. "Of that, I have no doubt."

On the monitor across the room, Nicholas Gregory threw back his head, his face a grimace of ecstasy, and pumped his release into the female beneath him. His arms were rigid, his hands clamped tightly around her neck, and beneath the monitor, the red light of the recorder beeped steadily.

CHAPTER ELEVEN

Through here." The Fae ambassador pointed to a floor-to-ceiling tapestry at the end of the hallway. Gold leaves decorated the borders of the wall hanging depicting a garden filled with climbing rosebushes and flowing fountains. When he touched a blood-red rose with thorns dripping golden tears, a panel swung open onto a passageway. The space beyond was black. Not just dark, but completely without light. Sylvan's wolf searched for signs of life and saw nothing. She sought the scent of others and smelled only emptiness. The silence was endless. Inside, close to her skin, her wolf paced restlessly, uneasy in the face of nothingness. She could not fight what she could not see or smell or hear.

Niki stepped forward. "Let me go first."

Sylvan gripped her shoulders, pulled her back, and captured her gaze. "Gather the others and return to the Compound. You are my second, and until I return with the Prima, the Pack is your responsibility. You know what to do."

"No, Alpha," Niki whispered, "please. Let me go and I will bring back the Prima. I swear on my life."

"I know." Sylvan cupped Niki's jaw and brushed her thumb over the arch of her cheek. "I trust you with my life as I trust you with the Pack. You must do this for me." She pushed her back a step. "Now go and do your duty."

Sylvan turned to the ambassador. "Take me through."

She could not imagine why she had sensed the darkness was without life. A thousand birds sang, an ocean of water cascaded over her body, and a hundred winds whispered through her pelt. Dancing filaments of light coalesced into a million sunrises blurring past her eyes. The ground undulated beneath her feet as if breathing, and when the dazzling colors faded and shapes emerged, she found herself standing on the edge of a sparkling grotto. The pool, dotted with pale green fronds resembling giant lily pads, was as transparent as glass but, unlike a clear mountain spring, was the sky blue of a spring morning. Fish with filamentous dark fins reminiscent of waving tresses of delicate hair, and slender bodies adorned with brilliant yellow, gold, and orange stripes flitted along the stony bottom and between the undulating stems of emerald plants that beckoned like seductive fingers. The smooth white rock walls on the far side of the pool rose into a hillside of riotous shrubs whose branches dripped with crystalline leaves that tinkled in the breeze. The air caressed her skin like the brush of pelts when she awakened surrounded by Pack, safe and peaceful and content. A longing so deep for the sensation of home flooded through her that she dropped to her knees. Her belly warmed as her wolf curled up beneath the shade of a giant palm.

"You'll be happy here," the ambassador whispered. "You'll have everything you ever wished for—the safety to run, to hunt, to be free."

Sylvan shuddered and her wolf struggled to rise. For just an instant the ambassador's glamour faded and she glimpsed brilliant green scales beneath his pale countenance and a crest of red flowing down the back of his neck. His red eyes glinted above a beak-like mouth and then his features morphed into the face he'd worn before—the face he'd assumed to move among the humans without calling attention to his otherness. Just as she kept her wolf at bay until she could run free. Freedom. Faerie didn't offer freedom, only silken chains. She staggered to her feet.

"How do I find Cecilia?"

The ambassador's smile was that of a *magister* toward a pup who wanted to hunt before he could run—indulgent and chiding. "Cecilia, Queen of Thorns and All of Faerie, Ruler of Dark and Light, and Mistress of All Seasons, will find you when she's ready."

Sylvan tipped her head back and drew deeply of the spice-scented air. If Drake was in this world, she would find her. "Then I won't wait."

"You cannot wander through Faerie." He smiled again. "Even if you *can* see glamour."

"No? And why is that?"

He lifted a shoulder. "Our realm is not what you're used to. What appears today may not tomorrow."

"Meaning?"

"The realm breathes and shifts like every other living creature. As the winds change, so do the paths and byways. You'll soon be lost."

"I don't need landmarks. I have something more powerful."

"You are of the earth. Your power is as a drop of water to your ocean here in Faerie."

"I do not speak of my wolf, although she does not need landmarks either."

He frowned. "Then what else is there?"

Sylvan smiled. He was a being of illusion and magic. He would not understand the power of the mate bond even if she had been inclined to explain. "We shall soon find out."

She turned her back and studied the verge between woodlands and the grotto that even now appeared to be growing smaller as the undergrowth tangled and curled around the shore. Paths radiated from the grotto like spokes on a wheel, each similar to the others. This might not be the world she knew, but her power drew from the elements that nurtured her wild spirit, and from the strength of her mate. She closed her eyes and opened herself to the wind and the water and the ground beneath her feet. She stretched and let her need and passion and love reach for the only one to complete her. When she opened her eyes, she stepped onto the path that called to her. Somewhere ahead, Drake waited.

❖

"We are approaching the Compound," Niki informed Callan as the Rover rocketed across Pack land just after dark. Callan had reported the Blackpaw defections to her when she'd called, and she and the *centuri* had returned as fast as they'd dared without attracting the attention of police or reporters. They'd seen no signs of intruders on their ride in from the highway, but she did not want to breach the Compound defenses unless all was clear. "Any trouble?"

"No. But we've taken precautions."

Double the usual number of *sentries* stood post along the ramparts.

"Understood," Niki said. "Open the gates."

"Yes, *Imperator*."

The gates swung open and Jace propelled the Rover through. Callan was waiting in the center of the yard.

"Report," Niki barked as she jumped down.

"No sightings along our border," he said.

"How secure is our perimeter?"

"We have patrols stationed at intervals a mile out from the Compound."

"Reserves?"

Callan grimaced. "We've called up anyone with training, but with some of our squadrons assigned to the Blackpaw camp, we're thin."

"Who commands there?"

"Val."

"Good. Make sure the patrols stay in radio contact and inform Val we may need to redeploy her forces quickly."

"Yes, *Imperator*." He glanced at Jace and Jonathan waiting with the Rover. "The Alpha?"

"Has business elsewhere."

He nodded and did not question her. "Max is here with Andrea. He says they need to speak with the Alpha."

"I'll speak with them. Alert me if anything changes."

Callan saluted and loped away.

"Get some food and whatever else you need," Niki said to Jace and Jonathan. "Then report to headquarters."

The twins headed for the dining hall, and Niki strode toward headquarters. She nodded at the *sentries* posted on either side of the door who shot to attention as she pushed inside. She followed Max's scent to the meeting room that took up half of the first floor. The *centuri*, a big rough-faced male with enormous shoulders and thick brown hair that tangled around his wide neck, stood by the massive stone fireplace in dark jeans, black T-shirt, leather vest, and biker boots. The female beside him was barely as tall as his shoulder, slight of build but powerful in appearance. She too wore a close-fitting dark T-shirt, jeans with a wide leather belt, and boots. Except for her finer musculature, she might have been a young Were soldier. She wasn't, though. She was human, and Niki wasn't yet convinced she was an ally.

"The Alpha is occupied. You have information?" Niki closed the door behind her and breathed the scent of dominant Were mating hormones. She lifted her brow in Max's direction. His eyes glinted and he slid his hand around the back of Andrea Hoffstetter's neck. Niki was mated, in all ways but the final one. Without the mate bite sealing her bond to Sophia, their chemistries would not fuse and Niki would broadcast like every other dominant Were. If Max was claiming this female, she was his competitor. He growled softly, an involuntary and perfectly natural warning, but she had no time for it. She'd been gone from Sophia for over twenty-four hours and she'd been continuously prepared to fight, prepared to defend the Alpha, and now, forced to leave the Alpha. The Pack was under threat of attack, and she could do little but wait. Her wolf was half-wild and she needed to tangle with her mate. Or to fight.

"Your human is of no interest to me," Niki snapped.

"That's what you say." Max took a step forward, his rumble growing louder.

Andrea grasped his arm and pressed her palm to the center of his chest. "Max, stop. Your *imperator* is right. There is nothing of interest for either of us."

As she spoke, she slowly stroked his chest, and to Niki's surprise, Max calmed. A human should not be able to affect a Were like that, but then Max's wolf should not want to claim a human as a mate, yet that was apparently the case. She just shook her head. Too many changes for her to fight.

"Make your report. I have other duties to see to." She knew she sounded short, but Max's mating hormones only made her wolf more insistent she find and claim her own mate.

"Andrea has news." Max dragged the human close, her back to his chest, and looped his heavily muscled arms around her middle. He rubbed his cheek against her hair and watched Niki warily.

Andrea didn't seem to mind his possessiveness, but instead grasped both his forearms to tighten his hold. "I've received intelligence from our people undercover in HUFSI that they are moving toward armed confrontation."

"Meaning what?" Niki asked. Humans United For Species Integrity was a radical underground group whose stated purpose was the eradication of Praeterns, particularly those deemed most dangerous—the predator Weres and Vampires. Their leadership was kept secret, as were the locations of their cells. Nevertheless, they had a vocal presence aided by the Internet where they released videos and manifestos and recruited others to their cause.

"We're not sure, but we know that Sylvan has always been a target, and we think they are stepping up their efforts to remove her." Andrea scratched her nails along Max's forearm in an unconscious gesture that had Max's eyes glowing. "The more militant members of the group want to attack the Compound."

"Do they think they can attack us in our own territory and survive?" Niki rumbled in disgust. She would welcome a chance to meet her enemies face-to-face at last and be rid of them.

"They seem to think you will not retaliate for fear of official reprisal."

Max snarled and Niki curled her lip. "We do not answer to human law."

"All the same, you are vastly outnumbered, and if public sentiment turns against you, many of your so-called friends, human *and* Praetern, will change sides."

"We don't depend upon humans, who have little in the way of honor, to stand with us."

"Be careful, *Imperator*," Max said in a low ominous tone. "Andrea and her people risk their lives every day."

"And you should remember you are a wolf." Niki stalked forward. "Be careful who you challenge."

Max stepped out from behind Andrea, shifting her to one side as if Niki posed a threat to her. His canines glinted and he growled again. Niki's wolf had had more challenge than she could tolerate, and she wanted to let her free. Andrea, though, would try to intervene if the two of them tussled. "I would gladly accept your challenge if the human were not here, but she would be in danger."

Andrea pushed Max with her shoulder, which had as much effect as if she had tried to move a mountain. "This has to stop. We are all on the same side." She faced Niki but did not challenge her eye to eye. "Max is afraid if he claims me I'll become a target too. He forgets I already am and have been for a long time before we met."

"Mating wolves don't think very clearly." Niki glanced at Max and snorted. "It seems to me your wolf has already claimed her. Finish it so the rest of us can have some peace."

Andrea laughed. "I've been telling him the same thing."

Max ducked his head. "My apologies, *Imperator*. I—"

"I know. Just listen to your wolf in this." Niki said to Andrea, "Do you have any more information about the location of the labs?"

"We've identified two, but the people we've been able to get inside haven't found any evidence of human or Praetern subjects."

"We believe several pregnant females have been abducted. We need to find them."

Andrea grimaced. "We know Veronica Standish is involved.

We've had her under surveillance, but we can't find her or her current lab. We're reaching out to all our informants. If anyone knows anything, we will too before long."

"We've already reinforced our perimeters, and the Alpha is always well protected." Niki uttered the lie with total confidence. No one could know that Sylvan was even now in mortal danger.

"We can support you here with personnel temporarily," Andrea said.

Niki frowned. "Human soldiers in the Compound? Impossible."

"With your patrols—each one personally vouched for by me."

"Federal agents."

Andrea nodded. "Sooner or later, you will have to accept human friendship."

Niki snarled. "We have survived millennia without it."

Andrea slid her arm around Max's waist and rubbed her cheek against his chest. "It's a new dawn for all of us."

"We will take the offer under advisement. Let us know as soon as you locate that lab."

Niki left them and hurried toward the infirmary. Her mate was there and she needed her. She bounded up the steps and through the door, drawn by her mate's scent. As she expected, Sophia was caring for the infected human females who'd been liberated from the labs and were now *mutia*. Niki would have destroyed them, but Sophia and Drake believed they could be saved, and the Alpha would not turn her back on a Were, even a mutant. When Niki entered the isolation room and saw Sophia sitting by the bedside of one of the comatose females, she was grateful that the Alpha was wiser than she. Sophia had been like these females once, and the Alpha had not abandoned her. Sophia looked up, heat in her eyes.

"I don't like it when you're away so long," Sophia said.

"Nor do I. Can you leave them?"

Sophia glanced at the monitors and set a chart aside. "For a short time."

"I only have a short time. I need you."

"I am always here."

CHAPTER TWELVE

Sylvan climbed up the twisting path until she reached a clearing where the trees parted to frame a view down the hillside. She stopped and looked back, but the grotto was gone and in its place a field of yellow daisies stretched as far as she could see. The ambassador was gone as well, and there was no indication the Faerie Gate had had ever existed. She suspected the Earthside entrances were fixed, but where the Gate led into the Faerie realm was likely determined by the destination of the one passing through or perhaps by the will of whoever was watching. And she was certain someone was watching.

Her wolf scented the presence of others but she saw no one other than the myriad insects, some flying species resembling butterflies but with three sets of iridescent wings and needle-thin bodies, and others with a dozen legs clinging to leaves and stems while spinning gossamer webs of shimmering green and gold. All were brilliantly hued and seemingly unperturbed by her presence, as were the multicolored birds that flocked in the nearby trees and swooped overhead, and the small prey—rabbit-like furred creatures with stubby ears, large orange eyes, and sleek catlike bodies who hopped along beside her for a while and then broke away, only for others to appear a few paces farther along. Perhaps the winged species were scouts of some kind, reporting her progress through the landscape that changed from forest to farm to jungle in the blink of an eye. For all she knew, the rabbit-y creatures might be Fae soldiers cloaked in glamour. Her wolf wanted to eat one, more to send a warning than to satisfy her hunger, but she was not here to hunt—at least not foreign prey who might very well strike back with weapons of their own. Her only goal was to find Drake and Misha and take them home.

She traveled what felt like an hour, although she could not trust her sense of time passing. Clouds drifted overhead, spinning and changing direction so quickly she could not judge the points of the compass. Sometimes she moved from sunlight to shadow, but she could mark neither distance nor time by the position of the sun because she couldn't find it. When she searched the heavens, the light was so bright she could only blink and look away after a few seconds. Perhaps all of Faerie was perpetually drenched in light, or maybe that was only here and some other part was eternally dark. No one knew, because the Fae kept their secrets better than all the other Praeterns, having withdrawn from Earthside millennia before when the Vampires and Weres went to war against the humans and all Praeterns fought for their lives. The Fae queens decided they needed none of what the earth had to offer except the fertility of human and Were males from time to time, and they had no difficulty luring Earthlanders to Faerie with the promise of eternal spring and everlasting youth.

Sylvan ran on along the ever-changing path, drawn by Drake's scent. Not her scent exactly, but the *sense* of her, pulling at some place deep in Sylvan's core. She moved from the high grasses and dense trees into a valley, where a wide river twisted through tangled marshes dense with flowering plants whose leaves were as huge as boulders, and let her wolf rise. She could move faster and less visibly in pelt, staying close to the ground under cover of the thick undergrowth. When she'd followed the river around yet another bend that led to yet another glade that hadn't been apparent until she'd emerged into it, she stopped at the water's edge to drink. The aqua water was cool and crisp and tasted fruity, like a delicate wine. She lapped at it cautiously. A shadow fell across the water and her wolf spun, snarling a warning. Only shadows danced behind her where there had been sunlight before. A weeping willow now arched high above her, its dangling branches thick with delicate tendrils that waved like sea grass in the sudden current of a floral-scented breeze. The path was gone, and she was surrounded by pale yellow reeds capped by blood-red petals edged in swirls of silver. A petal brushed against her foreleg and burned a trail through her pelt.

Sylvan rumbled warily and slowly padded through the lethal foliage, her ears pricked forward for any sound, her nostrils flaring to capture any scent. A dove rose from the willow, its pure white wings spread wide, lifting on the sweet air current and carried away like a leaf in an autumn breeze. The trail was gone but she wasn't alone. The reeds bent toward the taller undergrowth that ringed the glade as if reaching for a lover. Sylvan growled softly, her pelt rising along her spine, her canines exposed beneath her curled lip. Moments passed in silence except for whispers on the air that might've been music or the rustle of a thousand wings. A path appeared off to her right, and she heard a roar like thunder rolling over the mountains.

She kept the water at her back and hunkered down, belly low and muscles coiled. A boar the size of a small pony, with short powerful legs, a wide snout, and two foot-long, razor-edged tusks, charged out of the underbrush. Massive, red eyed, and wild, it lowered its tusks and raced straight for her belly. She waited until he was almost upon her to spring out of the way, slashing at its throat with her claws. His head swung around and struck a glancing blow across her hindquarters that drew blood. She chased it down before it could turn, caught it from the side, and snapped her jaws closed on its neck. Her strike was aimed for the jugular. The hide was thicker than any prey she'd ever hunted and her bite was too shallow to reach the vulnerable vessels. It roared and twisted while she hung on, clawing at its heavy body, hoping to damage a leg. If she could bring it down, she could kill it. If there weren't more.

The boar-thing tried to dislodge her, dragging her through the reeds where a hundred slender silver blades sliced through her pelt. She clenched her jaws tighter, gouged bloody trenches in its flanks with her claws, and the heavy beast slowed a fraction. Then she felt the other coming. The earth trembled, and a wall of hot air burst out from the undergrowth as if fleeing in the face of a raging storm. A rumble so deep her blood vibrated assaulted her ears. She released the boar and jumped free of its swinging head. It panted, blood running from his neck and side. She watched it warily and waited for something far bigger to emerge from the bush.

The boar let out a furious scream and raced off into the underbrush in the opposite direction.

❖

Sophia laughed softly in the dark. "What if someone sees us leaving?"

Niki pulled Sophia's head against her shoulder and nuzzled her neck. Sophia had been as ready as her, and she'd emptied in a fury almost as soon as she'd felt Sophia's legs tighten around her hips. The hot flush of release still burned through her belly. "What if they do?"

"The *imperator* sneaking off into the barracks for a quick tangle like some adolescent with no control?"

"They'll be envious." Niki grinned and rubbed her cheek against Sophia's hair, immersing herself in the scent of her mate. "And what does it matter where we couple?"

"You're right, it doesn't." Sophia scratched her claws up and down the trench between Niki's abdominals, and Niki tensed with a deep growl that might have been a warning if Sophia didn't recognize the rising scent of need. She kissed Niki's neck and teased her with a bite. "Everyone will know from the look in your eyes. You're always very proud of yourself after you take me."

Niki rolled on top of her and lightly clasped her wrists, letting her weight pin her to the bunk. "And why shouldn't I be? My mate is the most beautiful in the entire Pack."

"And I have the only one I've ever wanted." Sophia clasped her legs around the back of Niki's thighs and shifted her hips until they were fitted to one another again. She lightly bit Niki's neck. "Again."

Niki kissed her, still ready. Always ready and done with waiting. "Did your parents speak with you?"

Sophia grew still. "They didn't tell me they had spoken with you."

"We weren't trying to hide anything from you." Niki rubbed her cheek on Sophia's breast, making her arch and growl softly. "I was with the Alpha when your parents told her of the results. I didn't have a chance to see you before I left."

Sophia looked away and Niki cupped her face, drawing her gaze back. "Why aren't you happy?"

Sophia took a deep breath. "Because I know what you will want."

"You've always known what I wanted. You're my mate, I want us to be bonded. I want everyone to know you're mine."

"And you think I don't want everyone to know you're mine?" Sophia's eyes sparked. "You think I don't see how many females still try to catch your attention?"

"You know that's not what matters."

"I know it *does* matter, no matter what you say."

Niki rumbled. "You doubt me after all this time?"

"Never. I never doubt your love." Sophia stroked her face. "But we are what we are, and until your wolf is bonded, you will feel the call of others. You are free—"

"No." Niki caught Sophia's lip between her teeth and tugged, a reminder that she was a dominant wolf who had made her claim and would not be denied.

Sophia snarled and Niki kissed her until she stopped protesting. "I have the one I want. And now there's no reason that everyone shouldn't know what we know. That we are mates. Your parents said it was safe."

"No, they didn't. They said there was a better chance that it was safe, but there is still a substantial possibility that I could infect you." Sophia took a long breath. "Niki, you could develop the fever."

"That's not going to happen. You've never been sick. You survived. You won."

Sophia shook her head in frustration. "We don't know that. We can't know that for certain, and until we do, I won't—"

"Nothing is ever certain. There will always be threats, we will always have to fight. You are my strength."

Sophia's eyes filled. "As you are mine."

"Then it is time."

"Let's wait a little longer," Sophia whispered. "Let my parents test—"

"We don't need any more tests. It's time." Niki rocked her hips into the valley of Sophia's thighs, inciting Sophia to tighten around her. "Now. Together."

"I won't—"

"You will. I will drive your wolf to make the claim no matter what you think you want."

"I want," Sophia gasped. "But—"

Niki kissed her throat, grazed her canines along the swell of her breast, and closed her mouth over Sophia's nipple. She bit slowly, pressing her clitoris to the cleft awaiting her, until Sophia's need misted both their skins. "I'm not worried. It's time."

Sophia arched, her claws scraping down the center of Niki's back. Her snow-white pelt gleamed beneath her skin. Niki kept up the torture, holding her down, biting lightly, teasing all the places she knew would drive Sophia's wolf wild with the need to join, the need to release.

Sophia whined, the gold ring around her brilliant blue irises widening, her skin slick and shimmering. "Don't. Don't let me hurt you."

"I won't." Niki kissed the bite she'd placed on Sophia's shoulder, the bite that made Sophia hers, licking and sucking lightly, stirring Sophia's wolf to return the claim. "Trust me. I need this. We need this."

Niki sat up, pulled Sophia into her lap, and Sophia instantly wrapped her legs around Niki's hips until they were face to face, breast to breast, sex to sex.

"I am yours as you are mine. I have always been yours," Niki whispered. She lifted her hips and her clitoris slid beneath Sophia's, enticing her, inflaming her.

Sophia threw her head back, her canines gleaming, a high-pitched cry escaping from her throat. Her breasts flushed, her nipples tightened into peaks. A fine dusting of pelt feathered her lower abdomen. "Please, I need you."

"Not until you give me what I want."

The mate bite on Sophia's shoulder darkened, beckoning for Niki to bite, to send Sophia spiraling into her release. Niki's clitoris pounded, her vision narrowing until all she knew was the need in Sophia's eyes. The need to empty into her. She spread her hand into Sophia's hair and pulled Sophia closer to her exposed throat.

"Make me yours." Niki tilted her hips and notched her clitoris into the cleft between Sophia's thighs. "Let me be your mate."

Sophia buried her claws in Niki's back and rode her, milking her length, drawing her tight into her center. The pulsations in her glands pounded in time with her heart. The drive to release, to join, to surrender was so painful she whimpered.

"Complete me," Niki groaned. "I need you."

I need you.

I need you.

"I need you too." Sophia buried her canines in Niki's shoulder at the instant Niki pierced hers.

Niki exploded, blind with pleasure and filled with belonging.

Chapter Thirteen

Sylvan crouched as air rushed by her with the force of water cascading down the mountainside. The reeds on the far side of the glen parted as though a great hand reached down and scoured a path through the dense undergrowth. The earth beneath her feet vibrated. A great beast nearly six feet at the shoulders emerged. Its clawed legs, as large around as tree stumps, dug into the earth with every stride. It halted ten feet away, its dense hide dark and weathered, its immense head capped by short ears above deep-set fiery eyes and a long, broad snout. Its thick, leathery black lips skimmed back to expose rows of daggerlike teeth, half the length of Sylvan's forelegs. Hot breath washed over her, and the fierce rumble emanating from its massive chest rolled down her spine like ice.

Is this any way to greet a friend? Sylvan's wolf snarled softly, showing her teeth.

Gold shimmered as bright as sunlight and the Hound faded in a wisp of smoke.

"I was more interested in the bush hog planning to make a meal of you." Torren stepped toward her, long slender body encased in shimmering black from her booted feet to shoulders. A scarlet sash ran across her chest and ended at one hip, where a silver scabbard swayed as she walked. The ornate hilt of her sword gleamed with precious gems.

Sylvan circled, keeping the distance between them as she sniffed the air, testing, searching for a hint of illusion. *I would have had hog for breakfast.*

Torren laughed, her voice chiming with ancient power. "And that's not blood I see on your flank."

Satisfied, Sylvan shed pelt and rose. Her wound closed as she shifted. The hip still burned, but she'd had far worse, and injuries were of no matter now. "Where is Drake?"

"Safe for the moment." Torren put her hands on her hips, dark eyes glittering like diamonds cast upon a field of coal. "Come with me, and I'll take you to her."

Torren paused and waved a hand. Sylvan found herself wearing plain black trousers, short black boots, and a white shirt so soft it might have been woven from air. "Is it real?"

"As real as anything," Torren said, "and more comfortable than the alternative, I hope."

"I'm not worried about comfort. I want my mate and my wolf returned."

"Wolves are always so single-minded." Torren sighed. "Sylvan, they came here voluntarily, as did you. We did not seek them out and kidnap them. Technically, you are all trespassers in Faerie."

"So you have made my mate a prisoner?"

Torren's shoulder lifted. "She is a guest of the Thorn Queen."

"Is there a difference?"

The Fae Master of the Hunt only smiled. She had shown herself to be a friend of the Pack when she had joined Sylvan and her warriors at the battle to rescue a captive wolf and dethrone Francesca. But Torren was a royal Fae, an ancient and powerful Hunter, and her loyalty would always be to her Queen.

Sylvan growled. "Drake would not have willingly broken your laws. How did they pass through the Faerie Gate?"

"Come," Torren said without answering. "It will be dark here soon, and you would not like to meet some of the inhabitants of the Glen after moonrise."

Sylvan glanced at the sky and saw nothing to suggest that night was coming. "The Glen?"

"That's what we call this area. The ambassador is the Governor of the Glen when he resides here."

"And that's why his Faerie Gate brought me here?" Sylvan remembered the shimmer of green and hint of scales beneath the ambassador's glamour and wondered at what other forms hid beneath the animals she had passed.

Torren nodded. "Cecilia is most unhappy with him right now."

"His fate is not my worry," Sylvan said, "but I did promise him a painful death if he didn't guide me through."

"Of that I have no doubt. However, Cecilia prefers death to betrayal."

"I gave him my word I would speak for him with your Queen."

"And perhaps the Queen of Thorns will be receptive." Torren did not sound convinced or concerned.

Torren slipped back along the path through the reeds, and Sylvan followed. When she glanced back, the undergrowth was closing behind her as if a net were weaving itself shut. The river was gone and the trees pressed trunk to trunk in a solid mass as dense as stone. Night had fallen behind her but ahead the sky was still alive with light. The grassy path wound through an orchard of short trees with flesh-colored bark and fruit resembling apples hanging from gnarled boughs. Each orb was decorated with a cap of green leaves the color of mint and pale unblemished skin that glowed like the surface of fresh-fallen snow. The ground was littered with ivory petals that emitted a fruity perfume. The fruit swirled in a breeze she couldn't feel as she passed, and dark pits swam beneath the surface of the glowing skin. Her wolf rumbled as a thousand eyes followed her. "What are they?"

Torren smiled. "We call them watchers."

"Are they alive?"

"Of course. Everything in Faerie is alive, even the stones beneath your feet."

Faerie was a realm of shifting time and place and form, totally unlike the world of flesh and blood and instinct Sylvan and her wolves inhabited. The Fae and the Weres had nothing in common, but Torren had somehow called to Misha's wolf, had formed a bond with her. With all that divided them, what shape that bond would take was hard to imagine, and Sylvan wanted Misha back almost as much as Drake.

"Misha's bond brought them through the Gate, didn't it."

"Possibly," Torren said.

From a Fae, that was as good as a yes. Sylvan grumbled. "Are you going to let her go?"

Torren slowed, met Sylvan's gaze. "No."

"Misha is of the earth. Without the Pack, part of her would die."

"Misha, all of us, are part of a much larger universe. Her ties to Pack will not be broken." Torren smiled, a smile so beautiful Sylvan's chest ached. "Are yours?"

"Not to Drake, but the Pack—" Sylvan reached out, sought the familiar threads that bound her to the hearts and minds and souls of those she served, and felt the distant beat of hundreds of hearts, strong and steady. She frowned. "How—?"

"Faerie is a place of answered dreams. Before, your wolf sought only Drake. The connection you share with her is more powerful than all the others, and you felt only her. So it will be with Misha, but she will never lose what ties her to Pack."

"She must choose."

"She will," Torren whispered.

They rounded a bend and a valley opened before them, lush and green, spreading out between mountain ranges whose peaks disappeared into a cloudless sky. At the far end of the divide, the valley ended at the base of a huge vine-covered dome. The Faerie Mound of Cecilia's court.

"How near are we to Earthside?" Sylvan asked.

"As close as a breath and as far away as the night stars."

"The Gates are really curtains, aren't they?"

"You ask questions that cannot be answered."

"And you never give those of us who live beyond the veil the answers we seek," Sylvan said.

"What we seek may not be what we need," Torren said.

"It is for me. I seek my mate and my wolf."

Torren led her to the base of the Faerie Mound. "Then may I present the royal court of Cecilia, Queen of Thorns and Ruler of All of Faerie."

An archway appeared in the mound, a great gate carved from gold and guarded by helmeted soldiers with sword and spear. Sylvan followed Torren through the archway, aware of the path behind her disappearing into mist as thick as midnight fog.

❖

Dru pulled her motorcycle into the end of a line of bikes in front of Raptures, a Vampire club in a run-down neighborhood adjacent to a towering bridge crossing the Hudson. The narrow four-story building was squeezed into the center of a block of derelict and abandoned factories and apartment buildings. The upper stories were dark, with boarded-over windows and sagging eaves, and the club itself was marked only by an unlit sign hanging askew from a bent iron rod above the windowless door. On the far corner of the block, a solitary bar sported an erratically blinking beer sign in the streaked plate-glass window, but otherwise the neighborhood was deserted. The customers who frequented Raptures tended to be Weres and humans who didn't want their business known to anyone who might ask too many questions. The humans were mostly addicts, willing to do anything for a Vampire bite, including sell drugs, their bodies, or the bodies of their children. The Weres were all loners or renegades who had left their Packs and formed gangs, loosely ruled by leaders who kept order through violence or drugs. The submissives among them were often addicted to the street drug desoxyephedrine. DSX was a variant of methamphetamine, one of the few drugs capable of corrupting Were physiology. In addition to hyperaggressiveness, the drug intensified the Weres' naturally high sexual drive, creating sex slaves of the submissive, males and females alike, before they eventually spiraled into psychoses. Dru suspected some of the Weres who frequented the place had been part of the past attempts to assassinate Sylvan. The idea made her chuckle as she booted down her kickstand and swung her leather-clad leg over her tank and strode toward the door.

Only the quickest and the best would ever defeat Sylvan Mir, not a ragtag bunch of undisciplined street fighters and addicts. And it would either take numbers, which they did not now have, or a highly skilled strike force. Francesca had given her the task of recruiting an army, and she'd do her best to fulfill that order, but she wasn't interested in a suicide mission. She preferred to draw out Sylvan with a small cadre of soldiers—an ambush would be ideal. All she needed was the right bait.

First, though, she needed to recruit mercenaries who would be willing to risk their lives. Francesca had assured her that money was not an issue, but she wasn't certain that Weres would be swayed by monetary enticements. Humans almost always were. She did know what would sway a Were, though. In the world of predators, the currency was power.

She pushed through the door and into a long, narrow room ringed by tables and crowded with bodies. The bar ran along one side with blinking signs and bottles lined up in haphazard rows on several shelves along the wall. The overhead black lights cast everyone in the eerie glow of moonlight. Weres and humans and Vampires mingled in a seething mass, those who were hosting having made their bodies available by wearing nothing under their vests, to expose their necks, chests, breasts, and bellies. Those who offered sex as well as blood leaned against the walls, leather pants and denim jeans open to allow the Vampires to fuck and feed. The room was stifling and awash with the scent of blood and pheromones. Dru's cat was well satisfied after Francesca had drained her to the point of exhaustion, but her clitoris twitched all the same. She ignored the automatic response and scanned the room until she found a familiar face.

Marcus was a dominant wolf Were she'd often seen with Bernardo at Nocturne when the Blackpaws had come for sex. He'd been a lieutenant, although not one of Bernardo's inner circle. She worked her way through the crowd, brushing past Vampires feeding from the throats of Weres who spent themselves in empty air. A hand reached out and brushed her thigh, and she found herself face-to-face with a male Vampire whose eyes glowed crimson and whose incisors glinted beneath his seductive smile.

"I've always preferred cats to wolves," he said.

"Then you show excellent judgment," Dru replied. His hand slipped between her thighs, finding the base of her clitoris with unerring certainty. He massaged her lightly and she hissed.

"So much more powerful," he murmured, "and far sweeter."

Her pelt rolled beneath her skin and suddenly she was running, her heart thudding, her loins filled, her belly tight with the thrill of the chase. She shuddered. His thrall called to her and she could not afford to lose herself in sex frenzy. She gripped his wrist, stilling the rhythmic motion of his fingers as he milked her. "What are you doing in a place like this? Don't they offer you enough slaves at your Clan home?"

He lifted a shoulder. "I've always been a rule breaker."

She smiled. He was clever, and Francesca needed to rebuild her Vampire minions. She would appreciate a clever, handsome one like him who could draw human blood slaves as well as other discontented Vampires to her newly forming court. "So, you drained someone and have been banished."

"An accident." He leaned forward and licked her throat. His hand closed around her, and her clitoris stiffened fully, beating in his palm. "I could drain you willingly, though."

She was ready again and pelt streamed down the center of her bare belly. "Francesca has already done that tonight."

He jerked away and bowed his head slightly. "My apologies. I did not know."

She pushed him back into the shadows and clasped his neck, guiding his head to her throat. "A taste. Then perhaps you'll accompany me back to the lair. I'll warn you, though, Francesca will not suffer disobedience."

"I would rather obey you."

"You will." She opened his pants and gripped him before he could move between her thighs. "Just a taste."

His bite was smooth and sleek, nearly as practiced as Francesca's, but without her power. The hormones he released into Dru's blood made her burn and her glands emptied, but she held on to her sanity, something she could never do with Francesca. She massaged him as he fed and he spent against the wall in long, thin arcs. When she pulled away, he hissed in protest but sealed her throat with a swipe of his tongue. He hardened again in her hand, her blood giving him power.

"I would be honored to join Francesca and her Clan," he whispered, shuddering in her grasp.

She guided him back into his pants. "You've had enough tonight. Be ready to leave soon."

He nodded, his eyes still hungry. "As you command."

She laughed and left him. Marcus was watching her as she made her way to him.

"Francesca sends her greetings," Dru said.

He regarded her stonily. He was big and brawny with sharp, intelligent dark eyes. His biker garb was well-worn and fit him like the uniform it was. "I've seen you with her. Who are you to the Vampire, Cat?"

She smiled, letting him see a glint of her canines. "One of her army."

He snorted. "What army?"

"We have common cause," Dru said, ignoring the jibe. "You are a Blackpaw—unless I am wrong—and you are now Timberwolf."

He snarled and spat on the floor. "I would never show my belly to Sylvan Mir."

"What choice do you have as long as she controls all your territory and your wolves?" She looked around the dingy, stark room filled with scruffy renegade addicts of one kind or another. "Unless this is where you prefer."

"What do you offer?"

"A chance to take back what is rightfully yours—your Pack and its lands."

He smirked. "How?"

"Sylvan Mir is no friend to Francesca, and without Mir in power, the Timberwolves will not be able to keep the Blackpaws under their rule."

"You'll need more than an army to displace her."

"I don't want an army in numbers, only a skilled force willing to be bold."

"And follow you?"

"No." Dru smiled. "Follow us."

Chapter Fourteen

Just after moonrise, Gray drifted through the trees and hunkered down beside Tamara where she crouched on a rocky overhang above a game trail a mile from the outer perimeter of the Compound. "Anything?"

"Just deer," Tamara said. "Have there been any sightings anywhere?"

Gray shrugged. "Not that I know of." She hesitated, sensitive to Tamara's conflicted feelings about being part of a Timberwolf patrol lying in wait for Blackpaws. Still, she was Pack now and should be treated that way. Pack meant trust and loyalty. "Have the Blackpaws ever penetrated this deep into our territory?"

Tamara was silent for a long time. Gray waited, searching the forest for any hint of intruders. Small prey scuffled through the undergrowth and occasionally a deer wandered through. When the wind shifted and carried the hint of predator down the slope, the deer flicked a tail and dashed away with so much grace Gray didn't even mind letting it go. She hadn't hunted with the Pack since her rescue, except when the Alpha insisted. She still wasn't sure she could control her wolf enough to let her run with others. Once in pelt, she wanted to fight, or fuck, anyone who gave the slightest hint of challenge.

"You're not betraying anyone—not if they're planning an attack on our Compound. We have young there. What honorable wolf would attack a den with young inside?"

"I don't know if patrols ever came this far into Timberwolf territory," Tamara finally said. "I'm not that high ranking, and the only raiding party I was ever part of was the one where your...the Alpha captured us."

"I can't see why they would risk it," Gray muttered. "They must know we would outnumber them."

"Maybe they don't care. Or maybe they have help."

Gray bristled. "What do you mean, help? Do you think we have traitors among us?"

"It wouldn't be the first time." Tamara snorted. "I'm sure most everyone in the Compound would consider me a possibility for that role."

Gray shook her head. "That's not true. Not every Timberwolf is born in Pack. Lots of us came from somewhere else. Even our *medicus* was once a Blackpaw."

Tamara stiffened. "Who?"

"Sophia. The one who came to look at your back in the prison cell. She was a Blackpaw once."

Tamara frowned. "Then what is she doing here with you?"

Gray scratched at a bug crawling on her neck and used the diversion to sort out her thoughts. Maybe she shouldn't be talking about the *imperator*'s mate, but everyone in the Pack knew the story. And if it helped Tamara feel less like an outsider, she couldn't see the harm. "I don't know the whole story. It never seemed to matter. But I know she'd been in danger in the Blackpaw Pack somehow and her parents came to our Alpha for sanctuary."

"Danger," Tamara said softly. "From Bernardo?"

"I think so, or maybe the Alpha before him."

"From what everyone said, there wasn't much difference."

"She's like you, you know," Gray said quietly.

"I don't know what you're talking about."

"Yes, you do. I just don't understand why you don't want to talk about it."

"Everything's always clear to you, isn't it," Tamara said. "You've always known who you were and what you were. Everyone else did too. All you had to do was find your place somewhere along the line. You would tussle and tangle and dominate until you couldn't anymore and, when you finally submitted, that's where you belonged."

"What of it? We're wolves. That's our way."

"Not for everyone."

"What do you mean?"

"Did you ever want to tussle just so you could submit, just so you could feel another Were between your legs?"

Gray stared hard through the gloom, knowing what her answer would mean. "No."

"Why not?"

"Because I'm a dominant Were."

"How would you feel if you were about to submit another Were in the midst of a tangle and all of sudden you couldn't bring yourself to do it? When all you could think of was how good it would feel to drag them down on top of you?"

"I…" Gray didn't know, not exactly. But she knew what it was to crave something she'd never imagined wanting. "You don't know as much about me as you think."

"No? Then how am I wrong?"

Gray would rather fight a dozen Blackpaws with only tooth and claw than admit to anyone, especially this female, how far she had fallen from her place in the Pack. "Never mind."

"You expect me to show you my belly," Tamara said, "but you protect yours."

"Maybe I don't want you to see."

"It has to do with pain, doesn't it?"

Gray vaulted to her feet and Tamara grabbed the waistband of her BDUs and jerked her down. "Remember where we are. I'm sorry. I didn't mean—"

"No," Gray rasped. She rubbed her forehead as if she could reach inside and tear out the memories. "You're right. I was in a cell once too. In chains, real chains, and after a while, I gave in."

"I'm sorry." Tamara gripped her wrist. "You don't have to tell me—"

"I know I don't." Gray laughed under her breath to prevent the tears that trembled on her lashes from falling. "That's the price, though, isn't it? Secret for secret?"

"I suppose it could be. One for one."

"I didn't mind the beatings. My wolf was strong enough to take anything they could do, but there were other things. Drugs and torture—I couldn't fight those."

"I'm so sorry. Are they dead now, the ones who did this?"

"Some of them."

Tamara rubbed Gray's back, lightly scratching her nails between Gray's shoulder blades, up and down, up and down. "Are you still hurting?"

Gray shuddered. Tamara's blunt claws stroked her tenderly, the compassionate caresses filling her belly with warmth and more than comfort. Want. "Not really. I dream. I remember."

Tamara nuzzled Gray's neck, whining softly and kissing the side of her jaw. "You're strong, I can feel it. The memories will fade even if they never disappear."

Gray turned quickly and her mouth brushed the corner of Tamara's. Her clitoris tensed and her belly tightened. She gripped her shoulders. "You make me forget. You make me feel like I used to. Strong and sure."

Tamara took a stuttering breath. Gently, she murmured, "Gray, I think you'd better move away. Because you make me want things too."

Gray inched away until their bodies no longer touched and Tamara's hand was no longer stroking her. She couldn't bear to leave her, though, couldn't stop now. She kept watching the trail. It was easier somehow to talk about her fears that way. "I like the pain, sometimes. Such fire blazing through me, burning everything in its path, until there's only pleasure at the end." She rubbed her belly, trying to soothe the ache between her thighs. Knowing it would do no good. She glanced quickly at Tamara, saw her eyes glow gold, scented her desire. "I want to be between your legs right now."

"I know. I want you there." Tamara sighed. "And I want to be on top of you, riding you. It's not so simple for either of us."

"I don't mind that. I don't fear you above me."

Tamara laughed softly in the moonlight. "Most dominants would."

"I'm not like most dominants."

"Then you'll have to show me, soon."

"I will."

Tree branches rustled and Gray's wolf went on alert. She crawled forward and peered down the game trail. After a second, she relaxed. "Callan is coming."

"And someone's with him," Tamara whispered.

"Come on." Gray led the way down the hillside to the trail.

Callan emerged from the shadows with a human beside him. The male was about Callan's height, not as bulky in the shoulders, with light hair mostly covered by a dark watch cap, pale blue eyes just visible in the faint light, and a smooth, strong-jawed face with just a hint of softness around his wide mouth. He looked oddly happy, as if there was nothing else in the world he'd rather be doing than tromping through the forest in the middle of a cold, damp night.

"Gray," Callan said, "this is Clint. He'll be with your squad. Find him a place on the line."

"He's human," Gray said.

The male's grin broadened. "Through and through." He saluted. "Clint Edgemont, ma'am. Happy to—"

"You don't have to salute me," Gray snarled. She stared at Callan. "What am I supposed to do with a human?"

Callan rumbled at her challenging tone, and Gray dropped her gaze.

"Captain," Gray added apologetically.

"Put him in rotation. An extra *sentrie* will help everyone get more rest and time for food. You might be out here for a while."

"He's not going to be able to stand watch alone."

"Put him with a spotter. He's an expert marksman."

"I can spot," Tamara said.

The male glanced at Tamara and his smile broadened, making him look attractive for a human. "That would work just fine."

Gray's wolf howled. She didn't want this human anywhere near Tamara, even if he was a relative weakling. "I don't think—"

"That should work," Callan said, fixing Gray with a hard stare. "See to it, squad leader."

She fisted a salute. "Yes, Captain."

When Callan disappeared down the line, Gray jammed her hands on her hips and faced off with Clint. "How well can you shoot?"

He still looked like he was on his way to a party, but the expression in his eyes darkened and she recognized a hunter beneath his easygoing manner. "I was a Marine sniper. I can hit anything, day or night, a thousand yards or more."

"Set up at the top of the ridge over there. Tamara will show you where."

"Yes, ma'am," he said jauntily, tossing another grin in Tamara's direction. He bent to shoulder his gear as Tamara moved closer to Gray.

"I'll look out for him," Tamara said.

"If it comes to a fight, don't risk yourself for him. He won't be able to keep up."

"He came here to help us."

"We don't need his help."

Tamara stroked Gray's forearm, her touch warm and comforting. "Maybe we don't, but we might need his friendship, him and others like him."

"I don't like him."

Tamara leaned even closer, her mouth brushing Gray's ear. "Don't forget you have something to show me soon."

Gray growled in response and watched Tamara move off with Clint. She heard his deep voice murmuring, and Tamara laughing softly.

❖

The throne room was empty except for the rows of guards, silent and immobile as statues. Torren remained as still as them, not even a flicker of her perfect features suggesting she was anything other than a beautiful dream. The air, moist and sweet as honey, swirled in indolent waves over Sylvan's tongue—teasing her wolf to run with the promise of prey. A diversion, an illusion. Another dream.

Faerie is a place of answered dreams.

"Where is Drake?" Sylvan asked.

Torren turned to her. "In one of the garden chambers in Cecilia's court."

"I want to see her."

"Only the Queen can give you leave to do that."

Sylvan snarled and started to shift. "I don't need permission where my mate is concerned."

"If you threaten the throne, I'll have no choice but to fight you," Torren warned, the red glow of her Hound burning in her eyes. "You'll do none of us any good, including Drake and Misha."

Sylvan pushed her face close to Torren's until their eyes locked. Close enough to open her jugular with the flick of her head. "I will not be kept from my mate."

"Then think before you act."

"Sylvan, my dear," a voice like bells tolling rang through the air. "How unexpected of you to visit."

Sylvan inclined her head to the Queen of Thorns but kept her gaze level. Cecilia looked much as she did on her infrequent travels Earthside to meet with the other Coalition members—full-bodied and sensual—but here in Faerie she dropped her shields and allowed her rapture to emerge. She was almost too beautiful to behold—her skin a luminous glow, her hair gossamer strands floating about her long, elegant neck and bare shoulders. Her wispy gown appeared transparent but the voluptuous body beneath was only a whispered promise. More dreams. Sylvan let her wolf rise and spoke through heavy jaws. "Cecilia, I apologize for my unannounced arrival."

"You always have been unorthodox." She glanced at Torren. "And now I see the two of you are having issues."

"Not at all," Sylvan said. "Your Hound has been most clear as to her loyalties and responsibilities."

Cecilia's smile radiated with the heat and splendor of the midday sun. "Oh, I have no doubt. But what brings you to Faerie?"

"I've come for my mate," Sylvan said. "I understand she is your guest."

"Of course," Cecilia said, as if just now remembering Drake's presence. "Another unexpected arrival from Earthside."

"I know my mate," Sylvan said, "and she would not have knowingly breached your boundaries."

"And yet, here you both are." Cecilia laughed. "If you'd only let me know you desired an audience, I would certainly have arranged that."

"I'm afraid we were a little short on time. The situation Earthside has become volatile."

"Yes, I am aware that once again the Praeterns and humans are locked in battle. Not an unexpected result of your father's plans, I'm afraid." Cecilia's tone hardened. "And not a battle we in Faerie wish to join."

"It's not quite as simple as that," Sylvan said. "It's not just humans opposed to Praetern existence, but factions within the Praetern population attempting to undermine us as well."

"Old rivalries die hard," Cecilia said. "Why are you—any of you—here?"

"Drake was looking for Torren," Sylvan said. "We were hoping for information that would help us identify our enemies."

"Is that right?" Cecilia gazed at Torren, her expression tender except for the hard glint in her incandescent green eyes. "And why would that be, Master of the Hunt?"

"I'm sure the Prima would be happy to tell you that, my Queen."

"Oh, of course. I'm sure she will." Cecilia waved a hand and four guards stepped forward, two on either side of Sylvan. "Escort our guest to the gardens."

For one brief second, Sylvan considered killing them all. But another twenty guards stood behind her and she had no idea where Drake was being held. For now, she had no choice but to follow.

Chapter Fifteen

Dru returned to Francesca's new lair just before dawn. She left her motorcycle by the long garage housing several SUVs and a limo with blacked-out windows and led Dante up the walk to the rear entrance. The Vampire had complained about not being able to feed at closing time, but Dru had given him a choice. Feed now and continue on his own, or return with her and join Francesca's seethe. He'd silently followed her out when she left. "Luce is Francesca's second. You would do well not to antagonize her."

Dante smoothed his tight white T-shirt over his taut torso, lightly brushed his fingertips over the front of his jeans, and grinned. "I'm sure I can get on her good side."

Dru laughed to herself. The door opened before she reached it and Luce stepped out onto the porch. She was dressed in business attire— dark trousers, white shirt, and gleaming black shoes. She nodded to Dru and regarded Dante through narrowed lids. "Who is this?"

Before Dru could answer, Dante stepped forward with a blazing smile. "I'm Dante, and I understand you're the one to please."

Luce's cool expression never changed, but a sliver of crimson slashed through her dark eyes. "Then you are mistaken. The only one here whose pleasure is essential is our Queen, Francesca."

"Of course," he said smoothly, leaning so close his chest nearly brushed Luce's. "But the two needn't be mutually exclusive, I'm sure."

"What have you brought us?" Luce said, her question directed to Dru. "Besides an unschooled youngling with no manners?"

"Dante is without Clan, and despite appearances, he's clever and, as you can undoubtedly see, appealing despite his shortcomings. He has no trouble attracting hosts." She did not need to state the obvious—

Francesca was dangerously low on hosts and had no easy way to recruit more as long as she and her most trusted cadre were in hiding.

"We already have more mouths than we can feed," Luce said chillily.

"I can bring you at least a dozen hosts by evening," Dante quickly said.

Luce studied him expressionlessly. "Blood addicts?"

He shrugged. "Pleasure junkies, I like to call them."

"And they have no allegiance elsewhere?"

He visibly preened. "Only to me."

"If you reside here, you will share your hosts as Francesca dictates. You will feed when she deigns that you do. If you disobey or endanger the Clan house in any way, I will have your head."

Dante's smile disappeared and he glanced at Dru. She ignored him. Vampire business did not concern her. He raised his chin and said flatly, "I understand and I agree."

"Good." Luce stroked his cheek, brushed her fingertips down the center of his chest, and curled her fingers around his crotch. She squeezed slowly until he gasped, then leaned forward and kissed him. "See that you behave."

She let him go and said to Dru, "Francesca is waiting."

"Of course." Dru and Luce left Dante in the care of Daniela and Simon and walked together to Francesca's sitting room.

Luce knocked, and at Francesca's command they entered. Francesca lounged in the center of her bed, wearing only a long white shirt, unbuttoned, its tails lying across her thighs like a lover's hands. She was alone, and at dawn, she should have been surrounded by servants or slaves, waiting to serve her.

"Ah," Francesca said, "my two favorites." She opened her arms. "Come join me."

Wordlessly, Luce and Dru undressed and climbed onto the bed, taking up positions on opposite sides of Francesca. They stroked her in mirror-image movements, caressing her breasts and belly and thighs. She arched and purred approval.

"Tell me, my hunter," Francesca said, stroking Dru's chest, "what news do you bring?"

Dru leaned forward and kissed Francesca's breast, allowing her canines to tease at her nipple. "I believe I have recruited a wolf who will raise a mercenary cadre for us."

Francesca ran her fingers through Dru's hair and pressed Dru's mouth closer to her breast. "And what do you plan to do with him and his soldiers?"

"They want retribution against the Timberwolves. I think if we arm them and promise them control of the Blackpaws if Sylvan is defeated, they will be eager to attack her stronghold."

"Are they capable of destroying her?"

Dru raised her head. "I doubt it. But they can divide her forces, and if we're lucky, take captives. That might provoke her into coming after them and give us a chance to attack her away from her main forces."

"You will make me a fine commander." Francesca pressed Luce's shoulders to direct her down the bed. Luce kissed her lower abdomen while reaching over to caress Dru at the juncture of her thighs. "What else?"

Dru stretched and parted her legs as Luce toyed with her. "I brought home a Vampire who promises to provide slaves and servants. He has defected from another Clan and seeks a new master."

"And is he pretty?"

Dru hissed as Luce's incisors grazed her sex. "That would be for Luce to say."

Francesca laughed. "Luce?"

Luce looked up. "Very, my Queen. I think you'll enjoy him."

"Perhaps. But not nearly as much as learning that Sylvan has paid for her treachery. How shall we manage that if the wolf renegades fail?"

"I have some ideas, my Queen," Dru said.

Francesca cupped Dru's jaw and guided her upward until Dru's neck was exposed. "Tell me."

"We need to entice Sylvan to come to us." Dru gasped as Francesca flooded her with thrall.

"How?" Francesca licked Dru's neck.

"We might have to sacrifice someone." Dru's pelt thickened down the center of her abdomen.

"War always calls for sacrifice," Francesca murmured and struck deeply. Luce stretched across Francesca's body and drank from the large vein in Dru's groin. Dru shuddered and her mind blanked.

Francesca's voice commanding someone to enter roused Dru from a cloud of lassitude. The loss of blood didn't weaken her, but the repeated sexual draining left her reflexes slower and her mind dull. She needed to be more wary. If someone sought reprisal against Francesca here in her lair, she needed to be able to defend Francesca as well as herself. Luce sat up beside her, apparently unconcerned, so Dru feigned sleep and listened.

"Forgive me for not meeting you more formally, Ambassador," Francesca said, "but given the hour—"

"It is I who should apologize," a male said in a musical tenor, his voice like a sweet flowing brook, hypnotic and enchanting. The hair along the back of Dru's neck stood up. She didn't have much experience, but she recognized the seductive tone. Fae.

"What brings Cecilia's chosen here with such urgency?" Francesca asked.

"I have a personal message from Cecilia, Queen of Thorns, Ruler of—"

"Yes, yes," Francesca said. "I'm quite aware of all Cecilia's magnificence. What is the message?"

"Cecilia has an unexpected visitor and wishes an immediate meeting with you."

"I'm afraid that would not be convenient. Unfortunately, I am ill-disposed to travel at the moment."

"I shall relay that message. However, if…" He cleared his throat as if reluctant to speak.

"What is it?" Francesca's tone rang with impatience. She had just fed and was ready for sex before retiring. This was not a time Vampires did business.

"If I could secure a meeting place nearby, perhaps that would be acceptable?"

"Perhaps. Who is the visitor?"

Silence ensued.

"If Cecilia sent you, I doubt she wanted to keep me in suspense."

"My understanding is the wolf Alpha has paid a visit to the Queen."

Francesca laughed. "Do tell. Why, that is quite interesting."

"And what would you have me tell my Queen?" the Fae ambassador asked again.

"Tell *Cecilia* I would be most interested to hear her plans for her guest." Francesca returned to the bed and stretched out, indolently tracing a finger down the center of Dru's chest. "As to the meeting, I'll give it some thought."

❖

Niki climbed the ramparts as the sun came up and joined Callan at one of the lookout posts. The forest stretched out before them, treetops still cloaked in fog, sunlight beginning to color the distant mountaintops in swaths of red and gold. Her chest ached. If the Alpha had been here, if they did not have infected humans in their infirmary, if they did not have renegade wolves at their gates, they might have gone running. She might have felt the wind in her pelt and Sophia's shoulder riding along hers. She might have lost herself for a time in the glory of the hunt and the safety of the Pack. Instead, she stood alone. "Anything?"

Callan shook his head. "A few scouting reports of cats moving in the north. Nothing unusual. Everything is quiet along the Blackpaw border."

"Once the renegades left the camp, they could've gone anywhere. There's no telling where they might strike."

"You're right." Callan pulled a map from his pocket and spread it out against the wood rail. "We've accounted for that in terms of our patrol placement. So far, nothing."

Niki gritted her teeth. Expecting a fight that didn't come was far worse than the most brutal battle. Waiting was not something she was good at.

"The Alpha?" Callan asked.

Niki hesitated. Callan was a trusted captain, but he was not *centuri*, and the Alpha's comings and goings were not something the Pack needed to know. Still, he was as close to Sylvan's inner circle as most of them. "She has not returned."

Callan said nothing. He would not question her. He would not voice concern. He, like Niki and everyone else in the Compound, trusted that Sylvan would always be there to rule. Niki gripped his shoulder. "I'll be at Sophia's. Contact me if anything changes."

"How long do you want us to keep the patrols in place?"

"Until something happens." Niki turned and dropped down the wooden stairs to ground level. Max intercepted her in the center of the yard.

"Anything?" he asked.

Niki shook her head. "What about you?"

"Andrea has gone back to the city to contact members of the other cells. She's reaching out to informants, gathering as much intelligence as she can. Hopefully she'll turn up something." Max stared up at the ramparts, then over at the darkened headquarters building. "The Alpha?"

"She's in Faerie."

Max's lips drew back into a snarl. "How did that happen?"

"She went after the Prima."

He raked a hand through his hair and growled. "They're both there?"

"Yes."

"What are we going to do about it?"

"For now, nothing. Sylvan's orders were clear. Our first priority must be defending the Compound."

"We can't just let her disappear there."

Niki rumbled. She wanted to go after Sylvan more than she wanted anything except Sophia, but her duty was to carry out Sylvan's orders. And that meant she must remain at the Compound until all threat to the Pack had passed. "I don't plan to. But for now, we wait. And no one else is to know."

"Yes, *Imperator*." He sounded as if the words were painful to emit. He rubbed his belly as if to ease an ache. His skin dripped with sex-sheen and his erection jutted out beneath his BDUs.

"Your wolf wants to mate," Niki said, stating the obvious.

"She's human."

"That didn't make any difference to the Alpha, or any number of other wolves."

"She doesn't know what it would be like."

Niki laughed. "You really think you'll be too much for her?"

Max's eyes glowed gold and he took a quick step toward her. Under other circumstances she would have been ready to fight, but he wasn't rational. He needed to claim the female his wolf had already chosen. Until he did, his hormones would be uncontrollable, and so would his instincts.

"Maybe you're right," Niki said. "If you have so little faith in her, then maybe she's not worthy—"

Max snarled. "She is quick and strong and brave. She is everything she needs to be."

Niki poked him in the chest to remind him of his place. He rumbled again but stepped back. "Then you should be less of a coward or else she will find *you* unworthy."

"I don't want to leave the Compound now, not with the Alpha gone."

"You'll need to in order to check with Andrea about any new intelligence. When you do, let your wolf take charge."

Max blew out a heavy breath. "I'll try."

"Good. Get some sleep." Niki loped across the yard to the infirmary to find her mate and tell her it was time for them to go home for a few hours. Sophia was where she had expected her to be, with the mutants in the isolation room.

"You need rest," Niki said. "Is there someone here to cover for you until this afternoon?"

Sophia looked as if she was going to protest, then sighed. "Elena just came back. You could use some rest too."

"All I need is you." Niki rubbed the new mate bite on her shoulder and rumbled as her belly warmed. "The night was long and cold."

"After you're warm, then," Sophia said with a satisfied smile. "Then you sleep."

Niki grabbed Sophia's hand and tugged her down the hall to the main infirmary where Elena was checking the recuperating warriors. "Can we leave you for a few hours?"

"Go ahead." Elena tilted her head, her gaze traveling from Niki to Sophia. "You may need more than a few hours. I'll take care of them until you get back."

"Thank you." Sophia rubbed her cheek against Niki's shoulder. "Let's go."

Niki slid an arm around her waist and pulled her close as they started down the hall. "She's knows we're mated."

"Of course," Sophia murmured. "Everyone will."

"Good." Niki nuzzled her neck. "I love you."

"I—" Sophia halted as her parents hurried through the front door. "Mother? What are you doing here?"

Nadia Revnik carried a white Styrofoam cooler. "We isolated a plasma extract we want to administer to your turned Weres. We hope it will counteract the fever."

Sophia pulled away from Niki, her face alive with excitement. "If it does—if we could manufacture an antiserum, we might be free of the threat—"

"One step at a time," her father said, but his eyes glinted with enthusiasm. "Are you ready to get started?"

Sophia spun around Niki. "I have to stay. This is too important."

"The Alpha should be advised," Niki said cautiously. "Can it wait?"

Nadia shook her head. "We don't know how stable the proteins are—we need to start while the specimen is fresh."

Niki looked from Sophia to her parents. The decision was hers and she must act as the Alpha would act, for the good of the Pack. "Is it safe for all of you?"

Nadia and Leo exchanged glances. "There's a possibility the patients may only partially recover. They may regain consciousness, even shift. But—"

"They might be feral," Niki spat. A feral Were would kill anyone nearby. She wanted to protest. "Go ahead, but I will post guards in the room. At the first sign of violence, they will be executed."

Nadia gasped but Leo nodded.

"Agreed," he said.

Sophia kissed her quickly. "It will be fine. I promise."

Niki folded her arms. "I'll be staying, all the same."

Chapter Sixteen

Sylvan followed Torren from the throne room into a long, curving colonnade that ended in a stone archway decorated with carvings of dancing figures she could not identify. Beyond was a courtyard with marble walkways twisting among a jungle of greenery. Tall trees resembling palms with wide fronds dangled pear-shaped fruit the color of pumpkins from their boughs. Shrubs with spiny rainbow-hued petals leaned toward her like grasping hands. Grass as blue as the sky cushioned her steps like thick moss in the forest. Here and there small creatures the size of mice with filmy wings tucked close to their snow-white fur scurried among the undergrowth. Ordinarily such interesting prey would catch her wolf's attention, but all her senses were tuned to something that became sharper with every step. Drake's scent.

"She was here," Sylvan said. "Is this the garden where Drake was being held?"

"One of them," Torren said. "Be patient."

"I've been patient long enough." Sylvan looked behind her. Two guards stood at the open archway, their helmeted features covered, their slender bodies at attention, their silver spears crossed between them, glinting reminders she was a prisoner, far more than a guest. She could no doubt defeat them easily but for Torren, who would likely try to stop her. She could best the Hound as well but would not wish to call Torren enemy until forced to. "Why does Cecilia make an enemy of me?"

"Cecilia is Fae," Torren said in the familiar way of the Fae and their non-answers.

"Cecilia is also a member of the Coalition," Sylvan said, "by her own volition. She has taken common cause with the Praeterns in negotiating with humans."

Torren sighed. "You are too much a creature of the Earth—more than the Vampires, more than the Fae, more even than the Mage who seek to rule the elements, or the Psi who live in a place beyond flesh."

Sylvan snarled. "What does that mean?"

"When you face an enemy, you do not plot—you act as your instincts demand. You attack and you fight until the fight is ended."

"I am a wolf," Sylvan said, struggling to make sense of shadows. She stilled. "You showed me a vision when you first came to my land—Bernardo with Francesca and a human in a secret meeting. You were there, but you were not hunting as I thought. You were guarding. Guarding your Queen."

Torren stopped walking and a tangle of green vines as elegant as snakes curled around her feet, their tendrils brushing the gleaming leather of her boots. "I shared with you a glimpse of your enemies. Has that not proven to be so?"

"But perhaps not all of them. Cecilia has withdrawn to Faerie," Sylvan mused. "She is insulating herself from the struggles Earthside between Praeterns and the human radicals who seek our destruction. Perhaps her commitment to the Coalition goals was never real, but only, as you say, a move in some larger game."

"Cecilia's business is her own," Torren murmured. "And my Queen does not confide in me."

Sylvan thought this unlikely, but then Torren had been Earthside for a very long time and perhaps no longer knew all Cecilia's plans. The only thing she could be certain of was she had no friends in Faerie other than Torren.

"I have no quarrel with Cecilia. If she and hers are not my enemy, I am not hers."

"I'm sure Cecilia, Queen of Thorns, knows that," Torren said.

"We will have a quarrel if she keeps me from my mate."

Torren smiled. "Then you shall have no quarrel."

Sylvan felt her before she saw her step into the garden. Drake, dressed much like her in a plain white shirt, black pants, and boots, emerged through a wall of shrubbery that closed behind her like a door. Misha was by her side. The heavy hand that had squeezed Sylvan's heart from the instant she'd realized Drake was missing opened and joy flooded through her.

Sylvan closed the distance in three fast strides and pulled Drake close. "Are you hurt?"

Drake clasped the back of Sylvan's neck and kissed her hard. "No. And you should not be here."

Sylvan laughed briefly and slung an arm around Misha's shoulder, drawing her into their circle. "And where else would I be, when you and mine are here?"

"Of course I knew you would come." Drake rested her cheek against Sylvan's shoulder. "You've been fighting. Your hip is damaged."

"Barely a scratch and almost healed. The two of you?"

"We are fine." Drake pressed her mouth close to Sylvan's ear. "We did not intend to enter and have not been able to get word out. How long has it been?"

"Before I came through the Gate, only a day, but since I've been here…" Sylvan shook her head. "Time is a strange thing."

"I know. I can't find anything to use as a guide. Everything constantly changes."

"Yes." Sylvan pulled Drake hard against her body and drew deep of her scent, calming her wolf, assuring her that her mate was fine. "But this is constant. Our bond." She stroked Misha's hair. "And Pack."

Drake cleaved to Sylvan's side, breathing freely for the first time since they'd crossed into Faerie. Her wolf rumbled with a mix of contentment and uneasiness. Sylvan was here but now they were all prisoners.

"Have you been treated well?" Sylvan asked.

"We are unharmed," Drake said as Torren joined them. "But we have not been treated as guests."

"I will try to get you an audience with Cecilia soon," Torren said. "Until then, there is no use trying to leave. There will be no path for you to follow."

"We will not be prisoners," Sylvan growled.

"No, for now, you are free to walk about, but don't go far. It is easy to lose one's way in Faerie." She glanced at Misha, her expression guarded. "You should stay with your Alpha."

"I'm not leaving without you," Misha said.

Torren's smile was sad. "I cannot leave."

Misha left Sylvan's side and wrapped her arms around Torren's waist. "Why not?"

Torren cupped her cheek and tilted her head until their eyes met. "Because I am not of your world."

Misha kissed her. "That is." She drew Torren's hand to her chest, pressed it to her heart. "As is this. I feel the hawk and the Hound." She kissed Torren again. "And your heart. You know my wolf. I will not leave you."

Torren glanced at Sylvan over Misha's head. "I would not have you leave if you choose to stay."

Misha turned in Torren's arms to look back at Sylvan. "I have chosen her. I will not leave her."

Sylvan rumbled. "We will decide when the time comes for all of us to leave."

Misha's chin came up and her eyes shimmered with gold. Her wolf was sure, and brave, and foolish enough to stand against her Alpha. Only a mated wolf would dare. "I will always be Pack, but I am hers now, as she is mine."

Drake tightened her arm around Sylvan's waist, knowing Sylvan was hard-pressed to be patient and her wolf would be wild to fight. "For now, we're all together in this. Torren too."

"I will do what I can with the Queen," Torren said.

Sylvan snarled softly. "Do what you can, but know that we will not bide here long."

"I will return soon as I can." Torren kissed Misha. "Stay with your Alpha. Know I will come to you when I am able."

Misha looked as if she would protest, but finally let Torren go. "Do not think you will get rid of me."

"I know better than to try to outrun a wolf."

Torren left them in the garden, and the archway slowly dissolved into a solid stone wall as she passed through. She ignored the guards and slipped through passages only she and a few others knew to reach Cecilia's chambers. The carved oaken door swung open as she approached and she entered, going to one knee in the center of a thick royal-blue rug woven through with strands of gold. In certain light, the surface of the rug shimmered and a vast scene unfolded of the whole of Faerie with the Faerie Mound in the center and Cecilia rising from it like a goddess. She bowed her head. "Cecilia, Queen of Thorns, your Hunter seeks a word."

A warm hand caressed her cheek and fluttered down her torso. A voice like a thousand wind chimes fluttering in a breeze whispered, "Torren, my Torren, what have you done?"

Torren lifted her head. Cecilia reclined upon an ornate chaise in a royal-blue gown that shimmered and flowed over her body as if it were a living part of her. The outline of her breasts and the curve of her belly and the hollow between her thighs beckoned. Torren's blood warmed and she recognized the familiar spell, but she had never been Cecilia's plaything and doubted she would have lived long if she had been. Cecilia tired of those she could control. "Thank you, my Queen."

"I was about to send for you," Cecilia said. "We have a trip to make." She held out her hand, her bejeweled fingers glowing. "Come."

Torren rose and slid her hand into Cecilia's, feeling the rush of wind and power as the stars spun overhead. She stepped into a large room with a huge stone fireplace blazing on one wall, heavy drapes covering floor-to-ceiling windows on another, and a ring of heavy leather-and-wood chairs arranged in front of the hearth. Four Fae guards followed close behind them, more for show than anything else. Cecilia needed no other bodyguard than Torren, even with the six Vampires ranging in the shadows on either side of the female seated regally in the central chair.

"Cecilia," Francesca purred, "how nice to see you again. And I see you've brought Torren." Francesca laughed. "We've been looking for you."

❖

Niki stood with her back against the wall next to the closed treatment room door. She'd ordered two *sentries* to wait outside, armed with assault pistols. She doubted she would need them if one of the mutants became violent. They were frail, having been kept alive for weeks now with intravenous feedings and fluid and drugs. They would be no match for her wolf. All the same, she couldn't take chances with Sophia and her parents in the room.

"They're ready," Sophia said to her parents.

Nadia and Leo withdrew plastic bags filled with clear yellow fluid from the Styrofoam container and attached them to the intravenous lines that Sophia had inserted into each of the females' forearms. They hung the bags from metal poles beside the beds and opened the ports. The serum streamed down the clear plastic tubes.

"How long before you know?" Niki asked.

"I don't know," Sophia said, adjusting a temperature tape on the forehead of one of the girls.

When they'd been infected, they'd probably been no more than fifteen. If they survived, they might be able to remember who had abducted them, and what had been done to them. They were the only survivors of the labs except for Katya and Gray, who still had only fragmented memories of their captivity. Unlike these females, Katya and Gray were Weres, and they'd been poisoned with silver that had distorted their consciousness. These females had started out human. Now they were something else. Something Niki did not trust.

She watched the fluid trickle into the intravenous lines and disappear into the bodies of the emaciated females. Monitors beeped and numbers flickered on the screens. The Revniks and Sophia alternated between checking the females and recording the vital signs, but Niki watched only the females, waiting for some sign they were turning or wakening.

"Her temperature's spiking," Sophia said as she stood beside the dark-haired female with the coffee-colored skin. "One-oh-one point three. One-oh-two. One-oh-two point eight." She glanced at her mother. "Mother? Should we try an infusion of ibuprofen to bring it down?"

"Not yet," Nadia said calmly, also watching the monitors. "We're not at dangerous levels for a Were. Another two degrees higher and we'll intervene."

Leo adjusted one of the lines on the second female, a blonde with pale skin and long limbs that might once have been elegant but now seemed merely fragile. "Her temperature's rising as well."

"A viral shower?" Sophia asked.

"Possibly," her mother murmured.

"What does that mean?" Niki asked uneasily, moving away from the wall and going on alert.

"As their bodies try to fight the virus, breakdown products are released that can produce tissue damage."

"Are they contagious?"

"Possibly, but probably not. Not if the virus is no longer intact."

"They should be restrained."

Sophia gave Niki a sympathetic glance, knowing Niki was motivated more by concern for her than cruelty. "They're in a coma, Niki. There's no reason to restrain them."

"If we wait until they wake—"

"If they wake, even less so." Sophia stroked the unconscious female's arm. "That will mean the serum is working."

"That won't mean they aren't feral."

Sophia nodded. "We have to give them a chance."

Niki growled and paced, watching and waiting. Sophia was altogether too close to the bed, but if she tried to move her, Sophia would only protest. An hour passed, then another, and Niki started to relax. Nothing was happening. The test, or whatever it was, wasn't working.

"Vital signs are stabilizing," Leo said.

"Yes, within range of normal Were values," Nadia said, a thread of excitement in her voice.

"I'm getting rapid eye movement," Sophia said. "I think she's—"

The dark-haired mutant jerked up in the bed, her eyes shooting open, dark as pitch and slashed through with gold. She howled, an animal scream of pain, and claws shot from her fingertips as she lunged at Sophia.

CHAPTER SEVENTEEN

Sophia stumbled back as a red-gray wolf rocketed between her and the female she had secretly been calling Angela. Niki must have shifted the instant Angela showed signs of waking, and her howl of rage made Sophia's wolf cringe and lower her belly. Niki and the turned Were clashed inches away from her, filling the air with snarls and clouds of battle pheromones. Niki landed on top with her front legs on Angela's chest, and the pair thrashed in a clatter of tumbling equipment. IV fluid tinged with pink streaks of first blood spread across the floor.

"Stop!" Sophia rushed forward and was instantly scooped up by her father. He dragged her clear of the fray, his arms clamped around her waist. She struggled, her wolf ascending to the call of her mate's frenzy. "Let me go. Niki is—"

"No," Leo barked.

The door burst open and two armed *sentries* crowded into the room, pointing their weapons at the roiling duo on the floor. Angela had shifted or as much of a shift as she could manage—canines jutted from distorted jaws, patches of black and gray and white fur interspersed with bare hide covered her misshapen wolf form, and claws tipped the ends of elongated hands. Her torso was massive, her pelvis a shallow canyon, her limbs thick with ropey muscles. She was like nothing Sophia had ever imagined, even in her nightmares. Not a half-form, not a wolf, but something monstrous in between. She was larger than Niki's wolf, outweighing her at least twice, and wild. She snarled and clawed and bit at Niki, fighting with whatever Were instincts had somehow survived in her mutated DNA. Niki, lithe and quick and ferocious, twisted away from Angela's lethal jaws and struck back with her own teeth and claws.

The *sentries* pressed close, their weapons extended.

"Shoot the *mutia*," Leo commanded.

"I can't get a shot," Fiona, the *sentrie* in front, exclaimed.

"No," Sophia cried. "Don't try. You might hit Niki."

God, what had she done. She should have let Niki restrain them both, but she'd been so sure they'd either never regain consciousness or be too weak to pose a threat if they did. She'd never heard of this kind of transformation. She couldn't look away, could barely breathe, could feel her heart stopping in her chest. Dimly, she was aware of her mother briskly strapping down the other female. She'd foolishly named her too. Solara. Would she turn into a monster as well? None of them had been prepared for this.

What seemed like hours was only a minute or two before Niki backed away. Still snarling, she repeatedly lunged and then dodged to the side, taunting the mutated Were to attack again. Confused, Angela swung her head around, surveying the others in the room, her eyes a patchwork of gold and black, mad with rage and pain. Her lips skimmed back from jagged teeth too large to fit in her half-formed muzzle. She snarled, hunched forward on hind legs part human and part wolf. Niki flattened her belly to the floor and Angela focused on the nearest figure.

Sophia.

"Angela," Sophia said softly, her throat so dry the words were barely a whisper. "Angela, we're not going to hurt you. Angela."

The female tilted her head, eyed Niki and then Sophia, growled.

"Let us help you," Sophia said, her voice stronger. "We'll find a way—"

Angela jerked forward in Sophia's direction, and in the instant when her focus shifted away from Niki, Niki launched herself at Angela's throat. The kill was quick and certain. Angela fell and lay still, blood pouring from her gaping throat. Niki howled, a mournful, lonely cry.

Fiona snapped to the second *sentrie*, "Call for reinforcements." She swung her weapon to the restrained female who had yet to show signs of waking and glanced at Sophia. "Should we execute?"

"No," Sophia whispered, still stunned by how wrong she'd been. Angela was dead, and she might not have been if she'd been restrained long enough for them to sedate and possibly treat her. Her parents might have been injured or killed. And Niki had been forced to kill another

Were—an ill and possibly feral one, but still, the cost of executing one of their own cut deep. "We don't yet know what will happen to her. Just—be ready."

Cautiously, Sophia approached Niki, who had backed away from the body but still crouched, body shivering with battle frenzy. A steady warning rumbled in her chest.

"Niki. Niki, it's Sophia. It's all right now."

Niki's sides heaved and saliva dripped from her muzzle. Her eyes were shadowed slits, her lips peeled back and jaws agape, showing her teeth. She was deep in frenzy, her wolf completely dominant. Everyone was the enemy. Sophia crouched down a few feet away and extended her hand.

"Niki, love. It's me. It's all right. I'm fine. There's no danger now."

Niki's head lowered and her shoulders bunched as if readying to spring.

Leo murmured, "Sophia, come away. She's guarding her kill. She's dangerous."

"No. She has more control than that. She just needs to know she's not alone." Sophia crooned, "Can you hear me? Niki? Everything is fine now."

A long moment passed and then Niki's wolf shuddered, shed pelt, and Niki crouched naked in front of Sophia. Her head was down, her hair soaked with sweat, her body dripping with pheromones.

"Niki," Sophia breathed in relief. "Are you all right?"

"Don't come near me," Niki said.

Sophia's belly tightened. "Let me get you some clothes. You need to eat."

"No." Niki looked up, her eyes swirling with pain. "Fiona, take me to the holding cells and confine me. Now."

The *sentrie* stared. "*Imperator*?"

Niki rose and Sophia gasped. Blood ran from a long gash on her right side and trickled down her thigh. The skin was torn in a jagged line and the deeper muscles shredded. Sophia reached out and Niki jerked away.

"No. She bit me. I need to be isolated." She gestured to Fiona. "Do it. Quickly."

Fiona brought her assault pistol up and aimed it at Niki. "Come with me."

Sophia cried out, "No. You need treatment."

"I need you safe. All of you." Niki staggered slightly and headed for the door, Fiona close behind. Callan appeared in the doorway, followed by two more *sentries*.

"What happened?" Callan snapped.

"Get Max back here," Niki said. "I've been bitten and need to be isolated."

"Form an escort," Callan said, his voice hard and flat. "One on either side of the *imperator*. Keep everyone outside away."

Wordlessly, the *sentries* did as he had ordered, and the cadre of armed Weres led Niki away.

Sophia said to her parents, "I'm going with her. She's hurt. She needs to be tended to."

"The wound isn't fatal." Nadia grabbed Sophia's arm, holding her back. "Niki is right, she needs to be isolated. If she's been exposed to the fever, she'll show symptoms soon."

"She's my mate," Sophia blazed, jerking free of her mother. "Would you have me abandon her?"

Nadia's expression softened. "No, but I would have you safe. And so would Niki. You heard her say so."

"I've been listening to and watching Niki put everyone's life before her own since the day I arrived." Sophia showed her teeth, her wolf in a fury. *"Enough."*

Leo joined Nadia. "At least wait until they have her safely in a holding cell, then go to her, talk to her. But wait before you put yourself at risk."

"Like Niki waited to risk herself?"

Sophia turned her back on her parents and went to gather what she needed. She would not be kept from her mate. What Niki needed, she would give.

Callan blocked the stairs down to the holding cells, an assault pistol holstered on his thigh. Sophia hadn't seen armed warriors inside the Compound since Sylvan's mother had been assassinated. Every dominant in the camp would be on edge and ready to fight at the merest hint of challenge. She needed to lend her energy to the Pack, but she couldn't. Not until she saw to her mate.

"Let me pass."

"The *imperator*—"

Sophia snarled. "I don't care what she said. The sooner I see to her, the better."

Callan stared, his jaw clenched, and finally nodded. "She'll have me on my back for this."

"No, she won't." Sophia stroked his arm until his wolf quieted. "I'll call you if I need anything."

The passageway was narrow and dim, lit only by torches set into the wall. She knew her way—she'd been here before, tending a few captives and fewer feral Weres. She hated the place and what it represented—failure. Failure of hundreds of Were scientists over half a century to isolate and counteract the Were-fever contagion. Failure of all the Were *medici* to cure the illness once contracted. And failure of the Weres to unite and live in peace.

Today she would not fail.

Torren wondered briefly if Cecilia was about to make a gift of her to Francesca as she'd done once before. They were Earthside, and she considered where in case she needed to make an escape. She'd accepted imprisonment once to gather intelligence for Cecilia, but she would not do so again. They had to be somewhere close to Francesca's previous territory, since she doubted the hunted Vampire would want to risk traveling far from her new hiding place. And somewhere near a Faerie Gate, likely in one of the riverfront mansions on estates that friends of the Fae had held and quietly passed down for hundreds of years. Torren bowed to Francesca. "I'm sorry I left without thanking you for your hospitality. My apologies."

"I'll admit I was disappointed." Francesca sighed, her blue eyes cold and hard. "I rather thought you enjoyed the entertainment we provided."

"Daniela was most…accommodating," Torren said, referring to the Vampire who'd fed from her regularly while she'd been imprisoned. Francesca had meant to use Torren as a blood slave, but she was largely immune to Vampire thrall, something Francesca had not known and Daniela had been too young to recognize. When the time had come for her to shed her prison chains, Daniela had easily fallen under her persuasion and unwittingly aided in her escape. "I'm most grateful for that."

"And I understand you're now in Sylvan's debt," Francesca said, "since she helped you escape."

"The wolf Alpha was gracious enough to provide me sanctuary when I requested it, but she had nothing to do with my departure." Torren smiled faintly. "And I am in no one's debt except that of my Queen, for failing to gain her permission to depart your lair."

Francesca waved a hand. "That's of no matter now. Everything's changed, hasn't it, now that Sylvan has declared herself to be less of a friend than we once thought."

Cecilia murmured, "I'm not convinced of that."

"No?" Francesca's eyebrow winged up as if she were astonished, but Torren doubted anything could take her unawares or surprise her. "She led a raiding party into my lair, killed many of my guard, and aided Zachary Gates's heir in attempting to steal my throne."

"An attempt it appears was successful," Cecilia said mildly.

Francesca hissed. "What has been stolen can be recovered."

"Do you have the power to take on Zachary Gates and perhaps all the other Clans?"

"The Clan leaders are sheep," Francesca said. "They will follow the strongest, and if Zachary is defeated, they will flock to whoever defeats him."

"Then you will need an army, because Zachary's heir is allied with Sylvan." Cecilia paused, a look of consternation crossing her carved porcelain features. "Or so I've been told."

"I shall have an army," Francesca snapped in a rare fit of temper. "We are even now bringing Weres who are tired of Sylvan's rule into our fold."

"That is very good news." Cecilia sat in one of the large leather chairs and crossed her legs, her gown sliding up her full, milky thighs. Torren stepped behind the chair and her guards fanned out to stand between her and the Vampire soldiers. "Even with Weres in your forces, you will still have to face Zachary's allies, and they will outnumber you."

Francesca studied Cecilia with a dark, unwavering stare. "You could remedy that imbalance if Sylvan were to disappear."

"I have nothing to gain by destroying Sylvan, except the destruction of the Coalition. With her gone, the others will listen to reason, and we can stop asking humans for what is already in our power."

"Your goal as well as mine," Francesca pointed out.

"True. But you have more need for Sylvan to die than I." Cecilia delicately fingered the hem of her gown, an innocent movement that drew the attention of every Vampire in the room save Francesca. She was in high glamour, glowing, seductive, mesmerizing. She smiled and sunlight filled the room, dispelling the night's gloom. "What if I were to give you Sylvan, and you in turn demonstrated your power to all those you wish to rally behind you. If you are the one to destroy the Alpha, you can call the Weres and Vampires to you as you once did."

Cecilia was ancient, older than Francesca, and remembered the days when the Vampires commanded armies of Weres. Without a leader as strong as Sylvan, she could install a weak Alpha who was willing to do her bidding, and she could have her army again.

"And what is the cost for this...gift?" Francesca said.

"Your promise to destroy the Coalition or what remains of it, and once you have established your power, you grant me privileged land to create a Faerie Mound Earthside."

Francesca laughed. "There hasn't been a Faerie Mound Earthside since before you ascended to the throne."

"This is true," Cecilia said. "But all things change."

CHAPTER EIGHTEEN

W e'll sit in the back," Luce said as she, Dru, and Veronica left
the lair. They'd managed to escape Nocturne with only one of
Francesca's heavily shielded vehicles, and it sat idling a few steps
from the door under cover of the portico. The sun had just set, but
even the little bit of UV radiation scattered in the twilight would have
been intolerable for Luce. She'd be comfortable enough in the vehicle
with its UV-filtering tinted windows and fire-resistant body. And she'd
have Veronica at her disposal during the brief ride. She'd just recently
awakened and she wanted to feed. Dru got behind the wheel and pulled
out onto the heavily wooded private road leading toward the winding
river road into the city.

"Are you ready?" Luce murmured, stroking Veronica's neck as
she kissed her.

"Oh yes." Veronica reclined on the seat, drew her black skirt
up high on her thighs, and tilted her head back against the door. Her
lids drooped as she watched Luce lean forward and slowly slide her
incisors into the artery on the inside of her thigh. The sight was almost
as exciting as the jolt of heat that shot through her with the burst of
feeding hormones Luce injected into her bloodstream. She arched
and moaned softly as the orgasm exploded in her depths. She'd been
waiting all afternoon for this moment, waiting for Luce to come for
her, pacing in her room, the tray of food a human servant had delivered
untouched by her bedside, her body and her blood burning. This was
all she'd needed. Now at last, as the terrible pressure eased, she would
be able to think, be able to work. Luce sealed the wounds and sat up.

"You are beautiful. And delicious."

"Finished so soon," Veronica said, not nearly satisfied. Each day she seemed to need so much more to erase the constant urgency that pounded inside her. "You must still be hungry."

"I am always hungry for you." Luce hovered above her, her body weightless, floating, and kissed her. "Any more and you'll need to rest, and I know you want to work."

Veronica stroked Luce's face, sliding her fingers into her hair and drawing her down for another kiss. She pressed upward but could not feel Luce against her. "I do, you're right. But again soon?"

Luce smiled. "Soon. I promise."

Veronica straightened her clothes and tried to ignore the heavy ache in her loins. Luce would take her again soon and the pressure would ease. First she would work. The idea of what she planned gave her another kind of pleasure, and her clitoris twitched. Yes, soon.

Dru pulled the SUV around behind the factory that Nicholas Gregory had retrofitted as a laboratory for Veronica after Sylvan Mir and her filthy Vampire allies had destroyed Veronica's previous laboratory. Actually, Nicholas had destroyed it, but they'd had no choice but to abandon the facility once Sylvan knew of its location and what they had been doing there. The Were was to blame, regardless of who ordered the explosions.

Now she was forced to work in hiding in a building that looked, to anyone who cared to notice, like it should be condemned. As they neared the building, Dru used a remote to open a double-wide metal delivery door and drove inside, slowing at a security station where Luce ordered the armed guard to open a second reinforced door. Veronica had only been absent for a week—at least she thought it was only a week, perhaps it had been longer—but without her, active investigation was on hold. Only a few vehicles were parked in this section of the underground garage—those belonging to the mercenary security teams and the select technicians responsible for maintaining the test subjects. The guards were cat Weres, who were easy to buy. The technicians, who also had a price, were humans.

Dru stepped out of the vehicle and waited while Veronica and Luce exited. "How sure are you of the loyalty of these guards?"

"They're mercenaries," Luce said. "They have no loyalty."

Dru smiled, since she was a mercenary herself. "I'd like to interview them. We can use cats who still have connections to the Pride. It would be good to know what Raina is planning."

"The new cat Alpha hopes to unify the Pride." Luce laughed.

"That should keep her busy for quite some time. But go ahead. We'll be a while."

Dru nodded and walked off in the direction of the guard station. Luce and Veronica strode to the elevators that only Veronica or Luce could activate. Technicians were escorted to their posts through a separate entrance and required visual confirmation from Luce or Veronica, who cleared them and buzzed them in remotely. The technicians had been recruited from among the HUFSI members with the promise of a large salary paid in cash. For most the monetary incentive was secondary to their zeal for working on projects they believed would protect the human population from mutant diseases. As far as their loyalty was concerned, Luce made it clear that any hint of a security breach would result in the untimely and painful demise of both the individual responsible and anyone they might have shared information with. No one complained about spending weeks sequestered in the high-security lab, and no one ever talked about it and lived.

Veronica slid her hand through Luce's arm as they exited the elevator into a long, brightly lit hallway leading to her office and adjoining conference rooms. "You will stay, won't you?"

"Of course. I did promise you again soon, didn't I?"

Need, her own and others, was a tool Veronica had come to appreciate very early in life. Luce's ready availability assured her she and not Luce was in control. "You did. I have to examine the subjects and be sure they're still fit for the studies I have planned."

Luce pulled her near and kissed her throat. "Waiting for you is no hardship. I'll be in the lounge."

Trembling slightly, Veronica let her go. "I'll find you."

Luce disappeared and Veronica entered the code for her office. The stacks of files on her desk, the computer monitors, the lab coat hanging on a coat tree by the door were all a welcome sight. This was her world. She'd missed being here. She shed her suit jacket and donned her lab coat and left the office through a private entrance to the labs. The bright lights and clean, sterile surfaces created a sense of order and purity she found comforting. A female lab technician in her midthirties wearing pale blue scrubs and a green cover gown hurried toward her with a look of expectation and mild apprehension.

"Dr. Standish, we didn't expect you back from the conference until the end of the week."

"I left early," Veronica said. She, or Luce, must have explained her absence with a cover story, but she couldn't recall the details. Not that it mattered. She was back now. "Do you have a progress report for me?"

"Several. We've been running baseline labs as you requested, and the printouts are collated for your review."

"Good. I want to see them."

"The reports have already been uploaded to your—"

"No. I want to see the subjects."

The lab tech flushed. "Of course."

She hurriedly stepped aside as Veronica brushed by her and strode down the aisle, between long counters laden with equipment, to an airlock. She keyed in her security code, leaned down for the retina scan, and waited while the outer door to the airlock opened. She stepped in, the door closed behind her, and the second door slid open. Her nerves tingled pleasantly as she moved into the controlled chamber where the subjects were held in separate isolation cubicles. She stood at the observation window and watched for a moment. The subject, asleep according to the EEG electrodes taped to the scalp, looked deceptively human—a smattering of black hair on the head, surprisingly discrete features at only a few weeks of age, a healthy flush to the tan skin. Noticeably larger than a human of the same age, however.

"Have they shown any signs of shifting?" Veronica asked as the lab tech stepped up beside her.

"No, Dr. Standish. The only irregularity we've seen is in the basal temperature readouts, all of which are consistently four degrees higher than a human counterpart. Their metabolic rates are also substantially higher."

"Growth rate and weight gain?"

"Ninetieth percentile for humans with an accelerated curve."

"Yes, their physical maturity is enhanced." Veronica moved to the second cubicle and regarded the other subject. Another female, fortunately. A male offspring would not have been as useful. The Were genes were transferred through the maternal mitochondria, and only the females carried what she was interested in working with. As to the adult donors, they had been of little use to her and had been disposed of shortly after delivery.

"Well," she said with a sense of well-being she hadn't experienced in days. "It seems that we are ready to begin Phase One."

❖

"You shouldn't be here," Niki said.

"Where else should I be?" Sophia got as close to the silver-impregnated bars as she could.

Niki crouched on a bare iron cot bolted to the wall in much the same position Tamara had been when Sophia had tended to her wounds. Tamara had been a prisoner then, accused of attacking the Prima and under sentence of death. Niki did not belong here. She belonged in a treatment room, not a jail cell. "I'm coming in. I want to look at your side."

"No," Niki snarled.

"I'm afraid there's nothing you can do about it," Sophia said coolly and gestured to the *sentrie* who stood guard a little ways down the dim passageway. "Please open this."

The *sentrie* hesitated, glancing at Niki.

"Do not open the door," Niki said.

"The *imperator* requires medical attention, and seeing as she is the one in the cell and I outrank you, you will do as I order. Please do it now," Sophia said calmly. "It's all right."

The *sentrie* nodded briskly and came forward with the key. He turned the key in the lock and stepped back. "I'll stay right here, in case you need me."

"That's fine, but I don't think that I will." Sophia entered, closed the door behind her, and crossed to the bunk. "You are no risk to me. You know that. I am immune to the fever."

"You don't know what this is," Niki said. "This isn't Were fever, not as it occurs naturally."

"I know that. But then, neither am I. Whatever was done to those girls was probably done to me. Now, please be quiet while I take a look at you."

Niki sat on the edge of the cot and said to the *sentrie*, "If I show any signs of becoming violent, shoot me."

The *sentrie* swallowed audibly. "Yes, *Imperator*."

Sophia just shook her head and opened the medical bag she'd brought with her. She sorted through supplies and began to gently clean the wound on Niki's side. Niki never moved, even when the blood began to flow again. "You should shift and heal this."

"I don't think that's a good idea. I don't want to be in pelt if there's some kind of change going on inside me."

"You should learn to listen to those who know more than you do about some things." Sophia rested her hands on Niki's thighs and caught her gaze. "There isn't anything going on inside you. I would know. I would sense it. I'm connected to you now."

Slowly, Niki cupped Sophia's face and stroked her cheek with the pad of her thumb. "I love you. I would never do anything to hurt you."

Sophia rubbed her cheek against Niki's palm. "Of course I know that. Just as I know that you are brave and strong and so, so stubborn. Now hush while I take care of this."

Niki fell silent as Sophia disinfected and bandaged her side. "All your vital signs are normal. Your temperature is unchanged. This is a wound, like any other battle wound you've had before. I want you to come back to the infirmary so I can care for you properly."

"Not yet. Not until we're sure."

"I'm sure."

"You were sure those females weren't dangerous too."

Sophia caught her breath. "You're right. You're hurt and it's my fault. I'm sorry."

Niki growled and grasped her hand. "No, I'm sorry. None of that was your fault. I'm just worried about you—I'm sorry."

"I've never seen anything like that," Sophia whispered, remembering the horror that Angela had become. "It was as if she was trying to shift but only part of her body had actually transformed. I don't know what to make of it."

"It's been decades since you were turned by whatever agent they had constructed in the laboratory. Maybe these recent experiments haven't been as successful as they think. After all, they've been getting rid of their failures by trying to convince the humans they had Were fever."

"But the Prima was infected by one of the lab subjects and turned, and she is perfectly fine."

"Maybe it has something to do with who or what she was *before* she became infected. The Alpha recognized something in her right away. Maybe the recipient is a factor in how the mutagen acts in the system."

Sophia smiled and, before Niki could protest, kissed her. "You like to pretend you are only a soldier, but that's not true. And you're right, we can't forget that the host is as much a part of the equation as whatever mutagen they're using."

"What about the other one. Has she transformed like the one I killed?"

"Not yet. My parents are monitoring her."

"Be careful."

"I will." Sophia drew a blood sample from Niki's arm, labeled it with the time and date, and handed it carefully through the bars to the *sentrie*. "Take this to the infirmary and give it to my mother or father. They'll know what to do."

Niki said, "If they find anything—"

"They won't." Sophia repacked her medical supplies and sat on the metal grate next to Niki.

"What are you doing?"

"Waiting." She checked her watch. "We'll check your temperature every thirty minutes. If there's been no spike in six hours, I want you to shift and heal your wound, and then we're leaving."

"I don't want you in here with me."

Sophia leaned against Niki's uninjured side. "It's too late for that. You're mine now, and I'm not leaving you. Ever."

CHAPTER NINETEEN

Sylvan paced the perimeter of the garden, searching for an exit. The walls of the grove were not stone but masses of trees, growing so close together there was not even a hand's-breadth between. A forest like none she had ever seen. The trunks were smooth as glass and the color of coal, the lowest branches twice as far from the ground as she was tall and covered with pale yellow fronds that ended in needle-like spikes. Vines entwined the bases of the trunks like strands of a tapestry, interweaving until they formed a dense barrier with cords as thick as her forearm. She tore at them with her claws but could not penetrate more than a few inches into the growth before new tendrils sprouted and covered the damage. As she probed the walls, the shape of the grove subtly changed, as if it was a living creature adjusting its camouflage. "Torren said everything in Faerie is alive. If that's true, then there must be a way to kill it."

"I haven't been able to find any openings," Drake said. "In the first place they kept us, I discovered narrow passageways through the undergrowth, but those paths always led to another garden. There's nothing like that here."

Misha finished a circuit of their forested prison and shook her head. "I thought I would be able to follow the path Torren took when she left, but I can't. I can track her to the wall, but there's nothing there now except tree trunks and underbrush."

"We cannot stay here." Sylvan rubbed her side where a burning pain had begun not long before. "The Pack is stirring. They sense danger."

Drake pressed close, slipping her arm around Sylvan's waist. "I feel it too. Do you think it is just because we are absent? The Pack is anxious?"

Sylvan shook her head. "No, more than that. Something else is wrong. The Pack is unsettled, unsure. Cecilia is holding us captive, and the longer we are here, the greater the danger to the Pack."

"When Torren comes back—" Misha began.

"Torren cannot be counted on," Sylvan growled. "Look around. Even the guards are gone. This is a prison cell, and Torren knew what Cecilia planned when she led us here."

"No," Misha said, her chin lifting. "She would not betray us."

"What did Torren say about us trying to escape?" Drake asked.

"That it would do no good." Sylvan paced, frustrated and furious. The Pack needed her and she was helpless. Trapped by an enemy she could not fight. "That it was easy to get lost in Faerie."

"Why warn us not to try escaping if escape wasn't possible?"

Sylvan stilled by a small pool in the center of the garden where multicolored fish with long swirling fins and bright iridescent eyes circled lazily. "What do you mean?"

"What if the impenetrable walls are an illusion?" Drake said. "What if it's glamour and we're not actually imprisoned at all?"

"It's possible." Sylvan considered what she knew of the Fae and their love of secrets and subterfuge. "Anything Torren said to me would have been reported to Cecilia, but even if she was trying to tell me we could escape this place, that doesn't tell us how."

"We were drawn here by Misha's connection to Torren," Drake mused. "What if the way back is a similar connection? Only it's our connection to the Pack."

Sylvan almost laughed. "Torren reminded me I could still reach the Pack if I opened myself to them. We should shift and let our wolves guide us. They may not be as susceptible to glamour as we are in skin."

Drake grasped Sylvan's arm. "Your connection will be strongest. Let the Pack lead us home."

"Stay close." Sylvan called her wolf and shifted instantly, Drake following in another heartbeat, and Misha half a minute later. Sylvan peered at her surroundings, the brilliant colors morphing into shades of gray. Here and there, the foliage shimmered as if moving or drifting in a breeze she could not feel.

Follow me.

She trotted toward the largest area of motion and sniffed at what appeared to her eyes to be a dense wall. She caught the scent of honeysuckle and spice and felt the breeze waft over her tongue, a subtle call of life beyond their green prison. *Here. Can you sense it?*

Misha shook her head and whined softly.

Drake nudged her shoulder. *Yes. A breeze must come from somewhere, but what if the opening is only a crevice or it closes behind us and never opens? We could be trapped.*

We already are trapped. We must get free of this place before we can find a path out. Trusting her wolf, who had hunted prey for decades by scent and instinct, Sylvan stepped forward into darkness, Drake and Misha by her side. She seemed to be in a lightless tunnel, but she felt earth beneath her paws. Warm and…breathing.

Even the rocks beneath our feet are alive, Torren had said.

Sylvan trotted on, following the teasing scents that tickled across her nose, and in one step to the next emerged into twilight. She crouched, waiting for the guards to attack. Drake and Misha appeared by her side.

Take cover.

From the shadows, Sylvan surveyed her surroundings. The gilded, colonnaded corridor was gone. Cecilia's court was gone. They stood in another garden, but this was no prison cell. Nighttime in Faerie was ablaze with fireworks. Above them, crimson clouds streamed across a magenta sky. The path beneath their feet sparkled with colors as if littered with gemstones. Shafts of light sifted through the leafy canopy and set the trees on fire. Subtle sounds of life teemed in the underbrush.

Where are we? Drake nudged her shoulder.

I don't know, but I think we're outside the Faerie Mound. And we need to get as far away as we can. They will know we have left.

Sylvan reached out for Pack and felt the call of the hearts and minds of those she led, those she loved. She set off at a fast run down one of the paths twisting through the trees with Drake and Misha at her heels. As Torren had warned, the trail branched and doubled back and turned in no logical direction, disappearing behind them almost as fast as they traveled, but she let her wolf have her head and trusted her to find the way out. She had no idea if she could locate a Gate or if they would simply travel in a circle and find themselves at the mouth of the Faerie Mound again, but she was running and breathing free, no longer a prisoner. They were wolves, and they would fight anything that tried to chain them.

Time was meaningless. Nothing around them changed. Everything changed. Only the call of the Pack was unchangeable. Sylvan emptied her mind and senses of everything except that distant call and pushed on under the bleeding sky.

Drake growled suddenly. *Do you hear it?*

Behind them…in front of them?…a horn blared.

They know we've escaped.

They'll be coming. We will run until we are free or we will fight.

Yes, Drake replied. Misha howled and pressed close to Sylvan's flank.

They leapt over rocks as smooth as glass and the color of rich wine, down a hillside under a glowing sky. The short grass beneath her paws quivered as she sped over it. The call of the Pack was stronger now. The veil was thinning. They would find a Gate if they could escape detection long enough. The sound of many horns resounded behind them, drawing closer, and the ground trembled.

Mounted riders approaching!

Horses or dogs or whatever hunters the Fae had unleashed were closing in. The call of the Pack was a constant pull now. They just needed a little more time.

The Gate is near.

It will be warded, Drake warned.

There are wolves waiting. We must follow their call.

Misha yipped, a danger alert. *Behind us!*

Prepare to turn and fight, Sylvan signaled. *If they overtake us from the rear, we will have no chance.*

She whipped around and faced the direction from which they had come, Drake on her left and Misha on her right. The path they had traveled was gone and in its place a glade ringed by spiraling trees with white bark and gnarled branches that reached to the sky like skeletal fingers, leafless and glowing silver. A dozen Fae guards on silver stallions burst into the clearing, and the sky turned black. Steam poured from the stallions' gaping nostrils as they trumpeted a battle cry. Their forelegs were encased in silver gauntlets, their heaving chests in glowing armor plates. The guards astride their prancing backs were helmeted and armored and carried bows across their chests and spears in hand. The horses spread out in measured steps, their hooves striking earth like hammers on steel, and formed a semicircle around Sylvan and her wolves. The guards lowered their spears, a dozen gleaming, silver-bayoneted shafts of death.

The horses advanced in slow steps, closing the circle around them. The path behind them was their only escape route, and that would be gone in another few seconds. Sylvan edged out in front of Drake and Misha and howled, a battle challenge of an Alpha wolf. The horses shivered and snorted, prancing uneasily as the air cracked with fury.

If she could unseat the riders, she would have a chance, but first she must secure the Pack. Sylvan took another step forward and the riders angled their spears down at her. She would draw the spears to her and give Drake and Misha a chance to reach the Gate. She prepared to leap.

No! Drake snarled.

From the dark grove behind the guards, a thunderous roar split the air. The horses split ranks, opening a pathway, and a Hound as large as the horses with flaming eyes and fire spewing from its gaping jaws bounded into the clearing. Cecilia's Hunter had come at last.

Jump for the Gate, Sylvan commanded. *It's me they want.*

No, Drake cried again.

The Pack is in danger. You must go. I will find a way out.

I won't leave you.

Trust me! Do as I command. Our wolves and the lives of all the Pack to come depend on it. Go, if you love me. Go.

Drake shuddered, the choice an agony that shredded her heart.

The Hound breathed fire, its powerful forelegs pawing at the earth a dozen yards in front of Sylvan. Sylvan growled a challenge and the Hound raised its head and roared.

Torren's voice filled Sylvan's mind. *You for them. They may pass.* She roared again and a cold wind blew over Sylvan's back. She turned as two arched trees appeared out of the gloom, their branches intertwined to form a gateway. Nothing was visible beyond. Would the portal just take them back to Cecilia's prison, or nowhere at all?

Decide, Torren roared.

Sylvan rounded on the two by her side, snarling and snapping, forcing them away. *Go!*

Drake stared into Sylvan's eyes, the only one who had ever dared. *I love you. Return to me.* She turned and jumped for the Gate. The blackness swallowed her.

Misha hesitated, her gaze on Torren. The Hound snarled and a funnel of fire struck the earth at Misha's feet. Misha swerved and backed away but did not leave.

Torren's voice rang in Sylvan's mind. *The next time she will die.*

Sylvan rushed Misha, driving her to the Gate. She growled and lunged for Misha's throat. Misha cried out, a howl of loss and pain, and leapt into the space between the two trees. The outline of the archway was already fading. The Gate was closing.

Sylvan spun to face Torren. *Now at last it is you and I.*

You will die if you challenge me.

I will die either way. And before I do, you will bleed, Hunter.

Torren thundered forward, the earth opening beneath her feet and flame crawling out toward Sylvan, forcing her to back away from the ring of mounted guards. The Gate was just behind her but Torren's ring of fire was closing around her. If she leapt through the flames the Gate might already be gone and she would have no chance to fight. She would rather die fighting than burn. She gathered her haunches to spring and stared into Torren's eyes. Beyond Torren, the guards shimmered in a cloud of smoke.

The Hound rose up on its hind legs, immense, blocking out the sky and the mounted guards behind her.

Now! Torren shouted. *Jump through the Gate!*

Sylvan whipped around and sailed into the fire. Flames clawed at her throat and her pelt singed. Her lungs filled with smoke and tears blinded her eyes. Ahead in the dark, she heard Drake call.

Here! We are here!

Sylvan crashed down on hard-packed earth, panting, her chest on fire. From beyond the Gate came a scream of agony. Sylvan shed pelt and staggered to her feet.

"Torren," Misha cried, and raced for the archway.

"No!" Sylvan grabbed her and dragged her to the ground a few feet from the Gate.

"Torren!"

The blackness between the two tall, twisted oaks shimmered and the Hound burst through. She collapsed at Sylvan's feet, a dozen silver spears ringing her throat.

Chapter Twenty

Niki alerted at the sound of approaching footsteps. Hours had passed and nothing had changed—she felt no different. Sophia performed regular temperature checks and declared her well, but she didn't trust herself. Her body had so easily betrayed her before—the hunger for Vampire blood never left her, even though she no longer craved the sex. Sophia was all she wanted, but the distant whisper promising blessed oblivion remained. She knew it for an enemy and had learned to live with the enemy within. Now perhaps she would carry another foe inside her, one that would be a danger to all she loved. That she could not allow, but there was time yet to decide. With Sophia beside her, she could not help but hope.

Nadia Revnik stopped in front of the bars, a sheaf of papers in her hand. Beside Niki, Sophia drew a sharp breath. Niki jumped up and moved away from her.

"What is it?" Niki said.

Nadia glanced at Sophia and then Niki. "We have the preliminary results from your tests. We've isolated the contagion in your serum."

"Get out of here," Niki snarled at Sophia, vaulting to the far side of the cell. Not far enough. "Now."

Sophia shook her head, striding to the bars and stretching a hand through to her mother. "Let me see. Her temperature is normal. She shows no symptoms."

"That's why I wanted to see her—see you both. We can't be sure yet," Nadia said, handing the reports to Sophia, "but it's possible the contagion is not active. Or its end-actions are being blocked by something else. We just don't know."

Her back to the cold stone wall, Niki growled, uncertain of what Nadia was saying, but certain that she did not want Sophia anywhere near her if she was likely to turn into anything close to what Angela had been. "Now, will you leave?"

Sophia spun around, her normally calm pale blue eyes flashing with shards of gold. "I will *not*. And you will not try to push me away. You chose me, you are mine now."

Niki gripped the stone, wanting nothing more than to hold her mate and terrified that her touch might harm. She understood now why Sophia had stayed away from her for so long, experienced the terrible dread that she could hurt the one who mattered more than anyone. The enormity of her love hammered at her to push Sophia away, and yet the memory of the pain of being shut out was so much worse. Sophia was right—Niki had forced the mating, insisted, sworn that no matter what happened, she would face it. Sophia finally believed her, trusted her, accepted her. Now she was refusing to allow Sophia to do the same. She held out her hand. "I'm sorry. I just don't want anything to happen to you."

Some of the fury left Sophia's eyes and she took Niki's hand. "I know that. I understand, I do. But I need to be here. If I thought you were a danger to me or to anyone, I would take precautions. But you're not." She faced her mother, still gripping Niki's hand. "I'll take another sample now and send more every hour. You can monitor the levels. Find out if it's multiplying."

"I was going to suggest the same thing," Nadia said. "Even if the numbers are rising, it won't necessarily mean the contagion's active, but it's the next logical thing to do."

"How long before we know for sure?" Niki asked.

"A matter of hours." Nadia hesitated.

"What?" Niki snapped.

"A matter of hours if you develop the full-blown syndrome. It's possible you could have a subclinical infection, or even become a carrier." Nadia sighed. "I'm sorry, Niki, we need more time. We've never dealt with anything quite like this before."

"A carrier," Niki said, glad she was a soldier and not a scientist. "Like Sophia? Healthy, but with some part of it in my blood. That's what you mean?"

Nadia smiled. "More or less, yes."

Niki glanced at Sophia. "We won't know for sure until I shift again. And I can't do that with you in here."

"I'm a carrier, and I've never shown any signs of abnormality during a shift," Sophia said. "My wolf is normal."

"That's because there's nothing wrong with you."

Sophia laughed, a sound almost a sob. "You've always said that. Now you should listen to me."

"I'm trying."

Sophia cupped her face and kissed her softly. "I know."

Niki wanted more. She ached to wrap her arms around Sophia and bury her face in Sophia's neck. She wanted to be sheltered and protected. For once in her life, she didn't want to be strong. But she couldn't. Not for pride, not even for instinct. For love. Gently, she moved Sophia back. "At least keep some distance between us."

"Never," Sophia murmured. "Let's get that blood sample."

Niki sat while Sophia assembled her equipment again. As Sophia was filling the last tube, a door somewhere clattered and running footsteps approached her cell. Nadia stepped aside and Beryl halted breathless beside her. "Callan received word that a raiding party has crossed into our territory."

❖

Gray lay on her stomach on a rocky ledge halfway down a steep slope, watching a deer trail that ran along the shallow, rock-strewn creek. The sun was just coming up over the mountaintop behind her, and the twilight painted everything a soft, shimmering silver. Fog lifted off the water in small puffs of white as if the creek were breathing. The forest slumbered still, the birds not yet awake, the night creatures having already returned to their dens. The brief curtain of time between night and day was utterly silent, the only sound her own heart thudding faintly in her ears. This was her favorite time. The time of the hunter, the moment before the deer broke from cover and started to forage, when the rabbits left their burrows, when the pheasants abandoned their nests in the undergrowth.

The wolf in her hungered to hunt. The warrior in her wanted to fight. She had taken the last watch, and the night had been long and cold. Her small squad was spread out at twenty-yard intervals, wedged between Mira's squad somewhere higher up to her left and Jazz's down to her right. Two of her four, now five with the human, Clint, were asleep. Tamara and Clint had taken the same watch as her. She wondered what they had done over the last six hours while she had lain alone. Her wolf growled impatiently, unhappy with the inactivity. Unhappy that Tamara was out of sight, in the presence of an interested male. Not that it mattered. It couldn't matter. She wasn't interested in Tamara, but her belly tightened when she remembered their tangle by the creek. Remembered the feel of Tamara beneath her, above her.

How would you feel if you were about to submit another Were in the midst of a tangle and all of a sudden you couldn't bring yourself to do it? When all you could think of was how good it would feel to drag them down on top of you?

Tamara's words, her nightmare. She hadn't been brave enough to admit she knew just what Tamara meant. Tamara was braver than her on every front—she'd been injured in battle, endured captivity, lost her Pack, and still she fought back. Gray hadn't even been brave enough to admit she wanted Tamara's claws in her back, her teeth in her flesh. She'd never even thought about what an Omega wanted from a tangle.

Neither dominant nor submissive, what did that mean? How did Tamara find her way, grow to be so sure and strong? Gray had never questioned her urges—her wants had always been clear, unquestioned, simple. She was a dominant, she'd known it from the time she was old enough to tussle with Packmates, driven by the instinct to keep going until all the others had given up. When she'd gotten old enough to want more than a playful tussle, when she'd wanted the tangle that followed, that urge had been inborn too. Now those urges were entwined in different needs, leaving her confused and unsure. Far less brave than the Were who kept watch a few yards away. If she tried, she might catch Tamara's scent on the wind.

Gray grumbled softly and tried to put Tamara and what she might be saying to Clint out of her mind. She couldn't let herself be distracted, even if the constant level of alertness kept her loins tight and her clitoris tense. Her body seemed to know what it wanted—it was her head that didn't.

A vibration in the pocket of her BDUs saved her from more punishing imaginings of Tamara and Clint lying close together under cover, and she pulled out her phone.

I smell Blackpaw. T

Gray scanned the trail below and the forest beyond and saw nothing. She lifted her head, sniffed the damp cool air. Scented nothing. Settling her rifle across her back, she crept back from the ledge and, keeping low, cut through the underbrush until she reached the outlook where Tamara and Clint were posted.

"Do you see anything?" she whispered to Tamara.

Tamara shook her head. "I caught a scent just a moment ago. Wolf. And more than one."

"Are you sure it's Blackpaw? Maybe it's Mira's patrol. They might have moved downwind and you caught their scent."

"No, it was Blackpaw. I know their smell."

"All right. Watch for them to break cover." She eyed Clint, who had black camouflage paint under his eyes. He still looked fresh and happy. "If you have a shot, take it."

"Roger that." He grinned, showing straight, white teeth.

Small teeth. His bite would not be much to worry about. Gray growled softly and Tamara frowned at her.

"Be careful," Gray said and backed away. She texted the others in her patrol, then Mira and Jazz, and finally Callan.

Possible Blackpaw raiders approaching.

Gunfire broke out off to her right. Jazz's squad was under attack. She turned to head back to her post and leaves shredded overhead as if plummeted by a heavy rain. She threw herself to the ground a small distance away from Tamara and Clint. "Get down!"

Bringing her rifle around, she crawled forward on elbows and knees until she could look down on the trail. No one. She checked the creek, saw nothing on the other side, but the fog was dense and her vision was obscured. They could be right on the other side and she would not see them. She raised her head to sight along the crest toward Jazz's position, and another spatter of gunfire cracked the air. Splintered branches rained down. She called to Tamara. "Can you track where they're firing from?"

"Not yet."

"When you can, return fire and change position."

"I'm better off firing from a fixed location," Clint said.

"Not if you're dead! Follow orders."

Tamara said, "We will. Go! You need better cover."

Gray ran back to her post. Shouts from Jazz's position were drowned out by more gunfire. Dropping onto the ledge, she trained her weapon on the trail and searched for a target. The undergrowth was thick, and the raiders were firing from behind the cover of trees. She saw muzzle flash and fired in that direction. As soon as she did, she rolled to her right and took cover behind another tree. Bullets peppered the ledge where she'd just been.

From her left, she heard a steady string of measured shots. The human was firing. She tried to check Tamara's location, but more rapid fire from assault rifles scoured the earth and underbrush in front of her. They were blindly raking the hillside, hoping to hit the Timberwolves in the barrage.

She texted her team.

Take rocky cover.

All of her squad was firing now in the direction from which the raiders were shooting. Still no clear targets. Her team had the high ground.

Fire in quadrants to your front. Go.

She sprayed the trees downslope from her, rolling behind rocky outcroppings after each short burst. The Blackpaws returned fire every few seconds. Their force appeared to be concentrated just at the bend of the trail. She focused her next salvo there. Someone close by on her right cried out. Someone was hit. One of her squad? Jazz's? Tamara?

Gray waited for a break in the gunfire and jumped to another rocky outcropping. Immediately the air was filled with bullets. She waited again, jumped again. A minute later she found Acer, one of Jazz's recruits, writhing in a pool of blood, both hands clutching his thigh. She quickly pulled a tourniquet from her pocket and wrapped it around his leg. "Come on, grab onto my belt."

"I'll drag you down."

"No, you won't. We need to get out of the line of fire." She grabbed him around the waist. "Do it."

He pushed with his good leg while she tugged him up the hill toward a cluster of boulders where he would be shielded. The firing seemed to be lessening, but she wasn't sure who had the upper hand. If the Blackpaws overran their lines, Acer would be helpless. She couldn't let him be taken captive or executed. She pushed him behind the rocks, and he fell heavily on his uninjured side. Blood still seeped from the wound.

Quickly, she texted Tamara. *Have wounded. You in charge. Retreat to Compound if needed.*

She turned to brace her weapon on the largest boulder and the firing started again. They'd seen her. Rock chips flew into the air, grazing her face and neck. She blinked away blood and sighted down the escarpment. A shadow flickered between the trees, and she fired. A hammer blow struck her shoulder and she flew backward. She landed hard on her back, her rifle flying from her hands. A stream of fire scorched down her arm. She'd been hit. She clamped a hand to her shoulder and blood seeped through her fingers. Pushing with her legs, she crowded closer to Acer, shielding him as best she could.

She wasn't sure how long she lay there as the gunfire slowly ceased. Her vision was dimming even as the sky brightened. From below her, rocks grated and rolled downslope. Someone was coming. She scented the air and smelled only gun smoke and blood. With her good arm she fumbled for her weapon. Gone. Then a shadow fell over her face and a figure loomed above her, blocking out the rising sun.

CHAPTER TWENTY-ONE

Veronica checked the digital readout in the lower right corner of her screen again. She'd never before cared about the passage of minutes and hours. Time was an inconsequential abstraction—the only measurements that motivated her were the data scrolling down the screen, the only yardstick by which she measured success. She'd certainly never given a second's thought to the precise time of sunrise. Now her life was marked by the rising and setting of the sun, almost as rigidly circumscribed as Luce's existence. Dawn meant Luce would disappear into the depths of the lair with Francesca, to do what Veronica could only imagine, and envy. Feed, fuck, rest? No matter the answer, Luce would leave her to toss and turn restlessly, her body hungering for release until sunfall, when Luce would emerge from her protected shelter and seek her out to feed. Time was now her keeper, and she was late.

She'd taken longer than she'd intended reviewing the data that had been acquired while she was away. Her focus had been off at first, but when she'd settled into her familiar mental landscape, she'd lost herself in the planning and the projections and the pleasure of imagining a world where humans ruled without needing to worry about who might be hiding undercover among them. Of course, her thinking had changed recently. She no longer envisioned a future with only humans, but one inhabited by their carefully selected Vampire collaborators. Humans of course would always be in the dominant position, due not only to their superior numbers but by virtue of their greater intellect. Humans had learned very early to take pleasure from the other species that shared the planet, most often as food, and now, in a more primal form of pleasure. The urgency to experience that pleasure again soon made her tremble. Only one more thing to do before she could find Luce and they could return to the lair before full daylight. When Luce would want to feed.

Veronica dialed the number and waited.

"Who is this?" Nicholas asked, sounding as if he'd been awake and expecting a call he didn't want to take.

"Who else would it be, darling?" Veronica said. "Do you give this number to many people?"

"No one has this number except you," he said, "but I wasn't expecting to hear from you so soon after—well, so soon."

"Really? And did you think I was going to let the work stop just because Sylvan Mir managed a minor victory?"

Nicholas scoffed. "I wouldn't call it minor. She's unseated Francesca and thrown her support to the Regent who's taken her place."

"A temporary setback at best. Surely you haven't lost faith in Francesca?"

"Of course not," he said quickly.

"Good, because I'm ready to get back to work, and I need a full complement of technicians to do that." She'd been relegated to making do with a skeleton staff while the lab was being rebuilt, but now that she'd acquired the right specimens she was ready to return to full power.

"Finding individuals willing to accept your scheduling requirements isn't easy."

"None of this is easy, but it's necessary. By the end of the week, I'll need at least twenty fully qualified scientists. Marshall, my head tech, will contact you and we can begin screening right away."

"We can't draw attention to what we're doing here," Nicholas said.

"I'm sure you can see to it." Veronica tried to cloak her impatience. Really, Nicholas was rapidly approaching the end of his usefulness. "I know many of your members are scientists. That is how we met, after all."

"I'll need time to relocate some of them."

"That's excellent. I'm sure Francesca will be very pleased."

"And what of your progress? Are we going to see some kind of biological weapon soon?"

Ordinarily she would have found his question annoying, but when she thought of the subjects and the wealth of material she would have to work with, she could only smile. "I think I can safely assure you it won't be long before we will have the means to neutralize the Were population, if not eradicate them completely."

"How?"

"Remember your basic biology, Nicholas," Veronica said wearily. Why must she always go begging to the inferior for the means to do her work? "A species that cannot reproduce will very quickly disappear. Add to that a deadly contagion, or the threat they *carry* one, and we will have a perfect storm."

"Fine," Nicholas said grudgingly. "My *friends* will be happy to hear that."

"Give my regards to the senators. I'll have to go now," Veronica said, checking the clock yet again. "I have a pressing appointment."

She disconnected without waiting for Nicholas to reply, pushed papers into her briefcase, and hurriedly locked her office. Luce was waiting in the darkened conference room. "I was afraid you might have left."

Luce was beside her in an instant, an arm around her waist pulling her close, her mouth pressed to Veronica's throat. She drew in a long, slow breath as if absorbing her essence. "I told you I would wait, but I don't want to wait much longer. Are you ready to leave?"

Veronica tilted her head to expose her throat. "Always."

❖

"Torren," Misha cried out, dropping to her knees by Torren's side. She ran her hands over the Hound's heaving flanks and stared at the blood pouring from the wounds in the Hound's neck where the spear shafts protruded like a monstrous collar. "Get them out! Alpha, can't we get them out?"

"Daniel," Sylvan said to the young lieutenant who'd been waiting in the grove, "guard the Gate."

"Yes, Alpha." Daniel quickly moved behind her, facing the dark hollow between the giant trees through which Sylvan and the others had just emerged.

"Sylvan," Drake said urgently, "your back is burned. You need treatment too."

"It's not bad. Call for a Rover and a medic. We can treat Torren while we transport." Sylvan gripped Misha's shoulder. "I don't know what will happen if we try to remove these spears. The bleeding might get worse."

Misha looked up at Drake, her eyes wide and terrified. "Prima?"

"Daniel, let me have your phone." Drake quickly called Niki but got no answer from her, Jace, or Jonathan. Finally Callan responded and she told him where they were and what they needed. She listened a moment and said, "Have Elena load up a medical pack and put it in the vehicle. Hurry."

"Elena isn't coming?" Sylvan asked.

"Blackpaw raiders have attacked the perimeter. We have wounded arriving soon."

Sylvan snarled. "We need to get back there."

Drake clasped her neck. Squeezed. When she'd landed Earthside with Sylvan still trapped in Faerie, her heart had ceased to beat. She knew she must live for their young, for the Pack, but she couldn't imagine drawing a single breath in a world without Sylvan. Now they were together, and she could face anything. "We will. Soon." She crouched by Torren's head. "Torren? Torren, can you shift? If we pull out the spears, can you shift and heal the wounds?"

The Hound blinked, its deep red eyes as dull as the embers of a cooling fire. She seemed not to hear, or if she did, she couldn't answer. Drake had no idea how much blood a creature the Hound's size could lose, or what kind of wounds Torren could heal, especially outside of Faerie where her powers might be diminished. She'd heard that the Fae drew their power from the magic of Faerie itself. She did know with wounds like this, time was not their friend, and by the time a Rover arrived and they got back to the Compound, Torren could be dead. She glanced at Sylvan. "I think we have to try to remove them and hope she can shift. She's losing too much blood, and who knows what else is on the weapons. There could be a poison of some kind." She gripped one of the wooden shafts. The long silver spearhead was nearly completely buried inside Torren's flesh. Sylvan grabbed another and nodded.

"Pull," Drake said and yanked the weapon free. She and Sylvan methodically worked their way around Torren's huge neck until all the spear shafts had been removed. The wounds gaped through the leathery hide, revealing shredded muscle and a steady trickle of blood. The Hound lay still, eyes closed.

Misha wrapped her arms as far as she could around the Hound's chest and laid her head against Torren's heart. "You have to shift. You have to heal. Please. Torren, you can do this."

The Hound shivered, a huge groan emerging from its massive chest, but she did not shift.

"She's too weak," Misha cried. "Alpha, please. There must be something!"

Sylvan glanced at Drake, who slowly shook her head. "You're injured too. You can't risk—"

"Torren risked everything." Sylvan gritted her teeth. "She saved your life once, and Misha's. She just saved mine. I will not let her die."

She took Drake's place by Torren's head and gripped the great Hound's face in her hands. "Look inside me. Find my power, feel my Pack. Take our strength."

Torren's lids slowly closed and Misha sobbed. "Please, I love you. Please. Torren, don't let go."

The Hound shuddered and her eyes slowly opened. She searched Sylvan's face and found her eyes. Sylvan jerked as if she'd been struck. Drake pressed close to her, lending her power and her strength. The muscles stood out in Sylvan's chest and abdomen, sweat broke out over her neck and ran down her arms, and her wolf roared to life. Her face and body grew heavy with the power of the Alpha. The Hound gasped, the air crackled with power, and in a shower of light, the Hound disappeared and Torren lay naked in its place.

"Torren?" Desperately, Misha dragged Torren's head into her lap and stroked her face. "Torren? Can you hear me?"

Torren's eyes opened and she gazed first at Misha, then at Sylvan and Drake. "I take it we made it through."

Sylvan grinned, feeling as weak as if she had just run all day on a hunt and had yet to feed. "Thanks to you."

"No," Torren said wearily. "If you had not found your way to the Gate, I would not have been able to help. I couldn't leave Cecilia's side until she trusted that I had nothing to do with your escape. We'd been watching you the entire time, and when she realized you were going to find your way out, she finally ordered me to bring you back."

"All of us?" Sylvan asked.

Torren slowly shook her head. "No, it was always you she wanted. She ordered me to execute the others."

Sylvan growled. "She wanted you to kill my mate?"

Torren reached up and grasped Misha's hand. "And mine."

"We need to get out of here," Drake said. "Who knows what might come through that Gate next."

Torren tried to sit up, but blood still ran from her wounds and she was weakening. "I will stay behind—"

"No." Sylvan stilled at the sound of an approaching vehicle. "The Rover is here, and we are all leaving. No one stays behind."

❖

"Gray, lie still," Tamara whispered hoarsely, dropped down behind cover of the boulders.

"Tamara?" Gray muttered, struggling to focus through the fog that seemed to lie over her like a thick, wet blanket.

"Yeah, it's me." A hand brushed dirt and sweat from Gray's eyes. "How bad?"

"Not...too bad." Gray swallowed around the pain. Her vision cleared. Clint crowded in next to Tamara, and she frowned. They'd both left their posts. She would have done the same if one of them had been hit, but this was different. She was in charge, and she had to think of what mattered to the Pack. "Acer is worse. Get two of the recruits to take him back to the Compound. You both need to get back to the line."

"We'll take you both," Clint said in his deep, easy baritone. He leaned down, hefted Acer over his shoulder and stood, half-crouched, keeping behind the boulders. He glanced at Tamara. "I guess you can handle her?"

Tamara didn't bother to answer but lifted Gray easily.

"What's the situation?" Gray clenched her jaw against the burning in her shoulder. Warmth spread across her chest. Blood.

"The Blackpaws have fallen back. We can't tell if they've left the area yet."

"Have you heard from Callan?" Gray murmured. She was cold, colder than she'd been all night, despite the sunlight that slanted across her face. She focused on Tamara's face just above hers. Tamara's jaw was set, her eyes glowing fiercely. Her wolf was close to the surface, and Gray took comfort in her strength.

"Not yet."

"We can't spare anyone else from the line," Gray said. "I can wait until Callan sends reinforcements."

"You two can sort this out later," Clint said conversationally. "We'd best be getting down off this slope while it's still quiet."

Tamara slung her rifle over her shoulder. "Let's move. We'll follow you. If you see anyone, shout and I'll cover you."

"You can't leave the rest of them out here without a leader," Gray said as Tamara loped sure-footedly down the slope, "and you've got the most experience."

Tamara rumbled. "I'm no leader. You know that. You know why."

"All a leader needs is a strong, fearless heart, and you have that." Gray wanted to sleep. She rested her head against Tamara's shoulder. "You know I'm right."

"I know you think you are. That's what makes you the leader." Tamara brushed her cheek over the top of Gray's head. "Mira or Jazz can take our recruits into their squads until Callan gets more *sentries* here."

Gray was too tired to argue. Tamara's arm under her back held her still and secure as they moved from outcropping to outcropping down the sparsely wooded hillside into the denser forest. Her shoulder didn't hurt so much anymore. In fact, she wasn't as cold as she had been.

"You should stay awake," Tamara murmured.

"Trying."

Tamara's hand beneath her back was warm, and after a while it was the only thing she could feel. Her hands were numb but it didn't seem to matter.

"Gray?"

Gray jerked. "Are we home yet?"

"Not quite yet. How do you feel?"

"Pretty good. It's nice and warm now."

Tamara laid her cheek on Gray's forehead. "You don't feel warm."

"No problem. I'm good." She pressed her face to Tamara's throat. "Just sleepy."

"Gray," Tamara said firmly. "I want you to stay awake now."

Gray tilted her head back. Tamara's expression was stony, as fierce as if she were in a battle. "You mad?"

Tamara's eyes met hers. They were an amazing shade of green. "No. I'm not mad."

Clint stopped under shelter of thick, towering pines. "What are we going to do with these two? My boy's not looking too good."

"We're going to take them home."

Chapter Twenty-two

Dasha Baran, the tall, muscular dominant who had recently been promoted to *centuri*, appeared in front of Niki's cell. She saluted briskly. "*Imperator,* Callan sent me with a message. He is taking two squadrons of reinforcements to the perimeter and plans to pick up the wounded. He needs a medic and requests Sophia join him immediately."

Niki paced the confines of her cell, the space growing smaller by the second. With her imprisoned and both the Alpha and Prima missing, the Pack was without its most dominant members. She was the leader of the Pack warriors, and unable to lead. Callan was experienced and steady, but he would be more valuable at the front, directing their warriors, not behind the lines planning strategy. But they could not leave the Compound without a strong presence to assure the hundreds inside they were safe. "What's the situation?"

"Reports are scattered, but it appears only one raiding party of Blackpaws has attacked so far, though they came in significant numbers."

"Are we sure it's Blackpaws?"

Dasha nodded.

"How many injured?"

"We don't have a count. Communications between the patrols are erratic."

"What about security here?"

"We've doubled the guards on the nursery. The stockade is well enforced. We have plenty of arms, ammunition, and supplies. We can hold off anything except a full-out assault."

Niki turned to Sophia. "What about our medical supplies?"

"The infirmary can handle several dozen wounded." She looked worried. "With the Prima...away...Elena and I will have trouble managing more than a few with major injuries."

"Let's hope there aren't many." Niki stepped back until her legs touched the metal edge of her cot. "You need to go."

"Elena could—"

"No," Niki said gently. She grasped Sophia's shoulders and pulled her close. "We can't leave the Compound, and especially the young, without a medic. If we have wounded, you must go. You can heal more than just their bodies. And if you are gone, Elena must remain here."

Sophia framed Niki's face with both hands. "You know I would never leave you unless the need of the Pack was great."

"I know. Just as you know that I only leave you when I must." She started to kiss her, drew back. Sophia glared.

"Such a foolish wolf." Sophia threaded her arms around Niki's neck, brushed her cheek over Niki's, and kissed her firmly. "I told you, you're fine. Believe me."

Niki held her tightly. "You are my truth in all things."

"And you are my love. I'll be back as soon as I can." Sophia looked into Niki's heart. "And you will promise me not to make any foolish decisions about what is best for me or the Pack while I am gone. We all need you, me most of all."

"I love you." Niki wished as she so rarely did that Sophia could not read her mind as she seemed to. Sophia knew she would have one of the *centuri* shoot her down if she felt the mutation taking hold in her. Her fellow *centuri* would not shirk from doing what was necessary to protect the Pack, and they would be swift and merciful.

"Promise me," Sophia demanded, "or I will not leave this cell."

Niki couldn't let the wounded in the field go without treatment, and she would not lie to her mate. "I promise."

"Then I will go."

Niki stepped back and watched Sophia leave. The thought of Sophia anywhere near the fighting when she was not there to protect her had her wolf howling in rage. She met Dasha's eyes through the bars. "See that no harm comes to her."

"I will guard her with my life." Dasha had once been Niki's relentless competitor for Sophia's attentions, but that was natural between dominants when they both wanted the same unmated Were. Now that Sophia was mated, Dasha would respect the mate bond and protect the *imperator*'s mate as she would the Alpha's.

"As soon as you can," Niki said, "get word to me of how things stand."

"I will."

Dasha and Sophia left and silence fell throughout the detention area. Niki's cell was dim and cool and achingly lonely. She sat back down on the bare steel ledge to wait.

Outside, Sophia hurried across the crowded yard to the infirmary to gather a portable med kit and found Elena in the treatment room already packing one. "I can do that now."

"We need more than one," Elena said, pulling meds from a cabinet.

"Why? I thought Callan wanted me—"

Elena spun around, her dark eyes gleaming with excitement. "Callan was just here. The Prima contacted him. The Alpha and Prima are on their way back, or will be as soon as Callan gets a Rover to them."

"Oh, thank heavens," Sophia cried. "But is someone hurt? Why are you—"

"Callan says they have wounded and need a medic."

"Who?" Sophia's heart constricted. The Pack was so vulnerable right now—Niki was imprisoned, they were under attack, and now the Alpha and Prima were possibly injured as well.

"I don't know. You need to go—the *centuri* will take you."

"But I thought Callan wanted me to go with him to the perimeter."

"I'm sending Adam with Callan."

"Adam! He's only an adolescent, and we've barely had time to instruct him—"

"He has the makings of a medic, and he's smart and steady. He'll be able to stabilize the wounded at least, and if Callan gets them right back here, we shouldn't lose much time in initiating the critical treatment. The Alpha's cadre takes priority."

"Of course," Sophia said, taking the med kit from Elena. "You'll be all right?"

"I can handle things. Go. And be careful."

Sophia glanced once toward headquarters and the detention center below, almost hoping to see Niki come charging out to take control. But the great wooden doors remained closed.

Callan waved her toward an idling Rover and she hurried in that direction. All around her, *sentries* and soldiers just returned from patrols and still wearing forest-green camouflage gathered arms into the backs of Rovers or hoisted packs onto their backs and formed up into squads.

Jace and Jonathan were already in the front seat of the Rover. Dasha, an assault rifle over her shoulder, held the rear door for Sophia. As soon as she climbed in, Dasha jumped aboard and slammed the door.

"Go," Dasha shouted.

Jace revved the engine and they tore out of the Compound. Sophia grabbed the hand strap as the Rover jolted through the gate, and looked behind her. Callan directed Adam, loaded down with medical gear, into the last of three Rovers in a convoy of armed Weres waiting to leave.

She hoped Adam would be able to handle the wounded at the front. She swallowed and stared straight ahead as the Rover bounced along the single track through Pack land. She hoped she would be able to handle whatever was coming.

❖

The farther Tamara and Clint made their way down the mountainside, the more distant the intermittent gunfire sounded. The trees provided some cover and shaded them from direct sun, but Tamara's hair was drenched with sweat and her shirt clung to her chest as if she'd been hunting all day under a summer sun. They'd been carrying the wounded for almost an hour over rugged terrain and Clint was tiring, although he would never admit to it. His face was pale and his steps less steady than they had been. She probably had five times his strength, and she was aware of Gray's weight but not bothered by it. She was sweating more from worry than exertion.

Gray had stopped talking a few minutes ago, and although her breathing seemed normal, she was weak and blood still seeped from her shoulder. Tamara strained to hear the sounds of approaching vehicles or the voices of other Packmates, searching for some indication reinforcements had arrived to take the wounded back to the Compound. All she heard was Clint's ragged panting. "We should stop."

"No," he grunted. "I don't like the looks of this one. He needs fluid and this trip isn't doing the hole in his leg much good. The bleeding's picked up."

"I'm not even sure we're headed in the right direction," Tamara said. "Since we have to avoid the trails in case the Blackpaws are scouting them, we could end up walking way out of our way."

"As long as we're going down, it's the right direction. You think they're following us?"

Tamara stopped, turned, and scented the air. "I don't think so. Not yet at least."

He cocked his head and regarded her curiously. "You really can smell them?"

She stared. Clint had turned out to be as good a shot as he claimed, and he was brave enough. But he was human, and when he asked a silly question like that one, she was reminded just how different they were. Could they all ever really live in harmony? "Yes."

"Listen, I always heard…"

Her jaw tightened. "You always heard what?"

"I always heard you could heal anything. Why aren't these two healing? Shouldn't they be spitting out the bullets or something so the wounds can close?"

Tamara had never mingled much with humans. She kept to herself when outside the Pack, and unlike some of her Packmates who lived with humans in college or worked with them after, she had gone right into military training. Could it really be that humans were so ignorant? No wonder they feared the Weres so much. She didn't want to say too much. It wasn't her job to educate humans, maybe it wasn't even wise. But he was risking his life for them, and she owed him some kind of answer. "No, that's not right. We heal better after we shift, but we need medical treatment first. Fluids, sometimes removing the bullets or counteracting a poison, just like you would."

"Huh. Handy, though. Sounds like shifting makes recovery a lot faster."

The tension in her jaw disappeared. "It does."

As if realizing they'd stopped, he settled Acer a little higher on his shoulder and started working his way through the brush again. "Well then, we better get these two the treatment they need so they can go all furry and heal."

"Furry?"

"Well, what do you call it?"

"We don't call it anything—it's just who we are. But for the record, it's pelt. Not *fur*. Fur is for rabbits."

His usual jocular expression grew serious as he looked at her across the wounded Weres they both carried in their arms. "Do you think I could see someday? Your other self?"

"Why?"

"I guess I'd just like to know all of you."

Tamara lifted her chin, let her eyes go cold. She didn't want to be known. Not by anyone. "Let's get these two to safety."

He nodded and looked away. "Sure."

"Then I'll think about it."

He grinned. "Sure."

❖

"Daniel," Sylvan said, "vehicle approaching. Cover the clearing from behind the trees."

Daniel slipped away, and Drake joined Sylvan standing in front of Torren and Misha. She wasn't sure from where the greatest danger might come—through the Gate behind them or out of the woods ahead. A Rover burst into the clearing and careened to a stop, kicking up clods of dark earth and a flurry of leaves. Max jumped out from behind the wheel and Andrea emerged from the passenger side. Andrea held an automatic rifle and scanned the surroundings. Drake welcomed the protection but kept her attention on the archway between the trees. She could almost see the helmeted horsemen galloping through the Gate on wings of fire. If she ever had a chance to repay Cecilia for her hospitality and the injury to Sylvan that even now wept a steady stream of bloody fluid down Sylvan's back, she would do it face-to-face and not delegate some soldier to exact retribution. She'd do it with her own teeth and claws, and quickly. A wolf did not play with its prey.

Sylvan strode toward Max. "Did you bring a medic?"

"No," Max said. "We came from the city. We were closest when Callan informed the *centuri* of your position. Another Rover is on its way from the Compound with a medic. We thought you might want to get out of here. We're rendezvousing at Nocturne."

"I would like very much to get us out of here." Sylvan grabbed his shoulders, jerked him close, and held him for a second. He rubbed his stubbled jaw against her throat and she released him. "Can you get Torren in the back?"

Max stared down at Torren, who still lay across Misha's lap. Her eyes were closed, her breathing barely discernible. The wounds in her neck had not healed but the bleeding had stopped. Her skin, always translucent, was practically transparent, so thin and fragile she seemed almost made of air. "What the hell happened?"

Misha looked up, her eyes dark pits, and growled a warning.

Max raised an eyebrow. "I'm not going to hurt her."

"Misha," Sylvan said firmly. "We have to take care of her. You have to let her go."

Misha showed her teeth.

Drake crouched by Misha's side. "It's all right. We want to help her. You know you can trust us. You can stay with her the entire time. But Max needs to put her in the Rover. Let him take her."

"No."

"You can hold her hand. I promise you, she'll be all right."

"Come on, little one," Max said gently. "Let me help her."

Misha's jaw opened and her canines jutted forward.

Andrea looked down at Misha. "The only chance she has of surviving is with the Pack. How much do you trust your Pack?"

Misha shuddered and nodded. When she loosened her grip, Max slid an arm beneath Torren's shoulders and under her knees and effortlessly lifted her. Misha sprang to her feet, keeping Torren's hand clasped in hers, and followed Max to the Rover. He settled Torren in the back and Misha jumped in. Drake, Sylvan, and Daniel followed. Sylvan crouched just behind the front passenger seats to see out the windshield, Daniel took a position where he could watch through the rear windows, and Drake knelt by Torren across from Misha. Andrea got in front with Max, and he swerved the Rover around the small clearing and plunged into the woods. He kept the headlights off.

"Well done back there," Sylvan murmured to Andrea.

"Basic Psych 101."

Sylvan laughed shortly. "Does it work on Max?"

"Not yet."

Drake checked Torren's pulse, not certain if Fae physiology would be anything like human physiology, but needing to do something. She felt the thready beat of blood whispering beneath the skin of Torren's throat. She was in shock, at least that's what she would've diagnosed in a human.

"Max," she said, "I think you should hurry."

CHAPTER TWENTY-THREE

After Luce delivered Veronica back to the lair and gave her the reward she'd been craving, she left her asleep and went to Francesca's boudoir to report. The day was upon them, and she wanted to feed. From outside the room, she smelled Were and human blood and sex. Francesca had already begun her pleasures.

She raised a hand to knock just as Francesca's voice whispered through her mind. *Good morning, darling. Come join us.*

Luce let herself in and bowed. "My Queen."

Francesca reclined on the sofa in front of the fireplace, Dru stretched out beside her and a human servant on the floor at her feet, his head resting on Francesca's thigh. Francesca idly stroked the human's curly red hair, as she might any other pet. Dru flashed Luce a contented smile. Her shirt and pants were open, her skin still slick with sex.

"Where did you go?" Luce asked. The cat hadn't been in the vehicle when she and Veronica left the lab. A human servant had been waiting to drive them back to the lair.

"I thought a visit to Raptures might be a better use of my time."

Francesca smiled at Dru. "I'm afraid we've been too occupied to discuss business, but now that Luce is here, we'll want a full report."

"Of course," Dru said. "Our new wolf friends have been busy gathering recruits, including some cat Weres, to our forces. We now have a respectable new guard that will allow you to travel more securely, my Queen. And the Weres are all eager to host in exchange for their allegiance."

"Very good," Francesca purred. "You have done well."

For an instant, Luce considered disposing of the cat. Dru might only be a Were, but Francesca seemed inordinately fond of her. Perhaps when the cat had fulfilled her purpose, which hopefully would be soon,

Francesca could be convinced it was unwise to keep an outsider so close to the throne. Weres had their place in bed, but not in the council chamber.

Francesca turned her attention to Luce, a glimmer of amusement in her eyes, and Luce wondered if Francesca had been probing her mind.

"How is the good doctor?"

"Satisfied for the moment."

Francesca's dark brow winged upward. "You don't seem to be."

Luce schooled her features to nonchalance. Francesca had little patience for dissatisfaction among her ranks, and she wanted no cause for Francesca to doubt her. She was centuries younger than the Queen, but she'd existed long enough to witness the consequences of Francesca's wrath. She had no wish to be entombed and left to starve or go mad. "I'll admit to still being hungry. The human is too weak to satisfy any longer."

"I am sorry." Francesca smiled and stretched an elegant arm out along the top of the sofa until her fingertips touched Dru's shoulder. Dru rumbled and rubbed her cheek on Francesca's hand. "Humans are just so…lacking. I'll call for a servant to meet your needs."

"That's not necessary, my Queen." Until now, they'd shared Dru, since the cat had been one of the few Weres available, and the human servants were too frail to truly satisfy. Now it seemed Dru was to be Francesca's alone.

"Nonsense. The youngling Dru found for us has brought quite an interesting clutch of hosts to us. I haven't sampled all of them, and we mustn't let them go unsatisfied."

"As you wish." Luce bowed her head. The ache in her midsection intensified and her mouth flooded with feeding hormones. Veronica had succumbed to bloodlust the instant she'd taken her vein, and when she'd realized how weak the human's blood had become, she'd taken almost nothing. The craving was close to madness now. She shivered and Francesca smiled again.

A moment later, Daniela appeared in the doorway. "Yes, Mistress?"

"Bring a host for Luce. That young dark-haired wolf. The one with the very lovely mouth."

"Of course."

"Now," Francesca said to Luce. "Tell me about your evening."

"Veronica contacted Nicholas and wants the lab fully staffed. I heard her promise him results very soon."

Dru hissed. "What kind of results?"

"I gathered she thinks she'll be able to manufacture some chemical that will render them…impotent or fatally diseased."

"Neither will meet our immediate needs." Francesca sat up straight, her casual indolence gone in a flash. The lethal predator she was peered from her violet eyes. "I've always found the entire idea of a biological annihilation a little untenable. Really, Nicholas has been trying to achieve it for years and who's to say it won't take decades more?" She laughed. "Ordinarily, time is inconsequential, but with the state of human politics since Anthony Mir had the idiotic idea that all of us should live in harmony with humans, we need to move more quickly."

Dru grunted. "That's why we need some direct action against Sylvan Mir."

"Exactly," Francesca said. "The goal of the Shadow Lords is to work behind the scenes to undercut these negotiations with humans, but that seems to be failing. Sylvan remains the obstacle, and Cecilia has yet to deliver her as promised."

"The Fae are not the most reliable of allies," Luce said carefully.

Francesca laughed. "How can any creature whose reality is as shifting as the wind be trusted? But I had hoped Cecilia's offer to turn Sylvan over to us was genuine."

"Sylvan is clever," Luce said. "She might have escaped."

"If so, we'll soon know." Francesca sighed. "And we are not yet strong enough to eliminate her."

"We might have an opportunity sooner than you expect," Dru said. "My new sources at Raptures tell me the Blackpaws struck Sylvan's patrols early this morning. Just a small skirmish, but enough to get her attention."

Francesca frowned. "We really don't have the resources to go to war."

"No, we don't," Dru said, "but we don't want a war. We want an ambush."

Francesca smiled. "And I take it you have some ideas about that."

"I do."

The door opened and Daniela escorted an adolescent male Were into the room. His dark hair, tangled and thick, reached his shoulders, and his green eyes glittered with chips of gold. He was shirtless, wearing form-fitting trousers and no shoes. His torso was heavily muscled like all Weres, and a thick line of dark pelt bisected his lower abdomen.

From the looks of the cock trapped against his belly beneath his pants, he was more than ready to give his body as well as his blood.

Francesca held out her hand. "Come here, darling, and sit beside me."

He leapt to Francesca's side and settled between her and Dru. She kissed him and stroked his abdomen, slicing a thin path down to the top of his pants with a nail. His hips jerked as blood welled up, and she murmured, "Careful. Don't be in too much of a hurry."

She opened his pants and gestured to Luce. "There's room for you, my *senechal*."

Luce started. Francesca had been treating her as her second, ever since Michel had betrayed them all, but had not acknowledged her openly until now. "Yes, my Queen."

She knelt between the male's thighs as Francesca reached into his pants, gripped his cock, and pulled him free. He groaned and his dark skin misted with pheromones. Luce's hunger gnawed at her insides, and her incisors throbbed.

"This time, you can take as much as you want," Francesca murmured, stroking him as Luce slid her incisors into him.

Luce hissed as the sweet power rolled through her, his blood so much richer than Veronica's. As the lure of lust and blood swept her up, she reminded herself to take care that her usefulness to the Queen not be tied to Veronica's. The human's value was diminishing quickly.

Max propelled the Rover out of the woods, shot across Nocturne's nearly empty lot, and veered around behind the club. The back door burst open and an armed phalanx of guards in black trooped out and surrounded the vehicle. Max rolled down the window.

"How'd you know we were coming?" he asked.

Katya, also in black with a rifle slung over her shoulder, stood out among the slender, pale guards, her shoulders broader, her features stark and dangerous. She grinned in at him, her canines gleaming in the sunlight. "Jace called. They'll be here in five minutes."

A blond with the distinctive ethereal beauty of a human servant who was no longer quite human approached Katya. "We have a follow-car ready for you, Consort. Blaze will drive. Renee and Ricard will be in the second car."

"Thank you, Alon. See that the guards are doubled on all the doors and the Liege's quarters inside."

"Yes, Consort." He saluted and melted away.

"Fancy," Max grumbled.

Katya grinned again, leaned on the door, and looked inside. "Alpha, Michel extends her greetings and offers our guards to accompany you to Pack land. Our Were blood slaves have heard talk of renegade Blackpaws recruiting mercenaries. Rumors are you're the target."

Sylvan leaned forward. "They've already sent a raiding party across our borders. We appreciate the escort."

"We are at your service, Alpha."

"Are you sure you are secure here?" Sylvan asked. "We do not want to weaken your forces, especially during daylight."

Katya's eyes streamed gold. "Michel and our Vampires are well protected. And we are honored to assist the Pack."

"Your aid is noted and appreciated," Sylvan replied formally, as befitting the respect due the mate of an ally. "We stand ready to support you should the need arise."

"Thank you."

"And, Katya," Sylvan said, a note of command entering her voice, "do not forget you will always be Pack."

Katya bowed her head. "Yes, Alpha."

Katya signaled to her soldiers and they drifted away. Sylvan turned back to Drake. "How is Torren?"

"She hasn't shown any signs of waking." Drake shook her head. "I just don't know what that means. She could be healing. She might be too weak to heal."

"Help is almost here."

Drake's expression was grave. "Good."

Five minutes passed as slowly as an hour, but finally a Rover pulled around the corner and stopped beside them. Sophia jumped out with her med kit and ran toward their vehicle. Drake pushed the doors open and she climbed in.

"I'm glad to see you," Drake said.

Sophia glanced at Torren. "What happened?"

"Multiple deep punctures in the neck," Drake said. "I don't know if there's any systemic poisoning, but she's lost a lot of blood and hasn't been responsive for the last half hour or so."

"Max," Sylvan said, turning to the front, "let's go."

Sophia said, "You are injured, Alpha. Let me—"

"No," Sylvan said. "Just some burns. They can wait. See to Torren."

Sophia hesitated, then nodded. "Yes, Alpha."

As Drake filled her in, Sophia pulled out intravenous lines and catheters and began inserting them into Torren's arms. "There's not a lot I can do here except resuscitate her with fluids and cleanse the wounds."

"That will help," Drake said. "If there are toxins in the wounds, diluting them may give her the ability to heal."

Together they irrigated the punctures and bandaged them. As they worked, the edges of the wounds slowly drew closer.

Misha, who still held Torren's hand, murmured, "I think she's getting stronger."

"Talk to her," Sophia said, sending Misha an encouraging smile. "Your strength will be hers."

Drake said, "When she wakes, she'll require food to shift. Do you know what she needs?"

"I know what to get her," Misha said. "I brought her a tray many times when she first arrived—I'll fix something as soon as we get to the Compound. But she's so weak."

Sophia said gently, "I think the only thing that can heal Torren is Torren...and you."

Katya's escort left them at the border of Pack land, and fifteen minutes later, Max pulled into the Compound and drove up to the infirmary.

"I'll take her," Max said. He lifted Torren out, and he and Misha hurried inside. A moment later Elena appeared on the porch.

"Callan just returned," she said. "I have wounded in the treatment room. We put Torren in an exam room."

"I'll check her," Sophia said, glancing toward headquarters. "How many wounded?"

"Three so far, two seriously."

"Are my parents still here?"

"Yes. In the isolation room with the *mutia*. No change there...or anywhere."

"Thank you."

Sophia disappeared inside and Elena turned to Drake. "Prima, I could use your help. One of the wounded needs surgery."

"Of course." Drake glanced at Sylvan. "You need attention."

"Soon. See to our wolves. I must see to our defenses." Sylvan jumped down, showing no sign of pain or injury. She would not show weakness now when the Pack was under attack and anxious.

"If you're not back in half an hour," Drake said in a low voice, "I will come looking for you."

"I promise." Sylvan frowned as Callan hurried across the Compound to join them. "Where is Niki?"

Callan saluted and said, "She's in a holding cell."

Sylvan's eyes sparked. "What?"

"Voluntarily, Alpha. She—"

"Never mind," Sylvan growled. "I'll find out for myself."

She strode off in the direction of headquarters and Drake followed Elena inside. A female Were was in the first room with a relatively minor bullet wound to the upper extremity. Adam, the *medicus* trainee, was cleaning the wound. "Everything all right here?"

Adam looked over his shoulder and straightened perceptibly. "Yes, Prima. As soon as this is clean, we'll get her to the barracks where she can shift and rest."

"Very good." She continued on down the hall to the treatment area. Elena had two patients side by side on treatment tables. Gray and Acer. Tamara stood by Gray's side, a hand on her shoulder, watching fluid run into Gray's arm. Gray's eyes were closed, her chest rising and falling shallowly. A bullet wound in her right shoulder was crusted with blood. "Is that the only wound?"

"Yes," Elena said as she opened an instrument tray. "The bullet passed through her shoulder and missed the bone. The track needs to be cleaned, but she's stable."

Drake went to Acer's side. "What about him?"

"The bullet's lodged near the femur, and I don't think he can heal this until we get it out."

"All right. How is he otherwise?"

"Weak, but he's young. Once he shifts, he'll heal. So will Gray." Elena straightened, her gaze worried. "How can this be happening? Other wolves attacking us, trying to hurt us?"

Drake stroked her arm softly. "Bernardo's rule was flawed and he lost control of his Pack. They are lost, without a strong leader, without a home. For now."

Elena nodded. "I would feel sorry for them if not for this."

"Yes," Drake said grimly. "So would I…if not for this."

Drake used a claw to enlarge the wound another five inches, separated the damaged muscles, and probed gently until she located the bullet track. Sliding deeper, she grasped the bullet and pulled it out. "Can you take care of the rest of this? I want to see to the Alpha's injuries."

"She's hurt?"

"Not badly, but nothing to be ignored."

"Of course. Take her home, see to her there."

Drake frowned. "You might need me here."

"We need both of you well and strong more." Elena smiled, her gaze clearer and more assured. "Now that you're back, everything will be better."

"We won't be long. If you need us, just call."

"We know."

"Then I'll see what I can do to convince the Alpha to let me tend to her," Drake said.

Elena laughed. "Don't give her any other choice."

CHAPTER TWENTY-FOUR

W hat are you doing in here?" Sylvan jammed her hands on her hips and stared through the bars at Niki. Her second looked half-feral, her eyes hot and her skin shimmering with pelt about to burst free. She crouched on the iron ledge, her clawed fingers gripping the metal. Her wolf was close, and she was slowly losing the battle to keep her at bay. The last thing Sylvan needed was her *imperator* out of control.

"One of the mutants bit me," Niki growled. "I might be dangerous."

Sylvan took a long breath, scented the pheromones rolling off Niki. Familiar scents of aggression and power, and something new. A subtle strength entwined with raw muscle; a tempering of primal force with cool rationality. She smiled. "Finally, you and Sophia have done what has needed to be done."

Niki straightened, satisfaction flickering over her face. "You scent our bond."

"Of course, why wouldn't I? You are two normal, healthy Weres who have joined your essences. Now get out of the cell. I need you."

"But the Revniks haven't completed their tests yet."

"The Revniks will never complete their tests," Sylvan said. "They're scientists, that's what they do. And you are a warrior, and my general. I need you to do what you do."

Niki snarled and leapt halfway across the room. The seams of her dark T-shirt split, her torso broadened.

"*Niki*," Sylvan snapped. "Hold your wolf."

Niki's lips drew back and she growled. Sweat drenched her clothes as her wolf howled and thrashed to be free. Her voice thickened. "I know what my duty is. But you didn't see what that thing became."

"Then tell me. What happened?"

Niki told her of the serum and the test trial that went so wrong.

"She was caught somewhere between human and Were, a monster like one the humans think we all become when we shift. But..." She shuddered and looked away.

"But what?" Sylvan asked softly.

"Somehow, she was one of us. When I killed her, I felt her wolf reach for me. For Pack."

"You know it had to be done, but I'm sorry."

Niki shook her head. "It is my duty, but whoever did this to them must die."

"What about the second female?"

"She has shown no signs of transforming, or of improving," Niki said. "At least not before Sophia needed to leave."

"I'll see that Sophia gets free to find you. Your mate is fine."

Niki relaxed minutely. "And what of the ones who did this? No human court will punish them the way they should be punished."

"If we exact retribution," Sylvan said, "we will be seen as in the wrong. Humans experiment on animals all the time, and that's all we are to them."

"We are nonhuman," Niki said, "and that means less than human. We have no protection."

"Don't you think I know that," Sylvan snarled. "Don't you think that's why my father wanted the Coalition, wanted us to force the humans to abide by laws that protect us from just this kind of thing?"

Niki strode close until only the silver-impregnated bars separated them. She met Sylvan's gaze with the hunter-green eyes of her wolf. "And where has that gotten us? We are more hunted now than we ever were, only now it's done secretly in laboratories and behind closed doors in the legislature, and in secret meetings of radical extremists. And now the Vampires, with whom we've had a truce for centuries, are in league with the humans who would like to destroy us. What has the Exodus gained for us?"

Her words, her stance, her direct gaze were a challenge. Sylvan growled softly.

Niki shivered but held her place. "Gregory has been trying for decades to wipe us out. That mutant in the infirmary is proof he's still trying. They've tried to kill you, they nearly killed Lara, they *did* kill Andrew. Where will it end?"

"Not all the Vampires are our enemies. And we are making strides in counteracting the experimental agents—at least we know what and who to fight." Sylvan was no politician, despite her father's faith in her.

Her law degree was of no use to her now when there were no laws to address the needs of her Pack. She was first and foremost the Alpha of her Pack, the leader of her wolves. She had tried so hard to fulfill her father's wishes, to lead the Weres and all the Praeterns to a more secure future, economically, legally, and socially. That seemed a very far-off dream now. "I know this, Niki. I know that we have as much right to exist as any other species. That we should not have to hide, pretend that we are other than who we are, make excuses for our nature, or justify our society. If that recognition is all we ever gain in the human courts, that will be enough. We can rule ourselves, we've been doing it for millennia. And we will protect ourselves."

"What if the Nicholas Gregorys of the human world gain more power and sway the government into believing we are a danger to the human population? What then?"

"There are humans like Andrea and her brother and the organizations they represent who know that isn't true. Andrea is more than just one human fighting on our side—she's a federal agent, and there are others like her. We do have friends in the government." Sylvan stepped close to the bars. "And if we must fight, we will."

"Wherever you lead, we will follow."

"Then follow me now. There's nothing wrong with you," Sylvan said. "We have wounded in the infirmary and renegades within our borders. I need a patrol organized to run them down. I need you upstairs now."

Niki snarled. "What if—"

Sylvan yanked the cage open, breaking the lock. She strode forward, grasped Niki by the back of the neck, and dragged her out. She pushed her toward the stairs. "I'm tired of arguing. Do as your Alpha commands."

Niki spun around but carefully did not challenge. "If I turn—"

Sylvan grabbed her shoulders, yanked her up onto her toes, and glared into her eyes. "If you turn, I will kill you myself."

"Thank you," Niki whispered.

"Now, are you ready to do your duty?"

"Yes, Alpha," Niki said, relaxing in her grip. "More than ready."

"Good." Sylvan let her go, slung an arm around her shoulder, and pulled her close as they walked out into the late-day sun together.

Upstairs, Max and Andrea stood with shoulders touching by the great fireplace in the gathering hall. Callan worried a line in the floor striding back and forth in front of the tall windows, grumbling steadily.

Jace and Jonathan, guarding the doors, rumbled happily as Sylvan strode in with Niki. Everyone straightened as her power flooded the room.

Callan halted abruptly and his grumbling ceased. "It's good to have you back, Alpha."

"It's good to be here," Sylvan said. "Tell me what's happening."

Callan gave her a summary of the last twenty-four hours, finishing, "There's been no more activity along the perimeter since the last attack at dawn."

"What about pursuit?"

Callan shook his head. "We did not want to weaken the lines or reduce our forces here, in case this attack was a decoy action and a larger force is gathering to attack the Compound."

Sylvan nodded. "That's possible, but it seems too soon for them to have organized an army."

Max said, "Not if they have help."

"Explain."

"Katya heard rumors that rogue Weres and some of the Blackpaws who had refused to pledge allegiance to us are gathering. If they attract mercenaries too, they could marshal a sizable number."

"Even if that's true, they'll still need to be armed and organized." Sylvan curled a lip. "Renegades are undisciplined, unruly, and resist strong leaders. Attacking us would require an experienced leader...or a very crazy one."

"If we pursue them now," Max said, "they won't have time to consolidate significant resistance."

"Unless," Andrea said quietly, "they already have and are lying in wait."

Sylvan regarded her intently. "Do you have intelligence that makes you think that's likely?"

Andrea stepped forward and Max automatically laid a hand on her back, keeping contact. "Only that we've heard the same rumors as Katya. Someone is recruiting mercenary Weres—wolves *and* cats." She paused. "We believe the Vampires are involved."

Niki snarled.

"How do you know that?" Sylvan knew the government had agents undercover in radical groups like HUFSI. Why wouldn't they also have agents who gathered intelligence on Vampires and Weres? Perhaps all the agents weren't human. If a wolf Were entered her territory and petitioned to join the Pack, she admitted them. Would a Were actually spy for the human government? She couldn't believe it of a wolf, but she had to consider it. "Do you have agents involved with Vampires? Hosts perhaps? From the beginning?"

Andrea stared straight ahead, her gaze fixed on Sylvan's shoulder. "I can't answer that."

Sylvan nodded. "That's answer enough. Do you know where Francesca is hiding?"

"No, and if we find her, you will be informed."

"So we can deal with her?"

"The government is not interested in involving itself in internal Were affairs."

"I see." Sylvan grinned, showing her canines. The humans would be happy for her to risk her wolves, but at least she would not have to worry about *legal* repercussions if she eliminated Francesca and what remained of her seethe. "I'm very glad to hear that." She glanced at Niki. "*Imperator*? Your opinion?"

Niki shot out, "I agree with Max. We need to run these renegades down now, find out what we can, and send a message. Our borders are inviolate, and anyone who trespasses will pay the price."

"You heard the *imperator*," Sylvan said.

Everyone moved for the door.

"I'll ready a squadron," Callan said.

"No," Sylvan said. "You were right not to weaken our defenses here or on the perimeter. We will take a small team that can move quickly. You see to security here and coordinate the patrols on the border. I'll take Niki and the rest of the *centuri* and pursue the Blackpaws."

"What about me?" Drake said from the doorway.

Sylvan had felt her coming, their always-present connection growing stronger the closer Drake approached. "We need you here, Prima."

"You'll need a medic," Drake said. "The infirmary is full, and Sophia and Elena are needed here."

"We can manage," Sylvan said. "I don't plan on having wounded."

Drake slipped behind her and wrapped both arms around her waist. She pressed her mouth to Sylvan's ear. "You're not going anywhere until I've seen to your injuries."

Sylvan rumbled disagreeably.

"You know I'm right. I'll stay behind if you give me two hours."

"One," Sylvan said.

"Agreed."

Sylvan turned, gripped Drake's hips, and kissed her. "That's what you wanted all along, wasn't it?"

Drake grinned. "I can do a lot in an hour." She looked past Sylvan's shoulder to the others. "Bring back captives. We need information."

Niki's lip curled. "They should be shown no mercy."

"If you want to make an example of them, then let's find out who needs to learn the lesson. If they're dead, they can't tell us."

Sylvan looped an arm around Drake's waist and started for the door. "One hour. Be ready to hunt."

❖

Drake had a Rover waiting in front of headquarters. "I'll drive. Your hands are burned."

Sylvan silently complied.

"How did that happen?" Drake pulled out of the Compound in the direction of their den.

"Niki was being stubborn. I ripped the door off her cell."

"Expedient."

Sylvan laughed.

"I spoke to the Revniks. Niki's blood is clear. The contagion is fractured, degraded in some way. Eventually it will break down completely and disappear from her system."

"What does that mean? Do we have a cure for what infected those humans?"

"Possibly. The working theory is that the mate bite from Sophia transferred some form of immunity to Niki." Drake clasped Sylvan's leg and kept it there while she drove. "What Sophia and I have in our serum could be the makings of a vaccine."

Sylvan grumbled. "More experiments."

Drake smiled. "Yes. And, Sylvan, we need to test our young again. There's a good chance they're naturally immune to the contagion."

"Will it hurt them?"

"No more than when you bite them to remind them you're their Alpha."

"That's different."

"They'll be fine. I'll see to that."

"All right. Whatever the Revniks need." Sylvan sighed.

"Resistance to Were fever or at least protection against the manufactured variety will protect every wolf Were in the world. At least we will have defeated one of our enemies."

"You're tired and you're hurt." Sylvan started to protest and Drake cut her off. "No one knows that but me. Let me fight this battle—it's what I know how to do best. We will win this and all our battles."

Sylvan closed her eyes and gripped Drake's hand. "You make me hope."

"Believe me."

"Always."

Ten minutes later Drake pulled up in front of their cabin. Jace and Jonathan had followed at a distance and parked in the woods a hundred yards away. She'd long given up trying to prevent the *centuri* from standing guard wherever Sylvan was. Now that their borders had been breached, she wouldn't complain. Sylvan had always been a target, and probably always would be. She was grateful for the loyalty of the *centuri* and all those who guarded Sylvan's well-being. When their young began to run with the Pack, the Pack members would extend the same loyalty and protection to them. She was in debt to those who kept her family safe, now more than ever.

"In the shower," Drake said, leaping onto the porch. Sylvan followed and they stripped off their clothes together and stepped under the warm water.

"Face the wall."

Miraculously, Sylvan complied without argument. Drake lathered her back and carefully washed the burns, removing debris and dead flesh until raw bleeding tissue was all that remained. Sylvan made no move or sound while she worked. In some areas the muscle was exposed. Sylvan had to have been in pain, but she would have ignored it and probably gone out to hunt without even bothering to take time to heal. Drake kissed the back of her neck. "I'll fix you something to eat and then you should shift. This will heal once you do."

Sylvan turned, gripped Drake's hips, and spun her around until her back was to the wall and Sylvan's was under the warm water. She grazed Drake's neck with her canines and settled her hips between Drake's thighs. "I'll eat and I'll shift when I've had you."

Drake would have argued if she didn't need Sylvan so much. They'd been separated for what had felt like days in Earth time, had fought their way free of Faerie, and now faced enemies on every front. She needed Sylvan's touch, needed her body, more than she needed her heart to beat. Sylvan was her strength, her heart, her soul. She opened to her, readied for her. "You should be too weak for this."

Sylvan laughed and pressed her mouth to the mate bite on Drake's shoulder. "You underestimate me, Prima."

Drake gasped as need lanced through her. "Never."

She gripped Sylvan's ass, let her claws puncture skin, and wrapped her legs around Sylvan's hips. Her clitoris, full and hard, pressed into Sylvan's lower abdomen and she felt Sylvan slide into her cleft. She groaned. "Always so good."

Sylvan pinned Drake to the cool tile walls with the weight of her body and arched her back, driving into her. She grazed her canines over and into the mate bite, and Drake cried out. They clung together, rode each other hard, and spent at the same time, emptying with the force of long-awaited pleasure.

Sylvan leaned against her, panting. "The next time you decide to go through a Faerie Gate, make sure you know how to get back."

Drake laughed softly and kissed her. "I don't think I'll be returning to Faerie anytime soon."

"I am nothing without you." Sylvan leaned her forehead on Drake's shoulder and shivered.

Drake slid her hands into Sylvan's hair, raised her head, and kissed her again. "You are everything to all of us. And you are mine. I will not leave you."

"I need your counsel, and your strength. I cannot lead the Pack alone."

"You could, if you needed to, but you won't. And do not doubt your decisions. You know what must be done, and we know it too."

"Death is coming—for our enemies, perhaps for our friends. I don't want my wolves to die."

"We'll do everything we can to protect our Pack and our allies. As to our enemies..." Drake snarled softly. "We have been more than generous until now. It is time for us to strike back."

CHAPTER TWENTY-FIVE

Torren's eyes flickered open. The room was dim and warm, the air silent and empty. She reached out for the magic, found it in the distance where it had lain long buried under millennia of disbelief, dissension, and corruption. The tendrils whispered past her senses, wary and distrustful. A kiss so fleeting it could have been a wish. Heaviness settled in her chest. Earthside was a tomb for the Fae, a half-life where remembrance of beauty was an ever-present pain. She turned her head and met Misha's gaze. "How are you?"

Misha's eyes filled for an instant and she blinked hard. "Not bad." She brushed the hair from Torren's forehead. "How are you?"

"Hungry."

"Your neck…is there pain?"

Torren smiled. "No."

"I have some food here." Misha gestured to a tray laden with things she wouldn't consider food enough to sustain a shift in a wounded Were, but that she knew Torren liked. A loaf of grain bread, roasted turnips and potatoes and other things they grew in the gardens carved out of the forest at the edge of the Compound. Fruits from the cold storage cellars. Cheese from their larder. "And warm cider. I could bring juice but I thought—"

Torren grasped her hand. "This is exactly what I need." She pushed up to a sitting position and leaned her back against the rough wall of the barracks. "Thank you."

"I could get you meat?"

"I'll leave that for the wolves." She ate vigorously and silently for a few moments, watching Misha watch her. Misha watched her like she might watch prey—with utter stillness, barely breathing, only her dark eyes moving, following each sweep of her arm, each swallow. Dark intense eyes, wounded eyes. "I'm all right."

"I thought you were going to die."

Torren set the tray aside and held out her hand. Misha took it and Torren pulled her onto the bed and tucked her against her side. She kissed her forehead and then her mouth. "I knew you were there the entire time. I felt you reaching for me, holding me, keeping me from drifting away. I took your strength, depended on it."

Misha wrapped her arms tightly around Torren's waist, buried her face against her chest. "You were so far away. If I lost you, everything inside me would end. I would live, but I would be empty."

Torren stroked her hair. No one had ever said such words to her before. There were no endings in Faerie, only a transition when the spirit yielded to the magic and left the physical plane. When the heart is never given, it cannot be lost. "The Fae are not easy to kill."

"The Fae do not fight with honor." Misha leaned back, her eyes glowing with fury. "Your Queen tried to kill our Alpha when she came unarmed and in peace."

"Not everyone in the universe has the same beliefs. Honor to us is a strange concept. We follow the magic and the power."

"But you love me."

"I do."

"There is honor in love."

Torren sighed. "I should not have brought you through the Gate. I put you and the others at risk. But when you called me, I could not resist."

Misha bristled. "Did you think to leave me behind forever?"

"You have seen Faerie. That is not a world for a wolf."

"We will find a way. I will not let you forget me."

Torren sighed and kissed her. "The world to you is like the world your wolf sees, black and white and clear. Simple and orderly. Honor and loyalty guide your actions. But we are different."

"What guides you, then?"

"Survival."

"We fight to survive too." Misha stroked Torren's chest. "And there we are the same. Only our weapons are different."

"You are very stubborn." Torren rubbed her cheek on Misha's hair. Her scent carried the magic of forest and stream, earth and sky. She closed her eyes and the darkness receded.

"What will happen now?" Misha asked softly. "Will you stay here?"

"I'm afraid I will not be welcome in Faerie as long as Cecilia rules, which may be a very long time."

"What will happen to you? If you can't...go home?"

"My powers will not be full Earthside," Torren said, her eyes darkening. "I can call my Hound, I can call the hawk, I can reach my magic through your earth. But I will not be as I am in Faerie."

"I'm sorry. If you must go back, I will go with you. We will find Cecilia together and kill her."

"You would risk that for me?"

Misha's brows drew down. "Of course. You are my mate. Where you go, I go. What you need, I need."

Torren sighed. "In all the long cycles of my life, I have never been touched as you touch me. I don't understand it, but I do not question it."

"You will never need to." Misha touched the bandages on Torren's neck. "I know you're weak. I know you hurt. You need to shift again, to heal all the way."

"I will sleep awhile and then shift." Torren hesitated, unused to the need for another's touch. "Will you sleep with me?"

"Of course. Always."

Misha sat up and stripped off her clothes until she was naked like Torren. She lay down and pressed her flesh to Torren's, tucked her head beneath Torren's chin where she could feel the breath and blood and heat of her body. She let her wolf rise until their spirits touched. "My life is your life. My future your future. We will go back when it's time, together."

Torren pressed her palm over Misha's heart. Misha's wolf rumbled a greeting to her Hound. Her hawk took flight with a wild cry. Here was the magic. "Then I will make this my home."

"Do not call my wolf just yet," Misha whispered, entwining her legs with Torren's. Her wolf's steady rumble grew stronger and want arched through her. "You are not strong enough yet, and after a battle my wolf wants her mate."

Torren laughed. "Misha, my wolf, I am a royal Fae. At my weakest, I am strong enough for my mate."

Misha leaned up on an elbow. Her pelt line flared down her abdomen at the invitation in Torren's gaze. "Your arrogance has not been tempered by your wounds." She kissed her slowly. "I prefer to have you at full strength. Then perhaps you can handle me."

Torren slipped her fingers into Misha's hair and lifted her head to kiss her. "I love you, Misha of the Timberwolf Pack. There is a ritual you wolves perform to seal your mating. I can't give you that."

Misha nipped at Torren's lower lip. "We call it a mate bite, and mate bonding. It's a mark that shows we belong to each other." She slid her leg over Torren's hip and pressed against her, her essence warm and slick against Torren's skin. "We share our essences, our bodies merge, and we join."

"With me, you will always be incomplete."

"Oh no." Misha drew back, scowled. "You are not a Were?"

Torren frowned. "I thought you'd noticed that."

Misha laughed and kissed her. "Then do not think to act like one. I do not want a Were. I want you, Torren de Brinna of the Fae."

"And what of your wolf? Will she not be disappointed?"

Misha grew serious. "Never. When you and I tangled the first time, we joined more than our essences, more than our flesh. I felt the wings of your hawk beneath my heart, felt the Hound run with my wolf, mind to mind. We are already mated, bonded, spirit to spirit." She drew Torren's hand between her thighs and pressed her fingers to the tense glands on either side of her full clitoris. She gasped at the arrow of need and desire. "You call my body and my heart and my spirit. I am yours."

Torren kissed her and gently massaged the hot, full flesh beneath her fingers. "Let me have this now. And when I wake, I will want more."

Misha trembled, the fear that had held her captive for hours transforming to joy. "There will always be more."

Torren pressed Misha's mouth to her breast. "Then let your wolf take what is hers."

"Yes, now and forever."

Misha's canines erupted and when she slid them into Torren's chest, the magic flowed.

❖

Drake woke beside a great silver wolf, her face buried in its ruff. She sighed and stroked Sylvan's back. An ear flickered, and she felt her stir. *It's time.*

The wolf pressed close, and with barely a shudder, Sylvan shed pelt. Drake ran her hands over the flawless skin and the long, hard muscles beneath. For an instant, all that mattered in her world was beside her, and she knew peace. She rested her head on Sylvan's chest, listening to the beat of her heart. "How do you feel?"

Sylvan stretched, gave a supremely satisfied growl. She caressed Drake's ass. "Strong. Ready."

Drake laughed. "Then all is well."

"We have a few minutes. I want to stop and see the young before I leave."

"About this strike…" Drake caressed Sylvan's stomach, tracing the ridges between her abdominals with her fingertips. Power flooded from her, stirring Drake's wolf. The *centuri* would ready to the call. Every warrior in the Pack would go on alert. There was no turning back.

Sylvan kissed her. "What?"

"Andrea's right. This could all be a ploy to draw you out. Ambush you."

"I know."

"Then why are you going?" Drake knew better than to try to dissuade her from protecting the Pack. Sylvan was ruled by her wolf more than any other Were, her primal nature most untamed, her instincts the purest. And the wildest. But Drake was Sylvan's mate and Prima to the Pack. She was bound by blood and love to protect Sylvan. Even from herself.

"Because the Blackpaws invaded Pack land, attacked my wolves, injured some. Because this is my territory."

"Is it really that simple?"

Sylvan sat up and shifted Drake into her lap. She looked down at her, at her deep dark questioning eyes. "It is not simple at all. To outsiders, our laws seem rigid and harsh. But they do not know who we are, how we live, what fury and power drives our wolves. We are predators at the core."

"More than just that," Drake whispered. "Love and loyalty drive you too."

"Yes, we are more than wolves, and that's why a Pack needs a strong Alpha. Our wolves live to hunt and bear young and run free. But we are not wolves, we are Were, and some of us hunger for things our wolves do not understand—power and influence that do not come to us naturally. The Alpha is a peacekeeper—"

Drake laughed and raked her blunt claws down Sylvan's hip. "That is not a word I would use to describe you."

Sylvan grinned and growled softly. "Sometimes peace requires us to fight for it. My wolf protects what makes us wolves and defends against what would prevent us from living in harmony."

"What will you do when you find the renegades?"

"If they do not resist, we will bring them back and find out who they are and why they attempted such a foolish attack."

"And if they resist?"

"I would much rather bring them all into the Pack, but if they will not live with us, as we must live, and accept my rule, then they must leave our territories or die."

"You know they won't leave. They've already made the choice to live as rogues."

"I know." Sylvan sighed.

Drake pressed her mouth to Sylvan's abdomen. Sylvan would suffer if she was forced to execute Weres. Every Were in the Pack would feel the loss. "If Andrea's right and you run into a larger force, will you retreat?"

"My *centuri* are the finest fighters in the world. One is worth a dozen. We will fight as wolves. We will be fine."

"I want you to remember something while you're out there."

Sylvan snarled, pelt shimmering close to the skin as her wolf surged. "Do you think I need a reminder that you and my young and the Pack need me?"

Drake bit Sylvan's stomach, leaving a mark where her canines punctured. Sylvan tensed and rumbled, the pain an invitation more than a protest. Drake smiled against her skin. "Are you listening?"

"Do I have a choice?" Sylvan sighed. "What do you need from me, mate?"

"I do not need to remind you of what you were born knowing," Drake said. "What I need you to remember is that you are the power that maintains order throughout the Packs, not just ours, but all of them. If you must maintain order by force to keep all of us safe, then do not hesitate. Kill if you must."

"I will do my duty."

"Yes," Drake whispered. "And then come back to me."

CHAPTER TWENTY-SIX

Tamara looked over her shoulder, growling softly, as the door behind her opened. Sophia stepped into the light, the brightness behind her casting her face in shadow.

"You should get something to eat," Sophia said.

Tamara stroked Gray's arm. She hadn't left her bedside all morning, ever since the Prima had said Gray would be all right after a shift, and they'd moved Gray to a room in the barracks until she woke. She wanted to believe the Prima, wanted to believe this Pack was different, but those in power had lied to her before. Gray still slept—at least, she hoped it was sleep and that she was healing inside. "Not yet. She might wake up. She'll need help getting food then."

"Not might wake." Sophia came in and gently closed the door behind her. "She *will* wake up. She's strong."

"I know. I know about before…about how much she's already survived."

"She told you about being a captive," Sophia said, more a statement than a question. "I'm so glad."

Tamara swiveled so she could track Sophia's movements, knowing Sophia was there to help Gray but still feeling protective and strangely defensive. Gray was hers to protect. She'd been taking care of her since she'd been hurt. She would see that no one harmed her ever again. "Why? Why do you care?"

Sophia smiled. "I care about everyone in the Pack. Including you."

"You would." Tamara couldn't keep the envy from her voice. She was like Sophia, but not—not as strong, not as sure. Not as worthy. Everyone said she was Pack now, but how could she be when she had no place? She was a warrior, but not dominant like the others. She could fight for her place, would fight if she must, just as she always had, but she would always know she was less.

"I care not just because of what I am," Sophia said. "But because I am a Timberwolf, and all the Timberwolves are my family."

"I know it's supposed to be that way."

"In time, you'll believe it."

"Is it hard," Tamara said finally, "living in…some in-between place?"

"Is that what you think we do?"

"Isn't it?"

"Do you know what they call the Omega of a wolf Pack?"

Tamara grimaced. "Only that the Omega is the lowest rank in the Pack." Bernardo had never let her forget it, even after she'd won too many challenges for him not to allow her a place with the warriors.

"Some refer to the Omega as the joker, or the trickster. The Omega defuses aggression in a wild wolf Pack, particularly when higher-ranking dominants are frustrated or irritable."

"I don't know how to be Omega. I've tried all my life not to be."

"You don't have to try, you just are."

"What does that mean? The Blackpaws called me weak, humiliated me, beat me until I showed them they were wrong. I proved I was stronger than most of them. I won my place as a warrior. I'm not like you, I'm not a peacekeeper or a healer."

"Just because you're Omega does not mean you can't be a warrior. But you have something the other warriors don't."

Tamara regarded her warily. Hope was a foreign sensation, as was kindness. "What?"

"The ability to temper your fire with reason, to think before you strike, to search for compromise before combat."

"Doesn't that just make me weak?"

Sophia laughed. "Just the opposite. It's easy to strike out, and much harder to wait. Much harder to reason. Our warriors need calm as much as they need the courage to fight. You bring them both."

"Will they believe that?"

"Of course. You have proven your strength and your courage. You and Clint risked your lives for our wounded."

Tamara regarded Gray. "She's a Were. I couldn't let her die."

"Just a Were?" Sophia asked softly.

Tamara stared at her. "I don't know what you mean."

Smiling, Sophia came closer slowly, making no sudden move toward Gray. "Do you mind if I touch her?"

Sophia was mated, but she was still beautiful and powerful. For an instant, Tamara wanted to snarl at the image of Sophia touching Gray, even to heal her. The feeling was foreign and yet completely natural. "I...all right."

Sophia felt Gray's throat, put her hand on her chest, touched the back of her hand to her abdomen. "Her heartbeat is stronger. See how her skin is lightly dusted with pelt? That's her wolf growing stronger. She's healing. Give her time."

"Will she shift before she wakes?"

"She might, but I think she'll need a little more strength to do that." Sophia hesitated. "And the courage to trust her wolf."

Tamara bristled. "She doesn't lack the courage. She is the bravest Were I've ever known."

"You're right. She is very strong and very brave." Sophia reached to stroke Gray's hair and Tamara warned her off with a sharp growl. Nodding, Sophia drew her hand back. "She told you about being held prisoner, but she might not have told you when the Alpha freed her, her wolf was out of control. The Alpha almost had to put her down."

"She didn't say, but I'm not surprised. Her wolf is very strong, fierce." Tamara sounded proud. She *was* proud. "She has no reason to be ashamed."

"Exactly. Let her know how much you value that. How much you trust her. She needs to shift as soon as she's strong enough to heal completely. Don't let her hold back."

"What makes you think I can convince her?"

"Because you're Omega, and because she's yours."

Tamara caught her breath. "Is that what you think?"

"Isn't that what you feel?"

Something hard and tight relaxed inside Tamara's chest, and a flood of joy raced through her. She lifted her chin, smiled. "Yes, that's what I feel."

"Good."

"I'm not ashamed of what I am."

"No." Sophia stroked Tamara's hair, and the solace was so unexpected Tamara leaned against her. Sophia's power filled her with peace the way the Alpha's power infused the Pack with strength. Bernardo had feared the strength of others, and he'd never wanted her to know there was more than one form of power, and more than one way to serve the Pack.

After a moment, Tamara said softly, "I wish I could give what you do…the comfort and the strength, with just a touch."

"I think you probably can. Give yourself time for that too." Sophia held her close for another moment before stepping back. "Now, my young warrior, will you get something to eat?"

"Soon." Tamara looked up and smiled. For the first time, she knew who she was and what her place might be. She saw a future that had meaning and worth. She glanced at Gray and saw something else. A time when she wasn't alone. "Thank you."

"You don't need to thank me. We're Pack."

"Yes. We are."

As the door closed behind Sophia, Gray said quietly, "She's right, you know."

Tamara drew in a breath and glanced down. Gray was watching her. She was pale and hollow eyed, but awake. Tamara's heart soared, but she rumbled unhappily. "How long have you been listening?"

Gray smiled weakly. "A while."

"Maybe I didn't want you to hear that."

"You think I didn't know already? That you are Omega? That you are strong and brave." Gray tried to sit up, and failing, scowled. "Which part didn't you want me to know?"

"The part where I doubted. Stay still." Tamara drew the light sheet over Gray and cupped her cheek. "Are you hungry?"

"Starving." Gray caught Tamara's hand and held her in place. "Sophia said I was yours."

"You must have misunderstood."

"I didn't. Was she right?"

Tamara wanted to deny it all. Fear closed her throat. She'd kept hidden, kept away from everyone for so long, she trusted nothing. Gray was still watching her. "Would you care?"

"Yes. I would care." Gray's voice was strong and steady. "I would like it. Being yours."

"What makes you think I want a stubborn, arrogant, dominant Were like you?" Tamara tried to sound indifferent, but she couldn't stop herself from caressing Gray's cheek.

Gray grinned. "Because you carried me down the mountainside. Because you wouldn't leave me. Because I want you to want me."

"Those are pretty good reasons," Tamara said softly. She leaned over and kissed Gray. "You need to get well. We can talk about all of this later."

Gray moved over on the cot. "We don't need to talk about it. Just be with me for a few minutes."

Tamara shed her clothes, slipped under the sheet, and wrapped her arms and legs around Gray. "How is your shoulder?"

"It hurts worse than when Callan kicked my ass in *sentrie* training." Gray nuzzled Tamara's throat. "And I couldn't do much more than crawl after that."

"Ouch." Tamara kissed the uninjured tip of Gray's shoulder. "It'll be better once you've shifted."

Gray grew still.

"I haven't seen your wolf yet," Tamara said. "Let me feed you so I can see her."

"Will you stay with my wolf?"

"Of course."

"She's…wary." Gray swallowed, her throat tight. "And angry still. So angry."

"At who?"

"Everyone," Gray said quietly. "At me for being stupid enough to get captured. At Katya for living through the same thing and not being so fucked up by it." She hesitated. "At the Alpha for not finding me sooner."

"I guess the only one you can really punish is you, huh."

Gray laughed bitterly. "Yeah. Maybe."

Tamara tightened her hold, kept her voice light. "I'll shift with you. My wolf is Omega. She knows how to distract, to play, to quiet. You'll be all right."

"What if I'm not?"

"I can do more than play." Tamara kissed Gray again. "I'll just have to submit you until you behave."

Gray's eyes gleamed. "That's never going to happen."

Tamara nipped her chin. "Not unless you want it to."

Gray sighed and pressed her face to Tamara's chest. "I might, sometimes."

"Good."

❖

Sophia found Niki in the armory strapping on a sidearm. She wore forest-green fatigues and black lace-up boots. An automatic rifle stood beside her and extra magazines hung on a leather bandolier angled across her chest. She looked dangerous and distant. Sophia's stomach churned with want and worry. "My parents say you don't have any signs of disease."

Niki stilled, her expression blank but her gaze darkening. "They're sure?"

Sophia closed the door to shut them in. The room was long and narrow, lined with plain wooden shelves piled high with ammunition, cases of weapons, stacks of fatigues, and other supplies. One small horizontal window just under the roofline emitted a shaft of dim light. That little bit of illumination was enough to see Niki's eyes glowed gold around the edges, her wolf ready for the hunt.

"You can't wait to go, can you?" Sophia said.

Niki bared her teeth. "This is what I do. This is how I serve the Pack. This is who I am."

Sophia sighed and gripped her shoulders. "I know. I know who you are. And I love you." She kissed her. "Just remember the Alpha needs you in one piece. So do I."

Niki grinned. "I have just gotten out of a cell after almost twenty-four hours away from you. I have plans for when I return. I don't intend to be injured."

Sophia laughed despite her fears. "I see. I'm surprised you plan on waiting until you get back."

Niki growled and suddenly pushed her against a cabinet door. She bit her lightly on the neck while stroking her breasts and belly with a sure, arrogant touch. "I could be quick."

"You could." Sophia threw her head back, whimpering softly. Niki always knew what she needed. She grabbed Niki's forearm before Niki sliced open her pants and took her. "But I don't want you to be quick. I would rather wait until I can have you for as long as I want."

Niki rubbed her cheek against Sophia's. "I love you. You are everything to me."

"And you are my hero. So be careful."

"I'm really all right?" Niki whispered as if asking would somehow change the answer.

Sophia stroked her rigid back. "Yes. My parents think our mate bond is part of it. That when our essences blended, you developed some kind of immunity from me."

Niki buried her face in Sophia's neck, breathing in her scent. Coating herself with Sophia's pheromones. "You see, you save me in more ways than one."

"I hope so." Sophia fell silent and Niki leaned back, studying her intently. "What is it? Something makes you unhappy."

Sophia smiled gently. "Nothing that can't keep."

Niki scowled. "There is never a better time than now. What is it?"

Sophia smoothed her palms over Niki's chest, reveling in her strength. "I still can't give you young. I don't even know if I'm capable, but even if I were, I can't risk—"

Niki kissed her hard and kept kissing her until Sophia softened in her arms and whimpered again. She pulled back. "I don't need young. I need you. I never planned on a mate, so I have more than I ever expected. More than I ever dreamed."

"But you are so special," Sophia said. "You should have—"

Niki snarled. "I have what I want." Her expression softened and she kissed Sophia gently. "You will just have to believe me. And I'll keep saying it until you do."

"I do believe you."

"I must go," Niki whispered.

"I know." Sophia stepped back and handed Niki the rifle. "Fight well, *Imperator*. I'll be here when you come back. I'll always be here for you."

CHAPTER TWENTY-SEVEN

Sylvan and the *centuri* piled into a single Rover. Sylvan sat in front with Dasha driving; Niki, Jace, Jonathan, and Max took the rear. Everyone carried assault rifles and sidearms.

"Take us to the last sighting of the renegades inside our perimeter and we'll pick up the trail from there," Sylvan said as Dasha took them into the forest. "Niki, you'll go ahead in pelt from that point, and we'll follow as far as we can in the vehicle. Once you have a visual, turn back and alert us."

Niki leaned forward between the seats. Her scent was ripe with battle pheromones and excitement. "What if I come upon a straggler?"

She sounded hopeful. Sylvan shook her head. "Do not engage. We want the main raiding party, and I don't want to risk you being overpowered."

Niki snarled in disbelief.

Sylvan rumbled and Niki quieted. "Circle around any lone raiders if you can, if not, return and advise us of their direction. We may be able to flank them with the Rover."

"And when we engage, do you plan to fight on foot or in pelt?"

"I plan to fight to win, whatever form that takes."

"As you command, Alpha." Niki sat down, closed her eyes, and prepared for the hunt.

Nightfall had come by the time they reached their lines. Callan had radioed the closest patrol, and Mira waited for them. She saluted Sylvan as Sylvan got out of the Rover.

"How are Acer and Gray?" Mira asked instantly.

"Healing. How are your recruits?"

"We're all fine, Alpha."

"Do you need resupply?"

"We have what we need."

"And your recruits? Do they need relief?"

Mira shook her head vehemently, her eyes glowing in the twilight. "No, Alpha, we will stay at our posts as long as we are needed here."

Sylvan nodded. "Good. What do we know about the route the renegades took on retreat?"

"Jazz's patrol tracked them a short distance, but we did not want to weaken the line, so he pulled back."

Mira gave Sylvan the GPS coordinates and Sylvan passed them to Dasha. "Very good. Callan will coordinate. Let him know if there's any sign of activity."

"Yes, Alpha." Mira saluted again and faded into the night.

Sylvan climbed back into the Rover and they continued on along the riverbank in the direction the renegades had taken. Her wolf prowled close to her skin, looking forward to the battle. Her time in Faerie had left her feeling the need to regain control, not just of the new wolf Weres who had been annexed to her Pack, but of the direction she had taken since the Exodus.

When she'd taken the mantle of leadership from her father, she'd assumed his position that negotiation and compromise would reap the greatest gains for the Pack, but experience had shown her otherwise. The humans were distrustful and actively seeking to control the Praeterns, her allies were more enemies than friends, and the unity of the Were population was threatened by rogues and renegades. She still believed that her father's vision of a world in which the Praeterns lived openly had been the ideal to aspire to, but ideals were not reality, and the reality was that the Praeterns were vastly outnumbered and without the resources in arms, influence, or power that humans wielded. The one thing she could do to protect her Pack was to consolidate the Weres into a unified society that she could keep safe. Fighting other Weres was one of the hardest things she had to do. The thought of killing another wolf left her heart heavy and her spirit saddened. Her nature was to rule by force and strength, but she had learned from her mother that ruling was more than just power, it was also fairness and compassion. Her mother had demonstrated that compassion when she'd taken the Revniks into the Pack, even though Sophia was infected with Were fever, potentially contagious, and possibly a risk to those around her. Sylvan hoped every day she could be as wise an Alpha as her mother had been. But there was a time to fight, and that time was now.

Dasha slowed as they bumped along the narrow, rocky riverbank and pointed to the nav con. "If we are going to continue in the Rover, I need to veer off the most likely route the renegades would've taken. The forest is too thick ahead to follow directly."

"Niki," Sylvan said, "it's time for you to run."

Niki rumbled happily. Dasha pulled over, Niki jumped out, and by the time they set off again, a red-gray wolf streaked into the underbrush and disappeared.

The forest at night was one of Niki's favorite places to run. Under cover of the night, the shadows came alive—lit by the moonlight reflecting off the eyes of prey, drops of water caught on the undersurface of leaves, specks of fool's gold in the rocky escarpments. Every smell was bolder, brighter, teasing across her taste buds and calling her wolf like the pull of the moon. Except for those quintessential moments when she and Sophia joined, she was never more herself than when hunting. When she stalked prey, all her senses engaged, her muscles and blood and mind attuned, she was complete. Tonight, she hunted the ultimate prey, another predator as strong as her. She took no joy in killing another wolf, but she took joy in doing what she was born to do. Protecting her Pack, serving her Alpha with her body and her skill and her heart. She caught their scent—a mix of adrenaline, fighting pheromones, and lingering fear. They weren't that far ahead, moving quickly but not retreating at full speed, confident they weren't being pursued. She sorted the scents, a dozen, not many more, a small raiding party. Her nose quivered—not just wolves. Cat Weres. Her upper lip pulled back in distaste. More than one.

She padded along at a brisk run, her wolf tracking effortlessly while part of her mind considered the raiders and their intent in attacking inside Pack land. They had come to leave a message, a message she still didn't quite understand. Was their purpose simply to draw Sylvan out as Andrea had suggested? They were foolish if they thought the Alpha could be taken so easily, especially surrounded by her *centuri*. But then, they were renegades and foolish by definition. In the end, the intentions didn't matter. They had wounded several *sentries*, might have killed them, and violated Pack law. Her path was clear and she welcomed the chance to act.

Niki lifted her snout, tested the air, caught a sharper, stronger scent just ahead. They'd left a rear guard to alert them of anyone approaching from behind. Niki grinned to herself. She was downwind, and her position would not be discovered. She flanked right and circled around the single wolf in the rear. She would've liked to have taken her down, but the Alpha had said to exercise caution. Caution was not in her nature, but following orders was. The Alpha had said she could not engage, and despite the clawing in her belly to challenge the intruder, she raced on, one shadow among many. Before long, the trail freshened and she knew she was close. They were headed not for Blackpaw territory, but south, toward the city. They must have a camp somewhere outside the forest. She snorted, unsurprised. Renegades rarely kept a forest camp but congregated in abandoned factory buildings or flophouses. She did not pity them. They didn't deserve to sleep beneath the moon.

Certain now of their course, she quickly turned back and raced toward the riverbed and the Rover. She shed pelt when she stepped into the headlights and Dasha pulled to a stop a few feet away. Niki climbed into the rear and Jace tossed her clothes.

"They're headed for the city," she said as she pulled on a T-shirt.

"Then we need to cut them off before they leave the forest," Sylvan said. "A chase on the open highway will attract police attention."

Dasha already had a map up on the Rover's nav con and pointed to a section of highway that skirted the densely forested Pack land. She tapped the screen. "Here is where they've most likely left their vehicles. I can get there before them if I take this fire trail." She traced another line.

"Do it," Sylvan said.

Niki settled back to wait, content that she had done her duty. She closed her eyes, conserving her energy while her wolf remained on the alert.

Forty-five minutes later, Dasha pulled the Rover into a secluded turnoff a quarter-mile from the highway. "There." She pointed.

"Yes," Sylvan said with satisfaction.

Two dark SUVs were parked in the underbrush at one edge of the small clearing, nose out for a quick getaway. The vehicles could easily have carried half a dozen raiders each.

"Jonathan," Sylvan said, "disable the alarm systems and make sure those vehicles aren't going anywhere until we want them to."

"Yes, Alpha." Jonathan climbed out and skirted the edges of the clearing, keeping to the shadows. He knelt by the first vehicle, withdrew tools from inside his flak jacket, and worked for a few minutes before crouching by the side of the second. When he returned to the Rover, he said, "They won't be going anywhere in those."

"No," Sylvan said. "They won't be going anywhere at all."

The *centuri* rumbled their assent. Sylvan rolled down her window and drew in air so crisp the inside of her nose tingled. Finally, she scented them.

"All right," Sylvan said, "it's time."

The *centuri* practically climbed over one another in their eagerness to fight. Sylvan didn't try to settle them—she wanted them alert and ready. They'd be safer with their every sense on edge. She positioned her warriors along the mouth of the trail leading from Pack land into the clearing. They formed a gauntlet through which the raiders would pass to reach their vehicles.

"On my command," Sylvan said, "we take them. Don't fire unless you have to."

Niki snarled. "Why show them mercy?"

"Two reasons," Sylvan said, though an explanation was not required when she gave an order. "We need to know who leads them, and they are wolves. If they agree to my terms, I may let them live."

Jace growled. "They attacked us. They don't deserve to live."

"I won't argue that truth," Sylvan said flatly. "But do as I command."

Jace ducked her head. "Yes, Alpha."

They formed up on either side of the trail, Niki across from Sylvan nearest to the point the renegades would emerge, Jace and Jonathan as always a pair—one on the left, one on the right, and Dasha and Max closest to the vehicles. Six against twelve or fifteen. Poor odds for the renegades.

❖

They came in a tight group, a dozen or more dressed in combat fatigues, carrying automatic rifles at the ready. Sylvan stepped into a shaft of moonlight in the center of the trail and the wolf Were at the point of the phalanx of renegades halted abruptly, his face registering shock. Sylvan carried no weapon. She put her hands on her hips, her legs spread wide.

"You've trespassed on my territory, you've brought challenge to me and my Pack. I accept the challenge. Your leader may stand for all of you, or I and my *centuri* will judge you all guilty and render punishment."

The apparent leader in front, a tall male with thick dark hair, a beard scuffing his jawline, broad shoulders, and a bulky body, laughed. "I've heard you were invincible. I never heard you were this stupid."

Sylvan's eyes glowed gold, and silver pelt shimmered down her torso as she grew taller, her warrior half-form emerging effortlessly. Her limbs lengthened and claws emerged. Her face transformed, her jaws stretching to accommodate her canines. Most wolf Weres had never seen a half-form. Bernardo had never been capable of it. Some of the renegades cowered. "The punishment is death."

"Then death it is." The male lowered his assault rifle in her direction, confident in his supremacy.

Sylvan smiled, and before her smile registered in his mind, she shifted completely, sprang through the air, and took him down by the throat. Blood sprayed in an arc across the clearing, shimmering like drops of fire in the moonlight before falling to the earth. The kill was swift and more merciful than he deserved. She straddled his chest and raised her head to the sky, howling a cry of triumph. She backed away and crouched on all fours, waiting, studying the prey through sharp, patient eyes. The renegades drew closer together, a few raised their arms, and the *centuri* stepped from the cover of darkness and raised their own weapons.

Niki said, "Surrender your arms, and the Alpha may judge you mercifully. You have three seconds, or you will all die."

Sylvan howled again, and the force of her power shuddered across the glade and spread out into Pack land, igniting all the Weres within hearing distance and beyond. A cacophony of cries echoed back, and the renegades shuddered under the onslaught. Their primal nature was to obey the strongest, and resisting an Alpha of Sylvan's power was an internal struggle that most could not win. At least half instantly dropped their weapons on the ground. The others twisted uneasily, glancing from the *centuri* to Sylvan and back again. A cat quickly raised her rifle to fire in Sylvan's direction and Niki shot her through the forehead. The other cats immediately dropped their weapons and moved away from the wolves. Three wolf Weres attempted to run for the shelter of the trees, firing wildly as they ran, and the *centuri* cut them down.

"Wait!" a golden-haired female cat called. "We surrender and petition for a hearing before the cat Alpha."

"You are trespassers on Pack land," Niki repeated, "and therefore have forfeited your rights to petition for *anything*. You would be dead by now if not for the Alpha's mercy." She motioned to Jace and Jonathan to round up the cats. "Take them to the vehicles."

When the cats were herded away, less than a half dozen wolf Weres remained. Niki grinned as Sylvan prowled around them. Each time she circled, the renegades squeezed closer to one another, as if trying to disappear. "Time's up. *Centuri*, prepare to fire."

The *centuri* aimed their weapons on the raiders.

"One, two..." Niki intoned. Automatic weapons thudded to the ground and the renegades dropped to their knees. A single dark form broke from the center of the milling group and crashed into the underbrush, running in the direction of the vehicles.

"Round them up," Niki said.

As the *centuri* closed around the kneeling captives, Niki dropped her weapons and shifted. She bounded toward the clearing, saw a tall, thin male racing for the nearest vehicle. She launched herself just as he opened the door and slid inside. Her jaws closed on his shoulder and she dragged him from the driver's seat and onto the ground. He fell screaming beneath her, his shoulder shredded and gushing blood. She planted her paws on his chest and pinned him with the weight of her body. She stared into his eyes, saw hatred and fear, and snapped her jaws. He was the enemy. He would kill if not killed. She opened her jaws, prepared to strike.

Niki!

Sylvan burst from the forest and streaked toward them. When she reached them, she shed pelt and looked down at the writhing renegade. "We'll take this one back with us."

Niki growled and set her teeth against his throat. She slowly closed her jaws until her canines pierced his flesh. He whimpered and urinated in submission. Satisfied, she climbed off and shed pelt. "Why spare him?"

Sylvan stared down at him. Even in the moonlight, his pallor was clear. He was terrified, but his eyes still burned with hatred. "He's one of Bernardo's old lieutenants, and he smells like the leader."

Sylvan was right. He was a dominant male, more dominant even than the one Sylvan had killed—the one this male had allowed to stand for him. Niki wondered how a leader could lead from the rear, but that had always been Bernardo's style too.

"If this is an example of Bernardo's best warriors," Niki sneered, "it's no wonder he's dead."

"Put him in the other SUV," Sylvan said in disgust. "It's time for some answers."

CHAPTER TWENTY-EIGHT

D ru pulled up in front of Francesca's lair on her motorcycle at three in the morning. Lights glowed dimly on the wide front porch and behind the tall narrow windows on the first floor. From a distance, the mansion looked like any of the others that dotted the heights overlooking the river on the outskirts of the city. Only when one drew near were the armed guards along the drive and at the entrances visible. Luce pushed through the front door and walked down the wide stone steps as Dru kicked down the stand and swung her leg over the tank.

"You're back early," Luce said.

"I need to see Francesca."

"The Queen," Luce said, emphasizing the title, "is conducting business. She'll see you at sunrise."

Dru shook her head. "She'll want to see me now. Tell her it has to do with Sylvan."

"Do we need to prepare for an attack?"

"If she was in danger, I wouldn't be standing here talking to you. But I wouldn't let your guards stray very far from the lair."

"Come inside." Luce moved so quickly she was already through the door when the invitation left her mouth.

Dru followed inside, through the hall, and down the elevator to Francesca's quarters. The largest room other than her bedroom had been turned into an office. Luce knocked on the closed walnut-paneled door, although Francesca undoubtedly knew everyone who approached long before they reached her door. A moment passed, and then Francesca said, "Come in, Luce."

Luce entered and Dru followed. The room resembled a library in a mansion owned by an eighteenth-century land baron—and perhaps it was. The scrolled bookcases were solid mahogany, filled with leather-bound books that were probably first editions. Thick oriental carpets covered most of the gleaming hardwood. The ceiling was coffered with hammered tin tiles painted a creamy white. Heavy brocade drapes covered portions of one wall, adding to the opulent air of the luxurious space. Francesca relaxed in a high-backed, dark brown leather chair behind a broad antique desk, a laptop computer incongruously open before her. A cell phone rested by her left hand. She studied them with undisguised annoyance. "What is it?"

"Forgive the interruption, my Queen," Luce said, "but Dru insisted on seeing you."

"Oh?" Francesca switched her attention to Dru. Her expression softened. "Then it must be important."

"I've just come from Raptures," Dru said. "I'm afraid Cecilia won't be delivering the wolf Alpha. Sylvan is back in her own territory."

Francesca hissed. "You're certain?"

"Unfortunately, yes. We sent a raiding party to test their lines and lure some of her forces away from the Compound. Communications with the mercenaries ended before they were able to leave Pack land. Probability is high that Sylvan has them."

"Oh dear," Francesca said mildly. "How much do these mercenaries of yours know?"

"Very little," Dru said. "Their orders came from a wolf Were. They believe their goal is to overthrow Sylvan in order to place one of their own in power."

"And what of your role in all of this?"

"Most don't know me at all. The few who do know only that I support their cause and provided funds and munitions."

"None of which threatens our position long-term with the Weres or Clans," Luce pointed out.

"No," Francesca said, "assuming Sylvan is no longer in power." She pushed back her chair and paced in front of her desk. She had dressed in a sheer cream-colored silk shirt and deep green silk trousers for the videoconferences she held with her business associates and Clan captains throughout the country. Her nipples were pale crescents crowning the voluptuous swell of her breasts.

Dru imagined sinking her canines into their inviting ripeness. Francesca slowed, captured Dru's gaze, and a warm wave of indolent desire rolled through Dru's belly. Thrall. She curled her lip and hissed quietly.

"Sylvan," Francesca said briskly, her attention swinging from Luce to Dru, "will undoubtedly alert her allies of the attack. Eventually none of the Weres will trust us and our position *will* be threatened. We can't wait any longer for Nicholas's miracle drug or for a handful of pathetic mercenaries to win our war for us."

"I agree, my Queen," Luce said, a glint of triumph in her crimson eyes. "The longer we wait, the more likely we are to be forced into a position we can't defend."

"We can't challenge her directly," Francesca said calmly, leaning against the front of her desk. She rested her palms on the surface behind her, breasts pressing forward, straining the thin, delicate material. "If we can lure her out with just a few of her warriors, we could surprise her." She focused on Dru. "We have numbers enough for that, don't we?"

Dru shook off the cloud of lust leeching her attention. "We can assemble at least several dozen well-trained mercenaries and Vampire soldiers. That would be enough if we control the time and place."

"Then we need to bait a trap," Francesca mused, "that will force Sylvan to act." She paused, her nipples tightening beneath the translucent silk. "We must offer her something that she's willing to risk everything for."

"We have that," Luce said. "We have Veronica Standish's test subjects."

Francesca pursed her lips. "Yes, but I'm afraid if we sacrifice Standish's work, her usefulness to us will be over."

"If we're successful," Luce said, "in intercepting Sylvan and destroying her in the process of attempting to free the subjects, Dr. Standish will have nothing to complain about."

"And if the plan fails?" Francesca asked, studying Luce intently.

Luce shrugged. "Some sacrifices must be made during war."

"You're right, of course." Francesca sighed. "As much as I would hate to lose Dr. Standish, I'm afraid we will have to risk it."

"We'll need a credible way to leak the information to Sylvan," Dru said, "or else she'll expect a trap."

"You have an idea?"

"Luce reported Gregory was recruiting scientists for Veronica's lab. If someone pretending to be a member of HUFSI leaks the information, it won't be traced to us. Standish will blame Gregory."

"Luce?" Francesca said questioningly.

Luce nodded slowly. "It might work. It's a dangerous game, but we have the upper hand."

Francesca smiled. "That's the kind of game I like to play."

❖

Drake found Sylvan in her office, standing by the open windows. The sun was just breaching the horizon, the dawn not yet upon them. She brushed both hands over Sylvan's shoulders and kissed the back of her neck. "The interrogations are over?"

"Yes."

"Is there anything that requires urgent attention?"

Sylvan sighed, an uncommon weariness in her body and voice. "No, not really. I'll fill in the others in a minute."

"Can it wait an hour?"

Sylvan turned, her brows drawing together. "A problem?"

"No. I want you to come with me."

"All right," Sylvan said unquestioningly.

Drake took her hand and led her outside, across the Compound to the infirmary, through the silent halls, and past the guards who snapped to attention without speaking. As they walked closer and closer to the nursery, the exhaustion seemed to evaporate from Sylvan's stride.

Marta, one of the maternals on duty, had the pups ready, and when they saw Sylvan they rushed her, tails slicing the air madly, their high-pitched yips and yelps sharp and strong. Laughing, Sylvan gathered them both into her arms and glanced at Drake.

"It's time for a run," Drake said.

Eyes shining, Sylvan nodded.

They shifted together at the edge of the forest, the pups racing around them with ecstatic cries. Sylvan spun around and growled once, softly. Kira and Kendra instantly stilled, bodies quivering, ears alert, bright eyes fixed on the Alpha. Drake shouldered in beside Sylvan, licked her muzzle, and waited.

Sylvan lifted her head and howled, a long, strong call to hunt. Before the echo of the call died away, she pivoted and raced into the woods. Drake followed, keeping the two pups behind her uppermost in her senses. Sylvan would set the path and track the prey. The Pack would follow. She kept Sylvan in sight but didn't try to flank her as she often did when they ran together. The morning frost was crisp beneath her pads, the air crystalline and bright. The forest came alive with the first shafts of sunlight under a brilliant blue sky. Sylvan led them along pine-strewn paths, across brooks and winter bare clearings. They hunted small prey, the pups watching eagerly as first Sylvan then Drake took the lead on the chase. When they finally circled back to the Compound, the pups were lagging, their tongues lolling, their sides heaving, their spirits bright and eager.

When they delivered them back to Marta, Drake said, "These two will probably sleep all morning now."

Marta laughed fondly. "I'm not so sure of that. They're the Alpha's young, after all."

"That they are," Drake said, "especially when they're misbehaving."

Marta left to settle the two in with their Packmates, and Sylvan slipped her arm around Drake's waist. "You were right. I needed that."

Drake turned and wrapped her arms around Sylvan's waist. "We all needed that. This is why you do what you do. For them and all the others like them, now and in the days to come."

Sylvan rested her forehead on Drake's and closed her eyes. "I don't know why I ever thought I could do this without a mate."

Drake kissed her. "Because you're stubborn and strong."

Sylvan laughed softly. "I love you."

"I love you too. More than life." Drake kissed her again. "Now, tell me."

They walked through the Compound as Sylvan talked. Their wolves surrounded them, mated pairs slipping into the forest to run, *sentries* by the fire pits, recruits in the training yard, the *centuri* at their posts on the headquarters porch. "I've contacted Raina. We're sending the cats back to her for judgment."

Drake laughed. "I'm not sure the mercenaries will find that such a bargain."

"No, I doubt they will."

"And the wolves?"

Sylvan was silent for a long moment. "Three have sworn allegiance."

Drake spoke carefully. "Will you trust them? Will the others?"

"Not at first," Sylvan said. "They'll have to prove themselves. I'm sending them to the Blackpaw camp and promoting Val to captain. She'll watch them. There'll be no second chances."

"And the last?"

"I did not give Marcus a choice," Sylvan said. "He is exiled, banished from my territory, from that of my allies, and from all lands bordering ours. Niki will escort him to the far border. If he turns back, she will execute him. If he returns here or anywhere within our reach, she will execute him."

"What did he know?"

"One very interesting thing," Sylvan said, pausing before one of the fire pits where a pot of coffee sat steaming on hot rocks. "The recruiter is a cat Were."

"Not a Vampire?" Drake poured coffee and handed the steaming cup to Sylvan. "I didn't think the rogue cats were organized enough to pull off a raid like that."

"Oh, I suspect she's recruiting for a Vampire."

"She." Drake sipped from her coffee. "The cat who was with Francesca at Nocturne. The one who kidnapped Katya."

"Yes. And I know where she's recruiting." Sylvan growled quietly. "Raptures."

"The blood bar."

"Yes. Jody might be able to help us there. Someone will talk."

"Perhaps if we wait, we can capture the cat."

"I'm tired of waiting. I'm tired of reacting, rather than controlling events." Sylvan growled more loudly and several nearby *sentries* jerked to attention. "We still have missing Weres out there."

Drake stroked her back. "Any word from Andrea?"

"Not yet," Sylvan said, her frustration as sharp as a blade. "We're still fighting shadows."

"I have some good news," Drake said.

Sylvan sat on one of the huge log benches that ringed the fire pit and pulled Drake down beside her. "Tell me. I could use it."

"The Revniks report the second infected female has stabilized. Her fever is abating and her vital signs are stronger."

"What does that mean?"

Drake blew out a breath. "We're not sure yet, but it looks as if she will live. What happens when she shifts is still uncertain, but there's a chance she may have made the transformation successfully."

"Then that is good news."

Drake slid her hand inside the waistband of Sylvan's camos, wanting flesh beneath her fingers. "We're close, Sylvan. All we need—"

"Alpha," Max called, crossing the Compound at a run. "Becca Land is on the phone for you. She says it's important."

Sylvan's grin was bright as she rose. "Maybe we're about to get what we need."

CHAPTER TWENTY-NINE

S ylvan," Becca said when Sylvan answered, the excitement rippling in her voice. "I just got a call from someone who claims to know the location of Veronica Standish's laboratory."

Sylvan glanced at Drake, who stood close by, listening. This could be a break, or another trap. Drake's eyes narrowed. She was as suspicious as Sylvan. "I don't suppose you know who it is?"

Becca laughed, her deep melodic voice as smooth as molten chocolate. "I'm afraid I never get those kinds of tips. I can say for sure it wasn't Martin Hoffstetter. I recognize his voice now, and Martin would have no reason not to identify himself."

"What about the human who warned you of the infected girls being dropped off at the ERs?"

"I don't think so, but I'm not as positive."

"Does this one claim to be another HUFSI member?"

"The conversation was brief," Becca said. "According to him, and I'm quite sure the caller was male, there's a move afoot to recruit scientists for a top-secret assignment. And yes, according to the source, they're drawing heavily on HUFSI members. This individual claims to have had a meeting with a recruiter and has been told to report to the city before the end of the week."

"And then what?"

"They'll be transported to the lab. They don't have an address."

"Convenient."

"I agree it's not much, but the pattern fits what we know about these people—the multiple layers of camouflage, the secret locations, the focus on humans who wouldn't be opposed to anti-Were experiments."

Sylvan snarled. "Do you have any sense of how reliable this information is?"

Becca sighed. "None whatsoever. And almost no way to confirm. But if the information is accurate, and he calls me again, I can push for a meeting or, at the very least, his destination in the city. Then we can put a tail on him and find the location of this laboratory."

Sylvan smiled at Becca's language. "Jody's detective traits are rubbing off on you."

"Don't you believe it. I was following her from the beginning when she was still trying to pretend she wasn't interested."

Sylvan heard a dark chuckle from the background and suspected the Vampire was listening. "Do you think he'll call again?"

"It's impossible to know, but my guess is, yes."

"I like your plan. If he at least tells us where he'll be, even if we don't get a name, we can keep the place under watch. Sooner or later someone we recognize is going to show up."

"I agree with you. Is there anything we can do in the meantime?"

"Let me talk to Jody. We could use some help checking out another lead."

"I'll give her to you in a minute," Becca said. "But, Sylvan, this story is something I'm not going to be able to sit on. People need to know what these extremists are doing."

"I know, and I wouldn't ask you to keep it quiet." Sylvan paused. "Becca, some things may happen that might be hard for humans to understand."

"I live with a Vampire, Sylvan."

"Have you watched her kill?"

Becca caught her breath. "No, but there have been times I've wanted her to."

"Wanting and doing are two different things."

"Then I'll ask you to trust my judgment as to what the public can handle. And remember, I'm on your side."

"I will."

"Thank you."

A second later Jody spoke. "How may we be of service to the Pack?"

"We just intercepted a raiding party in my territory," Sylvan said. "According to the leader—one of Bernardo's previous crew—a cat Were is recruiting mercenaries at Raptures. If I send my people in there to see if we can find out who, they'll be identified immediately. I was hoping you might be able to help."

"I can send one of my younglings. If they're recognized, they can claim they're looking for a little more adventurous blood sport than they can find at the lair."

"I don't want to put any of your people in danger."

Jody laughed. "My Vampires can take care of themselves."

My Vampires. Since Jody had risen, she'd assumed her station as heir to her father's Clan completely. Sylvan was glad of it. Viceregal Zachary Gates was old and powerful and someone she didn't completely trust. Jody might not ascend to his position for decades, but even as his second, she had influence. "I think the cat is one of Francesca's. It's all related somehow."

Jody hissed. "Then I am doubly glad to be of service."

"If you track her to Francesca's lair, we want to be there when you take them."

"That is Vampire business," Jody said coolly. "Francesca has broken with the Vampire League and dishonored our truce with the Weres. She is subject to execution on sight."

Sylvan growled. "It is all of our business. Francesca has had a hand in these assaults on us and is in league with those who would destroy us."

"We will do our part to bring you justice."

Sylvan heard Becca murmur in the background and Jody sighed. "If we find Francesca's lair, we will welcome you as witness to our judgment."

"Agreed."

"What of this business Becca speaks of? The laboratory?"

"If we find it, we will destroy it. We have reason to believe they have captive Weres, and even if they don't, they are actively working on a contagion to infect us and humans. The human population will hunt us down if that happens."

"Do you have a plan?"

"We divide and conquer."

Jody laughed, a cold sound like steel slicing through air. "I like that idea very much."

"Then we have a plan."

❖

The *centuri* waited in the great room, in their usual places, Max by the fireplace, Niki inside the door, Jace and Jonathan flanking the windows. They snapped to attention when Sylvan and Drake entered.

A huge fire burned in the hearth, chasing the early evening shadows from the room. The scent of aggression thickened the air. Everyone was ready to fight.

"An informant contacted Becca Land. His information may be able to help us find the laboratory where the missing females were taken." Sylvan briefly outlined the discussion.

Niki snarled. "So we wait?"

"We have no choice."

"Andrea should be told about this," Max said. "She has people embedded in HUFSI throughout the country. She may be able to help us."

Sylvan regarded Max intently. "Andrea is human."

Max stiffened. His dark eyes glinted, and for an instant, he met Sylvan's gaze. "She and her brother and other humans like her risk their lives every day to help us."

Niki strode forward. "They do it to protect their own interests. They work for the human government. They will always place humans above Weres."

Max growled and took a step in Niki's direction. Niki bared her teeth. Smaller than Max by eighty pounds, she was nevertheless more dominant, and he shuddered.

"Enough," Sylvan snapped. "We all protect our own first. Andrea can't be faulted for that and she has proved herself a friend already."

Niki halted, pelt rippling beneath her skin. Max glowered.

"My point," Sylvan said with a bite, "is that our methods may not be acceptable to humans, whether they are our allies or not."

"Andrea knows what we are." Max would not contradict the Alpha directly, but he would defend his chosen.

"Max," Drake said, "Andrea is an agent of the federal government. If she knows we are planning retribution against those in this lab, some of whom are human, she could be placed in a compromising position. If we eliminate a human in the presence of witnesses, she might be forced to report it or be in danger."

"She will not betray us." Max rubbed his chest. "We are mated. She accepts what that means."

Sylvan had already suspected they were mated, although Max did not emit the distinct scent of a mated Were. Andrea was human and their essences could not fuse. Whereas once she would have mistrusted the strength of a bond between any except two Weres, she had learned that the mate bond was just as powerful when the spirit and the heart melded even if the body couldn't. "She is your mate, and you are my *centuri*. You and I are bound by blood as well as oath. If you trust her, so shall we."

She scanned the others, all of whom nodded, including Niki.

"Thank you, Alpha." The tension left Max's big frame and the fire banked in his eyes.

Drake slid her hand down Sylvan's back and addressed the others. "We have to wait, but we don't have to wait idly. We need to prepare the Compound in case of retaliation, gather as much intelligence as we can, and be ready to move quickly."

"Max," Sylvan said, "outfit the Rover with weapons and comm equipment. You'll drive." She gestured to Jace and Jonathan. "If we can track this human to the city, we'll need him watched. You two will do that. You'll need to be on the lookout for Weres and Vampires who might be meeting him or, most importantly, transporting him."

The twins nodded in unison. They didn't need much sleep and communicated effortlessly through their twin bond. They would make excellent spotters.

"Niki," Sylvan said, "you need to escort the Blackpaw prisoner beyond our lands and get back here as quickly as possible."

"I'll leave now." Niki's eyes glinted. "It may be a short trip if he decides to resist."

Sylvan laughed. "Be careful. And be swift."

Niki pivoted and left the room. Sylvan grasped the back of Drake's neck. "Our time for reckoning is near."

❖

Luce entered Francesca's study and bowed her head. "You called for me?"

Francesca rose from her leather chair and was beside Luce a second later. She stroked her face and kissed her. "The call went as planned?"

"Yes, my Queen. Simon was most convincing."

"How soon can we be ready to spring our little surprise?"

"We mustn't make it appear too simple. Simon will call again in a day or two."

"Very well. How is Dr. Standish?"

Luce grimaced. "I'm afraid she is…distracted."

"Addicted."

"Yes."

"Can she function long enough for us to pull this off?"

"Yes, but her colleagues will notice before long." Luce hesitated. "And so will Nicholas Gregory."

Francesca huffed. "Nicholas has become a liability. The humans simply can't be relied on. They are far too short-sighted and blind to their own inadequacies. I think it is time for us to end our partnership with him."

"We might be able to rid ourselves of both of them at once. Should some unfortunate fate befall them during Sylvan's attack on the labs."

Francesca laughed. "For a moment, you reminded me of Michel." She kissed Luce again. "So deliciously clever."

CHAPTER THIRTY

Sylvan's cell rang. Jody Gates. A surge of anticipation raced through her. Waiting was wearing on everyone's temper. The Compound was awash in pheromones, and Weres snapped and growled at each other over the slightest provocation. Even Sophia could not calm the more volatile dominants, and it didn't help that Sylvan was aroused and aggressive with the constant pulse of adrenaline and hormones boiling in her blood. Her call kept the wolves in a state of hyper-readiness that could only be tempered by battle. She answered her cell. "You have news?"

"My Vampires have identified your cat," Jody said.

Sylvan left Niki and Drake, who had spent most of the night discussing strategy with her, sprawled in the sitting area and walked to the office window. The sun crested the far mountain peaks, the sky a brilliant combination of orange and magenta that harbingered snow. Winter was coming. "Who is she?"

"A mercenary by the name of Dru."

Unsurprised, Sylvan growled. "Francesca's cat."

"Yes. She's recruiting other mercenaries and, from what we were able to ascertain, Vampires at odds with their Clans."

Jody's voice was as cold as the coming snow.

"She would be. Francesca needs to rebuild her seethe, so she needs Vampires. But she also needs to assemble an army that can fight in daylight." Sylvan inhaled a long breath of bitter cold air. Everything that had befallen her Weres—from the attacks on her, to the capture of Katya and Gray, to Andrew's death—was all part of one huge campaign to ensure Francesca's continued supremacy. "Francesca never wanted an alliance with humans, and I stood in her way with my support of the Coalition. All that matters to her is power. She will want her Dominion back."

"Yes," Jody said. "It will take time for her to become strong enough to challenge my father, but if you were out of the way and the Weres in chaos, she would not have to worry about an army opposing her."

Sylvan snarled. "Francesca has always been about the long game. She's patient."

"Her mercenaries will try to take control during daylight when we are weakest."

"Then it's a good thing you have Were allies. Tell me when to send my Weres and we will be there."

"My father may resist," Jody said. "He is not as fond of you as I."

Sylvan laughed. "That may change."

"Perhaps. You, however, have been an obstacle to Francesca's plans for too long. I think her patience is running out."

"Where is she?"

"If I knew that, I would've told you already." Jody's frustration showed, an unusual lapse for her. "Have you looked out the window?"

"I'm watching the sunrise right now."

"The cat is clever. She doesn't leave Raptures until just before sunrise when most of the Risen have already fed and returned to their lairs. My Vampires cannot follow her without risking being caught too far from the lair in sunlight."

"Then we will have to send a Were to track her."

"She won't be easy to track, but I agree."

Sylvan nodded. "Tonight."

"I will send a human servant to accompany your Were."

"That won't be necessary—"

"I wouldn't want you to find Francesca's lair and do anything rash."

"When we find her," Sylvan said, "I'll honor our bargain. We'll inform you."

"Then I'll leave the hunt to you," Jody said and was gone.

Sylvan stood for another moment feeling the tug of dawn on her wolf. A good time to hunt. She turned to Drake and Niki.

"As we expected. Francesca's cat is recruiting Weres and Vampires. Jody's Vampires can't follow her after dawn, so we'll need to send one of our Weres to follow the cat home."

Niki straightened. "I'll go."

"No," Sylvan said with finality.

"I will not arouse attention," Niki said quietly. "I've been there before."

"And that's exactly why you're not going," Sylvan said.

Niki growled. "I am of no use to you if you do not trust me."

Sylvan was on her before Niki had a chance to avert her challenging gaze. Sylvan, her canines down, her wolf ready for a tussle, gripped Niki by the back of the neck and thrust her face an inch from hers. "You challenge my orders one too many times, *Imperator*. I do not need to explain myself to you."

Niki shivered in Sylvan's grip. "No, you don't. But you need a second you trust."

Drake said mildly from beside them, "What *we* need, at the moment, is a plan. Bloodshed probably won't be helpful."

Sylvan whipped her head around. "Must I argue with everyone?"

"It's called discussion," Drake said, stroking Sylvan's back. "That's why you have us. Both of us."

Sylvan still gripped Niki's neck. "I would not risk you, whether you liked the flavor of Vampire seduction or not. I need you with me when we take Standish's laboratory, not trailing some feral cat across the state."

"I'm sorry," Niki said. "I thought you doubted my ability to resist the bite."

"I don't need you to be sorry. I need you to trust my judgment as I trust you." Sylvan shrugged. "The bite never incapacitated you half as much as your guilt, but that is of no matter now. If you say you are done with it, then it is so."

Niki ducked her head and rubbed her cheek against Sylvan's throat. "I trust you in all things, Alpha. And I understand why I can't go."

"Good." With a sigh, Sylvan released her. She glanced at Drake. "We can get Val back from the Blackpaw camp. She's one of our best trackers."

Before Drake could answer, another voice filled Sylvan's mind.

You already have the best tracker Earthside, or anywhere, for that matter.

Sylvan tilted her head and stared at the door. "If you're listening, you might as well come in."

The door opened and Torren and Misha entered. Torren had

her arm around Misha's waist. Both wore black camo, but somehow Torren's garb shimmered as if made from wisps of smoke. Her neck was unmarked.

"I wasn't planning on listening," Torren said with a musical smile. "But it's hard not to hear the shouting."

"I see you've recovered," Sylvan snapped.

"Completely, thank you." Torren glanced from Sylvan to Drake. "I owe you my life, and I am in your—"

"No," Sylvan said sharply. "You are not. You saved my mate and my wolf, and I don't want a Fae in my debt."

Torren laughed. "Superstitious?"

"Cautious." Sylvan stared. "Other than eavesdropping on our conversation, what brings you here?"

"I seek sanctuary with the Timberwolves," Torren said formally, "for myself and my mate."

"Your mate," Sylvan said flatly, eyeing Misha. *You're certain?*

"Yes," Misha said quickly.

"You consent to live under Pack law?" Sylvan asked Torren.

"I would live as close to the Earth as I can," Torren said, "and we would like to live where Misha may continue to serve the Pack. I will honor your laws."

Sylvan studied her a moment. The Fae were the most adroit bargainers in the universe. She trusted Torren, but she knew better than to leave any loopholes in a contract with a Fae. "You consent to be bound by Pack law as long as you live on Pack land."

"So be it." Torren gave a slight bow. "And I also would serve the Pack, in any way—"

"You may, from time to time," Sylvan said, "but right now I have other duties for you."

Torren's eyebrow winged upward. "Oh?"

"I intend to inform the Fae ambassador, if he hasn't already slunk back to Faerie, that Cecilia's presence on the Coalition council is no longer required. You will be the new Fae minister."

"I'm no politician."

Sylvan snarled. "Neither am I. But we can't abandon the Coalition regardless of its lack of effectiveness. The Praeterns are known to the humans now, and there's no going back."

Torren pulled Misha closer. "There is no going back." She nodded to Sylvan. "I will serve."

"I will grant you space to build your house," Sylvan said. "I don't imagine you'll want to live in the barracks."

"We are appreciative," Torren said.

"Thank you, Alpha," Misha said.

Sylvan fixed Misha with a hard stare. "You will continue to serve Callan as a *sentrie*. Being mated to the Hunter does not give you special status."

"Of course," Misha said, grinning.

"I can track Dru," Torren said. "I know her scent, and I've tracked her before."

"You'll also be recognized," Niki pointed out abruptly.

Torren smiled at Niki. "You really think so? I am the Master of the Hunt."

Niki huffed. "As if *that* explains everything."

"What would be the point of explaining something far beyond—"

Niki growled.

Drake raised a hand. "Enough competition tonight. The two of you can tussle some other time."

Niki continued to grumble quietly, but she grinned, and Torren laughed.

"I won't be recognized," Torren said.

"Then tonight you will find Francesca's lair for us."

"And when I do?"

"The first of our battle lines will be drawn."

❖

"They're getting stronger," Sylvan said when she and Drake returned to the den after another run with the young.

"I know." Drake pulled off her clothes, walked into the bathroom, and started the shower. "Did you notice they're switching places automatically as we hunt, first one then the other taking the lead?"

Sylvan joined her and they stepped under the spray together. Sylvan threw her head back and let the water run over her face. Spending time with the young was one of the only things that calmed her wolf enough for her to contain the crushing urge in her belly to kill. Somewhere out there, the enemy plotted and planned while she was forced to wait. She was a hunter by nature, she sought her prey, she tracked her prey, she chased it down, and she took it. Now she was forced into the position of being prey, and every fiber of her being resisted. "We might have been wrong about the natural order of things for them. But they'll work it out."

"They've got a long time to test each other," Drake said, soaping Sylvan's back. "Put your hands against the wall. Let me settle you."

Sylvan laughed harshly. "Is that what you call it now?"

Drake wrapped her arms around Sylvan's middle and pressed against her back, biting her lightly on the nape. "I call it taking what I want. Would you deny me?"

Sylvan growled softly. "Never, even though I know you're handling me."

Drake laughed against the back of Sylvan's shoulder and slid one hand down Sylvan's belly between her thighs. "It seems you want to be handled."

Sylvan pressed her palms hard against the tile wall and closed her eyes. The weight on her back felt right, Drake's hand enclosing her felt right. Letting Drake take her felt right. "You show me I am more than I thought."

Drake's teeth scraped against her shoulder. "You let me be more than I ever was. Now be quiet."

Sylvan rumbled and gritted her teeth, the urge to pin Drake against the wall and fill her raging through her blood like fire. But Drake wanted something else, and the need to please her outweighed everything. Her hips surged and her ass tightened and she let Drake empty her in long, stomach-clenching waves. She growled softly when she could breathe again.

"Better?" Drake asked.

"Yes." Sylvan started to turn, wanting Drake. Wanting to be between her thighs, filling her.

"Wait," Drake whispered, stopping Sylvan from turning.

"You ask much."

Drake pressed close against her, rubbing against her ass. She set her teeth into Sylvan's shoulder, gripped her hard and rode her until she released.

"Better?" Sylvan murmured.

"Better," Drake gasped.

Laughing, Sylvan turned and pulled Drake into her arms and kissed her. "You know me better than I know myself."

Drake brushed damp strands from Sylvan's forehead. "I would love you whether you let me or not, but I know you because you let me see you."

"I love you," Sylvan whispered.

Drake turned off the water, reached outside for a towel, and draped it around Sylvan's shoulders. She kissed her softly. "I'm yours."

The cell rang before they were dressed again. Sylvan picked it up, said, "Mir," and listened. When she put it down her eyes glowed gold. She looked at Drake. "Becca's informant called again. This time Becca kept him on the line long enough to trace the call. We have an address."

Chapter Thirty-one

Three blocks from Raptures, Torren slipped into a dark alley and emerged in the form of a young male wolf Were. Having been immersed in the pheromones saturating the air in the Compound for days, she had no problem assuming the alternate form. She'd likely be taken for a thrill seeker looking for adventure and dangerous sex, not a hard-core mercenary or rogue. No one would give her a second glance. Strolling into Raptures, she headed for the bar and ordered a drink. Nearing two a.m., the small dark room was packed with Vampires and Weres and the daring, or desperate, humans who had come to host. This was not a place where humans were safe. These Vampires accepted no Clan rule and were under no obligation to cease feeding before the host was terminally depleted. More than one human body, drained dry, had been discovered slumped in a doorway of a deserted building in the ten square blocks surrounding Raptures.

The Weres were mostly wolves and a few cats. Most cats didn't venture as far south as the city, not unless they'd hosted enough to become blood addicted. The wolves were rogues and the rare lone wolf passing through, keeping to the shadows and hoping not to arouse the attention of the ruling Alpha.

Dru wasn't among the cat Weres interspersed among the customers, but Torren caught traces of her scent lingering around the fringes of the crowd. Satisfied, Torren settled onto a bar stool and sipped the tepid beer. She'd never understood how any species could prefer the grainy taste of beer to the lilting fragrances of wine, but she pretended to savor it. After a few moments, a human female slid onto the seat beside her and leaned too close.

"You look too young to be here," the buxom blonde murmured softly. Her scent was heavy with arousal and something else—a drug to enhance sexual desire.

Torren produced her best grin. "Is there an age limit?"

She laughed. "There probably ought to be. I was wondering, are you interested in a threesome with one of the vamps?"

"I might be. Maybe a little later. I'm still looking. You have someone in mind?"

She pointed to a lithe, dark-haired Vampire holding court in a booth across the room. He was surrounded by females of all species and pretty, if you liked men with smooth faces, delicate eyebrows, and slender bodies. He reminded Torren of the form so many Fae males assumed Earthside, unconsciously tailoring their physique to reflect their evanescent spirits. "Who is he?"

"That's Dante," she said as if Torren should know. "He's got connections."

"Connections?" Torren feigned confusion. Could Francesca be so confident as to allow her Vampires to recruit this openly? Or maybe she didn't know. Her forces must be spread thin, too thin to monitor the activities of everyone in her seethe.

"He says he can take us to some really old Vampires." She leaned closer, her low-cut shirt gaping to reveal enhanced breasts barely constrained by a frothy bra whose scalloped cups floated under her magenta nipples. "Mmm-mmm. The sex is supposed to be fabulous."

"Really? I didn't think the really old ones ever came to places like this."

"They don't. But he says it's not far, and he'll take us at dawn. What do you think?" As she spoke, she stroked Torren's leg, cupping the organ between her thighs.

Male bodies were always curious, so unsubtle in their signals. Torren had not the slightest interest in this female but allowed her physical form to respond to the neurological stimulation, almost laughing at the anticipated response. The female's eyes widened, and she clutched her a little tighter.

"Oh," she said breathily, "you really, *really* have to come with us now. I'm going to be thinking about this for the rest of the night."

"So am I," Torren said, gently easing the human's grip. "Would you like a drink?"

"Oh yes. A pink lady. And then let me take you over to meet Dante."

"All right." Torren slipped an arm around her waist and signaled to the bartender. "I'd like that very much."

An hour and a half later, Torren was settled at a table adjacent to Dante's booth as the crowd around Dante grew. The humans and Weres were mostly young, and all bore signs of having hosted recently and repeatedly. Many were already addicts or almost there. Torren drank little, said less, and tried to avoid being fed from or otherwise sexually engaged. Dawn was still several hours away when Dru came through the door alone. Dante tried to appear casual, but he followed her movements uneasily. After making a slow circuit of the room, Dru approached and scanned the group surrounding the Vampire. "You've been busy."

Dante grinned cockily. "Just doing my part."

"The van will be here in half an hour."

"I was hoping we could party some before we left." He waved an arm expansively. "Plenty to choose from. I'm happy to share."

Dru's lip curled and her canines glinted. "You'll leave when the van arrives."

He quickly smoothed away the grimace of displeasure and smiled. "Of course."

Torren felt Dru's gaze linger on her for a moment, then skate away. Dru spent the next few minutes talking with several wolf Weres at the bar, paying Dante and his groupies no further mind. Torren couldn't be certain Dante would lead them all to Francesca and slipped away when the blonde was fawning over Dante. Outside in the shadows, she let the glamour fade and the Hound settled in to hunt the real prey. The cat would lead her to Francesca's lair, and she and Francesca had unfinished business.

❖

Sylvan, Drake, and Niki waited in the great room for word from Jace and Jonathan. The twins had been in position all night at the hotel where Becca's informant had made his call. So far, they'd spotted nothing.

"They might not recognize him," Niki pointed out. "One human among so many. How could they tell?"

"Someone will be coming to deliver him to the laboratory—a mercenary or blood servant," Sylvan said. "They'll be in a protected limo. Hopefully, the twins will recognize the transport or the escort."

"If he wants Becca to get the story, he needs to give her more information," Niki complained. "Don't you think that feels off? Maybe this is another trap."

"It might well be," Sylvan said. "But every trap can be sprung, and if we spring it, we'll learn something about our opponent."

Niki grumbled but didn't argue.

"So far, he's been careful," Drake said. "That makes sense if he's legitimate. He fears for his life, and rightly so. If exposed, he's expendable. He'll have to trust Becca not to reveal his identity."

Sylvan said, "And he doesn't know where he's going or who will be taking them there. Maybe he thinks he'll be able to recognize his destination and give Becca more information. He might be right, but I'd rather follow him and find the place on our own."

Sylvan paused, cocked her head, and smiled. "We have visitors."

The doors opened and Lara and Raina strode inside. The cat Alpha wore tawny form-fitting leathers, shirtless beneath the vest despite the cold. She was a mountain lion, and the winter weather bothered her as little as it bothered the wolves. The Vampire physiology was less vigorous unless just after a feeding, but Lara seemed as unconcerned as Raina in just a leather shirt and pants. Her amber eyes glittered with shards of fire as she tipped her head to Sylvan. "Alpha."

"Warlord." Sylvan held out an arm, and Lara stepped into her embrace.

Lara murmured, "It's good to see you, Alpha."

"And you." Sylvan released her and nodded to Raina. "Alpha Carras. I take it you received our delivery."

Raina hissed in disgust. "What a sorry crew. They've been dealt with and hopefully have learned a lesson. Time will tell."

Drake eased up beside Sylvan and wrapped an arm around her waist. "Somehow I don't think this visit is a coincidence."

Raina smiled and Lara shrugged the elegant shrug of a Vampire.

"My Liege called me back from the mountains," Lara said. "It seems we are about to go hunting a renegade Vampire."

"And a renegade cat," Raina said darkly.

"Francesca and Dru." Sylvan nodded. "Jody would want her warlord. And the cat Alpha wants her due."

"We're on our way to my Liege's lair," Lara said. "We can take a strike squad with us."

Sylvan looked to Niki. "Prepare our wolves to aid our allies."

"Yes, Alpha." Niki strode out.

"Torren has left to track Dru," Sylvan said. "We have *centuri* watching for the human who will lead us to Standish's laboratory."

Lara hissed. "If we don't hear something tonight, we'll have to wait until the next dawn. Francesca will be distracted then and her Vampires weak or somnolent."

"Your Vampires will be weaker too," Sylvan said.

Lara's canines gleamed. "Not all of us."

"Then I'm very glad Liege Gates called you back." Sylvan's cell rang and everyone stilled.

"Mir."

She listened.

"How many?"

Sylvan's face was as smooth and unreadable as a river-washed stone.

"Lara and Raina are here. I'll inform them."

Sylvan hung up. "Torren has found Francesca's lair, an old mansion by the river. She says Francesca has assembled a formidable seethe—at least two dozen vampires and mercenaries. There's no way to tell how many humans might be inside."

"It's too near dawn now," Lara said. "But tomorrow…"

Sylvan nodded. "Tomorrow we strike."

❖

"Do you think we've waited long enough to bait the trap?" Francesca said when Dru and Luce joined her at dawn.

"I am certain the reporter has contacted Sylvan Mir," Dru said. "Mir is almost certainly waiting for some evidence that proves the informant can be trusted. We don't want to be obvious, but forty-eight hours should be enough time for Simon's story to be credible."

"Can we have our forces in place in time?" Francesca unlaced the bodice of her gown and let it fall to the floor in a crimson pool.

Luce's eyes tracked every move, her hunger surpassed by her desire. Francesca had been allowing her to feed from her, just small sips, just enough to taste the power and know she was growing stronger. Soon, she would truly be Francesca's second, more powerful than any other Vampire in the Western Hemisphere, possibly in the entire world. Power was an aphrodisiac all by itself, and every Vampire knew the pull. Sex was an offshoot of the quest for power, the orgasm a side effect registered with pleasure but secondary to the main goal. Not so any longer. Francesca's body had become her obsession, and Dru her rival for Francesca's attentions. "The mercenaries can be placed before sunfall, and our guards shortly after. Sylvan will not strike during the day—there's too much risk of being observed. She will come at night, and we will be waiting."

"Then it's time we gave her a destination." Francesca ran her hands over her breasts and cupped them, rubbing her nipples, still pale rose, until they peaked. When she'd fed, they would blush scarlet.

Beside Luce, Dru growled and a cloud of pheromones drifted from her, stirring Luce's feeding hormones. She wanted them both, but she would have to wait on Francesca's pleasure. Francesca held out her hand.

"Dru, come join me."

Dru quickly shed her clothes, her skin already dusted with golden pelt. Francesca reclined on the bed, and Dru moved between her thighs.

Francesca laughed. "You seek to mount me, my eager lion?"

"I seek to fuck you." Dru braced herself above Francesca on both arms, her caramel hair falling around her face, a lacy curtain obscuring all but Francesca's fiery eyes. Her ass clenched rhythmically, and Luce hissed.

Francesca raked her nails down Dru's back, drawing lines of blood that trickled down the cat's sides.

"Move over," Francesca said, her voice like ice.

Dru's entire body trembled, and she growled. Luce took a step forward, ready to rip the cat from Francesca's body, but she didn't need to. Francesca thrust a palm to Dru's chest and the cat tumbled over on her back.

"My Vampire needs to feed first," Francesca said, her gaze caressing Luce's trembling body. "Come, darling. Take what you need. Before long we will have all the blood we desire."

CHAPTER THIRTY-TWO

R apid footsteps on the porch outside headquarters ended with a sharp rap on the door.

"Come in," Sylvan said abruptly, her gaze narrowing.

Gray strode in, dressed for battle in black camo. "Alpha, I—"

"Why aren't you in the infirmary?"

"I am healed, Alpha." Gray straightened her shoulders and raised her head as much as she could under Sylvan's glare. "I heard about the lab. Callan is organizing squads. I want to go with you."

Sylvan studied her. She looked strong enough. Her eyes had lost the haunted look that had colored them since she'd been freed. And if anyone deserved a chance to strike back at those in the labs, it was her and Katya. Although she knew the answer, she asked, "Can you control your wolf?"

"Yes, Alpha."

"And follow orders?"

"Yes, Alpha!"

"Niki will tell you where she wants you. Wait outside."

Gray ducked her head. "Thank you, Alpha."

"Niki," Sylvan said after Gray left, "keep a watch on her. I don't want her hurt."

"She won't be easy to handle."

Sylvan grinned. "Neither are you, but I manage."

Drake laughed and Niki joined in, and then they went back to waiting. At three thirty in the afternoon, Jace called with an update.

"We followed the informant to an abandoned factory on the river," Jace said.

"You are sure about who they are?" Sylvan asked.

"Yes, Alpha. The description of the human matched what he told the Consort. We saw him come out and get into a limo at the specified time. The windows were shaded, so we couldn't identify the driver."

"Tell me about the location," Sylvan said.

"It's several blocks long, six stories," Jace said. "The parking lot surrounding it is mostly empty, with the river directly behind it and the highway probably three hundred yards away."

"No evidence of occupants?"

"It *looks* abandoned, but we don't think so. The vehicle pulled around behind the building, and when we checked it out, it was gone."

"Underground garage?" Sylvan asked.

"We think so. Plus, there are at least a dozen storage containers on the wharf side that look new. Someone could have brought in a lot of equipment, or other things, in them. And there's a renovated docking platform in the rear too."

"Is there somewhere you can station yourselves to watch the building?"

"There's not much cover on the river side—we just took a quick run past to check it out. We can watch the front without much difficulty."

"Is the river side guarded?"

"We didn't see anyone. No cameras, but we could have missed them." Jace rumbled softly. "We're sorry, Alpha."

"Don't be. You've done well. I don't want you seen. Position yourselves as well as you can and send me the coordinates. Let us know if anything seems out of the ordinary. Niki will call you when we move."

"Yes, Alpha."

Sylvan disconnected and waited until she got a text from Jace. She punched in the coordinates and pulled up the map on her GPS. She tapped the location with her finger. "We have them."

Niki and Drake crowded around to look.

"Whatever security they have is well camouflaged," Sylvan said. "There may be only a skeleton staff inside or there could be dozens. From the outside, not much is visible."

"Crossing that parking lot, even at night, would be risky," Niki said.

Drake grumbled uneasily. "It's a perfect setup for an ambush. Anyone inside would be able to see us coming, and those upper floors make a great place to fire from."

"I agree," Niki said. "The water would be the best approach."

"Can we arrange it in time?" Sylvan asked.

"We'll need to mobilize now. We need to get the squads and weapons into the city, and we can't risk a convoy. Too obvious."

"Send the Rovers at irregular intervals and vary the routes," Sylvan said. "Can you get us boats?"

Niki grinned. "I have friends at the marina. I can get a few outboards without questions being asked. We should have plenty of time before a nighttime strike."

"Arrange it."

"Yes, Alpha." Niki grinned and headed for the door.

Sylvan called Jody. Becca answered on Jody's line.

"Hello, Consort," Sylvan said. "When Jody awakens—"

"Sylvan," Becca said, "just a moment. She's here."

Jody came on the line. "Good news?"

"Aren't you supposed to be in a coma or something?"

Jody chuckled. "You shouldn't believe everything you hear about us."

"I'm glad you're awake. We have a location." Sylvan filled her in. "We're going to strike tonight."

"As will we."

"An hour before dawn? Does that give you enough time to get your soldiers back to your lair before sunup?"

"We will either have succeeded well before that or it won't matter," Jody said flatly.

"Max and Dasha will bring a second squad to your lair now. Together with the squad Lara brought last night, you should have plenty of warriors to handle whatever mercenaries Francesca has gathered."

"We appreciate the Pack's support."

"I'm assuming your Vampires can handle Francesca's guards."

"I and my Warlord will deal with them."

"Just don't lose your head," Sylvan said. "I don't want to have to deal with your father for the next hundred years or so."

"I'll say the same to you. Although your Prima does tend to be more reasonable—"

"And don't let anything happen to my *centuri*."

"*My* Warlord," Jody corrected.

Sylvan grinned. "Rendezvous at your lair?"

"Until sunrise, then."

"Niki," Sylvan said when Niki returned, "send Dasha, Max, and a squad to Jody's."

"I was hoping we could dispatch Francesca ourselves," Niki said darkly. "She deserves retribution for kidnapping Katya."

"Our first obligation is to free our wolves. And Francesca is Vampire business."

"Francesca is everyone's business," Niki muttered.

"Not for much longer."

❖

At three a.m., Sylvan and Drake met Niki and the squads at the marina south of the city. She called Jace for an update.

"Perhaps a dozen cars left the facility at eleven p.m.," Jace said. "We saw no vehicles entering."

"The night shift going home?" Sylvan mused.

Jace was silent.

"What about the limo that delivered the informant?"

"A limo left at the same time," Jace said. "We couldn't be sure who it was and decided not to follow it."

"It's possible he wasn't in it and it doesn't really matter where they took him. He's not our quarry."

"If there is a substantial security force on site," Jace said, "they've been here all day. We didn't see anyone arriving since we've been here."

"Is it possible they could've brought a force in by water?"

Sylvan heard her murmur to Jonathan.

"It's possible, Alpha."

"Very well. We will be coming by water. Meet us at the landing dock in thirty minutes. If anything changes between now and the rendezvous time, call me."

"Yes, Alpha."

Sylvan called Jody. "We're leaving now. If you don't hear from us, good hunting."

"And to you."

❖

Luce answered Francesca's call while seated at the desk in Veronica Standish's office. The good doctor lounged, semiconscious, on the sofa, recovering from their latest blood exchange. Veronica rarely went more than six hours without demanding Luce feed from her. The feedings were by necessity brief and unsatisfying for Luce, although Veronica's orgasms seemed as epic as ever.

"Well?" Francesca said. "Did they take the bait?"

Luce shrugged. "It is difficult to tell, my Queen. We were obvious about picking up Simon from the hotel, so if they were watching, they would've been able to follow us to the laboratory."

"*If*—you don't know?" Francesca's tones flamed.

"No, not for certain. We couldn't ascertain that we were being followed." Luce didn't bother to disguise their conversation. Veronica was beyond awareness.

Francesca's sighed. She spoke to someone, presumably Dru. "Opinion?"

Luce had no trouble hearing the conversation, and Francesca would know that. The Queen seemed to enjoy taunting her with the cat.

"Sylvan will not wait if she thinks Weres are in danger," Dru replied. "They will be coming tonight."

"Excellent." Francesca's smile was nearly visible and Luce hissed. "Our forces are in place?"

"Our guards are in position," Luce replied.

"You're sure we shouldn't send Dru's mercenaries," Francesca said.

"I would not leave you unprotected, my Queen, and the mercenaries might not be as motivated as our own." Luce emphasized *our own*. She hadn't been happy leaving Dru and the mercenaries to guard Francesca, but she was needed to keep Veronica satisfied. Besides, some of the Vampire guards and all of the blood servants remained at the lair, any of whom would die to protect Francesca. Her dozen Vampires and handful of Were guards could handle a few wolves, and then she could return to Francesca's side victorious, having proved herself worthy of her place as *senechal*.

"Just be sure Sylvan does not escape."

"Do not worry, my Queen. We will finish this tonight."

CHAPTER THIRTY-THREE

The two outboards ran without lights beneath a shadowed moon. Sylvan tracked their course on her GPS and radioed the pilots to cut the engines close to shore, a hundred yards downriver from their target. They drifted to shore in silence and beached the crafts on the narrow strip of land between the black water and the sharp embankment.

The two squads piled out, Sylvan at the head of the first, Niki with the second. Drake was by Sylvan's side. She wouldn't have been able to keep the Prima safe in the Compound even if she hadn't needed a medic with the team, but she did. She could not send her warriors into battle without a medic, and she'd sent Sophia with Max and Dasha. Elena was needed at the Compound in case of another attack on their borders. So Drake had been needed, and despite Sylvan's personal wishes, the need of the Pack came first.

"Be careful," she murmured as they climbed the steep, rocky bank.

"You too." Drake pressed a hand to Sylvan's back for an instant.

The ridge was overgrown with scrub and good cover from anyone watching from the buildings that squatted along the highway. At one time, this area had been a busy industrial zone, but the businesses had long left the city and the factories had fallen into disrepair. The largest, a square brick behemoth, was their destination. In the scant moonlight, Sylvan could make out the rows of windows, blank and black. But none broken.

Closer now, skirting abandoned cars and rusted Dumpsters and a row of new-looking trailers, she could see the loading dock with the shiny double-wide steel security door Jace had described. No doubt the building had been recently rehabilitated and was likely occupied. A very good choice of location. The river was a perfect avenue to deliver equipment and personnel.

When they reached the wharves directly below the building, Sylvan signaled for Niki. "There has to be an underground delivery area or garage somewhere back here. When you've located that entrance, post half your squad outside and take the others in. Enter on my command and wait for further orders before advancing."

"Yes, Alpha," Niki said, quickly whispering instructions to her lieutenants. "Alpha, perhaps the Prima should stay with the rear guard."

Sylvan glanced at Drake. "She's right. If we have wounded we'll need you to evacuate them."

"If we have wounded, you'll need me at the front to take care of them. I'm going with you."

"I thought you would." Sylvan gripped Niki's shoulder. "We'll see you upstairs."

❖

Zahn Logan, Jody's human servant and chief of security, and Rafaela, the head of Jody's Vampire guard, ordered the drivers of their fortified vehicles to stop a mile from Francesca's lair. The team of a dozen Vampires plus the Were squadron headed by Max covered the remaining distance on foot, keeping to the back service roads that wended through the forested properties dotting the slope overlooking the river. At one time, the city's elite, including a few Vampires, had held court in the mansions along this stretch of river. Some were still occupied, others long abandoned. Fortunately, the owners had valued their privacy and kept as much wooded acreage between the houses as possible. Now Jody's forces advanced within fifty yards of Francesca's lair without coming across any security.

"She has grown overconfident," Zahn murmured. "Her perimeters are unguarded."

"Either that or she's desperate," Jody said. "If she'd been wise, or able, she would have moved every few days."

Zahn made a disgusted sound. "Francesca has become a creature of comfort and ego. She cannot bring herself to believe she could be attacked in her own lair, yet again."

"Always a pleasure to prove her wrong," Jody said. She studied the sprawling house. A single light burned on the wide front porch and a smattering of lights glowed behind windows on the first floor. Francesca would not be in any of those rooms. She would be underground, probably in a fortified bunker. Her guards would be close by, ready to fend off attackers and spirit her to safety.

"You have the explosives," Jody said to her security chief.

"Yes, Liege."

"Warlord? Assessment?"

Lara scanned the building, saw no forces other than two guards in the front and rear. The rest of the grounds appeared deserted.

"We need to disable any vehicles as soon as we commence the attack. Francesca's servants will try to get her out." Lara looked to Rafaela. "The limos will be in the rear of the building. Two of your soldiers with RPGs should be enough."

"I'll see to it."

Lara turned back to Jody. "Send the wolves to disable the guards on the outer doors. Wolves will be unexpected, and they'll be swift. Once they take down the guards, we enter en masse. We need to be quick and deadly."

Jody laughed. "Are we ever anything else?"

"Anyone we encounter must die."

"Max," Jody said without the slightest hesitation, "choose four of your fastest. Strike the throat. We'll be right behind you and take the heads."

"One minute." Max signaled to Dasha and two of his most seasoned lieutenants. They shifted together and, on a short bark from Max, tore across the moon-strewn grounds for Francesca's lair.

❖

Sylvan, Drake, Gray, and three other *sentries* raced for the loading dock. At the same time, Niki's squad broke from the shadows and ran down a ramp to the underground entrance. Sylvan flicked on her radio.

"Three, two, one."

She gripped the bottom of the steel security door with both hands and ripped it from its hinges. It rolled up like a window shade severed from its cord, revealing a two-story space lit by dim security lights at floor level. Huge furnaces, water purifiers, air conditioners, and other machinery, all controlling the internal environment of the building, hummed and clanged. From somewhere off to the left, she heard a quiet thump of another door being breached. Niki was in.

Sylvan led the squad forward cautiously. Where were the

engineers, the maintenance people, security for that matter? Why had no one tried to stop them yet?

"I don't like it," Drake murmured.

"No," Sylvan said. "It smells like a trap."

"Stairwells?" Drake asked.

"Probably—or the elevator shafts. That's where I would plan the assault." Sylvan radioed Niki. "Anything?"

"A Vampire limo and a few civilian cars. No guards."

"Stay away from the elevators and stairwells. Go up the parking ramp to the first office level and wait for my signal to enter."

"What about us?" Drake said when Sylvan finished.

Sylvan smiled in anticipation. "One thing all these old factory buildings had were exterior fire escapes. I'm betting they still do."

❖

The wolves sailed through the air and took Francesca's Vampire guards down in silence, tearing out their throats with savage bites. The injuries were not lethal to Vampires, but the attacks were swift enough that the Vampires couldn't begin to recover before Jody and the others landed beside them with drawn swords and took their heads. When Zahn fired a shock grenade at the front door, Dasha and Anya disabled the limos parked nearby. The wide, heavy front door splintered inward, blasted into thousands of toothpick-sized fragments. As Jody's Vampires and Weres flowed into Francesca's lair, the Hound burst from the shadows and followed them in like a black tide.

CHAPTER THIRTY-FOUR

Francesca was abruptly pulled from her pleasure by the startling sound of an explosion. She raised her head from Dru's neck, her heart pumping with the infusion of potent blood and the almost-forgotten sensation of fear. Daniela still crouched between Dru's thighs, her incisors buried in Dru's groin, oblivious to anything beyond the blood coursing down her throat. Dru's back was arched, her eyes blind, her body taut with release.

"Dru," Francesca said sharply, shattering Dru's trance. "Something is happening."

Dru shook her head, emerging from the erotic haze, and pushed Daniela away. With blood still streaming down the inside of her thigh, she sat up, her pupils mere slits in molten gold. Cat's eyes. A growl reverberated in her chest. "Intruders."

Dru jumped from the bed, her skin awash in adrenaline. Tawny pelt flowed down her chest and abdomen. Claws punched from the ends of her digits and her canines lengthened. She took two steps toward the door of Francesca's boudoir, halted as a crash reverberated through the hall outside, and spun to face Francesca. She scooped up the clothes they'd left on the floor and tossed them to her. "Take Daniela and get to the limo. I'll send Dante to drive you. Hurry."

Francesca listened to the footsteps above. Just entering the main part of the mansion. A dozen. "Where are you going?"

"To stop whoever's out there.

"No. Let the guards handle it. Leave with me."

"I will if I can, but without help up there, we could lose all of them."

Francesca sorted options. She'd had to run from enemies before, but she needed to win even in retreat. If she lost the entire seethe, she would be powerless and in danger of starving even if she escaped. If the attackers could be stopped, she still had a chance to recover and rebuild. She had fed, and she wasn't a coward. No Vampire on the continent matched her strength.

"I'm coming with you."

Dru showed her teeth, her eyes blazing. "Let me clear the way."

She pulled open the door and slipped out. Francesca took a silver katana from the top drawer of the stand next to the bed. Its gleaming blade glinted red in the glow of the light from the crimson lampshade.

❖

Sylvan and the others reached the roof in under a minute. The windows they'd passed on the way up had all been dark. The flat-topped roof was littered with broken boards, bits of rock and glass, and rusted metalworks. A bulkhead with dented double doors in the center of the roof was closed with a rusty padlock that looked as if it had not been opened in decades.

"Stairwell," Sylvan said. "Probably a maintenance shaft."

"If this is a trap," Drake said quietly, "they could be waiting for us to come down this way."

"If I were setting a trap," Sylvan said, "I'd be waiting on the floor where I placed the bait. Where's the most likely place for them to be holding captives?"

"Either the basement or the top floor," Drake said. "That way, only those individuals with clearance would have access or a reason to be there. The middle floors have too much traffic, with workers passing through to places above or below. We know they're not in the underground level."

"Then if they're here, they're right beneath us."

"If Niki comes from below and we come from above, we can catch them in the crossfire."

"Yes." Sylvan flicked her radio. "Niki, where are you?"

"Clearing the third floor. Office spaces, all of them empty."

"Let us know when you reach the fifth-level landing. We're coming down from the roof."

"Yes, Alpha."

Sylvan waved the squad closer. "Gray, take the *sentries* and go through the windows from the fire escape when the Prima and I come down from above. Niki will enter from the stairwell. Any armed resistance, shoot to kill."

Gray nodded, her expression set and steady, and led the young warriors across the roof and over the side.

Sylvan looked at Drake. "I can take more bullets than any of the rest of you."

"I know." Drake gripped her arm. "But you aren't invincible. So try not to."

"Ready?"

"Yes."

❖

"They're moving up, floor by floor," the Vampire guard reported to Luce. "ETA three minutes."

Luce glanced at Veronica, still stuporous on the sofa. The office adjoined the lab, and as long as the wolves never got that far, the human would be safe. If they did get past the guards, well…Veronica's usefulness had come to an end.

"Hold fire until they enter the hallway, then take them. I'm on my way."

"Yes, *Senechal*."

❖

The expansive marble-floored foyer was empty—no furniture, no guards, no servants. Jody raced into the main room, what had once been a formal living room with high decorative plaster ceilings, banks of floor-to-ceiling windows, and a huge marble fireplace against one wall. The great room was barren, save for two oversized sofas and a tattered brocade chair. Blood slaves stretched out on the sofas, arms and legs entangled. Two cat Weres lounged on the chair, naked and covered in blood and sex. The three Vampires who had been feeding from them when Jody shattered the front door rushed at Jody and Lara. The Vampires were too slow, and Jody and Lara took their heads in two swift arcs of their long swords. Max and Dasha gripped the snarling cats by the throats and slung them across the room. They flew into the stone mantel and fell senseless to the floor. Jody spun at a growl behind them and came face-to-face with the enormous Hound she'd last seen at Nocturne the night Francesca had been driven from power.

"Are you here to collect what remains of their souls?" she asked. The Hound's thick black lips peeled back and its fiery eyes glowed. "Take them, but Francesca is mine."

Jody signaled for the others to follow her on while the Hound prowled the room, dispatching the occupants to whatever underworld it ruled. Three more Vampires raced around the corner. Two held long swords, the third a handgun. Dasha shot the Vampire wielding the gun between the eyes and finished with two shots to the heart. Jody and Lara parried the blades of Francesca's guards in a quick flurry that ended with their swords buried in the hearts of their opponents. As they swept from room to room, humans and a few mercs scurried to escape through broken windows. At the rear of the first floor, Jody pointed to a stairwell leading down.

"This way."

She started down and was stopped short when a huge cat struck her full force in the chest. She flew backward, her sword flying from her hand. When she reached for her weapon, a silver sword drove through her shoulder and pinned her to the floor.

❖

"We're just below the fifth-floor fire door," Niki announced over the radio.

Sylvan contacted Gray. "Are you in position?"

"Yes, Alpha."

"Ready," she said to both teams. "Go."

Sylvan gripped the door's hinges, tore them off, and flipped it open. Avoiding the narrow, dark inside stairs completely, she dropped down the stairwell to the floor below. Drake followed. The sound of glass breaking clattered somewhere out of sight and another *boom* told her Niki had breached the stairwell door. Gunfire erupted from every direction. A Vampire leaned around the corner and fired at her.

"We're pinned down," Sylvan radioed to Niki. "Can you clear the corridor?"

"Not without exposing ourselves."

Another burst of gunfire, this time from farther down the hall, and the Vampire fell out into the open, an assault rifle by her side. Gray's team. The Vampire twitched and jerked, an arm reaching for the weapon. Not dead, merely injured. Sylvan loped forward, kicked the weapon away, and buried a blade in the Vampire's heart. She signaled to Drake, who crowded next to her at the opening of the stairwell. The hallway ran the entire length of the floor and ended at the far end in an airlock of some kind.

"That's the laboratory," Sylvan said.

Between them and that door were at least a dozen armed Vampires crouched in doorways, pinning them down with intermittent fire. Sylvan heard the doors above them clang shut and suspected there were more Vampires on the roof.

"We might be trapped," Sylvan said, "but so are they."

"They know where we're going," Drake said, "but we have them flanked."

"If we draw their fire, Gray's and Niki's teams will have clear shots." She glanced at Drake and grinned. "Do you feel like a run?"

Drake's eyes glowed. "Always."

Chapter Thirty-five

S ylvan's wolf charged down the hall, Drake close by her side, moving so swiftly the silver and black of their pelts streamed together like clouds racing across the midnight sky. The first bullet struck her flank, the second her shoulder. She didn't slow, neither did Drake. Her goal was the glass-and-steel door at the end of the hallway with the security pads and scanners mounted in the wall beside it. As she passed doorways, Vampires fired and a spiderweb of bullets crossed paths in the hall as Niki and Gray returned fire from either end.

She and her Prima raced on.

When she was ten yards from the door, she let her warrior form emerge, and she was suddenly looming over Drake, still in pelt, shielding her from fire. Niki and her squad moved in behind Sylvan and Drake, protecting their flanks. Ignoring all the security devices, Sylvan punched her claw-tipped hand through the reinforced glass, hooked her hands inside the metal frame, and, claws digging into the steel, yanked the door from its moorings. With a tremendous growl, she slung it down the hall like an errant Frisbee. It crashed from one side to the other, gouging the newly painted walls and tiled floors, now awash in blood. She glanced over her shoulder, saw Gray and the *sentries* moving en masse down the hall, dispatching the Vampires with sword and bullet, one after the other.

Are you all right?

Better than you, Drake signaled. *Just a few scratches.*

"It's nothing," Sylvan said, although the silver buried in her muscles burned like chunks of fire.

Drake rose beside her, shedding pelt, and extended a clawed hand.

Sylvan smiled at her Prima's emerging warrior form. "You grow stronger every day."

"Be quiet." Drake plunged her claws into the festering wound on Sylvan's shoulder. A minute later she dropped the bullet on the floor and said, "Turn." She extracted the second bullet from Sylvan's flank. "Now you're all right."

Sylvan strode through the destroyed airlock toward the inner door to the laboratory. "Let's see what they're hiding."

❖

Jody glimpsed Francesca's triumphant face gliding past her, power radiating from her like a tidal wave. The others would not be able to hold her, not with Francesca's cat Were running amok and scattering their warriors. Jody gripped the hilt of the blade impaling her and yanked it free, keeping it in her hand as she lunged to her feet. The hall was chaos. An enormous mountain lion batted a huge gray wolf with its powerful front paw, raking the wolf's side with four-inch claws. The wolf flew against the wall, blood streaming from torn muscles and fractured bone. A second wolf dragged a Vampire to the floor by its throat, and a fountain of blood gushed toward the ceiling. The air split with the screech of a wild cat, and another lion—larger and heavier than the first, with canines a foot long and claws nearly the same—soared above the roiling mass and tackled Francesca's cat. Raina.

Jody searched for her prey in the midst of the blood and fury. Weres fought mercs. The two great cats rolled and screamed, biting and clawing. Lara and Zahn wielded their swords with ruthless efficiency, cutting down the last of the Vampires.

Francesca was gone. She had seen too many battles not to know this one was lost. Blade in hand, Jody charged into the battle. Blood pumped from her shoulder, and she could not stop it or replenish it until she fed again. But she was strong enough to keep on fighting. Francesca would not escape.

An animal screamed in chilling triumph. Raina straddled the other lion, her muscular body pinning the cat to the floor. Blood seeped from gouges on Raina's shoulders and belly. Francesca's cat twisted and clawed, screeching in rage. With a roar, Raina opened her powerful jaws, buried her teeth in the cat's throat, and tore her to pieces.

❖

The laboratory was eerily silent. State-of-the-art equipment, gleaming and alien, covered every surface of the long narrow rows of benches. Monitors and gauges ticked away with scrolling lines of data and graphs. The room smelled dead—not the earthy decay of the natural world that carried the promise of renewal, but the absence of life.

"There," Drake said, pointing to the far end of the room. "Isolation cubicles."

Sylvan stalked down the aisle. Drake, Niki, and Gray followed. The first cubicle was empty. Bright lights shone in the second, spotlighting two rectangular glassed-in cages. The occupants were small, wide-eyed, helpless. She could not scent them, but she didn't need to. Their eyes were wolf eyes, searching hers. Sylvan roared, cracking the glass of the isolation chamber with one furious stroke.

"Newborns," Drake said, her voice wintry cold.

Sylvan backed up a step, her fury too large to contain. If she touched them now, she would frighten them. "Get them out."

Drake began opening the latches on the cages, murmuring softly to the pups. Sylvan turned away, rage narrowing her vision to laser points. "Niki, see to them. Jace, Jonathan—sweep the floor. Gray, with me. Everyone dies."

"Sylvan," Drake murmured, "if—"

"No, there are no innocents here," Sylvan roared. "Find the mothers."

She headed for the last door on the floor. The one that opened opposite the isolation cubicles. Before she reached it, she smelled the Vampire and the human. Finally, she had found the enemy.

The lock gave with her first punch. The room was dimly lit, a large comfortable space with a thick patterned carpet and carved wooden bookcases and a sitting area with a large sofa. The contrast to the arctic room she'd just left fired her fury.

A flicker of movement to her right, a glint of silver. She blocked the blade sweeping toward her head and gripped the wrist holding the short sword. For an instant she stared into the fiery eyes of the last Vampire. The Vampire hissed and struck at Sylvan's throat with razor-sharp nails. Sylvan yanked her closer and the blow glanced off her shoulder. They were face-to-face with barely an inch between them.

"You have been found guilty," Sylvan whispered and thrust her hand into the Vampire's chest. She gripped the pumping heart and squeezed, watching the shock in the Vampire's eyes slowly turn to emptiness as she pulled the organ from her body.

"No!"

A shot rang out. Sylvan dropped the Vampire and spun around. A wild-eyed human swayed beside the sofa, a gun in her right hand pointed at Sylvan. Gray's wolf sprang, striking the human with unerring accuracy. She dragged the screaming female to the floor by the neck and slowly clamped her jaws together until silence filled the room.

"Gray," Sylvan ordered, "leave your kill."

The wolf swung around, a low growl in her throat. A second passed and she shuddered. Gray rose naked and staggered to Sylvan's side. "She was the one. The one who took us."

Sylvan grasped her nape and pulled her close. "I know. And now we are done."

❖

Jody raced down the hall, leaving the carnage behind. Francesca would know the rear was blocked and her vehicles destroyed. Even with the sun coming, if she escaped out the front, she was old enough to tolerate it until she found shelter or stole one of their vehicles.

A roar shook the building to its foundation. Jody skidded around the corner into the main foyer, her bloodied sword in hand. The Hound's massive body blocked the shattered doorway and the exit to freedom. Francesca was trapped between the two of them.

Francesca looked over her shoulder at Jody with a wry smile. "We are still Vampires. Still the same. Would you choose the others, the weaker, over one of your own?"

Jody strode forward. "You are not one of mine."

"You would give me to the Hound?" Francesca mocked, her eyes laughing. "You are not your father's daughter."

"No." Jody raised the sword above her head in both hands. "I am not."

Francesca's gaze widened as the sword arced. A furious scream rent the air, and a crescent of blood streamed from the blade as if it were a brush painting the walls in a crimson sunset.

No body fell.

Jody stared where Francesca had been. The Hound growled, and an instant later, Torren stood in the doorway.

"Is she dead?"

"She should be." Jody sagged to her knees. "If she endures somehow, she will be alone and powerless. For Francesca, that would be worse than death."

Chapter Thirty-six

Sylvan's first stop was to check with Callan. Assured all was secure, she headed to the infirmary. Most of the less seriously injured had been treated in the Rovers on the way back to the Compound and were already in the mess hall eating or the barracks sleeping post-shift. Max needed more than just fuel and time spent in pelt. He lay on the treatment table, Andrea by his side. Elena cleansed a series of deep rips on his chest and hip with hemostatic solution.

"How is he?" Sylvan asked.

Before Elena could answer, Max growled, "Fine. I'd be better if these two would let me get up."

"Be quiet, Max," Andrea said, fingers lightly working through his hair. "Let Elena work."

Max's scowl faded and Sylvan smiled.

"He'll be fine," Elena said. "Half a dozen cracked ribs, some muscle tears, a bruised lung. It won't slow him down once he shifts."

Sylvan gripped his shoulder and glanced at Andrea. "Any word?"

"The wet work team is done at the lab. The AG should be arranging the warrant right about now. My team is set to go as soon as they receive it."

"I told you to go with them," Max said grumpily to Andrea.

"They don't need me to take down a civilian like Nicholas Gregory. He'll probably still be in bed when they get there." Andrea continued to stroke Max's hair. "Besides, I'd rather not be identified in any official capacity. His arrest will put a dent in HUFSI, but it won't put an end to it. This is just the beginning."

"The case against him is solid?" Sylvan asked.

"The link between him and that lab is the connection we've been waiting for. What's even better, we have preliminary evidence the funding goes all the way back to some very influential politicians." Andrea smiled a smile like that of a wolf contemplating prey. "Believe me, before we go to the grand jury, it will be airtight."

"He has powerful friends," Sylvan said.

"All the better." Andrea's growl was worthy of a Were.

Sylvan said to Max, "Do as Elena orders."

He grumbled even as he ducked his head and settled back on the table.

Sylvan continued through the infirmary and into the nursery. Drake was just coming out of the newborn area.

"Well?" Sylvan asked gruffly.

Drake slid an arm around Sylvan's waist. "They're healthy. We'll want to monitor them, but I can't find any evidence that they've been…"

"Experimented with?"

"Yes." Drake sighed. "They've been tested—there's evidence of blood drawing, but nothing more that I can see."

Sylvan watched through the doorway as Sophia lifted one of the newborns and handed it to Niki. Sophia took the other, and they sat side by side to feed them.

"There's no trace of the mothers," Sylvan said. "According to Tamara, the pups were sired by forced matings with Bernardo's lieutenants. They're dead too."

"The pups have a Pack now," Drake said gently, running blunt claws up and down Sylvan's back. "We couldn't have gotten there any sooner, and it was time enough."

"I can't help feeling that I failed them," Sylvan said.

"I know, because that's who you are. But you have to trust me when I say that you didn't. They'll be fine. They just need care and love, and they'll get plenty of that in the Pack."

"Yes, they will. But they need something more."

Drake studied her intently. "You're their Alpha. You know what's best."

Sylvan kissed her and slipped quietly into the room so as not to disturb the feedings.

Niki started to rise.

"Stay there." Crouching down beside Niki and Sophia, she studied the blue-eyed pups. Both females, both blond like so many of the

Blackpaws. Like Sophia and her parents. "They look hungry."

"They are," Niki said. "And strong already too."

Sophia looked up, eyes glowing. "You should name them, Alpha."

"No," Sylvan said, "you should. The two of you."

"I don't understand." Sophia glanced at Niki.

Sylvan said, "They won't need to stay here very long, but they're not big enough yet to join the other pups. Take them home."

Sophia's hand slid onto Niki's thigh and tightened. Niki covered it with her own and met Sylvan's gaze. "Our home?"

"Yes. They need connection to the Pack, but they need more than that. They need parents."

"Yes," Sophia said softly. "They do."

Niki grasped Sophia's hand. "We are honored, Alpha."

Sylvan laughed. "You say that now. Wait until they're a little bigger and start driving you crazy."

Niki swallowed hard. "Thank you."

Sylvan kissed Sophia's cheek, gripped Niki's neck, and whispered in her ear, "I can't think of a finer home for them."

❖

"Now," Drake said to Sylvan as they crossed the Compound to headquarters, "we can put our energies into unifying our Pack and building our future in the light."

"We will still need to negotiate with the humans."

"Yes, but at least now you will not be fighting a war as well."

Sylvan closed the door to her office and pinned Drake against it. "How do you feel about another litter of our own?"

"I'm not in heat."

"We can change that."

Drake laughed and bit Sylvan's lip. "I like the idea of trying very much. Are you ready now?"

"Always." Sylvan grinned. "Give me five minutes."

Drake pulled off her shirt, unbuttoned the top of her BDUs, and canted a hip against the edge of the desk. "I'm counting."

Sylvan growled and yanked her cell from her pocket.

"How is Jody?" she asked when Becca answered the phone.

"Torren was kind enough to carry the idiot back here so she could feed and heal. *What* is the matter with you?"

"Uh…"

"Really, Sylvan," Becca raged. "Must you macho types always be in the thick of things?"

Sylvan laughed. "I don't think that term really applies to Weres and Vampires."

"Then *idiots* will have to do." Becca paused for breath. "She's fine."

"Could I talk to her, then?"

A moment later Jody said, "You are well, I take it?"

"Fine." Sylvan rubbed her shoulder. The wounds had healed and the soreness would disappear after her first run.

"And your wolves?"

"None seriously injured. Your Vampires?"

"All recovering."

Sylvan rumbled. "What about Francesca?"

Jody was silent for a long moment. "Francesca was one of the oldest and most powerful Vampires in existence. She might have had powers none of us knew of. I can't say with certainty she's ended."

"Could she have gotten past Torren?"

"No," Jody said. "And no Vampire I know of has ever been able to teleport."

"You have a theory?"

Jody sighed. "Torren does."

"That is worrisome."

"Yes."

"Tell me."

"Passage between the realms usually requires a Faerie Gate."

"Usually?"

"Some Fae can cross the realms without a Gate. The power expenditure is tremendous, which is why Torren wasn't able to return to Faerie that way after her long period of imprisonment. But some royal Fae can."

"But Francesca is not Fae."

"Torren thinks a very, very powerful Fae might be able to transport others as well."

"Did Torren say who those very, very powerful Fae are?"

"No, but she didn't need to."

"Cecilia," Sylvan said darkly. "But we don't know that?"

"No. And even if somehow that were the case, Francesca is still without power, without allies, without servants, without soldiers. She is no longer a danger."

"So for now," Sylvan murmured, pulling Drake to her side, "we have won."

About the Author

Radclyffe has written over forty-five romance and romantic intrigue novels, dozens of short stories, and, writing as L.L. Raand, has authored a paranormal romance series, The Midnight Hunters.

She is an eight-time Lambda Literary Award finalist in romance, mystery, and erotica—winning in both romance (*Distant Shores, Silent Thunder*) and erotica (*Erotic Interludes 2: Stolen Moments* edited with Stacia Seaman and *In Deep Waters 2: Cruising the Strip* written with Karin Kallmaker). A member of the Saints and Sinners Literary Hall of Fame, she is also an RWA/FF&P Prism Award winner for *Secrets in the Stone*, an RWA FTHRW Lories and RWA HODRW winner for *Firestorm*, an RWA Bean Pot winner for *Crossroads*, and an RWA Laurel Wreath winner for *Blood Hunt*. In 2014 she was awarded the Dr. James Duggins Outstanding Mid-Career Novelist Award by the Lambda Literary Foundation.

She is also the president of Bold Strokes Books, one of the world's largest independent LGBTQ publishing companies.

Find her at facebook.com/Radclyffe.BSB, follow her on Twitter @RadclyffeBSB, and visit her website at Radfic.com.

Books Available From Bold Strokes Books

Twice Lucky by Mardi Alexander. For firefighter Mackenzie James and Dr. Sarah Mackenzie, there's suddenly a whole lot more in life to understand, to consider, to risk…someone will need to fight for her life. (978-1-62639-325-7)

Shadow Hunt by L.L. Raand. With young to raise and her Pack under attack, Sylvan, Alpha of the wolf Weres, takes on her greatest challenge when she determines to uncover the faceless enemies known as the Shadow Lords. A Midnight Hunters novel. (978-1-62639-326-4)

Heart of the Game by Rachel Spangler. A baseball writer falls for a single mom, but can she ever love anything as much as she loves the game? (978-1-62639-327-1)

Getting Lost by Michelle Grubb. Twenty-eight days, thirteen European countries, a tour manager fighting attraction, and an accused murderer: Stella and Phoebe's journey of a lifetime begins here. (978-1-62639-328-8)

Prayer of the Handmaiden by Merry Shannon. Celibate priestess Kadrian must defend the kingdom of Ithyria from a dangerous enemy and ultimately choose between her duty to the Goddess and the love of her childhood sweetheart, Erinda. (978-1-62639-329-5)

The Witch of Stalingrad by Justine Saracen. A Soviet "night witch" pilot and American journalist meet on the Eastern Front in WWII and struggle through carnage, conflicting politics, and the deadly Russian winter. (978-1-62639-330-1)

Night Mare by Franci McMahon. On an innocent horse-buying trip, Jane Scott uncovers a horrifying element of the horse show world, thrusting her into a whirlwind of poisoned money. (978-1-62639-333-2E).

Pedal to the Metal by Jesse J. Thoma. When unreformed thief Dubs Williams is released from prison to help Max Winters bust a car theft ring, Max learns that if you want to catch a thief, you have to get in bed with one. (978-1-62639-239-7)

Dragon Horse War by D. Jackson Leigh. A priestess of peace and a fiery warrior must defeat a vicious uprising that entwines their destinies and ultimately their hearts. (978-1-62639-240-3)

For the Love of Cake by Erin Dutton. When everything is on the line and one taste can break a heart, will pastry chefs Maya and Shannon take a chance on reality? (978-1-62639-241-0)

Betting on Love by Alyssa Linn Palmer. A quiet country girl at heart and a live-life-to-the-fullest biker take a risk at offering each other their hearts. (978-1-62639-242-7)

The Deadening by Yvonne Heidt. The lines between good and evil, right and wrong, have always been blurry for Shade. When Raven's actions force her to choose, which side will she come out on? (978-1-62639-243-4)

One Last Thing by Kim Baldwin & Xenia Alexiou. Blood is thicker than pride. The final book in the Elite Operative Series brings together foes, family, and friends to start a new order. (978-1-62639-230-4)

Songs Unfinished by Holly Stratimore. Two aspiring rock stars learn that falling in love while pursuing their dreams can be harmonious—if they can only keep their pasts from throwing them out of tune. (978-1-62639-231-1)

Beyond the Ridge by L.T. Marie. Will a contractor and a horse rancher overcome their family differences and find common ground to build a life together? (978-1-62639-232-8)

Swordfish by Andrea Bramhall. Four women battle the demons from their pasts. Will they learn to let go, or will happiness be forever beyond their grasp? (978-1-62639-233-5)

The Fiend Queen by Barbara Ann Wright. Princess Katya and her consort Starbride must turn evil against evil in order to banish Fiendish power from their kingdom, and only love will pull them back from the brink. (978-1-62639-234-2)

Up the Ante by PJ Trebelhorn. When Jordan Stryker and Ashley Noble meet again fifteen years after a short-lived affair, is either of them prepared to gamble on a chance at love? (978-1-62639-237-3)

Speakeasy by MJ Williamz. When mob leader Helen Byrne sets her sights on the girlfriend of Al Capone's right-hand man, passion and tempers flare on the streets of Chicago. (978-1-62639-238-0)

Myth and Magic: Queer Fairy Tales, edited by Radclyffe and Stacia Seaman. Myth, magic, and monsters—the stuff of childhood dreams (or nightmares) and adult fantasies. (978-1-62639-225-0)

A Spark of Heavenly Fire by Kathleen Knowles. Kerry and Beth are building their life together, but unexpected circumstances could destroy their happiness. (978-1-62639-212-0)

Venus in Love by Tina Michele. Morgan Blake can't afford any distractions and Ainsley Dencourt can't afford to lose control—but the beauty of life and art usually lies in the unpredictable strokes of the artist's brush. (978-1-62639-220-5)

Rules of Revenge by AJ Quinn. When a lethal operative on a collision course with her past agrees to help a CIA analyst on a critical assignment, the encounter proves explosive in ways neither woman anticipated. (978-1-62639-221-2)

The Romance Vote by Ali Vali. Chili Alexander is a sought-after campaign consultant who isn't prepared when her boss's daughter, Samantha Pellegrin, comes to work at the firm and shakes up Chili's life from the first day. (978-1-62639-222-9)

Advance by Gun Brooke. Admiral Dael Caydoc's mission to find a new homeworld for the Oconodian people is hazardous, but working with the infuriating Commander Aniwyn "Spinner" Seclan endangers her heart and soul. (978-1-62639-224-3)

UnCatholic Conduct by Stevie Mikayne. Jil Kidd goes undercover to investigate fraud at St. Marguerite's Catholic School, but life gets complicated when her student is killed—and she begins to fall for her prime target. (978-1-62639-304-2)

Season's Meetings by Amy Dunne. Catherine Birch reluctantly ventures on the festive road trip from hell with beautiful stranger Holly Daniels only to discover the road to true love has its own obstacles to maneuver. (978-1-62639-227-4)

Courtship by Carsen Taite. Love and Justice—a lethal mix or a perfect match? (978-1-62639-210-6)

Against Doctor's Orders by Radclyffe. Corporate financier Presley Worth wants to shut down Argyle Community Hospital, but Dr. Harper Rivers will fight her every step of the way, if she can also fight their growing attraction. (978-1-62639-211-3)

Never Too Late by Julie Blair. When Dr. Jamie Hammond is forced to hire a new office manager, she's shocked to come face-to-face with Carla Grant and memories from her past. (978-1-62639-213-7)

Widow by Martha Miller. Judge Bertha Brannon must solve the murder of her lover, a policewoman she thought she'd grow old with. As more bodies pile up, the murderer starts coming for her. (978-1-62639-214-4)

Twisted Echoes by Sheri Lewis Wohl. What's a woman to do when she realizes the voices in her head are real? (978-1-62639-215-1)

Criminal Gold by Ann Aptaker. Through a dangerous night in New York in 1949, Cantor Gold, dapper dyke-about-town, smuggler of fine art, is forced by a crime lord to be his instrument of vengeance. (978-1-62639-216-8)